THE GIRL
WITH NO
REFLECTION

KESHE CHOW

DELACORTE PRESS

This is a work of fiction. Names, characters, places, and incidents either are the product of the author's imagination or are used fictitiously. Any resemblance to actual persons, living or dead, events, or locales is entirely coincidental.

Text copyright © 2024 by Keshe Chow
Jacket art copyright © 2024 by Victo Ngai
Map copyright © 2024 by Virginia Allyn

All rights reserved. Published in the United States by Delacorte Press, an imprint of Random House Children's Books, a division of Penguin Random House LLC, New York.

Delacorte Press is a registered trademark and the colophon is a trademark of Penguin Random House LLC.

Visit us on the Web! GetUnderlined.com

Educators and librarians, for a variety of teaching tools, visit us at RHTeachersLibrarians.com

Library of Congress Cataloging-in-Publication Data
Names: Chow, Keshe, author.
Title: The girl with no reflection / Keshe Chow.
Description: First edition. | New York : Delacorte Press, 2024. | Audience: Ages 14+ | Summary: Selected by the royal matchmaker to marry the crown prince, Ying Yue finds her husband-to-be stoic and infuriating, leading her to escape into a secret parallel world through palace mirrors where a kinder prince awaits, but the two worlds have a long and bloody history and Ying has a part to play in the future of both.
Identifiers: LCCN 2023031322 (print) | LCCN 2023031323 (ebook) | ISBN 978-0-593-70750-0 (hardcover) | ISBN 978-0-593-70752-4 (ebook) | ISBN 978-0-593-81523-6 (international ed.)
Subjects: CYAC: Space and time—Fiction. | Arranged marriage—Fiction. | Princes—Fiction. | Fantasy. | LCGFT: Fantasy fiction. | Novels.
Classification: LCC PZ7.1.C54266 Gi 2024 (print) | LCC PZ7.1.C54266 (ebook) | DDC [Fic]—dc23

The text of this book is set in 10-point Ten Mincho Text.
Interior design by Megan Shortt

Printed in the United States of America
10 9 8 7 6 5 4 3 2 1
First Edition

Random House Children's Books supports the First Amendment and celebrates the right to read.

Penguin Random House LLC supports copyright. Copyright fuels creativity, encourages diverse voices, promotes free speech, and creates a vibrant culture. Thank you for buying an authorized edition of this book and for complying with copyright laws by not reproducing, scanning, or distributing any part in any form without permission. You are supporting writers and allowing Penguin Random House to publish books for every reader.

PRAISE FOR
THE GIRL WITH NO REFLECTION

"A unique, gorgeous novel that blends gothic horror with Chinese myths."
—SUNYI DEAN, *Sunday Times* bestselling author of *The Book Eaters*

"In this richly imagined world infused with legend and folklore, Chow has woven a mesmerizing tale of passion and betrayal that takes you on a thrill ride of nonstop action. Eerie and magical, *The Girl with No Reflection* will sweep you away."
—RACHEL GREENLAW, author of *Compass and Blade* and *One Christmas Morning*

"*The Girl with No Reflection* is everything I love about YA fantasy. Keshe Chow's debut novel is driven by compelling lore and clever prophecies, not to mention plot twists that keep the reader on their toes—and a romance story fiery enough to break and then mend the world. I absolutely could not put this book down!"
—KATIE ZHAO, author of *Zodiac Rising*

"Keshe Chow has built the most stunning world on a foundation of Chinese mythology and backed it up with a heroine and a romance you'll be rooting for until the end."
—NISHA J. TULI, bestselling author of *Trial of the Sun Queen*

"Dark secrets, heart-thumping romance, thrilling twists— *The Girl with No Reflection* has it all."
—LILI WILKINSON, author of *Deep Is the Fen*

"A dazzling debut full of magic and adventure, set against a background of rich mythology, with a heroine to root for and a romance to remember . . . I loved it."
—AMANDA LINSMEIER, author of *Six of Sorrow*

"A smashing debut from Keshe Chow, a compelling new voice in YA fantasy."
—SHER LEE, author of *Fake Dates and Mooncakes*

"Keshe Chow draws on lush Chinese mythology to create the secret history of two worlds. . . . Surprising, romantic, and thrilling."
—R.R. VIRDI, *USA Today* bestselling author of *The First Binding*

For my family,
who are my world

I think of you far away, beyond the blue sky,
And my eyes that once were sparkling
Are now a well of tears.
. . . Oh, if ever you should doubt this aching of my heart,
Here in my bright mirror come back and look at me!
—Li Bai (701–762 AD), "Endless Yearning II"

AUTHOR'S NOTE

This is a work of fiction, set in a fantasy world. While inspiration has been drawn from various historical and cultural elements of Imperial China, it should not be considered an accurate representation of the history, politics, social order, spirituality, philosophy, or customs of those eras.

The sky was strewn with pepper-pot stars, reflected in the pond below. On the water's surface, the mirror image of Ying Yue's face floated, pale and moonlike, distorted by ripples.

"My lady," a voice behind her said. "Shall I fill the bath?"

Ying was at the edge, on her knees, bent over the water. It was an unusual position for a noblewoman, but she had never been one for following rules. She didn't turn around or get up. Instead, she raised a hand, dismissing her handmaiden. "No thank you, Li Ming. I will bathe myself tonight."

Li Ming retreated, silent as the wind.

Ying sighed. She was supposed to be preparing for tomorrow, but her stomach was in knots.

She forced herself to breathe in, then out. *You'll be fine.*

Frustrated, Ying flipped her long hair over one shoulder to keep it from getting wet. Then, reaching down, she cupped her hands together and dipped them in the water. It was icy but crystal clear. Bending close to the pond's surface, she drew her hands up and sluiced water over her face.

Something caught her eye: a splash from the far side of the

1

pond. Ying jumped and sat back on her heels. Her heart sped up. The back of her neck prickled.

She wasn't alone.

The ripples radiated outward until the water lapped at the pond's edge. It was lucky the ground was paved with stones, else Ying would have been kneeling in mud.

She rose to her feet in one fluid movement and adjusted the skirt of her hànfú, its golden embroidery scarlike against the red satin of the robe. With her eyes trained on the water, she listened, heart fluttering like a caged bird.

The ripples faded. The pond became smooth again; reflective, like glass. Ying exhaled. *Just a fish,* she thought. Earlier she'd seen carp milling about at the surface, clamoring for food, their huge, muscular bodies glinting silver in the moonlight. Surely it was one of them that had caused the splash.

The pond was an ornamental feature in the expansive gardens wrapping around Ying's private quarters. On the morrow, she was to wed the emperor's only son, Prince Shan Zhang Lin, in an elaborate three-stage ceremony. As the future crown princess and, eventually, empress of the powerful Shan Dynasty, she was afforded certain privileges.

The garden was one. She'd always loved nature, and when she had first arrived at the Imperial Palace three months prior, she had been delighted to find her own private oasis. Her first day had been spent trailing her hand through the swinging willow branches, breathing in the lush fragrance of the abundant exotic blooms, and watching the colorful carp swimming in lazy circles beneath the water. She'd marveled at the pond, its surface a delicate green and dotted with lotus flowers. It had been so beautiful. It *was* so beautiful. At the time, she'd been touched. The prince obviously wanted to make her happy.

It hadn't taken long for her to realize that that was not the case. Now that she knew better, Ying suspected the task had been delegated to his team of advisors. *It is in the empire's interest,* they would have told him, *to keep the future empress content.*

He probably hadn't prepared her lodgings, didn't know how they looked or where they even were. He certainly never visited. And whereas back home her family was involved in every household matter, she'd quickly learned that the ruling dynasty distanced themselves from everyday, mundane life. The Shan family had servants for their servants' servants, each tier confined to their own set circle.

No, it would have been a small inner group of officials who'd deemed it prudent to keep Ying happy. But, she thought, if they'd wanted to keep her happy, they would have allowed her family to join her. If they'd wanted to keep her happy, they wouldn't have confined her to her quarters.

If they'd wanted to keep her happy, they would not have locked her door.

Ying sighed again. Three months—three long months she'd been kept here. And while the trees and flowers had lost none of their beauty, she now knew them so intimately, so well, that even with her eyes shut, she could trace each detail in her mind. She spent day after monotonous day staring at the garden's high stone walls, wishing she could take flight and escape.

Pushing her sleeves up to her elbows so as not to trip over

the draping fabric, Ying Yue picked up the fāngzhū, a concave mirror designed to collect moonlit dew. It had been sitting in her garden gathering dew every night for a whole lunar month. Considered the nectar of the gods, the dew was to be used to brew her ceremonial wedding tea.

Balancing the large square in both hands, she turned to make her way back to her room. But as she stepped away from the pond, she heard a strange sound.

She whipped around, catching a glimpse of something just slipping below the water. Her knuckles blanched around the edge of the fāngzhū. Once again, ripples marred the surface of the pond.

In the distance, a warm glow spilled from the glass door of her room, but it was too far for the light to reach her. She should be going inside. She should be preparing for her hair-combing ceremony, traditionally held on the eve of a wedding.

But something filled her mind, a silent song, reaching out to her from the pond. She couldn't explain it. After all, the garden was quiet save for a few chirping crickets.

As much as she tried to ignore it, something was calling her. The lure of the water was strong, too strong.

Carefully, she placed the fāngzhū down on the pebbled path, crept toward the water's edge, and peered at the surface. It was smooth again, reflecting the stars, the moon, the skeletal branches of the surrounding trees. And once again on the water's surface was her face, looking pale and drawn and more than a little worried.

It's nothing. Ying pressed a hand to her chest. Nothing more than her reflection. Surely it was just the stress of the impending wedding, the weight of filial expectations that rested on her shoulders. Her anxiety was getting to her. She was starting to imagine things.

But then she noticed something. Something that made her heart pound, her palms grow clammy, her head throb with heat. Something was wrong—something terrifying.

It was her reflection. Yes, her reflection in the water looked exactly like her. Small, dainty cherry lips. Big, doelike dark eyes. A cascade of black hair tumbling over one shoulder.

But that wasn't the strange thing. The strange thing was that in the water, Ying's reflection was smiling.

And Ying Yue was not.

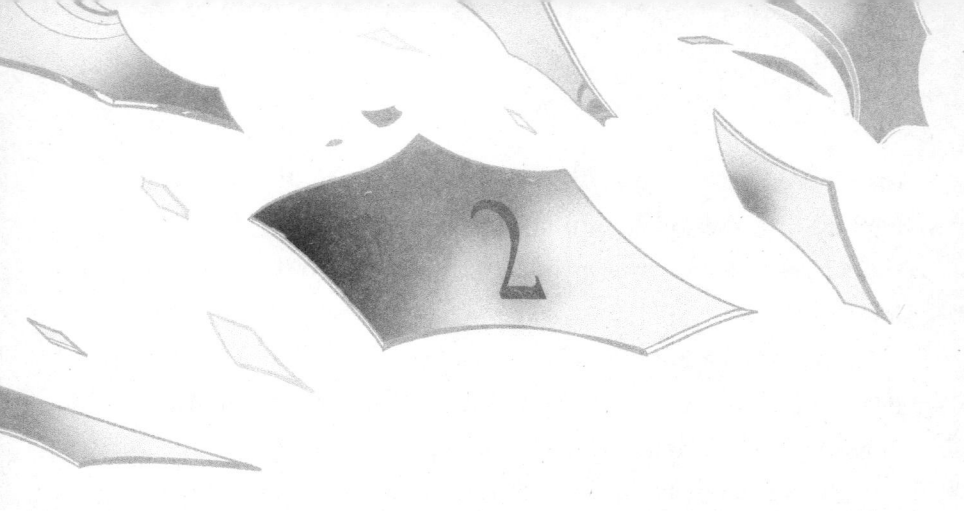

2

Ying caught a glimpse of what looked like a ghostly white hand reaching from the water before she turned and ran. She ran and ran, stumbling toward her rooms, panic clouding her vision. She didn't dare look back. The noises were bad enough; she thought she heard the wet sounds of something emerging, something splashing up onto the shore. In the still, almost-silent night, every sound echoed as loudly as a gong.

As Ying ran, her sleeves dragged down and tangled around her legs. She tripped and fell, palms scraping the paving stones. She heard a strangled cry and was shocked to realize it had been her own. Ignoring the grazes on her hands, she scrambled to her feet and threw a glance back at the pond. Her pounding heart slowed when she took in the surface, still and smooth.

Ying blinked. Had she imagined what she'd seen? Maybe she *had* been smiling, bent over the lake, studying her reflection. Whatever had happened, she wasn't smiling now; her face ached, as though frozen in a scream.

Squinting into the dim night, she stared harder at her surroundings. A breeze sighed, ruffling the water's surface. Was it a trick of the light, or were there arms stretching from beneath the water, glinting white and pale in the moonlight, trying to lure her in?

Ying's pulse accelerated as she slowly backed away. She'd better not wait to find out. Gathering up her sleeves and skirts, she resumed hurtling toward her rooms. Would she make it? And even if she did, would she have time to bolt the doors? Would the creature try to follow her? What *was* it?

The creature is me, thought Ying. She forced herself to focus, to think only of the glass doors. She ran, her feet slapping the stone pathway, the cold air cooling the sweat on her brow.

As she passed the fāngzhū, movement flashed within. Ying dodged away from it, gasping, but then paused—the mirror was now empty, her reflection absent. As if she herself had disappeared.

Her heart hammering, Ying leaned closer, not daring to breathe. A moment passed, deceptively calm. Then her reflection slammed against the glass, face up close, hair disheveled, teeth bared. The creature raised both hands as though it—or she herself, or whatever it was—might haul itself right through the mirror.

A scream caught in Ying's throat as she realized: She couldn't outrun it. She couldn't escape.

She had to face it.

She was not supposed to know how to defend herself, was not supposed to know how to fight. As the youngest child and only daughter of the aristocratic Jiang family, she was supposed to learn to play the èrhú, to embroider silks, and to serve tea. But she'd railed at the injustice of her brothers learning to fight but not her. Her parents, who were accustomed to indulging her every childish whim, allowed her to join in while her brothers trained with their masters. They never seriously believed she'd stick with it, but she did. She would memorize what she'd learned so she could practice by herself, secretly, in her room. Slowly, over the years, she built up her strength and the power behind her kicks. No one but Ying knew about the hours she spent training by herself in front of her mirror when she was meant to be in bed asleep.

She was glad of it now.

Throwing her entire body weight behind the movement, Ying stamped down on the fāngzhū. Pain shot through her foot as the mirror shattered, cracked lines feathering the glass. The creature in the mirror jerked away. With both hands, Ying raised the mirror, then swung it down, smashing it on the ground. Again and again she smashed it, until it was pulverized into a mess of glittering fragments. Tossing away the last two pieces, Ying sank into a defensive crouch. Her sleeves were long—ridiculous, even. Perhaps she could use them to strangle the beast.

With rising panic, she scanned the now-serene scene. The pond was smooth, quiet. But she knew the creature might try to emerge again.

"Lady Ying!" It was Li Ming.

Ying spun around. Her handmaiden was framed by the doorway, carrying a neat pile of underclothes in her arms. "Whatever is the matter?" Li Ming's eyes widened as Ying Yue sprinted toward her.

"The . . . water!" Ying cried, her voice garbled. She grabbed her maid's shoulder. As if in response, she heard a loud splash behind her. "Get out! I'll fight it off!"

"What is wrong, my lady?" Li Ming craned her neck, trying to see what Ying meant. Then she spotted the smashed mirror and gasped. It was considered bad luck to smash a mirror. Even worse, a fāngzhū mirror. According to the local superstitions, with insufficient dew to make the wedding tea, Ying's marriage would be cursed forever. "What happened?"

Ying spun Li Ming around and tried to push her back inside. "Never mind that. You need to run!"

"Run?" Li Ming repeated, her eyebrows knotted in confusion, before she twisted out of Ying's grasp.

"Don't go near the water!" Ying cried. But the maid was already walking toward it. Clearly, to her, *nothing* could be as horrific as smashing that damn mirror.

Li Ming edged toward the pond, Ying following. The creature had vanished—as if it had never existed.

Ying, still panicked, surveyed the empty garden. Nothing. The maid was staring at the water, looking puzzled. The pond was calm, the specter of Ying's reflection having completely disappeared.

"What is wrong with the water, Lady Ying?" Li Ming, clutching the pile of nightclothes, turned back to face her mistress. "Shall I call a guard? Or perhaps the animal keeper? Was it a wild creature that frightened you so, my lady? Did it cause you to drop the mirror?"

9

Ying shook her head and forced herself to quell her rapid breathing. Perhaps she was hallucinating. Or perhaps this was a nightmare. Perhaps she would wake soon, refreshed, ready to fulfill her obligations, all memory of aberrant reflections lost to the murky world of dreams.

Whatever it was, it was gone. She couldn't explain it, or tell anyone, not even Li Ming. They would conclude she was of unsound mind and throw her in the dungeons.

Or worse.

"It's nothing." Trying to steady her shaking hands, she took the pile of clothes from Li Ming and clutched it to her chest. "Probably just a carp leaping from the water. It gave me a fright, that's all."

Li Ming nodded. She was a small thing, short in stature, with a pixie-like face. Looking at her made Ying want to cover herself. Compared to the maid's neat little bun and pale-blue muslin frock, Ying's shoe, crumpled hànfú and messy hair felt scandalous.

It was not the untidiness of Ying's dress, though, that caught Li Ming's attention. It was the blood blooming on the gold silk of Ying's shoe. "Lady Ying!" She pointed, the whites of her eyes showing. "You're . . . you're bleeding!"

Ying shot a glance at her foot. By now, her shoe was drenched. Seeing it made her dizzy, but she forced her voice to stay level. "It's just—the glass. The broken glass."

Li Ming took Ying by the elbow. "Come," she said with heartbreaking gentleness. "The hair combing starts soon. We should get you cleaned up."

Allowing herself to be steered back to her rooms, Ying risked one last look at the two remnant mirror shards. It was hard to tell from a distance—but she could have sworn an eye appeared, staring out from the broken glass.

Watching her.

3

Ying winced as Li Ming dabbed at a cut on the sole of her foot. Not wanting to distract her maid, she bit her lip, trying not to cry out at the pain.

Assiduous as always, Li Ming bent her head to the task, stopping only to splash more spirit on the wound. She was used to patching up Ying's various cuts and scrapes. As she worked, she hummed a song, the same one she always sang when she was concentrating.

Previously an underservant at the Jiang family mansion, Li Ming had struck up a close friendship with Ying when they were both children. So when Ying came of age, the girl was raised from obscurity and trained in the arts of hair styling and dress to be Ying's personal attendant. When Ying's betrothal to the crown prince was announced, there was no question that Li Ming would accompany her mistress to Jinshan province, seat of the royal family.

Ying, who'd had to leave her family behind, was grateful for Li Ming's presence. Here at the palace Ying had no other allies, no confidants, no friends. In her lonely existence, she clung to the only person who showed her kindness: her maid.

Shifting in her seat, Ying turned away from the mirror. Now that she was back in her bright, cheery quarters, the idea of her reflection rising out of the water seemed far-fetched. Nonsensical. Still, her palms remained clammy, and her pulse roared in her ears. Had it all just been in her mind? Out there, under the wan light of the moon, it had seemed so real. . . .

Li Ming finished winding the gauze bandage. "There you go, my lady," she said, snipping off the loose end. "Hopefully, it won't make walking too difficult tomorrow."

Ying groaned, letting the hem of the silk nightgown she'd changed into drop back to the floor. "Please. Don't remind me of tomorrow."

The maid gave Ying a sympathetic smile and began busying herself with preparations for the hair-combing ceremony. It was nearing the Hour of the Rat, which meant Ying's family would be arriving at any moment.

Normally, Ying relished having her hair combed. It reminded her of childhood—of how her mother brushed her hair back home. Usually, it lulled her into a sort of trance. But tonight? Tonight she was dreading it. The hair combing meant two things.

One, that the day had almost arrived—she was well and truly going to be getting married to a most indifferent husband.

And two, she'd have to sit and face the mirror.

She almost jumped at the sharp staccato sound of someone rapping at the door. A eunuch servant swept in, kowtowing low. "Announcing the arrival of Lord and Lady Jiang, of Shuijing He, and their four sons, Jiang Hao Yu, Jiang Hao Qiang, Jiang Hao Zhuang, and Jiang Hao Zie."

The Jiang family were the rulers of Shuijing He, a southern region crisscrossed by an extensive network of lakes, streams, and rivers. Ying had grown up on the water, had spent her childhood watching the fishing boats—the province's primary source of trade—as they hauled in nets full of wriggling fish.

Ying's ancestors had sat on the Shuijing He thrones for millennia. According to legend, they were once demigods who turned carp into dragons and rode them along riverbeds. Of course, Ying knew these were merely fables. Dragons didn't exist, after all. But the Jiangs had nevertheless adopted a carp as their mascot, maintaining a long tradition of riverboating that spanned centuries.

Ying hurriedly kowtowed to her parents and elder brothers as they filed in one by one. As soon as she had completed the formal greeting, she rushed into their arms, hugging each one tight. The royal family, being fiercely protective of the palace precinct, had not allowed the Jiangs to accompany Ying to the palace. Her parents and brothers had arrived earlier that day, ushered in through a secret side gate, specifically to attend the wedding festivities. Tonight was the first time she had seen any of them in months. Hugging them felt incredible.

It felt like home.

"Little one," her mother said, holding Ying at arm's length and scrutinizing her features. Her eyes misted with tears. "I cannot believe you will soon be—"

"Mā." Ying cut her off. She did not want to be reminded of her marriage. She thrummed with nerves, terrified of the new life she would soon lead. Tonight, she didn't want to think of princes and weddings and her future duties producing heirs. All she wanted was to soak up the limited time she had with her loved ones.

From tomorrow onward, Ying would officially be part of a new family. It was likely that after the wedding she would never see her parents or four brothers again.

Her mother led her to the dressing table, upon which sat Ying's considerable collection of combs and brushes, as well as the room's only mirror. Ying fought the urge to pull away but allowed Lady Jiang to guide her onto the plush seat of the chair.

The sooner she got this over with, the better.

Ying closed her eyes, trying to clear her mind. But visions of the horrific water creature flashed behind her eyelids. Trying not to hyperventilate, she opened her eyes, gripping the edge of the dressing table, her fingers splayed upon the lacquered wood.

In the mirror, Ying's face was pale, her eyes wide. Otherwise, though, everything *looked* normal. When she moved, her reflection moved. When she blinked, her reflection did, too. All utterly, boringly normal.

She flinched when she felt her mother's fingers on her scalp.

"My, Yiyi," Lady Jiang said, using Ying's pet name. "You *are* skittish tonight. What is wrong?"

"Nothing," Ying lied. "Just wedding nerves."

For several minutes, the only sound was that of the comb pulling through Ying's hair.

"Māma?" Ying said eventually, chafing her fingers in her lap. Her eyes drifted to her mother's reflection. Lady Jiang had a look of intense concentration, her deft fingers partitioning the hair into sections before giving each a pass with the bone-handled comb. "Do you ever imagine something so strongly it seems real?"

The comb faltered for half a second before Lady Jiang resumed her steady pace. "Whatever do you mean?"

"I mean, you can see it. Really, truly see it. Right in front of you, even though you know it isn't there."

Ying didn't miss the silent look that passed between her mother and father. Ying knew that look. It said, *Here she goes again.* "No, Ying Yue," her mother said. "Why do you ask?"

Ying paused. "I thought I saw something." She stretched out a finger and placed it delicately on the cool glass. Her reflection did exactly the same. "Out there." She gestured to the garden with her eyes.

"Saw what?"

"My . . . my reflection." Ying's eyes met her mother's. "It *chased* me."

Her mother stared at Ying for a long moment, then shook her head. "It's just your fancy, bǎobèi. You're stressed due to the wedding—"

"No, it isn't that, it's—"

"The wedding," Lady Jiang said firmly, refusing to listen further. "Li Ming tells us you've been having nightmares. It seems your imagination is running away with you."

That much was true. Every night for the past few weeks, Ying had dreamt about lying in an open grave. In the dream, her future husband stood over her, his skin glinting silver in the moonlight. He'd smirk, then toss a shovelful of dirt over her face.

She'd wake screaming, heart thumping, absolutely drenched in sweat.

But tonight was different. She hadn't been asleep. She'd been very, very much awake.

As usual, the practical-minded Lady Jiang did not want to talk of ghosts and monsters. From childhood, Ying had always had a morbid fascination with horror stories. Even back then, she was intrigued by the Shan family and the rumors surrounding them. Ever since they'd conquered the noble kingdoms and founded the empire, the ruling family had completely closed the palace gates to outsiders. No staff members, except a few of their closest guards, were permitted to leave the precinct. Thousands upon thousands of Shan family servants, soldiers, guards, and bureaucrats were born, lived, and died all within the confines of the palace walls.

From that had sprung whispers: whispers about strange happenings, tales of secrets, witchcraft, disappearing women. . . . People whispered to each other that the Imperial Palace was cursed. Ying loved to speculate about the royal family, to gossip, to discuss rumors. And her curiosity had only burned brighter when she received the summons to wed the prince.

But her mother had always quickly shut down talk of anything supernatural. Lady Jiang's mind lived firmly in the present. She dealt with the touchable, the tangible. To her, Ying's interest in the occult was nothing more than a passing fancy. Of course Lady Jiang would dismiss Ying's story.

I know what I saw, dammit, Ying thought. *It was real. It was real.*

Or was it? a more sinister voice whispered within her mind. Ying fiddled with the cuffs of her sleeves, her mind racing. Since she'd arrived at the royal palace, she'd felt jumpy. Off. The truth was, this wasn't the first time she'd noticed something strange. For months now, she'd sometimes catch an odd movement, or a fluttering shadow, always just beyond the edges of her vision. Occasionally, she'd see colorful lines across her mirrors; she'd just assumed it was light hitting the glass in a very particular way.

She had dismissed it, because every time she'd turned to look, the movements had disappeared. How could Ying expect her mother to believe her when she wasn't sure she could believe herself?

"You're right." Ying kept her tone light. "It was probably just a hallucination. A vision. My nightmares have become so vivid they're happening while I'm awake."

"Very good," murmured her mother, and continued to comb Ying's hair.

After Lady Jiang had recited the last of the Four Litanies—*May you both be blessed with longevity*—the family took their leave. All except Hao Yu, Ying's eldest and most beloved brother. Hao Yu was the one who had taught her the most about fighting, the one who'd never complained when she tagged along on the brothers' adventures.

The one who once, long ago, had saved her life.

"Sister," he said, wrapping her up in an embrace. "I suppose this is where we say goodbye."

Ying's heart contracted for a beat. She blinked, her tears refracting, hazy, in her vision. But she couldn't cry. Would not cry. Crying would just waste the precious few moments she had left with her brother. Instead, she clutched his forearms and stared up at his face, trying to imprint it on her mind. She wanted to be able to recall it in detail when her loneliness became overwhelming—which would be often, if the past three months were any indication.

Hao gave her a faint half smile. "I have a present for you," he said, pulling something from the sleeve of his hànfú. "Although"— he raised an eyebrow in warning—"you're not to tell anyone what it is."

"Oh?" Ying's curiosity burned, momentarily distracting her from grief. It was so characteristic of him. He'd always loved indulging her with sweets and small trinkets, even when they were children. As they'd grown, his gifts had become more sophisticated, but the sentiment behind them had remained the same.

Tonight's gift was a silver ring set with a glittering black opal. "It's beautiful," Ying whispered, sliding it over her middle finger. Its cool tones contrasted with the warm gold of her betrothal bracelet—her old life and her new, side by side.

"It's not just a pretty ornament," her brother said, and one corner of his lip turned up in a grin. "Go on, press the stone."

She did so and gasped as the opal swung open to reveal a hidden compartment holding a small measure of fine gray powder.

"Essence of the Living Dead," Hao Yu explained at Ying's questioning expression. His voice dropped lower, and he took a step toward her. "Listen, if that husband of yours tries anything funny—and I mean *anything*—let me know. But give him some of this first, and it'll knock him out cold."

"Oh, Hao, you don't think—"

"I don't know," Hao said, his expression grim. "I mean, he's handsome, of course. Just my type. But in my experience, attractive men can still be pigs. And he just seems . . ." Her brother shook his head. "Plus, you know the rumors about the Shan family. All those empresses disappearing . . ."

"But, Hao—"

"All I'm saying is be wary. Don't fall for his pretty face. Or his pretty words." He cast a dark look at the ring on Ying's finger. "Just keep it on you, okay? In case you need it."

Ying clamped her mouth shut and nodded. The women who had disappeared—seven of them, if the rumors were true—had vanished over a span of centuries. Every princess who had married into the Shan family had faded from public view, never to be seen again. Until the current empress, that is.

But then, who was to say that they'd really disappeared? Sure, they had entered the palace and never reemerged. But so had thousands of other people, servants and nobility alike. Perhaps those other women just preferred not to interact with commonfolk.

Seven of them, though? Ying swallowed, squashing the thought. What she *knew* was true was frightening enough: that she'd be marrying into a proud, aloof family and joining a legacy that spanned centuries. That she'd be giving up her entire known existence for a man who was essentially a stranger.

No. If she thought too hard about the fate of past empresses, she'd crack, and worry Hao Yu even more. He was always worried about her safety. Once, when they were children, he'd almost lost Ying in the river. And although he had saved her, he'd never forgiven himself. Since then, he'd always been somewhat . . . overprotective.

It's because he loves me, thought Ying, hugging her brother again, not wanting to let go. Somehow, letting go seemed symbolic, as though her old life was crumbling to ash in her arms. Already her brother seemed less solid, more insubstantial.

But she had to let go. She had no choice. "Goodbye, Brother," she whispered into his shoulder, suddenly unable to stop her tears from flowing.

Finally, they parted. But as Hao went to slip out of her chamber, he stopped and turned back around. "Ying," he said, fixing her with his gaze. "One last thing. You won't go . . . *looking* for trouble, will you?"

Ying dried her eyes on a corner of her robe, her sadness replaced by mild irritation. "What do you mean?" she replied. "Of course I won't."

"Good. Remember." He paused, one hand on the door handle. "The lakes feed the rivers—"

Ying finished his sentence: "And the rivers feed the sea." The Jiang family motto. She'd said it countless times over the years, but this time the words felt so forced, so final.

Giving her a small bow, Hao finally left the room. The door snicked shut behind him. Ying wiped her tears and turned her face toward the window. The crescent moon hung suspended, a sharp-edged sliver in the sky. It was the same moon that had accompanied her, in all its phases, on her long journey to the palace. The same moon she used to watch back home. A reminder, perhaps, that out there, beyond the palace walls, real life still existed.

Even though she'd been locked up here for months, a prisoner in the palace, back in her home province, folk lived and loved and toiled and grieved under the light of the very same moon.

Ying stroked the surface of Hao Yu's ring with one finger, then closed her fist. It would stay with her always. A talisman; a memento of her brother's affection. The poison within would protect her if the prince tried anything untoward.

She shut the window, fastening the bolts. Then, drawing a steadying breath, Ying clutched her ringed hand to her heart. She could do this. The vision she'd had earlier . . . was just a vision. She was stressed out; it had been dark; she'd been spooked by some shifting shadows.

It was nothing, Ying reassured herself. As she climbed into bed and drew the covers up, the dim, guttering light from the candle swooped and flickered, blown by an errant breeze.

Ying froze.

She'd bolted the window. Which meant . . .

There was no breeze.

As she scrambled upright, she caught sight of her reflection, and the pale, ghostly hand emerging from it.

She screamed. Without thinking, she grabbed a heavy brass

ornament from her nightstand and threw it—hard. The mirror smashed; her reflection hissed and yanked back its arm.

Trembling, Ying flattened herself against the headboard, staring. Her reflection, cleaved in half by a jagged line, stared back. Its face was ashen, its chest heaving with apparent fear.

Ying could have almost convinced herself it was another hallucination, were it not for the deep crack that had appeared in her reflection's arm . . .

And the rivulets of black blood dripping from it.

4

By the time morning dawned, cool and crisp, Ying was a complete mess. She hadn't slept. Instead, after smashing the mirror to smithereens, she'd crouched in the corner of her locked bedroom, holding a candlestick aloft as a weapon and watching the candles burn down to stubs. Now her eyes were struggling to adjust to the pale creep of dawn.

Her head spun. Pain expanded from somewhere deep in the base of her skull. She felt like both crying and deliriously laughing: today, she would marry the crown prince of the Jinghu Dao empire.

She had never felt less ready.

By the time the gongs heralded the first daylight hour, Ying had already downed a tumbler of báijiǔ. She'd spluttered a little; her first taste of wine burned going down, but eventually it had turned into a faint, diffuse warmth.

Once her handmaidens finished readying her, she still had time to spare before the prince was due to arrive. So she occupied herself by drinking two more cups of wine. Then, to fill her queasy stomach, she swiped an orange from the fruit bowl, broke it open, and devoured it, pushing the peels through the window casings to hide the evidence of what she'd done. The fruit was supposed to be ornamental, a symbol of good fortune; it was not there to be actually *eaten*.

When the prince finally arrived, Ying was so lightheaded she fancied she felt, rather than saw, him enter. She trembled, facing him, drawing her robe close around her.

"Princess." His face was in shadow, his expression inscrutable.

He moved silently toward her. The morning light silhouetted his broad shoulders, making him loom even larger than usual. The dove-gray hànfú he wore was tight around his toned arms, the linen crossing over at the neckline and exposing a glimpse of tan chest. His shoulder-length black hair, in contrast with its normal artfully disheveled state, was neatly combed back into a topknot. The effect was almost otherworldly—he looked like an immortal, come to claim her virtue.

Ying's mouth went dry. This was the first time he had ever been in her room. It was the first time *any* man—apart from her father and brothers—had been in her room.

He looked too big for it. Though she herself was not tiny, she felt like a winter flower in the shadow of a mountain.

And he is just as stern and cold as a mountain, she thought. What little hope Ying had held for their union shriveled and died in her chest as he approached. There was no affection, no sympathetic light in those glittering, catlike eyes. Just grim resignation; resentment, she assumed, over their arranged marriage.

Ying straightened her spine and forced herself to look at him. It was difficult. As a warrior, he intimidated her; as a man, even more so. At only twenty years of age, Prince Shan Zhang Lin had already commanded armies, won battles, earned a reputation as a gifted archer. All these accolades made Ying feel like a naïve, provincial girl.

The prince sauntered over to the table, Ying watching his every move. He unstoppered the decanter of báijiŭ, freezing when he caught sight of its depleted contents. "I see you have already started . . . celebrating," he said, arching a brow at her.

Heat crept up Ying's neck. "I have, Your Highness." What else could she say?

With a steady hand, he poured a measure of wine, then frowned at the smashed mirror. Glittering glass dust littered the carpet around it. He turned to her, frowning. "Are your lodgings not to your taste, Lady Ying?"

Under his gaze, Ying felt completely exposed. Had his voice always been so deep? So resonant? She'd never noticed before. Though, to be fair, their opportunities for conversation had thus far been limited.

"It's not that, Your Highness. My rooms are lovely." She crossed her arms across her middle in an attempt to shield herself. "It's just—" She stopped. How could she explain the broken mirror? Would she tell her soon-to-be husband she was having hallucinations of her reflection emerging from the glass?

Of course not. The idea was ludicrous.

"I tried to furnish it in a way that would please you," he continued, moving closer. "Does it . . . not?" His voice had taken on a dangerous edge.

Ying raised her head at his words, her eyes fixing on his. She'd never been physically this close to him before, close enough to catch his scent. Wood smoke. Pine. She was suddenly acutely aware of the rhythm of her heartbeat and how pitifully erratic it had become.

"You . . . *you* furnished my rooms?" she said, unable to mask her surprise. This was so unexpected. He'd never given the slightest impression that he had any interest in, or even awareness of, her presence. Now he was claiming credit?

His eyes narrowed. "Of course," he bit back. "You are going to be my wife. What did you expect?"

Ying's insides clenched: she'd offended him. This was not an auspicious start to their wedding day. What was he going to do?

She flinched as he stepped into their shared space, but he only offered her his elbow. She held her breath as she took it; this was the first time they'd ever touched.

"Time to go serve tea," the prince said, his expression pained, as though he was attending his own funeral and not their wedding festivities.

Outside, Ying's handmaidens were waiting to help carry the heavy brocade of Ying's train. The group fell into complete silence as the prince escorted Ying toward the central rooms of the palace. As she hurried to keep up with the prince's long strides, Ying wondered how the two of them would learn to tolerate each other, let alone fall in love. Their marriage had been sanctioned by the fortune tellers. Weren't they supposed to be compatible?

Traditionally, tea ceremonies were held in the bride's family home, but since her whole family had traveled from their distant province, today's ceremony would be held at the palace. Ying walked into the tearoom by her future husband's side, her feet clumping in high-heeled wooden clogs. She would much rather have worn her supple leather slippers, in which she could prowl around, soft and silent as a cat. But she was not allowed. Not today.

The room was long and narrow. Murals depicting forests and mountains covered the walls, but, to Ying's extreme relief, there were no windows or mirrors. Several armchairs were scattered about. A long, gilt-framed sofa stood in front of an enormous fireplace at the far end of the room. As she was sweltering under her heavy dress, Ying was relieved that the fireplace wasn't lit.

She and the prince took their respective places, he making a point to keep an arm's length distance between them. Ying longed to say something, to start some sort of conversation, spark, connection—*anything*—with this man to whom she'd be bound for life. Today, she would join his family and then share his bed. She had never lain with a man; at eighteen, she had never even kissed one.

She was a loving creature. She craved touch and warmth, friendship and love. But her parents, knowing she was destined for at least a noble wedding, had kept her in a protected idyll her entire life. They had carefully curated her friends, allowing her contact with only the children of landed gentry. It was fortunate that she enjoyed a close relationship with her parents, her maids, and her siblings, for otherwise Ying's childhood would have been very lonely indeed.

Yet, despite her parents' ambitions, they had never expected a betrothal letter from the emperor himself.

One couldn't say no to the emperor, who was regarded as a deity. Nor would they want to. Marrying the crown prince meant that Ying would one day be the empress, the most powerful woman in Jinghu Dao. So Ying's mother and father had sent her away on the monthlong journey to Jinshan province, to the home of the ruling dynasty.

Lord and Lady Jiang had gifted Ying their finest horses. They'd bundled her into their most expensive carriage. She'd ridden nestled among piles of gold, gemstones, and fine fabrics intended as her dowry. The only thing that had sustained her through the long days and even longer nights was the thought of meeting her future husband. She'd passed the time picturing the moment their eyes would meet. The shimmering heat that would swirl around them, drawing them ever closer. Their hearts beating together, a timeless symphony proving they were intended, they were each other's anchors. That they were meant to be.

But Ying's fantasy had not come true. When she'd finally stumbled out of the carriage, nearly delirious with fatigue, Zhang was waiting, along with the entire royal family, their consorts, concubines, servants, and the house staff. Ying had kowtowed to the emperor and empress, kneeling in the mud and dirtying the skirt of her hànfú. When she'd finally struggled to her feet, Zhang's family were formally introduced. She'd stepped forward, her eyes wide, reaching her hands out toward her betrothed. But Zhang had not returned her warm gesture. He hadn't taken her hands in his. All he'd done was stare down at her for several long moments. Then he'd turned and walked away.

Ying forced her mind back to the present, to where she and Prince Zhang stood, side by side, waiting for the elders to enter.

At the first sight of her parents, Ying's heart ached. Today was a day of formality; she would not be allowed to go to them. Her mother, dressed in a dark burgundy hànfú, was beaming. When she caught sight of her daughter, she inclined her head. *Such a formal gesture,* Ying thought, plastering on a smile and inclining her head in return.

The betrothed couple bowed to Ying's mother and father as the servants prostrated themselves on the floor. Then a set of heavy carved mahogany doors inlaid with mother-of-pearl and gold accents was thrown open. A flautist began playing a haunting melody, and an opera singer warbled high, discordant notes, heralding the emperor and empress's impending arrival.

Zhang's parents entered in a stately parade. First came some servants, scurrying around and sweeping the floor ahead. Then the emperor came in, the empress on his arm. They moved so slowly that they appeared to be floating. Both were robed in yellow silk, swathes and swathes of it, and wore golden headdresses resplendent with precious gems.

Her heart hammering, Ying looked past the rotund frame and downturned mouth of the emperor, her gaze lingering on Empress Shan. What was it about this woman? Ying wondered, examining her future mother-in law. How was she the first empress in two centuries to escape the infamous palace curse?

Apart from the way her looks belied her age, the empress

seemed unremarkable. She was handsome, tall, her face smooth and unlined. The only gray in her hair was a single streak sweeping back from her widow's peak. Otherwise, though, there was nothing special about her appearance. Nothing that hinted at how she had avoided the fate of her seven predecessors.

Not that she had managed to escape tragedy altogether. There had been another son, her firstborn, Prince Zhang Lin's older brother. He had been the designated heir but had died in battle, and folks said after this the Shan family was never quite the same.

Ying's study of the empress was interrupted by the prince's hissed reminder to get down on the floor and *kowtow*.

It took a long time for the room to fill up. Although there were hundreds and hundreds of people, it was still just a fraction of the imperial household. Still, for Ying, this was more than enough of an audience. While she knew that Emperor Shan's household was vast, Ying had spent her time at the palace primarily locked in her own quarters. She'd never seen the palace's inner circle all gathered together like this.

The emperor and empress came to a stop in the center of the room. The air was heavy with silence. Every single person present was on the floor, even the elderly. When Emperor Shan finally commanded, "Rise!" Ying climbed to her feet. Her heart thudded, and she forced herself to take deep, slow breaths.

Raising her chin, Ying Yue squared her shoulders, and prepared to enter her second life.

5

The tea was carted in by a procession of eunuchs, who bore trays carrying porcelain teapots and an array of dainty, shallow cups. Each cup was embossed with the Shan family emblem: a three-peaked mountain encircled by a dragon.

Emperor and Empress Shan settled on the long sofa, their silks billowing about them, and looked at Ying expectantly. In fact, the whole room was watching her, waiting for her to make the first move. Everything was so silent, Ying could almost hear the buds of the tea leaves opening within the pots.

She made another bow, touching her forehead to the ground. Then she stood and approached the low table. Her heart thumped within the caged confines of her chest, and her hands shook as she poured out the dark amber liquid. A deep sense of foreboding had flooded her body—since she'd broken the fāngzhū mirror, this tea had been brewed with regular water instead of lunar dew, and she couldn't shake the idea that something bad was about to happen.

The tea sloshed out of the teapot, hitting the bottom of the cup. Tiny flecks of loose leaves flurried within the swirling liquid. Ying filled the first teacup to the top, then the second. She placed the pot back on the tray and picked up the first cup. The crowd drew in a collective breath.

"My respects, Holy Highness, Son of Heaven, Lord of My Kingdom for Ten Thousand Years." Ying bowed as she presented the cup to the emperor. He plucked it from her hands with the tips of his long, finely tapered fingers. His skin was remarkably smooth.

She picked up the second cup. The surface of the tea was so dark and still that it clearly reflected her face. Raising the cup, she bowed as she presented it to the empress.

"My respects, Empress Shan, Lady of My Kingdom for Ten Thousand Years."

But the empress didn't take the cup from her. Ying felt the weight of the pause, heard the beat of her pulse in her ears as the empress remained silent.

A chill trickled down Ying's spine. Why did the empress hesitate? Glancing up, Ying stole a look at the tea.

What she saw made her stomach flip. The tea was rippling, though no breeze blew. And reflected on the surface was an eye. Her own eye, judging by the sweep of gold along the lower lashes—yet it wasn't reflecting *her*.

No, this eye was right at the surface of the liquid, pressed up against it, staring at Ying.

Then, it winked.

Ying startled. Just slightly, just once, but enough for it to happen. . . .

The teacup slipped from her hand. Helplessly, Ying watched

its descent, time slowing like a dewdrop clinging to a branch. It hit the stone floor and smashed into a thousand pieces.

Hot tea splashed across Ying's shoes. She jumped backward, scalded. Beside her, she sensed the prince stiffen. Disapproval radiated from him in waves.

The room immediately descended into chaos. Hordes of servants rushed forward to help clean up the mess. Ying bent to pick up a broken bit of porcelain, but Prince Zhang went to grab her. He stopped himself, however, his hand hovering just above her arm. "Don't," he said, his voice tight.

Ying's anger spiked, and she shot him a glare. A shard of porcelain lay by her feet, and in her temper, she purposefully picked it up and held it out to a frenzied servant.

"Here, take this," she said. The servant, half bent over, squinted up at her for a moment. Then he took the piece of porcelain from her hand and tossed it into his basket. "Xièxie nǐ, xièxie nǐ," he said, clasping his hands together at his chest. "Thank you, Lady Ying." He backed away from her, performing a series of exaggerated bows. Next to her, the prince exhaled strongly through his nose.

Ying straightened, avoiding eye contact with Prince Zhang, and stared straight ahead. What had she just done? It wouldn't do to anger the prince, her future husband. She'd need to learn to rein in her temper. This wasn't like home, where she was the youngest child, the most indulged, where she could get away with almost anything.

The emperor was red-faced, his fists clenched. Ying's throat tightened—she'd already enraged him. The empress patted his arm in a soothing gesture before motioning to someone in the crowd. The audience parted as an old man shuffled forward—from his blood-red robe, Ying knew this was the head priest, Truth Master Chen.

The master passed the emperor an intricately carved bronze tumbler. After gulping down its contents, the emperor smacked his lips and flung the cup away.

The empress's gaze snagged on Ying's. She raised one eyebrow, her dark eyes boring into Ying's. It was as though the woman was trying to communicate something very important, but Ying didn't know what. Ying averted her eyes, feeling a flush creep up her neck. She was grateful, in that moment, for the white face powder Li Ming had applied this morning.

Whispers swept through the crowd, burgeoning into murmurs. Within minutes, the room was perfectly tidy again, and a replacement cup had appeared on the tray.

The crowd fell silent. No one stirred. They all held their breath, waiting for Ying to pick up the new teacup. Waiting to see if this time she would perform her task with the required degree of decorum.

She steeled herself, walked stiffly forward, and poured the tea. Forcing herself not to look at the cup, she clutched it with both hands and presented it again.

After the ceremony was complete, the emperor and empress left the room, and Ying began tottering after them, unsteady on her wooden heels.

"Why'd they have to give you such awful shoes?" Ying's second handmaiden, Fei fei, grumbled, trying to lift the heavy swathes of satin away from Ying's feet. Fei fei was originally from the Shan household and had been assigned to Ying upon her arrival.

Ying let out a long, protracted sigh. She was so clumsy in the clogs that she kept tripping on her skirt. "Probably so I don't run away."

Li Ming grabbed her corner of Ying's train and hoisted it up. "At least they're heavy enough, my lady," she said, a smile hovering about her lips, "that if the prince is an asshole, you can kick him in the—"

"Not now." Fei fei threw a frightened look over her shoulder at the prince, who was talking with his generals. "He might *hear* you."

Li Ming snorted. "Did you see how he treated Lady Ying? The man deserves whatever she can give him."

Ying felt a rush of gratitude at the loyalty of her maid, but she knew Li Ming's words would only bring trouble. "Quiet now, Li Ming. He is coming."

Both maids lapsed into silence and averted their eyes as Prince Zhang approached.

Ying fell into step beside her future husband, her handmaidens trailing behind. At first, he didn't say anything. He barely even acknowledged her. He certainly didn't touch her.

But then he spoke.

"That was some display," he said, his voice curt. He glanced sidelong at her ruined shoes. "You'll need to change."

"I needed an excuse to get rid of these things." Ying gestured at her feet, trying to lighten the mood. "I mean, look at them. They're hideous."

The prince paused abruptly, causing Ying to almost trip as she, too, came to a halt. "This is not a joking matter, Ying Yue," he snapped. "That ceremony was important. And it's not your place to help the servants. I won't have my wife scrabbling around on her hands and knees."

Ying bristled. "Why do you care?" Her loud whisper drew looks from several passing servants. "Why now? You haven't paid attention to anything I've done since I arrived! Not until today."

"Why do I care?" The prince's lip curled. "Such disrespect from my *beloved betrothed*. And on our wedding day!" He leaned closer, his face only inches from hers. "My father will have you flayed alive if he hears you speak to me this way." His eyes flicked toward the emperor's retreating figure, as though their conversation might indeed be overheard.

"I'm not afraid of your father," Ying shot back, her cheeks flaming. "Not as much as you are, apparently."

The prince hesitated for a moment. Fire flared in his eyes, a spark of embers on black coal. The air tremored within the narrow space between them, and Ying could barely catch her breath.

He leaned even closer. His hot breath fanned her lips. For a moment, she imagined he might kiss her. Or throttle her. She couldn't decide which.

He did neither.

Instead, he turned and stalked down the corridor in the opposite direction.

Ying's chest squeezed tight. Clearly, her words had cut deep—immediately, she regretted them. "Wait," she called after the prince's retreating figure. She hitched her skirts and stumbled along the corridor in pursuit. "Where are you going?" Huffing, she kicked off the wooden clogs and sprinted after him barefoot.

He ignored her, flinging open the closest door and striding through. Ying caught the door just before it slammed shut and barreled through after the prince, into a room dominated by a massive platform bed.

The prince, shoulders tensed, stood facing away from her, drawing rapid, ragged breaths.

"Your Highness?" Ying took a tentative step into the room. "I'm sorry if I offended you. But I *won't* apologize for helping the servants."

The prince whirled around. Advanced on her. Ying backed away, accidentally shutting the door behind her with a click.

"I'm only going to say this once, Ying Yue." He braced both arms against the door, his voice shaking with repressed rage. "You are going to be the crown princess. You are going to be my *wife*. You need to start acting like it."

Ying, refusing to be cowed, straightened, bringing herself nose-to-nose with the prince. She was furious at how her heartbeat sped up, at how her face heated at his proximity. "What about you? *You* need to—" She stopped, her heart dropping into her stomach like a stone. "The mirror!"

The prince stared at her a moment, then turned. "What about it?" he snapped, meeting Ying's eyes in the mirror.

"I—I . . . ," Ying stammered. She'd fancied she had seen her reflection smiling at her over the prince's shoulder. She'd thought she'd seen her reflection *beckoning* her with one finger. "I saw something. I mean, I thought I saw something." She caught a glimpse of the prince's expression and shook her head. "Never mind."

The prince turned back to her, scowling. "You saw something?" He leaned forward, forcing Ying to flatten herself against the door once again. "You *saw* something?"

"Please, I—"

"Gods!" He pushed off the door and backed away, his voice rising, and raked both hands through his hair. "Exactly *how* much have you had to drink, Ying?"

"Nothing. I mean, not much! You were late, and I—"

He dropped his head and shook it slowly from side to side. "First the tea, and now this. You've obviously had far too much." Sweeping past her, he reached for the door handle. "Stay here until the ceremony." Not a question. A command. Gesturing vaguely at the bed, he said, "Sleep it off or something."

Ying grabbed at his shirt. She needed to stop him from leaving, needed to keep him from walking out that door. Even if she embarrassed herself, even if she lost face. Anything to stop him leaving her in the chamber with her . . . that creature. That *thing*.

"Please!" Ying stared up at the prince, tears beginning to spill down her cheeks. "Don't go. Don't go. Please."

The prince stared down at her for one cold, measured moment, then pried her fingers from his clothing. "Collect yourself, *Princess*," he snapped as he jerked open the door. "And do better next time." The door slammed behind him, followed by the familiar sound of the key turning in the lock.

Ying collapsed, sobbing, her face pressed against the cold wood. She dared not turn around, dared not look at her reflection. She heard footsteps and started to rise, steeling herself for a fight.

Too late. She felt a hand twist into her hair. Her head was yanked back with unchecked force.

Her sobs turned to screams as Ying Yue was dragged by her hair across the floor and through the mirror.

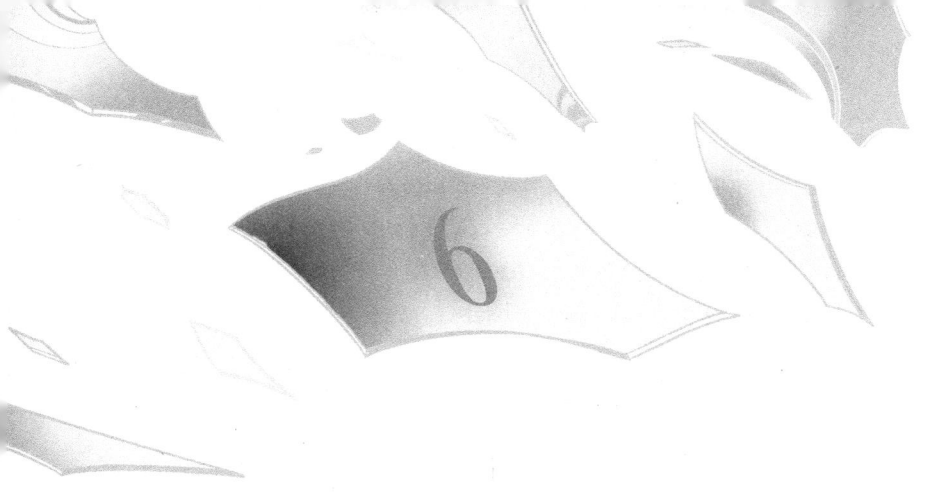

6

Ying must have passed out, because when she awoke, she was sprawled out on the bed.

She groaned and rolled over, pushing herself up to a sitting position. It must have been a dream. Her vision was blurry, but she tried to focus on her surroundings. She was in the same room where she'd argued with the prince.

Any hope she'd had for a harmonious marriage shriveled and dropped away—the crown prince was *insufferable*. Her very existence seemed to provoke him. How angry must he have been to have locked her in a strange bedroom rather than send her back to her own?

Not just any bedroom, she realized, hugging the bedpost to steady herself. This was easily the most sumptuous bedroom she had ever been in. The bed, an enormous carved-wood monstrosity, was elevated, accessed by a series of glossy wooden steps. Its surface was strewn with furs and gold pillows, and on three sides hung intricately embroidered curtains. A teak sideboard sat beside a black lacquered armoire adorned with colorful inlaid flowers, gold leaf work, and ornate iron handles. Ying didn't know what room this was, but with its refined luxury and proximity to the central rooms, she could guess.

The bridal chamber.

In one of the armoire's paneled doors was a mirror, though from this angle, Ying could not see her reflection. The idea of it frightened her, so she turned away, leaning her forehead against the bedpost, her mind churning.

Had this morning's horrific events been an extremely realistic nightmare? She must have fallen asleep, curled up on the large, empty bed. Which, she realized suddenly, was a problem.

"Mā de!" Ying leapt up, hurriedly trying to smooth the covers to erase any evidence of her repose. She was not supposed to touch the bridal bed before her husband. Supposedly, it would bring bad luck.

"Don't worry about it," a voice said from the shadows. A familiar voice. A *very* familiar voice.

Her own voice.

Heart pounding, Ying shifted her gaze to the source. In the dark corner of the room was a chair she hadn't seen before. A chair that hadn't been there. And sitting in the chair, with her long legs crossed and an exultant half smile . . .

Was her.

Ying Yue. Sitting in the chair.

With growing horror, Ying realized that the room was back to front, the wardrobe and window on the opposite side from usual.

She understood now. She was not in the bridal chamber. She was not in the same room. Or, rather, she *was* in the same room, but also she wasn't. This was the *reflection* of the room.

Ying was in a reflected room, looking at her own reflection.

Immediately, she backed up against the wall. She cast her eyes around in desperation, looking for something—anything—she could use as a weapon. Perhaps the fruit bowl would work if she hit hard enough. Or the chair, which was closer, fashioned crudely out of twisted branches. Ying stared at it, trying to figure out how long it would take to sprint over, wrench a stick out, whack her own reflection over the head, and escape—

"I suppose you're wondering about the chair." The reflection's voice cut into Ying's thoughts and made her jump. Could her reflection read her *mind*?

Reflection-Ying stood, matching Ying's height perfectly. She looked identical to Ying but somehow off-kilter. It was unsettling, seeing her reflection "in the flesh"—if you could even call it that—with shadows and curves and undulations. A mirror image is flattened, the irregularities smoothed out, but here Ying was, staring at herself in full, three-dimensional glory.

"It's made of scavenged branches," Reflection-Ying continued. She approached slowly, as though Ying were a wild animal. "It's all we have to work with in this world. Otherwise, we would have nothing for ourselves."

Ying finally managed to choke out, "What do you want?" It was meant to sound courageous, but it came out as a squeak.

"Just to talk, I promise. Listen, I'm sorry if I frightened you. I had to find a way to bring you here. You didn't seem to want to come." Reflection-Ying stopped a few paces away.

"Do you blame me?" Without taking her eyes off her

reflection, Ying sifted through her options. The reflection was now in front of the mirror, blocking Ying's escape.

Her pulse throbbed in her neck, in her stomach, on the insides of both wrists. Maybe she could still make a run for it. If she got through the door and to another mirror, she could try to go back through.

What were the chances, though, that the bedroom door was unlocked? Slim, if this world was anything like her own. Fear vined around Ying's neck and lodged inside her throat.

"No, I don't blame you." Reflection-Ying's voice was soft. Sincere. "But I promise I won't hurt you. I *am* you, remember? Hurting you would not be wise."

"Why have you brought me here, then?" Ying demanded, lifting her chin, fisting her hands to stop them from shaking. "Why've you been stalking me?"

"*Stalking* you?" The reflection raised her perfectly manicured eyebrows. "That's a funny way—"

"You know what I mean," Ying snapped. She had no time for semantics.

The reflection sighed and shifted, obscuring the mirror further. "Yes. I know exactly what you mean." She raised her large, luminous eyes at Ying. "The truth is, I've been trying to reach you for a while now, Ying Yue. But you haven't taken notice. You look not *at* me but *through* me. You'd never noticed me before, right? Before I tried to reach you through that pond in your garden?"

"Of course I noticed you. You're my reflection."

The reflection shook her head and frowned. "No, not really. I mean, we reflections are sentient creatures. We're individuals.

But when you humans look in the mirror, you only see yourselves."

"I never knew—"

"It's okay." Ying's reflection gave a small, sad smile. "You're not supposed to know. We're supposed to perfectly mimic you. If you don't notice, then we're doing our job well."

This gave Ying pause.

She knew she should be scared. And she was. After all, this was the person who had tried to lure her into the water, had watched her through the ceremonial tea, then hauled her bodily through a mirror. But Ying's fear was gradually dissipating, making way for a morbid sort of curiosity. It felt so oddly familiar to be standing here talking to her reflection. She'd done it countless times before, hadn't she? She'd just never, *ever* expected that one day her reflection would talk back.

Could this be the secret the Shan family was keeping? The reason they were so reclusive, so reluctant to let anyone inside their palace walls? It seemed like within the Imperial Palace the reflections were sentient, the mirrors permeable. Were the missing empresses actually *here*? Had they just escaped through the mirrors to run away from terrible husbands? Ying fought the urge to unleash a maniacal laugh.

Instead, she simply asked, "But *why* do you have to mimic us?"

Her reflection shrugged. "It is our duty."

Duty. Ying wrinkled her nose. She knew all about duty. She'd grown up being shackled by it. Hell, she was being forced into an unwanted marriage because of it.

Ying's reflection reached out cautiously and took both Ying's hands in her own. Strangely enough, although the reflection looked exactly like Ying, she felt nothing like her. Her hands were smooth and hard, like glass. And they were ice-cold. Ying flinched but stopped herself from pulling away.

"Ying, I need your help," the reflection said, then took a deep breath. "I've been trying to contact you for a reason. The thing is . . . I'm dying." She dropped Ying's hands and turned away.

Ying's stomach lurched. "What? Why?"

For a long time, the reflection didn't say a word. Instead, she sank down on the bed, twisting her fingers in her lap. When she finally spoke, her voice was so quiet. "Do you . . . do you remember that day on the water?"

"Which day?" Ying said, though she thought she could guess what Reflection-Ying meant.

"The one when we ran away from Hao and you fell into the water."

Of course Ying remembered that day, even though she'd not yet turned five. Hao Yu had been charged with watching his feisty little sister. And while he was distracted setting up nets for fish, little Ying Yue had slipped away and jumped into a wooden boat.

It'd been a game at first, paddling away from her brother's shouts. But then something—Ying could barely remember what—had enticed her into the water. She was a strong swimmer, but her ankle had become ensnared. And little Jiang Ying Yue had nearly died under her brother's watch.

Ying drew down her eyebrows. "Sure I do. I nearly drowned."

Then she paused, a memory crashing into her like a wave. "Wait. It was you. *You* made me jump in!"

It was coming back to her now, in bits and pieces. She'd been leaning over the side of the little boat, watching the ripples distort her reflected face, when suddenly her reflection had started thrashing and screaming for help. Ying, being too young to question it and too young to be alarmed, hadn't hesitated to go to her rescue.

"Something attacked us, remember?" The reflection gestured to her ankle, and Ying felt a shadowy memory of something—kelp perhaps—wrapping around her own. "And it wasn't just you who almost drowned. It was me, too. An old woman pulled you out."

Ying squeezed her eyes shut, trying to piece together the fragments of forgotten memories. Yes, there were glimpses: an old woman who had rescued her. And Hao running up, shouting, as Ying coughed up lungfuls of water.

Who *was* that old woman? Somehow, she looked familiar, though Ying couldn't place how or from where.

Feeling weak, her heart thudding as though struggling to keep up, Ying leaned against the wall. Last night, she'd thought her reflection had suddenly come to life. But that wasn't true. She had just forgotten. All those years, all those times she'd seen strange movements in her mirror. Just beyond the edges of her vision, always stopping when she turned to look.

And then, more recently, the colorful lights that danced on the palace mirrors, which she'd just chalked up to odd reflections. An overactive imagination.

It wasn't her imagination, though—she knew that now. It was real. It had always been easier to dismiss the truth as make-believe. Easier to forget.

Ying shook her head, trying to make sense of the words. "But why is it still affecting you now?"

"The woman who pulled you out did something to heal you. But in my world, no one came for me. Not until your brother found you, and mine found me." Reflection-Ying held her hand up in the lantern light. It was slightly translucent. The reflection's sleeve had dropped back, revealing deep cracks along the woman's arm, like damaged porcelain. Ying swallowed, her throat thick, guilt flooding her. She must have hit her reflection pretty hard last night when she'd thrown the statue.

"My brother tried to revive me," Reflection-Ying continued, "but I was teetering on the edge of death. His efforts came too late. Technically, I survived, but I've been getting weaker ever since. Like I'm living but only just. It's happening slowly, of course, but I feel it more and more as time goes on."

Ying stared at the ephemeral outline of her reflection's hand. She'd heard stories about the spirits of the underworld getting angry when they failed to claim their victims. Such people often suffered ill-thrift, wasting away like their souls were barely tethered to their bodies.

Pity was starting to soften the hard edges of Ying's heart. What must it have been like for her four-year-old reflection, being left to die while Ying was saved by the mysterious woman?

"So you're dying," Ying repeated. "And now you need my help. How? What can *I* do?"

"All I need is for you to stay in here. Just for a little while."

"Stay . . . stay here? In this world?"

"I'm a reflection. I'm made of light. But all we have here is the reflected light from your world. I need to spend time out there, soak it up, get strong again. We can't both be running around on the same side of the mirror, though. Think about it. People would get suspicious." Reflection-Ying's voice dropped to a whisper, as quiet as the flutter of a moth's wings. "It's a win-win, right? You want freedom. I see how the prince keeps you caged. The prince in this world isn't like that. In here, you can go where you want. Do what you want. And meanwhile I'll get a second chance." She drew a deep breath. "A chance to live."

Ying fiddled with her brother's ring, weighing her reflection's words. It was true, the part about the almost-drowning, and the old woman who had pulled Ying to safety. Was that the whole truth, though? Could she trust her reflection? This creature that had terrified her just hours, just minutes, earlier? This sounded risky, very risky.

In her peripheral vision, the lantern light in the mirror threw out a lustrous sheen. For the first time that night, Reflection-Ying had moved away from it.

For the first time, the mirror was unguarded.

Mentally calculating how many steps it would take her to reach it, Ying flicked her gaze toward the mirror and then back again, locking onto her reflection. Reflection-Ying was close, but the mirror was closer. Ying's bandaged foot might slow her down a little, but she didn't have far to go, and if she could just make a run for it . . .

Reflection-Ying followed Ying's line of sight and took a step toward her. "I can offer you something else," she said.

Ying turned her head slowly to face her reflection. She knew she should be ignoring this, going back through the mirror, back to her previously prescribed life. And yet . . . Her curiosity piqued, Ying asked, "What's that?"

"I can take your place." The reflection gestured at the mirror. "In the wedding. I can replace you. You need never get married to the real prince at all."

Ying's scalp prickled, her entire body flooding with a very specific sort of need. This was her one chance to escape a loveless marriage. A promise of freedom, of adventure. Wasn't that what Ying wanted? She had lived her whole life clawing at societal confines. Caged, not just by locked doors but by decorum and social mores. Trying to live up to whatever was expected of her.

For all her speculation, Ying would *never* have guessed the Imperial Palace was a gateway to another world. And here she was, being offered not just a chance to go through it but to explore it, to experience it, to live it. To escape. To live.

At any rate, it would only be temporary.

Wouldn't it?

Ying narrowed her eyes at her reflection. "So after the wedding, and after you're well again, we'll swap back?"

"I can stay for as long as it takes for the prince to lose interest in me—" She stopped and corrected herself. "To lose interest in *you*, I mean. Once his attention wanders, as usually happens with these noble men, he'll run into the arms of his concubines. We can swap back then—if that's what you still want."

Ying closed her eyes. Perhaps this was fate. Doing this meant they would both get what they wanted. For Ying, an escape from performing marital duties with a cold, uncaring man. For her reflection, a chance to heal, to get better.

Finally, Ying drew in a deep breath, opened her eyes, and nodded. "Okay," she said. "I'll do it."

Her reflection exhaled, tears gleaming in the inner corners of her eyelids. She smiled and placed her hand on Ying's cheek. It was like being caressed by a shard of ice. "Thank you," she said. "You've saved my life." Then she strode right through the glass.

Ying ran to the mirror, but her reflection was at the door on the other side, jiggling the handle.

"Don't bother," Ying called through the other side. "It's locked."

Reflection-Ying frowned. "I figured. Still had to try, though, right?" Her voice was muffled, as though she were trying to talk from the bottom of a lake. She went to the armoire and opened a drawer, rifling through the abundance of silks within; Ying herself went to her reflected drawers and opened them. They were bare.

She began to panic. The outfit she wore—her tea ceremony hànfú—was far too stuffy and formal to wear anywhere else. How would she get changed without clothes? She knocked on the mirror. Her reflection looked up.

"Excuse me," Ying said. "What do I do? There are no clothes."

"Don't worry. You'll be able to get dressed when I do." Her reflection turned and lifted up an elegant purple hànfú with embroidered edges. Ying reopened the drawer and, sure enough, the gown was there. Clearly, this world was not like her own. Clearly, it pulsed with its own deep magic.

She picked up the shimmering garment and slipped into it, mere seconds after her reflection did.

She knocked on the mirror again. "I'm not going to be able to mimic you properly," she called to her reflection. "I don't know how."

Reflection-Ying waved a hand. "It doesn't matter. No one will notice I don't have a reflection. They're all so wrapped up in their own problems. Besides, the wedding will distract them." She gestured in the general direction of the door. "Go and explore. Enjoy yourself. You deserve *some* benefit for agreeing to help me. I promise I'll let you know when we can swap back."

Ying hesitated. She glanced at the door of her mirrored world, then back at her reflection. "Will you be all right? Out there, on your own?"

"I'll be fine. You forget I've been watching your world our whole life." Her reflection gave Ying a small but encouraging smile. "Go!"

Feeling completely disoriented, Ying went to the door. Her hand tightened around the handle. In her world, the door was locked. In her world, she was a prisoner. In her world, she couldn't get out.

But this wasn't her world.

She glanced at the mirror, then back at the door. As she turned the handle, she held her breath, her pulse beating double time in her ears.

With a soft click, the door opened.

She was free.

7

When Ying had slipped through the bedroom door and shut it behind her, she leaned against it, shallow breaths fluttering in her throat. She was in the long corridor outside the bridal chamber. It was uncanny—everything looked exactly as it did on the outside. It also felt the same: The patterned wood of the door against her back. The flickering heat from the wall-hung lanterns. Even the plush carpet yielded the same way beneath her feet—softer, if anything, than the real thing.

She was thankful for both the carpet and her bare feet when she started creeping soundlessly along the corridors. The last thing she wanted was to be caught by any mirror people. Even though she'd been brought here and invited to stay by her own reflection, she couldn't shake the feeling that she was in the wrong. That she was an imposter. And what would happen if, in this world-that-was-not-her-world, she ran into someone who realized she was out of place? What would they do to her? Would they throw her back out? Hurt her? Or even worse, kill her?

She couldn't risk her one chance at freedom, even if the freedom was in another world. She'd spent so many months locked up. This was an opportunity to explore, to enjoy herself before being tossed back into her own mundane existence. Judging by his actions toward her, she had no illusions that life with the real Prince Zhang Lin would be anything but lonely, weighed down by the pressures of running the entire empire.

In the real world, she was a princess, the future empress, a noblewoman, a Jiang.

Here, she was no one.

She would just have to make sure she remained unseen.

Peering around the corner, Ying saw another long corridor. Everything was silent. She was used to the normal night-time sounds of crickets, the servants' whispers and shuffling feet, the occasional hoot of an owl. But there was none of that here. The only thing she could hear was her own heartbeat. In the eerie quiet, it sounded unnaturally loud.

Gathering her courage, she ducked around another corner. Before her was a hallway, the walls and floors made of stone. It was unfamiliar. From her studies, Ying knew the palace was composed of several discrete wings, with rooms of increasing importance closer to the center. But that was where her knowledge ended. She had no idea where she was or which wing she was about to enter.

What she needed was to get back to her own room somehow. It would not do to remain in the bridal chamber, where Prince Zhang Lin's reflection might show up. But where *were* her quarters? In her stress and confusion, she had failed to note the route they had taken to the tea ceremony that morning.

She stole along the passageway, yellow lantern light pooling on the floor and casting strange, otherworldly shapes in the shadows. Ying paused, listening for the sound of anyone approaching.

Her gaze landed on an ornate, gold-framed mirror mounted on the wall beside her. She wasn't going to look, didn't want to look, but habit made her head turn. What she saw—or didn't see, rather—drenched her in cold dread.

There was no reflection. Nothing. Just empty space and the opposite wall.

It took her some moments to collect herself, for her racing heart to slow. She raised her hands to touch her face, just to prove that she was there, that she was still alive. Of course she didn't have a reflection. Her own reflection had climbed through the mirror and taken her place. And she herself was here, stealing ghostlike along the corridor.

She shook off her unease and kept going, hoping she was headed in the right direction. Stepping through an archway, she found herself in a different wing, in an enormous antechamber paneled entirely with patterned wood. Painted vases as tall as Ying herself stood like sentinels around the perimeter. Between each pair were eight carved-mahogany double doors, leading to the different rooms within the wing. All of them were shut fast. Here, the floor was marble, and through a skylight, stars winked and stretched, distorted by the glass.

The room was richly furnished, with several clusters of carved-wood chairs surrounding little tables. This was decidedly *not* her wing.

Ying pushed open the first set of doors. She froze.

For in that room, standing in front of the mirror, was Prince Zhang Lin.

Well, the creature looked like the prince, at least from the back. Dressed in a light cotton tunic, he leaned against the mirror, one arm above his head and one hand resting on his thigh. He appeared to be gazing intently into the mirror, deep in thought. Behind him stood a colossal bed with four ornately carved teak posts that stretched toward the ceiling.

Horrified, Ying realized this was the prince's bedroom.

He hadn't noticed her. Stifling her fear, Ying bit her lip, wondering if she could escape, if she could steal away as noiselessly as she had come.

She was slipping back through the double doors when the prince's reflection spoke.

"Lady Ying," he said. "Why are you leaving?"

Ying stopped, her heart hammering, and slowly spun around.

"You looked occupied, Your Highness," she replied, her voice wavering. "I did not wish to disturb you."

"You aren't disturbing me." He stepped away from the mirror and turned to face her. "Are you ready?"

Ying's blood froze. "Ready for what?"

The Mirror Prince smiled, and Ying's breath caught. The real prince had never smiled at her as this man was doing now. "For the wedding, of course."

Ying went still. Fear flooded her, sharp and cold. She hadn't thought through the fact that, despite having avoided her real-world wedding, she'd still have to get married in here. And worse, she'd have to mimic her own reflection in order to get through it.

Reflection-Ying had said the Mirror Prince was nothing like the real Prince Zhang, though. All Ying could hope for was that her reflection was right.

She closed her eyes, her mind spinning. If she were her reflection, what would she do? Would she be friendly, would she be familiar, would she be calm, would she be shy? Would she tamp down her discomfort and pander to this Mirror Prince? Would she be happy? Would she *lie* about being happy?

Summoning all her courage, she sank into a respectful, if somewhat rigid, bow. "I am ready, my prince," she said, dropping her eyes, her posture demure. She gritted her teeth against the lie. "I am excited beyond measure."

"Me too," said the Mirror Prince, his voice low. He moved closer to Ying as she straightened—his gaze so penetrating that Ying flushed—and reached for her hand.

When the prince's fingers brushed hers, however, he recoiled as though burned. His skin was freezing, the surface as hard as glass, just like that of her own reflection. And Ying realized, horror dawning, that to him she must feel hot. She'd focused so much on how to act, she hadn't thought about how she might physically feel.

"What's wrong?" His eyes widened; he ran a hand through his tousled hair. "Your skin is burning. Are you ill?"

Heat flooded Ying's entire body. Scrambling to think of a believable explanation that would not give her—or her reflection—away, she shook her head, mortified, embarrassed, but mostly just angry at herself. It had been barely ten minutes, and she'd already been discovered.

"Do you feel all right? Do you feel weak?" The prince put his cold arm around her shoulders and led her to the bed.

Ignoring his questions, she sank onto the plush mattress.

The prince sat next to her, concern etched across his face. Even with his eyebrows knitted and his lips pressed together, he was exceptionally handsome. Being this close to him was making Ying's mind cloudy. She could barely breathe, let alone think, let alone frame a half-coherent response.

He gazed at the mirror, thoughtful for a minute. Through it, Ying saw the prince—the real prince—sprawled out upon his own bed. He was flat on his back, his head tipped back, his mouth open. He was snoring.

Fury spiked through Ying's body, so jagged that it hurt. Her husband-to-be had locked her in their bridal chamber . . . and then gone for a *nap*? How little regard he must have for her! Her hands fisted in her skirt, the silk crinkling like paper.

The Mirror Prince turned back to her. "You're one of them, aren't you?" He gestured at the mirror.

Ying's gut clenched. There was no way to spin this, no other rational explanation. Besides, Ying was and always had been a terrible liar.

She gave a tiny, almost undetectable nod.

Abruptly, the prince stood up, paced to the mirror, looked through it, then returned to stand in front of her. "You swapped?" His eyes were in shadow, their expression unreadable.

Ying gripped the edge of the bed. Cold, clammy sweat had

begun to gather on her brow, on her palms, across the back of her neck. She was unsure how much of the truth she should divulge. Would he even believe her? Would he be angry? Inwardly, she chastised herself for not asking her reflection more questions before they swapped.

She looked up at the Mirror Prince, her mind churning. "I . . . agreed to."

He shifted slightly into the light, throwing his features into sharp relief. "Why?"

The breath snagged in Ying's throat. She couldn't get the explanation out even if she tried. The silence between them thickened.

"Is it because of him?" He motioned toward the real prince's image on the other side of the glass. "Is it the wedding?"

Ying did not respond; the prince took her silence as an answer. Reaching out, he tipped Ying's chin up with the very tips of his fingers until their eyes locked. "You know what? I don't blame you. I've seen how he treats you." He pulled a face. "I've even had to mimic it."

With just that small touch, Ying's senses went into overdrive. Her skin burned beneath his fingers, even though his skin was ice-cold. It was beautiful. It was terrible. She gasped, flinching away, goosebumps peppering her skin.

"Sorry," the prince murmured, his gaze boring into hers.

Ying's chest tightened; her throat constricted. She took a breath, feeling as if she'd forgotten how. "It's . . . it's okay."

Suddenly, the real prince stirred. He was waking up.

Immediately, the Mirror Prince grabbed Ying's shoulders and yanked her behind the curtains of the four-poster bed.

Ying's breath hitched at the contact; at the coldness and foreignness of it all. The Mirror Prince glanced at the mirror—the real prince was getting up.

"I have to go."

The Mirror Prince reached up and grabbed his sword belt from a hook beside the door. "Perhaps you should get some rest, Princess." He began hurriedly strapping his ceremonial sword around his waist. "You must be exhausted after everything that's happened. You can stay here if you like."

"But . . . what about the wedding?" Ying asked. "It must be starting soon. Won't we both need to be there? To . . . mimic?"

A sad smile ghosted the prince's lips. "Don't worry about the wedding. You've gone to great lengths to avoid going through with it, and I . . . I'm not going to force you. Not like—" He paused and frowned, considering. "I'll find someone to stand in for you. It's lucky that brides are always veiled."

Ying was overwhelmed. "Thank you. I . . . appreciate it."

The prince gave a small nod in acknowledgment, his fingers tightening momentarily around the hilt of his sword.

"Well," he said, "I guess I'd better go. Will you be all right on your own?"

Ying gave a small nod.

He made to leave, but at the last moment, he turned back to face her. "Will you . . . still be here when I get back?"

Ying closed her eyes, turned things over in her mind. Would

it be better to return to her rooms—the reflected version, at least—or should she stay here, with the strange Mirror Prince?

When she opened her eyes again, they met his, his gaze burning with an intensity that made her heart flip.

She'd be safer with him, surely.

"She"—Ying took a deep breath—"the other me, I mean. She said she's sick. She said she needs to spend time in the real world to get better. She wanted me to . . . stay in here for a bit." Ying looked up at the prince. "Stay here with you."

His expression turned serious. He gazed down at her, his eyes dark and hooded.

"Good" was all he said.

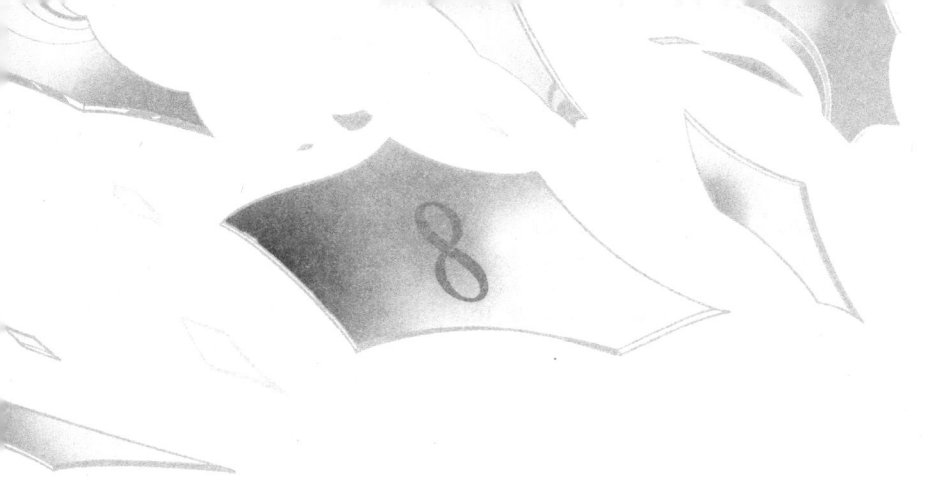

8

That was the first night she dreamed of fish.

In her dream, she was back in her garden, leaning over the pond. And once again, as she had last night, she'd noticed a flash of movement in her peripheral vision.

When she looked in its direction, she caught a glimpse of rainbow-hued iridescence. Entranced, she leaned closer.

The colors were the shimmering scales of dozens of fish, swimming in languid circles in both directions. As she watched, they sped up, swimming faster and faster until the center of the pond became a multicolored whirlpool. The water's edge rose. A wave crested over the bank, engulfing her. She tried to scream, but the rushing water muted her voice, filling her mouth, filling her throat, dragging her into its turbid depths.

As she sank, kicking and struggling against the torque, the fish began circling her. But they were no longer colorful. They were no longer iridescent. They were gray. They were slimy.

They had teeth.

When the first fish sank its fangs into the tender flesh of her thigh, she screamed again. But no sound came out, only bubbles. And then the rest of the fish descended—

Ying awoke with a start, swaddled in furs and covered in sweat, her purple gown clinging to her skin.

Still half-asleep, she thrashed under the heavy bedding. It didn't budge. She cursed, getting more and more tangled, her movements becoming increasingly frenzied as she drowned in the sheets.

Eventually, she became aware of her surroundings. She wasn't in muddy water being attacked by fish. This was the mirror world, and she'd spent the wedding night in the Mirror Prince's bed.

Not that she'd actually spent it *with* the prince. He must have been delayed by the wedding festivities.

It had taken her a long time to drift off; not only was the whole situation utterly surreal, it was awkward knowing that either prince might return at any moment. Finally, though, sleep had enveloped her—the stress and fatigue taking over, warmth returning slowly to her extremities.

She wasn't sure if he had returned. At one stage, she'd opened her bleary eyes and fancied she saw him sitting on the sofa, watching her, but she couldn't be sure she wasn't dreaming.

Now, despite the frosty air, she was too hot. Throwing off the covers, she stretched out her arms, luxuriating in the loose-limbed feeling. Swinging her feet to the floor, she smiled at a pair of silk slippers sitting by the bed.

Had the Mirror Prince left them there? Probably, Ying guessed. He would've seen Ying tottering around in her infernal wooden clogs from the other side of the mirrors, might have noticed she'd kicked them off before pursuing the real prince.

And now he was replacing them with something more comfortable. It was such a thoughtful gesture, and Ying was touched. It was true: he really was different from his real-world counterpart.

She took a moment to savor the softness of the slippers before turning her attention to the prince's room. It was large, with high ceilings. There were three windows on the opposite wall, all perfectly round, set in recessed alcoves and hung with embroidered silk.

Wondering if the outside view was the same in this world, Ying drifted to the windows. One by one, she tugged open all three sets of drapes, revealing patterned fretwork shutters. Light streamed in, chasing away the gloom. When she reached the last window, she pushed the shutters open, wincing as the chilly air bit her skin.

She shivered. Rubbing at her upper arms in an attempt to warm up, she leaned out of the window.

It looked onto the central courtyard, which even at this early hour was bustling with activity. Beyond lay the mountain ranges that ringed Jinshan province. The sight of the familiar landscape was a comfort—even though she felt wrong, felt out of place here, this world wasn't so unlike her own.

Except for the fact that it was *freezing*. Her face was numb; her muscles ached. She had unconsciously clenched her jaw to stop herself from chattering. Although this world looked the same, it was far, far colder.

Taking one last, longing look at the scenery, Ying pulled the shutters closed.

At precisely the same moment, the bedroom door swung

open and Ying, stifling a gasp, quickly withdrew into the recessed alcove and yanked the curtains shut.

She peered through a crack in the drapes, her neck growing clammy. A shadow slid across the surface of the mirror, and Ying's second handmaiden—the reflected version, that is—entered the room. On the other side of the glass, the real Fei fei entered the real-world chamber.

"Fei!" The whisper involuntarily fled Ying's lips, and she cursed inwardly. Luckily, the reflection hadn't heard her; seemingly unaware of Ying's presence, she walked to the bed, fluffed the pillows, and smoothed the sheets.

The real-life Fei fei was doing the same thing on the outside—this Fei fei was simply mimicking her.

With her pulse pounding in her ears, Ying studied the mirror version of her maid. Reflection-Fei fei was identical to the one Ying knew: the same round face, the same thin, straight hair. The maids on both sides of the mirror were tidying, picking up small ornaments from the tables and wiping the surfaces below. Ying watched Fei's reflection as she, copying her counterpart, carefully placed the trinkets back in straight lines.

Reflection-Fei's expression was curiously blank, as though she was looking not *at* things but, rather, *through* them. The hair on Ying's arms prickled. It was unsettling: here was someone who looked identical to her sweet, soft-spoken handmaiden—but it wasn't Fei. Not really.

Having finished wiping the table, the maids gathered their tools, turned to the first window to draw the curtains, and—

Too late, Ying realized her mistake.

The drapes on the other side of the mirror were closed. The drapes on this side of the mirror?

Open.

Reflection-Fei reached for the curtains' nonexistent seam and froze. For a moment, she seemed suspended in time, immobilized, while on the other side of the mirror the real Fei continued her work. Ying held her breath, shrinking farther into the alcove, wondering what Reflection-Fei would do. The room was silent, and after several thudding heartbeats Ying risked opening the curtains a crack and peeking through.

The maid turned her head slowly. Her eyes, so dark they looked almost black, snapped into focus, her gaze suddenly piercing Ying's.

With a gasp, Ying whipped the drapes closed again and held them fast. Her pulse accelerated, her breaths coming hard and fast.

She heard quick footsteps. The drapes were ripped from Ying's grasp as the maid yanked them apart. "You should not be here." Reflection-Fei glared at Ying. "You need to *leave.*"

Ying almost screamed, but fear strangled the sound.

The reflection is lucid, Ying thought, trembling all over. It was a shocking transition from the trance-like state the maid had been in before. *She's lucid.* But just as quickly, the shutters came down over the maid's eyes. Their blank expression returned. And Reflection-Fei—copying the real-life maid—promptly turned and walked out the door as though nothing had even happened.

A chill tore through Ying's body. What had Fei's reflection meant? Had she sensed Ying's foreignness and abhorred her for it? Was it supposed to be a warning? A threat? Ying had half a mind to go back through the mirrors and demand that her reflection swap back. Immediately.

It's probably nothing, she told herself, trying to soothe herself. *She just prefers her own mistress, that's all.*

She was so disturbed by Reflection-Fei's words, by the panic that now flooded her mind, that she didn't even notice the door click open.

"Princess Ying?" Startled, Ying looked up. The Mirror Prince had returned. He was carrying a burgundy cloak folded over one arm. His brow furrowed. "Are you quite all right?"

Rising from her seat on the windowsill, Ying placed her hands behind her back to hide their shaking. "It's . . . ," she began, her mouth dry. "It's my maid."

The Mirror Prince's thick black brows drew down farther. "Your maid?"

"The mirror version. She just left." Ying threw a fearful glance at the closed door. "Did you see her? When you were coming in?"

After dumping the folded cloak onto one of the tables—knocking the neat formation of ornaments into disarray—the Mirror Prince approached Ying, stopping an arm's length in front of her. "I did not," he said, looking carefully at Ying's face. "Did she frighten you?"

"She told me I should leave," Ying blurted out. "That I don't belong here, and . . . and . . ." She trailed off, her eyelids burning hot with the painful portent of tears. Blinking hard, she managed to stave them off. "She looked at me with such *hatred*. My Fei would never—"

"She did *what*?" For a fractional moment, anger limned the prince's features. But then his expression softened.

"Oh, Princess," he said. He took a step forward. Iciness radiated from his body, penetrating through the thin fabric of Ying's gown. She shivered, and not just from the cold.

"The people of this world," the prince continued, his voice as soft as new snow, "we are . . . different from your versions. We are forced to act like you, but we are not you. You must know how different I am from the other prince—"

"I do," Ying cut in. "I do know." And she raised her eyes, her breath catching at the Mirror Prince's expression. His high cheekbones, his sculpted lips. The way he was staring at her with such intensity. He was leaning slightly toward her, as though he wanted to touch her but didn't dare. Ying only just managed to stutter out, "B-but what if she's right?"

"Ignore her," the prince replied with a confidence that actually did make Ying feel better. Then his lips turned up in a half smile. "How about I give you a tour of the gardens? If you're interested, that is. It might help take your mind off your maid." He grabbed the cloak off the table and shook it out until the soft fold of its drape hit the floor. "I brought your cloak."

To keep me warm. Ying's mind finished off the sentence for him, and something swooped in her belly. The slippers and now this. It was true. He really was the polar opposite of the other Zhang Lin. "What about the other prince?"

He shrugged. "He's out on a hunt this morning. In the mountains. And at this time of year, the lakes up there are all frozen over. No reflections."

Ying chewed on her lip, thinking. She loved the outdoors. She loved greenery, and nature, and had always wanted to see the famed palace grounds. But was she safe? Outdoors? In this mirror world? Was she safe indoors, come to think of it?

The Mirror Prince seemed to read her thoughts. "You'll be safe," he reassured her. "As long as you're with me." He draped the cloak around her shoulders, his cool fingers brushing her neck. Ying froze at his touch, her breath running ragged, her heart thrashing as though trying to escape. When he stepped away, she pressed a hand to her chest, trying to calm herself.

As she clutched the cloak tightly around her, Ying suddenly remembered she could only get dressed in things her reflection was wearing. What was Reflection-Ying doing that required her to wear a cloak?

She brushed away these thoughts. "Yes," she said, looking up at the prince. "I'll come."

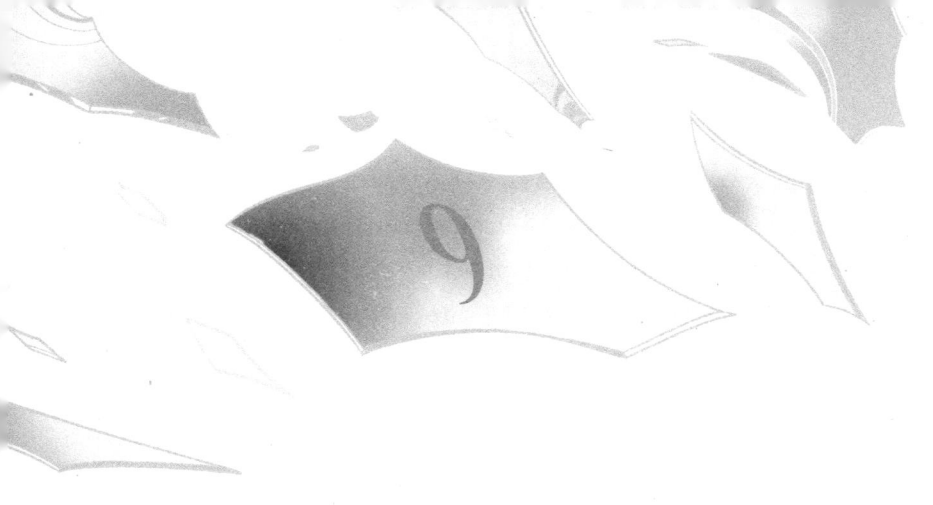

9

Ying spent the morning rambling through the expansive imperial gardens with the Mirror Prince as her guide. They plucked flowers in the Lotus Garden, sat under the shade of towering trees in the Garden of Blissful Repose, and burned incense at south-facing shrines in the Garden of Celestial Worship. From a distance, the prince pointed out the mausoleum, its cool stone walls a striking contrast to the Garden of Perpetual Solace surrounding it. In the Garden of Everlasting Immortality, he climbed a fruit tree to pluck the choicest plum. After breaking the fruit in half, he offered it to her, the pit nestled within the blood-red flesh.

The prince was a most gallant guide, allowing Ying to take his elbow. It gave her a thrill to be so close to him, for her small hands to encircle his strong forearm, his body's chill leaching into her skin and making her shiver.

He'd indulged Ying's every whim, showing her anything that took her fancy. He'd even allowed her an illicit peek into the emperor's private Holy Harmony Garden, where the empire's rarest, most beautiful and fragrant flowers were kept. She'd stood at one of the many circular moon gates, staring at the riotous color, listening to the low, languid drone of bees, inhaling deeply as though she could imbibe the sweet, wondrous scent and permanently brand it upon her mind.

But as they approached the gated Garden of Verdant Splendor, the prince hung back, tugging on Ying's arm. "Not there," he murmured.

"Why not?" The words slipped out. Ying quickly shut her mouth, not wanting him to think her impertinent.

He remained unruffled, however. "The Lake of Tranquility is in there," he said, jerking his chin at the closed gate. "We can't risk it. The reflections."

"Oh. Right." Ying bit her lip and nodded. Despite her disappointment, she understood his reasoning. "Of course."

Instead, he drew her gently toward him. "How about we do something else? Something fun?" He gestured toward the stables, to their right. "Do you like horses? Would you—" He paused, as though not quite sure how Ying would react. "Would you go for a ride with me?"

Ying's heart leapt. She loved horses. In fact, she'd spent most of her childhood on horseback—when she wasn't playing at swords, that is. And since she'd arrived at the palace, she'd been forbidden to ride.

"I'd love to," Ying said, smiling up at him.

The prince smiled back, but his smile morphed into a grimace.

Reflexively, Ying reached out and grabbed his arm. "What's wrong?"

His eyes dropped to where Ying was gripping him, and he

winced again. "It's just . . ." He took a shaky breath. "The other prince. He's coming back."

"Wait. It *hurts* you?"

"Yes." The prince closed his eyes, grimacing again. "We're always in pain. And it worsens with distance. It's particularly bad if our counterpart is nearing a reflective surface and we are not." He opened his eyes, his face smoothing into a mask of stoicism. But the lines of tension in his neck, in his shoulders, betrayed him. "We're tied to you folk—not just out of duty but physically, too."

Ying's fingers tightened around his bicep. She stared up into his eyes. Opalescent eyes that were not quite black but punctuated with flecks of violet light. He was breathing hard. It seemed so unfair. What must it have cost him—what was it still costing him—to have spent the entire morning with her and not his reflection?

Some feeling that she couldn't quite parse flashed through her body like fire. He had chosen to bear that pain—for her.

"Go," she said, releasing his arm and taking a step back. "Do what you need to do."

He raised his hands, as though he would grab her again, but then dropped them. "Are you sure?" His words were strangled, as if he could barely breathe.

"I'll be okay," Ying replied, worried. "I'll retrace our steps and go back to your room. I'll wait for you there."

He paused, hesitating, but then nodded once and sprinted away.

After a brief pause to get her bearings, Ying started along the path, heading back the way they'd come. Every now and then, a servant passed by, each one bowing low in greeting before hurrying away. She realized that she looked exactly like Reflection-Ying. Unless they touched her, they would not know the difference.

She took a left turn where the pathway forked—noting the familiar arbor beneath which she and the Mirror Prince had previously passed. If she followed the curved path, soon she would reach the fruit orchard in the Garden of Everlasting Immortality. Cutting through there would allow her to reach the inner courtyards.

However, the orchard never appeared. Ying walked and walked, wondering why it seemed so much farther on her own than it had with the prince. Her footsteps crunched on the gravel path as she trudged.

Then she stopped short.

She was back at the Garden of Verdant Splendor, in front of the very same gate. The gate through which lay the Lake of Tranquility.

She was back where the prince had left her.

Ying blinked at the gate's carved-wood motif and shook her head. Where the pathway had forked, she must have taken the wrong turn, somehow straying onto a path that looped back on itself. While she had been certain she needed to turn left at the arbor, perhaps... perhaps she'd been mistaken. To be fair, she'd been a little distracted on the way here, walking beside the Mirror Prince, clutching his cold, sculpted arm.

This time, when she reached the arbor, she took a right turn instead. It was disorienting—nothing looked at all familiar. The palace looked as distant as ever, the imposing structure nestled among the mountains. In fact, it looked as though it was getting farther away. Lost in thought, and utterly confused, she suddenly found herself . . .

Back at the same gate.

What is going on? Ying's forehead grew hot, and she placed a hand on it. Why couldn't she get back to the palace?

She tried several times more—taking right turns, taking left turns, even trying to crash through one of the neatly manicured gardens—but each time, no matter which direction she tried to go in, she ended up back at the same gate.

By now, the morning chill had dissipated, and Ying was sweating. Even stripping off her cloak hadn't helped. She glanced up to see if she could estimate the time based on the sun's position but could not see where in the sky it was.

A creeping fear was beginning to pervade Ying's mind. It seemed as though the mirror world was corralling her toward the lake. But for what reason? Maybe it was because she didn't belong here, in this realm. Maybe it was shunting her toward the closest reflective surface, trying to correct the anomaly. Trying to get her back to the real world, back to where she belonged.

What if she got stuck for good? What if she could never get back to the palace as she'd promised?

Licking her dry lips, Ying pressed a hand to her belly. She was famished—the plum from the gardens hadn't been nearly enough to fill her up—but more urgently, she was thirsty. She'd now been circling the gardens for several hours; she needed a drink, and soon. And she knew that past the wall directly before her, through this ornate gate, was a lake. The Lake of Tranquility. The lake that the prince had expressly asked her *not* to visit.

She swallowed, the dryness rasping her throat like cut glass.

Surely it would do no harm if she just snuck in there quickly, just to get a quick drink, perhaps wet her face and arms. She would conceal herself first and watch; she'd make sure there were no reflections, or real-world people, to see her. Rehydrating would rejuvenate her, allow her to continue trying to find her way back to the palace. Besides, it wasn't as if the mirror world would let her go anywhere else.

Making her mind up, she smoothed her skirt. After folding the cloak neatly and stowing it at the base of a tree, she strode to the massive wooden gate and pushed.

The gate swung open, and Ying gasped.

It was a garden. But not just any garden. The focal point was the lake, overwhelming due to its gargantuan size. Even when she squinted, she couldn't see the far side.

The water was a glassy green. Sprinkled across its surface were clusters of white flowers floating among their lily pads. Rocks tumbled along the shore, punctuated by patches of white, pink, and purple blooms. The low cadence of rushing water came from a small, elegant waterfall to Ying's left. Dozens of willow trees, all bent as if obeisant to the wind, trailed their long leaves in the water. Surrounding the lake in every direction were vast, grassy lawns.

There was no one around. Ying's body felt abnormally light, as though she were filled with air and bubbles instead of flesh and blood. She breathed in, absorbing all the scents and sounds and colors. The Garden of Verdant Splendor was aptly named indeed.

Standing over the lake on stilts was a héhuā tíng, a Lotus Pavilion. It had a curved, peaked tile roof. The walls were open, made up of an intricate cubed fretwork. The pathway leading up to the building's entrance was covered by a large archway draped in wisteria, which hung down in a fluttering canopy of purple, green, and white.

She trailed her hands through the hanging flowers as she walked the path to the lake house. She traced the carved-wood banisters with the tips of her fingers. And as she mounted the steps, she noted two dragon-headed statues, mounted on either side of the lintel.

From the platform, she had a sweeping view of the scenery, with the distant backdrop of the mountain range. The snowcapped peaks were reflected in the calm, still water of the lake.

Out here, she was exposed, the cold air stinging her skin. She rubbed at her goosefleshed arms. The back of her neck prickled, as if someone was watching her.

A crow was perched on the pavilion roof above her. A moment later, a few more fluttered down and landed there, watching Ying with beady eyes.

Trying to ignore the gathering birds, Ying knelt at the platform's edge and dipped cupped hands into the water. She drank, the water cool and sweet on her parched tongue.

The fish that lived in the lake must have sensed her presence, for they congregated at the surface, waiting to be fed, their bright-orange bodies gleaming in the sunlight. She shuddered, remembering her dream. But these fish were not rainbow, just standard red-gold carp.

"I'm sorry. I don't have any food." Ying touched the water's surface with the tip of one finger.

One bold fish nibbled at the finger. Then another fish joined. Then another. Ying giggled. Before long, the entire shoal was crowding around her hand, jostling for a chance to check for food.

But suddenly, they all darted away. The lake appeared empty, as though they'd never been there at all.

Strange. . . . Perhaps she'd startled them.

She withdrew her hand and dried it on her skirt, still kneeling. Everything had fallen silent—too silent.

It was then that she noticed. . . .

The lake wasn't empty.

A dark shadow skimmed beneath the surface. In an instant, the crows took off into the air, flapping away in a flurry of noise.

Ying stared, frozen to the spot, unsure what she was seeing. She barely had time to rise to her feet when the creature erupted from the water.

All she saw was a huge, shiny black body and a great big, open jaw. The creature launched itself at Ying, hundreds of fangs glistening in its cavernous mouth. Ying jumped backward, and the creature snapped its jaws shut exactly where she had been standing just a second before.

She didn't stop to see more. She turned. She ran.

A loud thump told her the creature had launched itself out of the water; it must have flung itself onto the viewing platform. Ying cursed. She had hoped it wouldn't be able to leave the lake.

Throwing a look back over her shoulder, she watched in horror as an enormous black snake uncoiled itself and reared its huge eyeless head, ready to strike.

Ying bolted. But the creature was quick. As she dashed through the wisteria-lined archway, the snake crashed right through it. Its jaws snapped at her again, barely missing her shoulder. Its next snap caught the edge of her hànfú, ripping it. Ying had made it past the archway, but the creature was gaining on her fast. It raised its head, ready to strike again.

Desperately, Ying reached for the first thing she could find, snatching a fallen willow branch off the ground. Then she turned to face the creature.

"Get back!" she screamed, then whipped the snake across the nose.

It balked for a moment, then reared up, its huge head swaying, its mouth unhinging.

Ying backed up and brandished her branch. But she wasn't sure it would work a second time.

The snake slithered toward her. Ying retreated, striking it over the head again and again. This time it didn't flinch. Its maw gaped open, dripping venom.

It was blind, Ying suddenly realized. Of course it was blind. With no eyes, it couldn't see her.

Ying stopped whipping the willow branch. She stilled, trying not to breathe, hoping her thumping heart wouldn't give her away.

The creature's head swayed from side to side, its forked tongue flicking, trying to detect her taste in the air. Ying briefly considered trying to silently back away, but she could not risk the creature sensing the vibrations. So instead she chose the reckless route. She'd once read in a book that the only way to restrain a snake was to grab it just below its head. This way it couldn't bite you. And this creature was a snake.

Just a very, very big one.

In a split second, she had thrown herself at the creature, grabbed its neck, swung her legs over its glistening body, and fastened herself to its scaly body. It writhed, its barbed tail slapping the ground.

Ying held on as the serpent thrashed. She screamed when one of the barbs raked her arm, but she ignored the pain, ignored the danger. There was only one way out of this mess, and that was to choke the beast.

She squeezed with every fiber of her being. Squeezed as though her life depended on it. And slowly, slowly, the creature stopped moving. It dropped its head to the ground. Ying let out a sharp exhale.

Her relief was short-lived. Panic rose in her chest as she realized what the snake was doing. It began slithering backward, into the lake, dragging her toward its fathomless depths.

10

She tried to jump off, but it was too late. The two of them plunged into the frigid lake. Water bubbled around her face, rushed up her nose, shot under her gown until it billowed like a sail. Struggling, she fought to reach the surface. But with one twist of its muscular body, the snake coiled its tail around Ying's torso, the barbs raking her upper back.

A noiseless scream escaped her, and water flooded her mouth. All she could hear was the rush of water past her ears. The snake's body tightened, crushing, hurting, and she clawed at its smooth, slippery scales. Around her, fish swam in increasingly tight circles, mimicking the fish from Ying's dream. Blackness crept around the edges of her vision. She began to weaken, her escape efforts becoming feeble.

Then came a sound. Screaming. Endless screaming. As though the entire universe was railing against Ying's dire situation. It was everywhere: above her, around her, even within her own head. Clamping her hands over her ears, she jerked and twitched, unable to dispel the piercing pain.

Her pulse became quick and fluttery, and her limbs grew heavy. Her fuzzy mind tried to orient her.

Right before she was about to black out, an arrow shot through the water, narrowly missing her. It plunged straight into the creature's neck. Another arrow flew by and skewered its head. The tight coil of the snake's body loosened.

Mustering one last effort, Ying pulled an arrow from the monster and stabbed it over and over into its soft, black-scaled flesh. The screaming escalated, augmented by the creature's keening cry.

It started to shrink away, its tail slackening even more. Ying fought her way out of the creature's grasp as it sank, writhing, into the murky depths. Hands hooked under her armpits and heaved her unceremoniously onto the shore.

Slinging his bow onto his back, the Mirror Prince rolled Ying over. She coughed, struggling to sit up, cold water gushing from her mouth. He held her upright and thumped her on the back.

"Are you hurt?" His face was pale.

Ying felt faint. "My . . . my arm." She'd been clutching her forearm; when she held her hand up, it was covered in blood.

The prince glanced down and uttered a low curse.

"Come with me," he said, sweeping her up into his arms.

At first she was numb, but as the prince rushed her through the palace hallways, the pain hit.

He burst into a small room atop the West tower and laid her on the narrow bed. Ying moaned. Her arm hurt badly. She was soaking wet and cold. But the searing pain across her back was the worst of all. Her head felt light, as if it were barely attached to her body. The Mirror Prince cursed again.

The room was dark, even in the daytime. Incense imbued the air with the intoxicating scent of sandalwood and musk. Ying's head was already woozy from blood loss, but if it hadn't been, she might have keeled over from the fumes.

"Mei Po!" the prince bellowed. When there was no answer, he yelled again. "Mei Po!"

Through the haze of incense-laced smoke, Ying saw a woman shuffling to her bedside. The woman was possibly the oldest living creature Ying had ever seen. She had a cloud of wispy white hair. Her skin was mottled, her face as wrinkled as leather. And her blueish eyes were so pale they were almost clear. She looked as though she had lived so long she'd been leached of all her color.

So this was the famous Mei Po. The matchmaker. One of the oldest fortune tellers in the emperor's household, and according to legend, hundreds of years old. It was said she kept herself alive with alchemical elixirs; that she'd once had another name but had lived so long people had forgotten it, so now she was simply called Mei Po.

The emperor, like all the emperors before him, held Mei Po's ability to predict auspicious marriages in the highest esteem. No self-respecting highborn family would allow their offspring to wed without first consulting Mei Po. According to legend, she always chose well. And according to legend, she always got it right.

Except for me, Ying thought, her mind casting back to the awkward silences between herself and the real prince.

Mei Po approached Ying, waving away the Mirror Prince, who retreated to a corner. The old woman leaned over Ying's arm, inspecting it thoroughly. Then she rolled Ying onto her side and prodded the wound with her finger. Ying sucked in a breath and clenched her jaw. The Mirror Prince made a move toward them, but one look from Mei Po pinned him in his place.

She frowned at him. "What was it?"

"Gōushé," he spat out. "Serpent."

"Aiyo." The old woman raised her eyebrows, then shook her head, tutting. "Lucky to be alive." She produced a vial of liquid attached to a leather cord that was threaded around her neck. "Take this," she said, putting the vial into Ying's mouth and tipping out a few drops. It tasted foul, but Ying's pain immediately dulled, and a somnolent feeling settled in her bones. She quieted.

Mei Po straightened and shuffled over to a small stone fireplace in a corner of the room. It was empty, but Mei Po grabbed something—powder, perhaps—from a ceramic urn and threw it onto the hearth. Immediately, green flames erupted. The smell of incense grew even stronger. Mei Po took something from a jar—to Ying, it looked like a brittle, molted snake skin—and tossed it on the fire. The flames flared, throwing off sparks. The old woman then balanced a crucible over the fire, poking and prodding its contents with a pair of porcelain chopsticks, humming to herself.

By now, Ying's wounds had settled into a dull, throbbing ache. The warmth of the room, too, had thawed her chill, though her torn robe still clung uncomfortably to her skin. Ignoring these unpleasant sensations, Ying watched Mei Po's activities intently.

Her mind was scrambled with so many unanswered questions from her morning spent in the mirror world. Might this woman have the answers?

She didn't get a chance to ask before Mei Po turned and dumped a cupful of liquid over Ying's exposed arm and shoulder. It sizzled. Ying screamed, her wounds burning, and curled up in a ball. At the sound of her cry, the prince rushed to her side and caressed her face, smoothing her hair away from her sweaty forehead.

The heat gradually dissipated, then disappeared altogether. And, to Ying's surprise, so did the pain.

"Can you stand?" Mei Po asked.

"I'll try." Leaning on the prince, Ying rose unsteadily to her feet. Her back felt a little tight but not too painful. The wound on her arm was gone, except for a long, red, jagged scar.

Mei Po smiled, her clear eyes crinkling at the edges. She reached out and ran her cold fingertips along the scar. "You will always have this, I'm afraid. And another upon your back. Gōushé venom leaves its mark." She bowed and gestured to a cluster of low wooden stools. She herself settled onto a tufted gold divan and smiled at her guests. Her teeth were small and white, like sun-bleached river pebbles.

"I have wanted to meet you for some time, Princess Ying." She held her hands together at her heart and bowed. "Congratulations on your union."

The prince cupped his hands at his chest and returned her bow. "Xièxie, Mei Po."

Mei Po waved her hands over a side table. Ying blinked

when a pretty porcelain tea set appeared out of thin air. The old woman poured two small cups of tea. "Chá?" she asked, holding them out. She bobbed her head. "Take, take."

The prince and Ying sat, each taking a cup. Ying brought hers to her lips and swallowed. Grasping it in both hands, she rested it on her knee, warming her stiff, chilled fingers. She glanced down but then looked away, not wanting to risk seeing her reflection in the tea.

Mei Po poured herself tea and drank a mouthful. Then she eyed Ying over the rim. "Pray, child, how long are you staying in this world?"

Ying tightened her fingers around her cup. *Of course Mei Po knows. She'd touched Ying's skin, felt her heat.*

She and the Mirror Prince exchanged loaded looks. "I don't know, Madame," Ying replied. "I did not expect to be attacked by the . . . what did you call it?"

"Gōushé. Yes, of course you would not expect it. It exists only in our world, not yours. And it does not hunt our kind."

"Why not?" Ying asked.

Mei Po took another sip of tea. "It craves flesh," she said simply. "It must have sensed your life force."

"I—I heard screaming." The memory made Ying shudder. "What *was* that?"

The old woman gave her a shrewd look. "Souls protest when they leave the body. It is . . . against nature."

"Gods!" the Mirror Prince exclaimed. His face had turned deathly pale. "The screaming," he said to Ying. "It must have come from you. From *your* head."

Ying's heart jolted. Had she really been that close to death? She'd been injured, yes, but it hadn't felt like dying. She'd already almost died that time Hao Yu had found her, but she didn't remember any screaming then.

Perhaps things worked differently in the mirror world. Perhaps there was some other explanation, something the Mirror Prince—and Mei Po's reflection—did not want her to know.

Mei Po turned her clear eyes on Ying. "You have had quite the ordeal, Ying Yue. I would suggest you take some rest." She directed her next words at the prince. "Be sure she rests!"

"Of course, Madame," he replied, inclining his head respectfully.

The old woman went back to sipping her tea. She seemed so harmless despite her obvious occult abilities. Ying gripped her cup, burning with more questions, but she didn't even know where to start.

Ying had always been drawn to anything supernatural. Her parents had tried to stamp out her interest, of course, branding it as nothing but cheap tricks and quackery. They had no faith in that sorcery, they'd tell her. *Best you study the arts and sciences. Learn music. Learn your manners.*

Learn to be a lady, was what they'd really meant.

But that hadn't stopped her from sneaking books out of Master Yuan's extensive library. Instead of memorizing poetry like she was meant to, she'd pore over books on witchcraft and alchemy, on demons and the dark arts. She'd devour whole volumes devoted to mythical beasts. In her safe home back in Shuijing He, they'd seemed so fantastical. But now she knew better.

Now she knew they were real.

Thinking back to the serpent, she was sure she'd seen something just like it in one of the ancient texts, where they were described as guardians of other worlds. Why had the garden pathways herded her to the lake? Were they simply steering her back toward her own world—or was something hidden there, in an unseen realm, something so precious it needed to be protected by an ancient monster?

And if so, Ying thought, what did it want with *her*?

Mei Po said nothing more. She just sat and looked at Ying, a benign smile playing at the corner of her pale lips.

A shiver rolled through Ying's body. She was beginning to realize that this world was less like her own than she initially thought. It contained vicious monsters, for one. And mirror people. Pathways shifted; direction lacked meaning. And then there was the most unsettling thing of all: Ying's growing uncertainty over who to trust.

Perhaps, she thought, if she could stay and talk to Mei Po, she might learn more about the mirror world and how to navigate it. Perhaps one needed magic to survive in this world. Or maybe trying to survive here was a fool's endeavor. Maybe she should be going back.

But that would mean abandoning her freedom, and her reflection, and, well . . . *him*.

Involuntarily, she glanced at the prince and reddened when she realized he'd been ogling her. He looked away—a little too late—and cleared his throat. "We had best be going," he said, breaking the silence. He placed his untouched cup back on the tray and rose to his feet, giving Mei Po a small bow. "Thank you, Mei Po, for all you've done. I am indebted to you for your service. Come, Princess."

Ying placed her own cup back on the tray. "Thank you, Madame Mei Po." She hugged herself, trying to stop shivering, for the cold in her bones had suddenly returned. Still, she tarried, her eyes lingering on the rows of dusty books and potions lining the shelves along one wall. If only she could stay, find out a bit more—but the prince was holding open the door, waiting for her to go through.

Ying bowed to the old woman and began to walk out.

"Wait." Mei Po stopped Ying with a wrinkled, icy hand on her forearm. She gestured for her to come closer. "Remember," she said. Her breath was cool. "Remember who the monsters are."

The old woman pointed to a mirror mounted next to the door. Ying hadn't noticed it before. It was a round disc, made of highly polished bronze. She'd seen ones like these before, in her own world: mirrors designed to ward off demons.

In it, Ying could see the cluttered shelves behind her. But although both she and Mei Po were standing in front of the mirror, neither had any reflection at all.

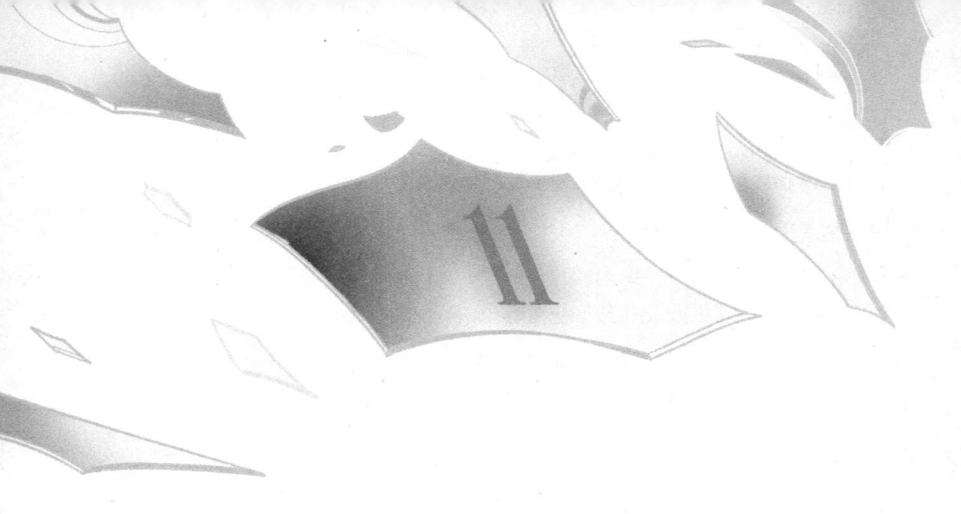

11

The Mirror Prince helped Ying down the stone staircase, leading her away from Mei Po's stuffy tower room. He didn't speak as they descended. Every now and then, Ying stole a glance at his face, at his drawn-down eyebrows, his dark and distant eyes.

"Does it hurt very much?" Ying asked eventually, just for some conversation. "Right now? To be apart from him?"

The prince paused in his descent and frowned. "Not as much as it hurts to be apart from—" He stopped short. Went silent.

"From what?"

He glanced sidelong at her, then looked away. "From nothing," he said, continuing down the stairs.

When they reached the bottom, he caught her wrist and whirled her around to face him. "Ying," he said, and sighed. "Why did you go to the lake? I was so worried when I got back to my room and you weren't there—"

"I tried to get back!" The visceral panic of that morning flooded into Ying's body. She could feel the dread again; she could almost taste it. "I tried, but I couldn't."

The prince looked alarmed. "What do you mean?"

"The path." Ying drew a shaky breath. "The path kept leading me back to the lake."

The prince's face fell, and he dropped her wrist. "Oh."

"Was it your world?" Ying asked. "Does the mirror world—I don't know—hate my being here or something? Is that why it pushed me toward the lake?"

"Honestly? I don't know." The prince swiped back a lock of hair that had fallen into his eyes. "Things here . . . work differently. Sometimes light bends in strange ways. Things can be reflected in directions that differ from your world. All I can think is that perhaps—perhaps you just got caught up in a weird trick of the light."

Ying felt faint. "So the mirror world funneled me into the lake, where I nearly died. And then my soul started screaming."

The prince buried both hands in his hair. "Oh, gods." He flung his hands down again, his face stricken. "I got there just in time. Gods, Ying, if I'd arrived but a minute later—"

"You didn't, though, did you? I mean, I'm fine—"

"You are not fine!" he bellowed. "I *was* too late. You got hurt. Badly! I wish . . ." He trailed off.

"What do you wish?" Ying prompted.

"I wish I hadn't left you." His eyes burned into hers. "I am sorry. So very sorry."

Ying shook her head, and choked out, "No, no, don't be sorry."

He grabbed her shoulders. "You almost *died*, Ying!" His fingers tightened, almost painfully. He was angry. But not with her—with himself.

"That's not what I meant," Ying said, trying to placate him. "I meant it's not your fault—"

The prince scoffed. "You're right. It's not my fault. It's *his*."

His. A loaded, bitter word. He hadn't said the name, but Ying knew who he was referring to: the real prince.

"He leaves you, and I'm forced to follow." The Mirror Prince took a step closer, backing Ying into the stone wall, his hands planted on either side of her head. Ying's breath hitched at the dueling sensations: the prince's cold body pinning her against cold stone, her own body surging with heat. "If you were mine," he growled, "I would never—"

"No," Ying whispered, her heart thudding at the casual way he'd said *mine*. She was not allowed to be *his*. Not really. Not when she was promised—and by all appearances, already wed— to someone else. But it didn't stop certain images, certain yearnings, from crowding into her mind.

She pushed them away. Shoved them into a box within her heart that she reserved for secret things.

"Don't blame yourself," she continued. "Please. You had to go. You had no choice. But I did. I chose to explore the gardens. I chose to swap with my reflection. I chose to stay here, in this world." She placed a hand on his chest, watching the way his shoulders strained at her touch. "Believe me, I'd rather face a thousand giant serpents in here with you than be safe out there with him."

Their eyes locked. They were so close their breaths mingled, hers warm, his cool. Ying felt faint. For several slow heartbeats, they did nothing, said nothing, just stared at one another.

The prince tilted his head forward even more, and Ying's heart raced so quickly she thought she might just faint.

"Qīn'ài de," he said finally, his voice breathless. "You are supposed to be resting."

This was so unexpected that laughter burst from Ying's lips, short and sharp and deliciously sweet. He'd almost kissed her, then called her sweetheart, then told her she should go and rest? Surely, that was the wrong way round? For a moment, she considered protesting, but he was right: her chest was burning, and the ache from her wounds had flared again. Perhaps Mei Po's medicine was starting to wear off.

"Shǎ guā," she said, still smiling. "Then you should let me."

The Mirror Prince insisted Ying go back to his chamber to rest. Since the Mirror Prince could sense the real prince's movements, he reasoned Ying would be safer with him.

There were no dry clothes available for her to change into, so instead, he stoked the fire and helped settle her in an armchair right before it. As she sank into the lush softness, however, her stomach growled.

He froze. "You're hungry."

Ying nodded, sheepish, and her stomach growled again. Having missed her wedding banquet, she had now gone a full day without eating anything except for an orange and half a plum.

"My apologies," the prince said, frowning. "I've forgotten to feed you. It's not something I normally have to think about."

Ying's stomach lurched. "You don't have to . . . you don't *eat*?"

"No. I mean, we do if you do, to mimic you. But we don't need to." He sank to a squat before her, his hands on the arms of the chair. "I'll fetch you some food. But can you promise me one thing?"

Ying arched her brow, her pulse thrumming. "What's that?"

Leveling his gaze at her, the prince said, "Stay in this room. I need you safe."

"But—"

"No buts, Ying. After what that—*monster*—did to you earlier, I can't take any chances." He took her hands and flipped them over, before running one of his thumbs lightly across the gōushé scar.

It was as though his touch had a direct line to her core. As his skin brushed hers, fire shot up Ying's arms, warming her body despite the coldness of his touch.

"All right," she said, her breath hitching. How could she say no to him when he was touching her like *that*?

The prince rose to his feet and, taking her hand, kissed it. "I'll be back soon." He lingered a few moments, waiting for her permission.

"I'll be right here." Reluctantly, she let him go.

Once he had shut the door, Ying turned her attention to her surroundings. Though she had spent an entire night in the Mirror Prince's room, she'd been too exhausted to pay much attention. This was her first opportunity to inspect it properly.

Clambering out of the plush armchair, she swung a blanket around her shoulders, feeling small in her vast surroundings.

The walls were soft red, womblike. Just below the cornices, a row of characters were daubed in elegant calligraphy. She moved closer, squinting up at them. It was just the imperial family name, Shan, inscribed over and over, spanning the entire perimeter of the room. The gold paint shifted and glowed in the flickering light of the fire.

The bed, a four-poster behemoth, was swathed in golden bed linens shot through with silver threads. On one wall was an enormous fretwork window, through which Ying could see a gray, bloated sky. The opposite wall was lined with furniture: a long midnight-blue tufted-velvet ottoman, a large wardrobe, and a compact mahogany writing desk. In the corner stood a freestanding oval mirror.

Trying to find something to occupy her time, Ying stopped in front of the mirror. It was empty; Ying wondered if she'd ever truly get used to having an absent reflection. To distract herself from the unnerving sight, she raked her fingers through her damp hair, then braided it with practiced hands. Then she went still, staring into the mirror, staring into the room beyond.

It looked innocuous enough. She wondered, if she tried, whether she could . . .

Raising her hand to the glass, she touched the surface with all five fingers. It rippled, as though liquid, and her fingers sank in up to her knuckles. She gave an involuntary cry, snatched her hand back, and cradled it to her chest. The mirror's surface shivered for a moment before settling into stillness.

She had lived eighteen years without falling through a mirror. Why had that suddenly changed?

Ying contemplated what the Mirror Prince had said. Vaguely, she wondered how his people sustained themselves, if not with food. Could it really just be light, as her reflection had said? Ying had no idea, but she wouldn't be surprised if this prince drank blood like a vampire or ate human flesh. She supposed she should be afraid of his otherness. But strangely enough, he didn't frighten her at all.

This world looked, felt, and smelled so much like her own that sometimes it was easy to forget. But then something would become apparent—monsters like the gōushé, or pathways that kept looping back on themselves, or the reflections not needing to eat—and it would jolt her back to reality. She was not in her world. She was, in fact, very far from home.

I should be on my guard, Ying told herself, waiting for the prince to return.

A movement in her peripheral vision caught her attention, and she turned to see her reflection in the mirror. Reflection-Ying looked small and pale within the dim cavern of the real prince's chamber.

Sudden guilt flashed through Ying's body. Of course her reflection would come to find Ying, positioned as she was in front of a mirror. She'd seen the pain it had caused the Mirror Prince; she felt terrible not having realized that her reflection might suffer from it, too.

With deliberate slowness designed to mask her anxiety, Ying approached the mirror. Her reflection mimicked her until they stood on opposite sides of the glass, staring at one another.

Ying was the first to speak. "How are you feeling?" she said. "Better?"

"A little," her reflection replied, sounding distant through the glass. "But not enough to swap back yet."

Unexpected relief swooped through Ying's chest. And she knew why. It was because of the Mirror Prince. Going back meant saying goodbye. Staying meant being with him for just a little while longer.

She knew she shouldn't be having these thoughts. Her time in this world was temporary; the Mirror Prince was not her own. But however much she denied it, she couldn't help the fleeting visions that would flash through her mind whenever her thoughts were otherwise unoccupied.

Visions of a life lived here, with him.

Reflection-Ying's gaze skated down Ying's soiled clothing, unkempt hair, and bruised body, and she raised her eyebrows, alarmed. "What *happened* to you?"

The question pulled Ying's attention back to the physical: her upper back tingled where the serpent's tail had gouged her. "I was attacked." She plucked at her torn hànfú. "You didn't tell me about the monsters."

"Oh." Her reflection frowned, seeming genuinely remorseful. "Sorry. I forgot to warn you. They don't usually attack us. Which one was it?"

"Gōushé, I think it was called." Ying frowned at the way she'd said "which one," implying that there were more. "It came out of the lake."

Her reflection drew in a sharp breath. "The serpent? A formidable opponent. How did you escape?"

"Prince Zhang." Saying his name sent a flare of heat through Ying. "He saved me."

"The prince?" Reflection-Ying's forehead creased, but she quickly rearranged her face into a neutral expression. "How valiant. You're lucky he was there. Those things are lethal to your kind."

Ying didn't elaborate. She hadn't missed the look that had flashed across Reflection-Ying's face. Perhaps Ying's reflection was in love with the mirror-world prince. The two were supposed to be married to one another, after all. Ying's guilt intensified at the thoughts she'd been having about the Mirror Prince, and she resolved to do better.

Theirs was a love story that was not meant to be.

Shifting topics, Ying asked, "What was the screaming I heard in the lake? When the serpent dragged me in." She still wasn't sure that Mei Po and the Mirror Prince had given her the full story. Perhaps they'd been trying to protect her. Perhaps they didn't want her to know how close she'd been to death, how close she'd come to losing her soul.

Another perturbed look flashed across Reflection-Ying's face. "Oh, that." She paused, seemingly in thought, before continuing. "They're people. Souls that have been trapped."

Ying swallowed her gasp. So it hadn't been in her head after all—the prince must have been trying not to frighten her by telling her it was. "By the serpent?" she asked, a shiver running down her spine. Is that why she had been lured to the lake? Had the monster drawn her there somehow, like an angler reeling in their prey?

"I told you, that thing is dangerous, Ying," Reflection-Ying said reproachfully. "I think—I would suggest that you stay inside for now. Keep out of trouble. Don't forget the promise you made to your brother. He's expecting you back in this world whole."

Her brother. Just thinking about Hao Yu caused a hollow ache in Ying's chest. So much had happened since he had visited her in her chamber on the eve of her wedding and gifted her the opal ring. Ying thought of that night. The night when everything changed. It was mortifying to think that her reflection—and that of her brother—had been on the other side of the mirrors, watching their every move.

It seemed impossible that only two nights had passed since.

Catching Ying's expression, the reflection touched the surface of the glass. "Come," she said, her voice softening. "You cannot stay in that ruined dress. I'll get changed so you can put on something clean and dry. And then perhaps you can get some rest."

The reflection was true to her word. As soon as she'd slipped on a pale pink silk nightgown, Ying was able to get changed, too. She dressed, then sank onto the bed, curling her left hand into a fist. Her brother's ring felt foreign on her finger.

A sound pulled her back into the present—the sound of the Mirror Prince returning. Ying glanced automatically at the mirror.

But her reflection was gone.

The mirror, empty.

12

The Mirror Prince entered, balancing a tray loaded with bamboo steaming baskets. The luscious-smelling steam curled toward Ying's nostrils, pushing out every other worry until all she could think of was her hollow belly. She watched intently, hungrily, as the prince placed the tray on the bed, unstacked the baskets, and opened the lids one by one.

Inside were dumplings: plump prawn xiā jiǎo, roe-topped shāo mài, and clusters of taro that looked like miniature haystacks. One plate held slippery, savory cháng fěn rolls with tiny baby shrimp and a sprinkling of scallions. On another plate sat three small white buns, their surfaces pristine, like untouched snow. Ying picked one up. It was still warm from the oven. She broke it open, revealing a center of sweet red bean paste. Holding it to her nose, she inhaled deeply, her mouth watering.

The prince sat down beside her. He looked amused. "Is this acceptable to you, Princess?"

"Acceptable?" Ying breathed in again. "This is amazing." She crammed half the bun into her mouth, then the other half. Bliss.

"This might be blasphemy," she said, her mouth full, "but I think the cooks in here are even better than ours."

The prince chuckled, then paused. "Well," he said, his voice dropping an octave, "there *is* one thing from your world that's much, much better." His gaze lowered, lingering on her lips.

Ying could only manage a short "Oh?" Suddenly, she was aware of every sensation. The tightness of the collar around her neck, the flush of warmth to her cheeks, the rise and fall of her chest. She swallowed, the bean paste sticking on its way down. The prince's gaze was so blistering it felt to Ying like being torched by the sun.

Her heart sped up. Mei Po's prophecy. What if her guilt was misplaced? Perhaps this, right here, was what was meant to happen.

Perhaps *this* was the prince she was foretold to marry.

Leaning in, the prince reached up and touched his finger to a corner of Ying's lips. Involuntarily, her lips parted, and she inhaled sharply.

He was close. So close, Ying could feel the whisper of his cool breath on her cheek. "You have something"—he brushed a crumb from her lips—"just here."

Ying leaned into his icy hand, and his touch morphed into a caress. Slowly, reverently, he traced the tips of his fingers down her cheek, then the line of her jaw. His eyes darkened.

Although her heart was hammering like thunder, Ying managed to remain deathly still. Was this it? Was he actually going to . . . kiss her?

He dropped his hand, and Ying just managed to stop herself from protesting. "I hate to say this, Ying," he whispered, "but you should rest."

"I feel fine!" Ying was shocked at how breathy she sounded.

"You must, qīn'ài de," he said, so gently. "You need to recover from your injuries. And if you don't, Mei Po will have my head." He gave her a small smile. He was joking, but only just.

Once again, Ying dreamed of fish. This time, though, she was not surrounded by them. This time she *was* one. She couldn't see herself, of course, but she sensed her body, sensed her movement, sensed every eddying current in the water through which she swam.

Her body was powerful, pure muscle. Her tail was long, forked, and covered in small barbs. And her mouth? Her mouth was lined with long, thin fangs, each as slim as a needle, wickedly sharp and carved from bone.

As she circled the lake, near the bottom, she tasted something in the water. It stirred something in her, whipping her into a frenzy. She had to have it, had to find it, had to taste more, taste more, taste more.

It was blood. Human blood.

She swam toward the source. The taste became progressively stronger as she approached the surface. And then she saw, up ahead of her, the body of a woman. Ying swam closer, her shiny-scaled body surging through the water. And when the woman spun in the current, Ying caught a glimpse of the face.

The woman was her.

It was Ying Yue. Ying the fish was swimming toward her own human body. As the woman turned over again, Fish-Ying saw a gash across the human's back. The gōushé wound. A thin plume of blood streamed from it. The woman tried to speak, but only bubbles came out. And then Ying, in her fish body with her fish fangs and fish tail, shot toward her, mouth open, teeth exposed, her belly hungering for blood—

Ying burst into consciousness all of a sudden, with the sound of souls screaming and her sheets tangled around her legs.

It was dark.

The silence was oppressive. There was no screaming. The screaming must have been her—the dream her.

"Ying! Ying, it's me!" The Mirror Prince hovered above her, his face in shadows. "What happened?" He stroked her hair, brushing the sweaty strands from her face. His cool hands felt heavenly on her overheated skin.

Gradually, Ying stilled, coming to grips with where she was. The room's only light was the dim, ghostly glow from the fire's dying embers. "I'm fine," she lied. She tasted the iron tang of blood; she must have bitten her tongue in her sleep. "Just a nightmare."

"I understand," he said, and Ying knew he was thinking of the gōushé. She didn't dare tell him about her fish dreams. What did they even mean? And why had she had one *again*?

She rolled to face him, startled to find the prince so close. They were nose to nose, both breathing just a touch too fast. His fingers, still tangled in her hair, toyed with a lock before tucking it behind her ear. Cool fingers brushed the sensitive part of her neck, raising goosebumps along her skin

Kiss me, Ying's mind screamed. She'd forgotten all about feeling guilty, or the fact that he was not truly hers. *Please.*

And he did.

He leaned in. Instinctively, Ying responded. Her stomach flipped when his lips pressed against hers: cold, hard, unyielding. He started to move, tentatively at first, slow and steady. But then he groaned, and his movements became faster, more urgent. His hand flattened against her lower back, pressing her body against his.

Her first kiss.

Ying yielded to it, her mind swarming with the sensation, her body responding to his touch. She wrapped her arms around his shoulders and held on tight. Like the rest of him, his shoulders were rock-hard and cold. His muscles rippled under her hands. He felt alien and familiar all at once.

His smell, his taste, his smooth, cool lips. She couldn't believe she was kissing the prince. The famous, handsome, fearless prince. How many times had she imagined this scene before they'd even met? Well, she'd imagined kissing the real Prince Zhang, and now she was kissing his reflection. But real prince, reflection prince . . . to her, in this moment, they meant pretty much the same thing.

Ying's thoughts were silenced when he rolled on top of her, the entire length of his frame pressing her down into the bed. He cradled her face with his icy hands, pinning her in place as their lips collided. She wrapped her arms around his neck, breathing in his heady scent. It was like lotus flowers and petrichor—the smell that lingers after rain.

By the time he broke away, Ying could barely breathe. She wanted more. Did he? In the low light, she could barely make out his features.

"Are you okay?" he whispered. "You're sure you want this? With me?"

His question made her hesitate, just for a moment. Was it considered infidelity if it was with her should-be husband's own reflection?

A single kiss was one thing. It could be considered a mistake, could be rationalized as a momentary slip of self-control. But a second kiss?

A second kiss was a choice.

Before she could reply, the prince bent his head and brushed his cool glass lips over her neck. A trail of ice followed where he traveled. Ying's thoughts dissipated, leaving only wanting in their wake.

Every touch left a chill. Embracing him was like stepping out on a winter's morning, endless possibilities in the unmarked snow. But she herself was still flushed, feverish. She had enough fire to burn them both. She had enough fire to burn up the world.

He was supposed to be her husband. She was meant to be his wife. Even if they were from different sides of the mirror, fate had brought them together. Hadn't their love been foretold by the fortune tellers? Really, the only thing the seers hadn't predicted was that their love would transcend worlds. Unknowingly, they'd picked the wrong prince. *This* one—this prince—was her destiny. She knew it.

Perhaps this was why she was suddenly able to pass through the mirrors.

Ying held the Mirror Prince's face and gazed into his eyes. "I do want this." She bit her lip. "I want you."

The prince groaned and pressed his lips on hers, kissing her hard. He made his way to her ear while one of his hands slid up and along her thigh, pushing up her silk nightgown until it bunched at her waist.

Ying glanced at the mirror in the corner. She hoped her reflection was elsewhere, or at least asleep. But even as the prince slipped the strap of her gown off her shoulder, she was distracted by anxiety that someone might, at any moment, look through the mirror and see her. The thought was sickening. She definitely did *not* want an audience.

"Wait," she said, wriggling out from under him. "The mirror. Let me cover it."

The prince raised a quizzical eyebrow. "Why, Princess?"

"I don't want to be seen." The Mirror Prince was used to this, but Ying was not.

She dragged one of the silk sheets from the bed and crossed the room, peering into the mirror. The reflected room—the room in her own world—was shrouded in shadows. She could make out an outline, a silhouette, moving in the darkness. As she peered at it, her eyes adjusted, and she saw her own reflection sitting astride the real prince, pinning him to the bed.

Letting out a short gasp, she averted her eyes. She didn't want to be caught acting like a biàntài, a pervert. Whatever was between those two was not hers to see. In a way, it was ironic: she *was* mimicking her reflection. Or soon would be. She quaked at the anticipation of what was to come.

But as she made to toss the sheet over the mirror, something caught her notice. She paused, her hands twisting in the silk.

"Ying?" the Mirror Prince said from the bed, but she ignored him. Staring harder into the darkened room, trying to make out the scene, she saw something that stopped her.

Something was wrong.

At first glance, it had looked as though her reflection was atop the prince and he was writhing in pleasure. But now she could see that the real prince was not writhing.

He was twitching.

And Ying saw that her reflection was not making love to him. Her reflection was strangling him.

Ying clamped a hand over her mouth, silencing her scream. What was happening? What was she *doing*?

"She's killing him! My reflection's killing the prince!" Ying cried. "I have to go through!"

"What?" The prince scrambled off the bed. "No!" He grabbed her hand. "It's not safe."

"I have to. I'm sorry. I can't just let him die." Ying clutched her forehead, her mind spinning. This must have been the reason for Reflection-Fei's warning. The maid had tried to tell Ying not to trust her own reflection. But bound as she was by her duty to mimic, the poor girl had been unable to explain further.

Or maybe she had just been afraid.

"Please . . . Ying." The prince spun her around to face him and put his big hands on her shoulders. "She's dangerous. And I can't follow you. The mirrors don't open for me." His voice cracked. "Please stay. Stay with me."

Her heart raced as she stared up into the Mirror Prince's eyes. For a moment, Ying considered listening to him. Staying with him. It would certainly solve all her problems. If the real prince died, she would never have to go back, never have to suffer through a loveless marriage, never again have to worry about the real world.

But then she'd be condemning the real prince to death. And although Ying didn't know what was happening, or why her reflection had decided to attack, what Ying did know is that she had agreed to the swap. She was partly at fault for this. If the real prince died, it would forever be a burden she'd bear.

Ying rose on tiptoe and gave the Mirror Prince one last kiss before shrugging out of his grasp and turning away. Tears pricked her eyelids.

"I'm sorry," Ying said over her shoulder. Then she dove right through the mirror and back into her world.

13

When she landed in the real prince's room, it took a moment for her eyes to adjust. She hadn't noticed at first, but everything in the mirror world was slightly sharper, brighter, more glaring. It wasn't long before the murkiness of the real world crystallized and she could make out the shadowy figures on the bed. The prince's jerky movements had slowed, almost stopped. Ying's reflection had him in a choke hold. She shook with the strain, her eyes trained on her victim, her teeth bared.

Ying ran over and, thinking only of saving the prince, grabbed a handful of her reflection's hair and pulled—hard. As her reflection's head arced backward, Ying delivered a jabbing punch to her exposed neck. Reflection-Ying exhaled sharply, and her hands briefly loosened from around the prince's neck.

Ying did not waste the opportunity. She dragged her reflection off the now-still prince and dumped her onto the floor beside the bed.

In less than a second, Reflection-Ying flipped onto her feet. She sank into a deep fight stance, her fists at her face. In the candlelight, the reflection was glowing—just slightly. It was subtle, and perhaps not evident to normal human eyes, but Ying had now spent enough time in the mirror world that the difference was apparent.

Ying let out a piercing cry as she charged. She pirouetted, kicking out at her reflection's head. Pain reverberated up Ying's leg—she wasn't used to fighting something that was as hard as rock.

Her reflection's head whipped to one side. Thrown off balance, she quickly regained her footing and drove Ying backward. Ying blocked and ducked, avoiding most of the blows.

Neither could gain an advantage. One would push the other back a few feet, and then the other would go on the offensive and the tide would turn. Ying anticipated everything her counterpart did, and vice versa.

Damn, Ying thought. *This woman knows all my moves.* Of course she did. She was her reflection. All those nights Ying had spent in front of the mirror . . .

They'd trained together for years without Ying even knowing.

A loud groan from the bed pulled Ying's focus from the fight. The prince had rolled to his side, clutching his head. His nose was bleeding—he wiped at it, smearing a little on his cheek.

It was then that Ying felt an icy forearm across her neck. Cold, even pressure across her trachea. That brief moment of distraction had cost her.

Ying couldn't breathe. She struggled, but to no avail. Her opponent was strong, hard, immovable.

She was going to die. The edges of her vision wavered. The pain was enormous. In her oxygen-starved mind, memories of the past few days flashed by, silver-bright. She saw the hair combing, the tea ceremony, her reflection crawling out from the pond. She saw the palace gardens, the huge lake, the giant serpent, Mei Po's cluttered tower room. And most of all—most of all—she saw the Mirror Prince, smiling at her, touching her, kissing her, caring for her.

Through blurred vision, she saw that the mirror was empty. The prince's reflection had disappeared. Why? Had he gone to get help? Or to figure out some way to smash through the mirrors? To follow her?

Regardless of the reason . . . if she didn't fight back now, she'd likely never see him again.

With a superhuman surge of strength, Ying curled her body and lurched forward, throwing her reflection over her shoulder and onto the floor. Reflection-Ying landed flat on her back and lay there for a second, seemingly stunned. A second was all Ying needed to launch herself at the wall and grab a hanging ornamental sword. By the time Reflection-Ying had risen to her knees, Ying had grabbed her by the hair and pulled her head back, exposing her pale neck. In her other hand, Ying held the sword, pointed directly at her reflection's heart.

"Tell me why," she roared. "Why are you trying to kill us?"

Her reflection spread her lips in a smile. Her teeth were stained with blackened blood. "It's our time."

Ying twisted her hands in her opponent's hair, firming her grip. "Your time? What does that *mean*?"

By now, Ying could see in her peripheral vision that the prince was sitting up. He was swaying slightly, still with one hand on his head. When he spoke, his words were slightly slurred. "Ying? Ying Yue? What's going on?"

"Bì zuǐ!" Ying snapped, not daring to turn her head. "Shut up!" Her attention shifted back to her reflection. "Speak!" she yelled. "Or I'll skewer you with this sword!"

Her reflection glared up at her with flat black eyes. "We've mimicked you for long enough," she said. "It's time we reclaim what's rightfully ours."

"And what is that?" Ying's arms were shaking like a struck zither string, but she fought to keep control, to keep her voice even.

Her reflection grinned. "This world."

Ying's mind shattered. So this was the plan all along.

"Well," Ying said, her sweaty hand gripping her sword handle tighter, "you won't get away with it." And throwing all her strength into her right arm, she drove the sword right into her reflection's heart.

14

Except the sword didn't penetrate.

Instead, it glanced off, unable to pierce Reflection-Ying's hard, glasslike skin.

Pain exploded up Ying's arm. Her entire body turned cold. Every single muscle seized.

Her reflection grinned again. Wrapping both hands around the sword blade, Reflection-Ying jerked the sword downward until Ying was only inches from her face.

"I *will* get away with it," her reflection sneered. "And the prince?" She let out a short, derisive laugh. "Dead, by the time I'm finished."

Which prince did she mean? A vision of the Mirror Prince pleading for her to stay flared in Ying's mind like a struck flint. Anger spiked hot in her chest. With a roar, she wrenched the sword away from her opponent and swung it, bringing it down in a wide arc. Her reflection leapt to her feet, parrying the sword with her rock-hard arms.

"You can't cut me," her reflection mocked as she deflected the blade over and over, predicting every one of Ying's moves. A sense of hopelessness spread through Ying, like blackness, like a disease. Her fighting became sloppy. A strategic blow knocked Ying flat on her back, her reflection pinning her down with the sword at her throat.

"You can't cut me," the reflection repeated, "but I can cut you." And ever so slowly, she dragged the sword across the soft skin of Ying's neck. The sting caused Ying to cry out. Her reflection only laughed.

"It's a shame I can't kill you. Not yet, anyway." The sword's movement stopped. "But I'll be more careful from now on."

Ying mustered all the courage she had left inside her and spat in her opponent's face.

For half a second, Reflection-Ying's face contorted in fury, and Ying thought the woman might kill her after all. But then came an almighty crash, a shower of porcelain, and the reflection's eyes rolled up as she slumped forward, unconscious.

The real Prince Zhang Lin was standing behind her, looking horrified, the remnants of a ceramic floor vase held in both hands.

Ying gave a grim smile. The reflections couldn't be cut, it seemed, but their skin was brittle and cracked like glass.

Which meant they could certainly be knocked out.

Ying rolled the reflection's prone body off her. Fine cracks, like spiderwebs, radiated across Reflection-Ying's forehead, black blood beading along the lines. The Prince opened and shut his mouth a few times, then pointed. "Who the hell is that?"

"Just some biǎozi," Ying said. "Quick, help me get her to the mirror."

Bending over, Ying pressed open her opal ring and tipped the entire measure of sleeping powder into her reflection's slack-jawed mouth.

Thank you, Hao Yu. With any luck, it would keep the monster asleep for at least a little longer. Just until Ying could figure out the next step.

The prince gave her an odd look, then ran a hand through his hair. "She looks just like you." His eyes slid to Ying and narrowed. "Do you have a twin sister I don't know about?"

"Gods," Ying said, trying and failing to shift her reflection's dead weight. "Shut up and help me, will you? We don't have much time. Unless you want to fight her off again."

The prince sighed, resigned. Grabbing the reflection's floppy arm, he hoisted her onto his shoulders. "Mā de! She's heavy."

Ying chivvied him toward the mirror. He staggered over to it and dropped his cargo on the ground. Together, he and Ying rolled Reflection-Ying over and over. His eyes widened as Ying pushed the unconscious body straight through the mirror as though it were liquid and not glass. Raising one finger, he tentatively touched the mirror surface. But nothing happened. It seemed mirrors were still impermeable to him.

"We need to smash it." Ying cast her eyes around the room, settling for a heavy jade ornament. She heaved it up with two hands and hurled it at the mirror.

It shattered. Shards of glass sprayed onto the floor, prompting Ying to jump backward. It was only a temporary solution, but it would buy them time.

She ripped a bit of fabric from the bottom of her gown and

handed it to the prince. "You have blood on your face, by the way. You might want to clean it."

He took the cloth without comment and scrubbed at his face.

Ying watched for a moment, then said, "I'm glad you decided to help. I was starting to think you'd lost most of your brain cells when she choked you back there." She raised her eyebrows at the rumpled bed.

The prince's nostrils flared. "I still don't know if I should've helped you." He scrubbed even harder at his face, his next words a torrent of rambling, barely coherent sentences. "All I remember is going to bed with my wife. The next moment, she—you—were on top of me, strangling me. Who the hell are you? Who the hell was that? Which one of you tried to kill me? Was it her? Was it you? *How do I know it wasn't you?*"

And with that, the prince's hand shot out and closed around Ying's neck, raising her to her feet. She yelped, her face growing hot. He held her at arm's length, his grip tight enough to immobilize but not enough to cut off air.

"Feel me," she gasped. She grabbed his free hand in hers and held it to her heart. "She was cold, remember? Feel my heat."

The prince sucked in a breath, hesitating. His eyes, the pupils so dilated they looked black, bored into hers. For several silent seconds, they remained like that, his hand hot on her chest, Ying's pulse roaring in her ears.

Then the prince's eyes unclouded, and he released his hold. "Okay," he conceded, tossing the soiled cloth onto the bed and passing his hand over his eyes. "You're not her, then. But can you tell me what is going on?"

Ying looked over her shoulder. Any moment now, her reflection could recover, enter the palace through another mirror, and burst right through the door. She had to warn the prince about her reflection's malicious intent. But not here, in a place full of reflections, where there could be mirror spies.

"We need to go," she said. "Somewhere with no reflections. I can tell you about it then."

The prince hesitated but then gave a curt nod. "I know of somewhere." He grabbed a jet-black travel cloak from the lacquered wardrobe and swung it over his shoulders, lowering the heavy cowl to obscure his face. He slung his bow and quiver over his back and secured his sword belt around his waist. Then he draped Ying in a cloak—exactly like the burgundy one she'd worn in the mirror world. His fingers brushed her collarbone as he did up the clasp at her neck. Every touch felt so hot, like sparks showering her bare skin.

The two of them hurried through the palace toward the stables. Once inside, the prince helped Ying mount a horse with a glossy, night-black coat and mane. Jumping up behind her, he lifted the reins, shouted a command, and spurred the horse into a gallop. Ying was thrown backward against the prince as the horse took off, neck extended, hooves pounding the ground. When they burst through the door of the stables, Ying's hood was blown back. The frigid night air chilled her cheeks.

As they galloped through the cobblestone streets toward the palace gates, Ying's nerves thrummed, taut with tension. It felt good to be on horseback again, but the farther the horse's clattering hooves carried her from the palace, the more her heart was left behind. The other prince—her prince, the Mirror Prince—was there, somewhere, on the other side of the mirror. Not realizing Ying was riding away, cutting off all access.

Was he safe? Did he know about Reflection-Ying and her plans to take over the world? He'd said she was dangerous. Was he in danger?

Ying thought hard. The real prince was strong, with a reputation as a skilled fighter. She had to believe that, if needed, the prince's reflection would be able to defend himself, too.

Ying dragged her attention back into the present. By now, they were on the open road, the guards having opened the precinct gates when they confirmed she was with the prince.

"What's his name?" Ying said over her shoulder, referring to the horse. She gripped the front of the saddle, her hands frozen, her knuckles white.

"Jué Yǐng," the prince replied, his warm breath stirring the baby hairs at the nape of her neck. "Shadow Runner."

Ying jumped at his proximity; he'd spoken right into her ear. Now that she took notice, his whole body was up against hers. She could feel his thighs nestled against the backs of her legs, and his strong arms encircled hers as he steered the reins. After her time in the mirror world, his heat felt scorching, even through her cloak.

Ying's hands tightened. The saddle's leather was smooth and well-worn under her palms. On either side of them, a blurred, darkened forest sped by.

"Shadow Runner," she whispered, half to herself and half to the horse. "It suits you."

Hours later, the horse had slowed to a walk. Ying was almost swaying from fatigue. To keep her upright, the prince had encircled her waist with one arm. The moon, not quite full, hung high in the sky. It must be around midnight, Ying thought. The few hours of restless sleep she'd snatched earlier in the mirror world hadn't been enough.

A thought suddenly occurred to her: Did the mirror people sleep? She'd never seen one do so. Not truly, anyway. The Mirror Prince had spent her first night in his room watching her from the sofa. And her own reflection's attempts to impersonate Ying in the real world—sleeping in her bed, wearing her nightgown—didn't count.

The horse began to pick its way up a winding mountain path. Not far up, a small wooden hut was set in the eaves of a rocky outcrop. The mountain loomed above. Around them, a thick forest of pine trees stood like solemn soldiers, stretching as far as Ying's eyes could see, silhouetted black against the purplish night sky.

"Where are we?" Ying murmured, her voice thick with fatigue. Shadow Runner tossed his head and snorted.

"Just a place I come to be alone," the prince replied, sliding off the horse. Putting his hands around Ying's waist, he lifted her down. "To hunt. To think."

He spoke a few low words to the horse, which wandered off to nuzzle hopefully at a small patch of grass. Then the prince strode off toward the hut, leaving Ying to navigate the uneven dirt path behind him.

He pushed open the door, which yielded with a low creak.

The hut was small but cozy. It consisted of a single room, with log walls, exposed roof beams, and a small stone fireplace in one corner. In front of the fireplace stood a scarred wooden table and a chair, and in another corner was a single, narrow bed.

The prince lit a candle, then unshouldered his bow and leaned it carefully by the door. His robe he threw over the back of the chair. Last, he undid his sword belt and hung it on a hook.

He slid the chair out and gestured to it. "Sit." It was not a request.

Ying sank down, gathering her cloak around her. With no fire lit, the hut was bitterly cold. At least the frozen air would keep her awake.

"Thank you for helping me," Ying said, rubbing her hands together, trying to bring feeling back into her numb fingers.

The prince sat on the bed and threw her a look. "You are my wife," he said, though there was no trace of love in his words. "It is my duty."

Duty, Ying thought dully. There was that word again.

"Now"—the prince leaned forward, elbows on his knees—"tell me what happened back there."

Ying hesitated. The prince had helped her roll her reflection through the mirror. Surely he would believe her?

"Well," she ventured, "that . . . that . . . creature. It was my reflection."

The prince sat upright and ran his hand over his chin. His tousled hair was loose around his square jaw. Below it, his shirt was slightly open, revealing the top of his broad chest and a flash of smooth, bronze skin.

He looked identical to his reflection—the reflection that, only hours earlier, had been lying on top of her, pressing her into the bed, running his hand up her leg. . . . Ying swallowed, her mouth dry.

Not the same, she told herself, like a mantra. *Not the same man.*

The prince finally spoke. "Your reflection came out of the mirror and tried to kill me." His voice was flat, the words a statement, not a question.

Ying nodded.

"And where were you in the meantime?"

"In the mirror. She brought me through into her world, told me she was dying, told me she needed to spend time in the real world to get better. I believed her. I thought I was helping." Ying shook her head sadly. "I'm so foolish."

There was a pause. "Not foolish," the prince corrected. "Kind."

Ying blinked, and a couple of tears dislodged themselves and ran down her face. "It wasn't just that," she continued, her voice small. "She offered to take my place—in the wedding."

The prince gave her a sharp look. "You mean it wasn't you? At the ceremony?"

The tears were flowing for real now. Ying shook her head.

"So we are not"—the prince paused for a second—"actually married?"

"No."

"Well." He grimaced. "This is a problem."

"Why?" Ying, indignant, swiped her tears away. "Aren't you happy? I mean, you don't even like me. And I sure as hell don't like you."

He gave a grim laugh. "We are royalty, Ying. We're not expected to *like* each other."

Ying didn't respond. Instead, she just pressed her lips together. He was right, of course, but that didn't make the situation better. Why, out of everyone the matchmakers could have paired her with, was she doomed to suffer a lifetime with *him*?

It made her realize exactly how much she preferred the Mirror Prince.

Ignoring her reaction, Zhang continued his interrogation. "What is on the other side of the mirror, Ying?"

"It's just like here." Ying paused, then added, "Except there are monsters."

"Monsters?"

"Yes. I was attacked by a giant serpent. Mei Po—Mei Po's reflection, that is—healed me."

The prince raised his eyebrows. "And these—reflections—what do they do?"

"Their job is to mimic us," Ying said, trying to recall all the information she had gleaned over the preceding few days. "They're not supposed to let us know they're separate from us."

"And each of us, even me, has a reflection in there? There's a separate version of me, with its own free will?"

"With *his* own free will," Ying corrected, thinking of the Mirror Prince. "But yes."

"And you met this other version of me?"

A pause. "Yes." Her face burned.

The prince narrowed his eyes. He hadn't missed the flush that was rising up Ying's neck.

"Did you—" The prince hesitated, then cleared his throat. "Did you go to bed with him?"

"Like you can talk!" Ying snapped. "You were in bed with *my* reflection!"

The prince gave a short, mirthless laugh. "The difference is, Ying, *I* didn't know!"

Ying scoffed. "How did you not know? They're ice-cold! And their skin is rock-hard! Didn't you notice?" She knew there was unveiled sarcasm in her voice, but she didn't care.

"Of course I noticed." The prince paused, then shifted in his seat. "I wasn't really thinking about it."

Ying narrowed her eyes. "You weren't thinking with your head, were you?"

"Well, no." His lips twitched; there was a hint of a smile.

"Figures," Ying muttered, crossing her arms.

There was another awkward pause during which neither of them spoke. Ying dropped her eyes to the table, staring at the coarse, knotted woodgrain and countless razor-thin scratches.

Finally, the prince broke the silence. "So. Why attack us? What do they want?"

Ying threw up her hands slightly and brought them down on the table. "I don't know for sure." Her fingers splayed out, feeling the rough-hewn wood. "She said she, or they, wanted to take our places. Take over our world." She clenched her hands into fists, mainly to subdue their shaking.

The prince blew out a breath. "Wǒ cào," he said, the curse harsh on his lips. Then he glanced at Ying. "Sorry."

Ying gave a dismissive wave of her hand. Profanity felt appropriate for the situation. Now that Ying was here, face to face with the real prince, she finally felt the full magnitude of how closely he'd skirted death. As her mind began to fully grasp what had occurred that night, her body began reacting, too. Shivering, she wound her arms around her middle, pretending she was just cold.

The prince rose to his feet and walked to the empty fireplace. He leaned with one hand on the mantel, lost in thought. Eventually, he spoke again.

"Well, there's a lot to think about. You'd best get some sleep. I can see you're tired."

Ying started. She'd almost fallen asleep at the table. "Yes, Your Highness," she murmured, rising unsteadily to her feet. Her gaze swept the room, then landed back on Prince Zhang.

"Is there a problem, Princess?"

Ying felt a blush rising in her cheeks. "There's . . ." She squared her shoulders. "There's only one bed."

"Yes, and?"

"Well, I—"

"We are supposed to be married, are we not?" His voice turned bitter, and he muttered, "Even if you did not think it necessary to attend your own wedding."

"Yes, but—"

The prince let out an exasperated growl. "It's my reflection, isn't it? Did you"—his lip curled into a sneer—"did you *fall in love* with him?"

"Are you jealous?" Ying tried, and failed, to keep the derision out of her voice.

"No. Just perplexed." He spread his arms. "You have me here, flesh and blood. But instead, you prefer a fucking *monster*."

Anger blazed in Ying's rib cage. "He is *not* a monster!"

The prince rubbed his face with both hands. When he lowered them, he was shaking his head. "Fine," he said, his voice terse. "Have it your way. You take the bed. I'll take the floor." He rolled himself in his cloak and threw himself down across the hearth, facing away from her.

Ying unfastened her travel cloak, undid her braid, and climbed into the bed. The quilt was thin, almost threadbare. She wondered why the prince didn't replace it.

Drawing herself into a fetal position, she drew the quilt and her cloak up, tucking them around her face. She'd taunted Prince Zhang Lin for being jealous, but she knew he wasn't really. He didn't care about her; he'd admitted as much. He didn't even *like* her. And she didn't like him.

Clenching her teeth to keep them from chattering, Ying curled up tighter and shoved her hands under her armpits. This goddamned hut was freezing, as though cold had curled in through the cracks and seeped right down to her bones. Even with her cloak spread out on top, she still couldn't get warm. The entire bed shook with her tremors.

"What's wrong, Ying?" The prince's voice was muffled by his cloak.

"Nothing."

"Are you cold?"

There was no point lying. "A little."

The prince sighed and sat up. Ying drew the bedclothes tighter around her, trying to hide her trembling.

"There's no firewood," the prince said, a brittle edge of impatience creeping into his voice. "I haven't stayed here in a while. Shall I collect some?"

"No. It's too dark." Ying thought of the woods, full of bears and wolves and goodness knows what else. "You'll get yourself killed."

The prince stood up and gave a drawn-out, long-suffering sigh. "Do you need me to come and warm you up?" His tone suggested that the idea was downright repugnant.

Ying's protest came a bit too quickly. "No! I definitely do not. Go to sleep. I'll be okay."

"Don't be absurd. I can hear you chattering from here."

Ying weighed things in her mind and decided that, on balance, her pride was less important than not dying from the cold. "Fine." She scooted over, pressing herself closer to the wall. "Just . . . don't expect anything. This is strictly about body heat."

The prince gave a quick bow. "Of course, Princess. I am at your service." The subtle condescension did not go unnoticed.

He came to stand by the bed and drew the bedsheets back. Ying curled up tighter, gooseflesh rising across her skin. "Gods, Ying. Is that all you wore under your cloak? What were you thinking?" He climbed into bed next to her, careful not to touch her. Heat radiated off him like he was the sun personified. Ying sighed, basking in his warmth.

"I didn't exactly have time for an outfit change," she said, trying to surreptitiously shift closer. "Besides, you were there. You saw what I was wearing."

"I didn't notice. I was too distracted by the homicidal monster we'd just pushed through the mirror." He settled on his back and put his hands behind his head. "Get some sleep, Ying."

"Yes, Your Highness," Ying murmured. She rolled to face away from him. Even with the prince's proximity, only her back felt warm. The rest of her was still cold.

She wrapped her arms around her torso and curled up again. But despite her best efforts, she couldn't stop shivering.

The bed dipped as she felt the prince roll over behind her and prop himself up on his elbow. For a few moments, he was silent.

"Oh, for gods' sake," he said, putting his arms around her. "Come here."

15

When Ying awoke, the prince was still curled around her, his arms wrapped around her middle. The heat was suffocating, and Ying's face and chest were clammy. Careful not to wake him, she peeled his arms from her waist and wriggled out of his grasp. He murmured and rolled onto his back. He looked untroubled, almost innocent, his strong features softened by sleep.

Ying realized that, for the first time in months, she hadn't dreamed. She actually felt rested, restored. Ready.

Throwing her cloak over her shoulders, she pushed open the front door to the hut and wandered outside.

She'd expected cold, but the sun was high and brilliant, its warmth wrapping around her like a blanket. Ying raised her face to the light, closed her eyes, and breathed in the crisp morning air.

A soft whinny broke her reverie, and she opened her eyes to see Shadow Runner nearby. He was alert, his ears swiveled toward her, an inquisitive look in his eyes. In the daylight, he was even more magnificent. His raven coat shone with an almost iridescent sheen, throwing purplish hues that winked and flashed in the sun. His mane, too, was jet black. In fact, there was nothing about him that wasn't black save for his clear blue eyes.

"Hello, beautiful," Ying cooed, inching toward him. He stamped a hoof and tossed his head but otherwise didn't move. "Hello," she said again, quieter this time, for she was nearer to him by now.

Shadow Runner took two steps forward, then nuzzled her below the ear, blowing her loose hair about. She giggled and rubbed his nose, and he snuffled more, nuzzling optimistically into her hand. Ying laughed, stroking his silky neck.

"He likes you." The prince's voice rang out in the relative quiet of the mountain air. Ying spun around. He had his arms crossed, leaning casually on the side of the hut, a hint of a smile at the edge of his lips.

"He's friendly," Ying replied, almost forgetting to breathe. When she remembered, she took a deep gulp, then went red.

The prince strolled over to her side. Cradling Shadow Runner's head, he rubbed the horse between the eyes. "No, he's not," he said. "He's actually an asshole. He hates people." He side-eyed Ying, who was resting her head on Shadow Runner's neck. "I was a little surprised he let you ride him last night. Maybe he's a good judge of character."

She laughed. "I feel extra privileged, then."

"Well, Princess Ying. What's the plan for today? Saving the world from more mirror monsters?"

Ying closed her eyes, the horse's velvet neck beneath her cheek. Her reflection was likely still out there, planning an attack. And the Mirror Prince—was he all right? She hoped he wasn't in any danger. She'd have to go back soon and check.

The magnitude of it all was overwhelming. Pressure built up behind her eyelids, threatening to spill out as tears, but Ying blinked and forced them away. She needed a plan this time. She couldn't be reckless. She couldn't get emotional. It wouldn't help anyone, least of all her prince.

"Yes," she said finally. "We need to save the world. But first, we need to eat."

They spent the rest of the morning wandering the forest, hunting and scavenging for food. The prince shot two hares in quick succession. Meanwhile, Ying found a loquat tree bent against the bitter wind, growing a little apart from the ubiquitous pines. She was in luck; it was fruiting earlier than usual. *A brave soldier with bounteous gifts,* she thought, stripping the tree of the small orange fruits.

The prince built a small fire in a clearing spattered with dappled light, gutted his prey, and speared the carcasses on sticks. When Ying returned with her skirt full of fruit, he was turning his catch above a crackling fire, whistling.

This caught Ying by surprise—he was whistling? She'd never have expected it. Perhaps he was just less guarded away from the palace and all its attendant duties.

Pretending she hadn't noticed his off-tune melody, Ying busied herself by stripping off her cloak and spreading it on the ground as a blanket. Then she stacked the fruit onto a bed of leaves and settled herself cross-legged atop her cloak.

The prince stopped whistling. His gaze shifted. Having no change of clothes, Ying was still wearing her flimsy pink nightgown. She sensed his eyes roaming over her barely clad body, and she blushed. But then he uttered an expletive and jumped to his feet.

"Ying!" He strode over, lifted her chin, and examined her neck and chest. "What in the gods' name happened to you?"

Ying looked down and was shocked to see her top half almost completely encrusted in dried blood. In the darkness of the night before, she hadn't noticed.

"She cut me," Ying said, feeling queasy. "My reflection."

Another expletive. "Are you all right?"

Ying tried, and failed, to give a nonchalant shrug. "It feels okay." Then, deflecting the focus, she said, "How do *you* feel? You're the one who was nearly strangled to death."

"Just a headache," he said, waving away her question. "We should get you cleaned up. Come." Gone was the carefree, whistling prince. The commanding tone was back.

Ying crawled closer, kneeling before him. With surprising gentleness, the prince pulled out his handkerchief, wet it with a splash of water from his leather water bladder, and spent considerable time sponging away her blood.

His closeness made Ying shift uncomfortably. In the stark light of day, the night she'd spent wrapped in his arms was like a distant, awkward memory.

Mostly awkward.

She watched him as he worked, her entire body tense, fighting her instinct to lean away. Then, purely to break the uneasy silence, she spoke.

"Zhang?"

"Mmmm?" He was distracted, his head bent in concentration.

"What are we going to do now?" Ying was cognizant of the time that had already passed since they'd pushed her reflection through the mirror, and anxiety was expanding in her chest. They needed to get started. Needed to do *something*. Anything.

The prince continued his ministrations, not looking at her. "About what?"

"About the monsters in the mirrors! I mean, do we ask your parents—"

"No," the prince said, a little harshly. "They . . . would not understand."

"What do you mean?"

"My father . . ." the prince started. He shook his head. "Never mind."

What did *that* mean? Ying wondered. Was the prince's father already aware of the truth about the mirrors? Were they all in on this, this Shan family secret?

Ying narrowed her eyes. "Wait," she said. "How much do *you* know about it?"

He paused and looked up at her. "About what?"

"About the mirrors."

Immediately, he lowered his head and went back to his task.

"Nothing," he said, and recommenced cleaning her wounds—a little too hard, a little too fast. "I know nothing."

"What about all those empresses who disappeared?" Ying continued. "Your ancestors? Were you told anything about them?" A mess of theories was swirling around Ying's mind, getting muddied. Not for the first time, she wondered if the women had escaped across the mirrors into a reflected world.

The prince pursed his lips. "I was just told that they fell ill and died."

"And you never thought that was *strange*?" she asked, incredulous. "Seven consecutive empresses dying young? You never thought to question it?"

"No." He stopped and threw down the handkerchief. "Of course I didn't question it! When literally everyone—your parents, your advisors, the imperial healers, the officials . . . even the history books—say the same thing, you don't *question* things, Ying."

Ying pressed her lips together. Of course he wouldn't question it. Historically, women weren't even remembered by their names—only by their relationships to the men in their lives. It figured that the crown prince, raised in a society that saw men as being inherently superior, wouldn't think twice about women who had disappeared before he'd even been born. "But what about the rumors? People say—"

"Listen, Ying." Exasperated, he snatched the soiled handkerchief up, crushing it in his fist. "We're royalty. People talk. If you're going to be part of this family, you better learn the difference between gossip and truth." He shoved the slip of fabric into his pocket. "And fast."

"Right," Ying muttered, crossing her arms. "Gossip. Truth. Got it."

The prince knew more than he was saying. Ying was sure of it. There was something special about the royal palace, some unknown quality that allowed the line between this universe and the next to blur. Yet the more Ying tried to make sense of the past few days, the more questions piled up in her head. Why had her reflection asked to swap with her and take her place, instead of simply letting her disappear like all the other vanished empresses? And why had Reflection-Ying attacked the real prince and not her?

Ying couldn't help feeling she was *so* close to the truth. Still, it remained elusive, flitting just beyond her consciousness, just outside her vision, just a tiny bit beyond her reach. Just like the strange movements she used to see in the corners of her mirrors.

"Well, I'm done." The prince narrowed his eyes and examined his handiwork. "It's shallow, but you'll need to keep it clean so it won't fester." He scrutinized her neck wound again, then touched the pouch strung around her neck. "We should remove this or it will rub. I can carry it for you."

"No," Ying protested. "Not that. Please."

"What is it?"

It was a lock of his hair. When she'd been sent it, following the announcement of their betrothal, she had added a lock of her own hair, twisting the two together. She was wearing it when she'd been dragged through the mirror and had almost forgotten it was there. Now she felt a little silly. She didn't want him to see she'd kept it, this fool's relic of foretold love.

The prince seemed to recognize it, because he was careful as he slipped it off her neck. "I'll keep it safe," he said, stroking it with his thumb. "I promise." He put it around his own neck and tucked it under his tunic, against his chest.

They ate. Ying didn't dare broach the topic of the mirrors again, because for the first time ever, things felt natural between them. Unstilted. It was almost as if they were a normal couple having an open-air picnic. Not awkward, estranged newlyweds who had both been seduced, or attacked by, their alternate-world doppelgängers.

Being away from the palace suits him, Ying thought. Or maybe he was just more genial once fed. Most people were, Ying knew. In the Jiang household, there was no hurt that could not be soothed with a hot, hearty bowl of rice porridge.

As the sun approached the midpoint of the sky, however, their meager conversation dwindled to complete silence. Ying sensed the prince's gaze on her, and the hairs on her neck prickled. She looked away.

"I can see why you're wearing that," the prince said suddenly. Ying gave him a sidelong glance.

"Oh?"

"It suits you." He gave her a wicked grin.

Ying, turning fully to face him, raised her eyebrows. "I'm only wearing it because it was what my reflection wore. In the mirror world, things seem to appear only when they appear out here."

"Huh." The prince contemplated this for a few seconds, then grinned again. "Well, I'll thank *her* when I see her next, then."

Ying picked up a loquat and threw it at him, narrowly missing his head. He chuckled. Then they both went quiet and simply stared at one another.

The silence was heavy with meaning. Prince Zhang finally broke it. "I really did think she was you, you know. I wouldn't have done it if I didn't."

"Done what? Lie with her?"

He grimaced. "We didn't get *that* far. But yes."

Ying picked up a loquat, rolled it in her palm, then placed it very deliberately back on the pile. "I wasn't ever—with—the other prince, in case you were wondering," she said, her cheeks reddening. "I haven't been with anyone."

The prince gazed at Ying for several long moments. Then he crawled over to her and took her face in his hands. Her cheeks seared with heat, partly from embarrassment, partly from something else.

"Maybe we should change that," he said, leaning in.

16

He'd only just brushed her lips with his when Ying pulled away.

"I'm sorry," she said, turning her head from the prince. For a split second, she had imagined the Mirror Prince in his place. Then she'd been flooded with guilt. Her feelings were not something she could just pretend away.

"No, it's okay," he said, clearly disappointed. But he sat back and didn't push things further. "We should be heading home anyway." He stood up, kicked dirt over the fire, and stamped it out with his boot.

Ying rose onto her knees. "Can we stop at the lake on the way?" she said, trying to change the subject. "I . . . I rather fancy a swim."

He stopped. Stared at her. "A swim? Why?"

"Why not?"

"The world is in danger of being overthrown by mirror people," he said slowly, enunciating each word, "and you want a *swim*?"

Ying's mind scrabbled for an excuse, but she came up empty.

"Wait." The prince crossed his arms and narrowed his eyes.

"The gateway to the mirror world isn't just through mirrors, is it? It's through any reflective surface. Am I right?"

"Well..."

"Ying!" Exasperated, he raised his hands, then dropped them. "You're going back? Why? Why put yourself in danger? Again!"

"My reflection's still in there. I don't know exactly what she's planning, but it can't be good. And there are people in that world who need to be warned."

"Right." The prince gave a small, derisive snort. "The *prince*, I'm guessing."

Ying opened her mouth to protest but couldn't think of what to say. So much had happened with both the real prince and the Mirror Prince. She barely knew how she felt, let alone what to think. But the prince took Ying's silence for confirmation.

Shouldering his bow with unnecessary force, he shot her a petulant look. "Fine. Do what you like. You obviously aren't going to listen to me."

He turned and strode away. When Ying failed to follow him, he spun back around.

"Well?" he said, impatient. "Are you coming or not?"

Ying didn't answer. She didn't move. Instead, she tilted her head to one side. The forest had fallen silent. Unnaturally silent. There wasn't even any birdsong.

But then—what was that rumbling?

She got to her feet, her head still cocked. Now the prince had heard it, too. He glanced at her, his face giving away his concern.

"Come, Ying." Taking her hand, he tried to tug her up the

hill, but she was frozen, immobile. The rumbling was getting nearer. Great plumes of dust wafted up into the sky, like columns holding up the heavens.

"Ying!" the prince said, pulling at her arm more urgently. "Come *on!*"

It was then that she saw what was making the noise. "Oh," she said. "Oxen."

The prince turned and stared at the stampeding animals swarming up the mountain. Their hooves striking the ground were like thunder. Their hair looked like dried-out straw. And each of them had four large curved horns protruding from their heads.

Except oxen don't have four horns; they have two. And they don't run uphill—not at this speed, anyway.

"Not oxen," the prince yelled, grabbing her arm. "Áoyīn. RUN!"

Mā de. Man-eating beasts. This finally spurred Ying into action. The two of them scrambled uphill as fast as they could. Not fast enough. The beasts were gaining ground. The prince stopped and whirled around to face her.

"Take the bow," he said, tossing it to her, closely followed by his quiver. "Get up a tree."

"But . . . but I can't shoot!"

He drew his sword. "Then learn. Quickly!"

Ying shimmied up a tree and nocked an arrow. On the ground, the prince braced himself, ready for a fight. They assumed their positions, holding their breaths, waiting to face the stampeding beasts.

The áoyīn were larger up close than Ying expected. When

they charged over a crest in the mountain, Ying saw how they towered over the prince. Her blood ran cold. Bile rose in her throat. They were not supposed to exist—not in this world, anyway. The tales told of their supernatural strength, their ravenous appetite for human flesh. They would crush him. And then they would swarm the nearest village, decimating the human population there.

But she'd underestimated him. Before this moment, she hadn't seen him fight. When the first creature was within striking distance, he slashed out at its neck. Blood spurted from its wound, spattering the prince. The animal uttered a bloodcurdling cry and collapsed onto the ground.

As it fell, the prince grabbed one of its horns and vaulted onto its broad back. He leapt from one creature to another, never losing his footing, as agile as a cat. As he went, he drove his sword down into each beast. As one fell, he would leap onto the next creature's back. Stabbing, slashing, bringing them down.

Ying drew her bow, her arm quivering with tension. Not brave enough to shoot too near the prince, she instead aimed at one of the stragglers at the edge. She let the arrow fly, missing by a long mark. She cursed and nocked another arrow.

Before long, the herd of beasts had been whittled down to three, mostly due to the prince's efforts. The three áoyīn pawed the ground, snorting, circling him.

He was in a half crouch, spinning around, keeping them all within sight. His hair was plastered to his forehead, his face spattered with blood. Ying sucked in her breath as he launched his attack, the silver of his sword flashing in the sun. He drove one creature back. Stabbed a second in the eye. As the third áoyīn charged, he did a low spin, driving his sword up through the creature's chin.

But as he yanked his bloodied sword back out, the first one charged from the side, gouging him with a huge horn. It ripped right through his leather jerkin. The prince was thrown against a tree. There was a sickening crack on impact. He slid down the tree trunk, slumping into a heap at the base, then lay there deathly still.

The enormous oxlike creature advanced on him, baring its fangs, rumbling a low-pitched growl.

The prince screamed as the creature's teeth sank into his torso. Ying screamed, too. The áoyīn was too close to the prince. She wasn't a good enough shot. What if she hit the wrong target? But she had no choice. If she didn't try, the prince would die.

She nocked her arrow and, without thinking, let it fly.

It whizzed through the air and—by some virtue of the gods—lodged deeply in the creature's broad back. Its growl transformed into an anguished bellow. The prince grunted and drove his sword upward into the creature's throat; blood spurted as it staggered sideways several steps, then crumpled onto the ground, dead.

Ying dropped out of the tree and ran to the prince. He groaned.

"How bad is it?" Her fingers roamed across his face and neck, feeling for any breaks or bumps. However, she knew the real damage would be where the áoyīn had gored him. Already, his tunic was soaked through with blood. The smell was sharp and metallic, and Ying almost retched. "Can you stand?"

The prince's face was pale, his forehead slicked with sweat. But he gave a weak nod, accepted Ying's proffered arm, and struggled to his feet.

He leaned on Ying as they inched their way toward the hut, wincing with each step. Ying's belly rolled with worry. Zhang Lin could barely stand, let alone walk all the way back to the hut. How would they get back to the palace?

The answer came as if on cue. Ying's chest constricted at the sound of galloping hooves. Thankfully, this time it was Shadow Runner.

"Thank goodness you're here," Ying said, awash with relief. The horse bent his forequarters low to the ground. Even beasts bowed to the future emperor.

The prince, panting hard, grabbed Shadow Runner's saddle and swung his leg over, dragging himself onto the horse.

Ying sprang up behind him. Luckily, they were close to the road. But she had no idea what commands to give to make the horse run. In the end, she settled on shouting, "Go!"

That was enough. Shadow Runner gave a whinnying neigh as he bolted off, bringing the injured prince home.

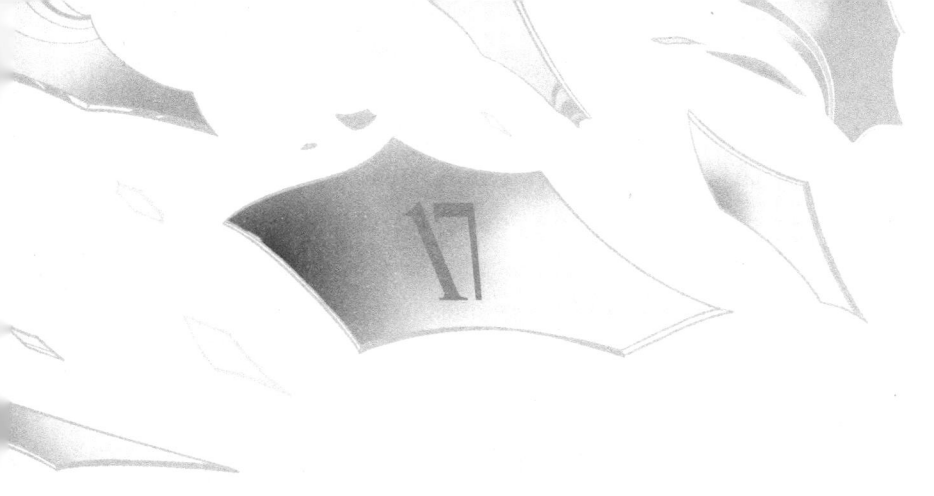

17

Ying called to the guards as they approached the palace gates. "The prince! Prince Zhang Lin! He's injured!" As the gates swung open, a horde of servants materialized, hauling the prince off his horse and onto a stretcher made of leather and bamboo. They hefted the stretcher up a short flight of steps to the infirmary, shouting commands to passersby.

The servants transferred Prince Zhang from the stretcher onto the surgeon's table. As they sliced away his jerkin, the prince moaned in pain. At the sight of his injuries, a few of the servants blanched, and from this Ying knew the wounds were bad. Very bad.

Her mouth went dry. She rubbed her upper arms, the action anchoring her. While a group of healers worked on the prince's mangled torso, Ying cast her thoughts back to the mountain and the attacking áoyīn. Áoyīn were supposed to be mythological creatures—terrifying flesh-eating beasts rumored to be especially fond of human brains. They weren't supposed to exist in this world. Which only meant one thing.

They had come through the mirrors.

As far as Ying knew, the mirror gateway was still closed. They were solid for the real prince, and ostensibly for the Mirror Prince, too. Sure, she had made her way through easily. But she doubted that a herd of stampeding áoyīn had accidentally stumbled from their own world to the next. There had to be something else, some explanation for their presence.

Ying could only think of one: the barrier was breaking down, and something—or someone—had let them through.

She was jolted out of her thoughts by one of the healers. The lead healer, judging by the embellished robes they wore. They were shouting at her, trying to get her attention. Strands of hair had escaped their topknot and were frizzing around their face. "Princess Ying! Princess Ying! Tell us what attacked him!"

"I—uh, what do you mean?" She wasn't sure if she could trust them.

"The wound... We cannot stop the blood. What caused this injury, Princess?"

What should she say? Should she tell them the wound was inflicted by a mythical beast? Would they even believe her?

In the end, she said the only thing safe enough to say. There was only one person at the palace who might have seen this before. Who might understand. "Call Mei Po!" she ordered. "She'll know what to do."

The healer hesitated for a second. But then they performed a perfunctory bow and rushed off.

The other healers milled about, pressing táixiǎn over the

large gash in an effort to staunch the blood. The wads of moss kept soaking through, and the healers had to replace them as fast as they packed them on.

Ying wove through the crowds congregated around the prince and knelt by the table. His face was gray. His eyes were closed. His hair, damp with perspiration, was stuck down on his head. He looked like a corpse. When Ying looked carefully, though, she could see the subtle rise and fall of his chest. She brushed his hair away from his face. He was colder than usual, almost as cold as his reflection.

"Why'd you insist on facing them?" she whispered. She squeezed her eyes shut to keep from crying. "Why didn't you hide, like me?"

She could guess why. This prince, the real prince, clearly had a keen sense of duty. He would not, could not, risk letting these creatures—beasts that hungered for human flesh—reach his people. And perhaps a tiny part of him had wanted to protect Ying. To have her armed but out of the way.

Was it because he cared for her, even a little? Or was it only that he felt he had to because she was meant to be his wife?

As she opened her eyes, a teardrop rolled down her cheek and onto the stone floor.

"Just stay alive, okay?" was all she could manage. Then, not knowing what else to do, she took a cloth and gently bathed the blood from his face, just as he had done for her.

The lead healer returned not long after, carrying Mei Po in their arms. The woman was swaddled in thick furs and held a walking stick—a piece of twisted wood with a phoenix head on top. The phoenix's long plumed tail wound around the shaft, and a pair of huge, glittering red rubies were inlaid into the handle to represent the eyes.

Ying stared. It was still deeply unsettling how identical the humans were to their doppelgängers in the mirror world.

The lead healer set the old woman down. The rest of the healers immediately stopped what they were doing and kowtowed to her.

"Get out," the old woman said, pointing at the door with her stick. The group of healers scrambled to their feet and scurried out. The lead healer, however, hadn't moved. Mei Po gave them a narrow look. "*All* of you."

Ying turned to follow, but Mei Po raised her palm. "Not you." Ying nodded and backed away into a corner.

Mei Po approached the table, her walking stick clacking on the hard stone floor, and bent to examine the prince's wound. "What was it?" she asked, shifting her gaze to Ying, her lychee-white hair sticking up in all directions. Ying couldn't help feeling a sense of déjà vu—she'd witnessed a similar conversation between the Mirror Prince and Mei Po's reflection in the tall tower of the mirror world.

"Áoyīn," Ying said, wondering if this version of Mei Po would be shocked by the mention of the mythical beasts. Mei Po only nodded and got to work.

After leaning her walking stick against the table, she waved her hands in the air, leaving a trail of flame that flashed brightly for a split second before dissipating into lilac-colored smoke. She then pulled a glass bottle out of a pocket in her robe, swung the bottle through the smoke, and stoppered it. Finally, she pulled the layers of moss off the prince's wound, bent low, opened the bottle, and gently blew smoke over his gash.

As the wisps of lilac smoke rolled over the prince's wound, it simply knitted together and disappeared. By the time the smoke had dispersed, the only evidence that he'd been injured was a thin, pale line that transected his abdomen.

Ying gasped, astonished. Of course she'd known that Mei Po possessed magical abilities—not only had the woman kept herself alive for longer than a mortal lifespan, but she was also renowned for her unnatural healing prowess. Rumors of her powers had become so rife that, over the years, whole factions of priests and healers had banded together to protest her presence at the palace. Their alchemy was science-based, their practice spiritual; Mei Po's brand of witchcraft, they'd argued, had no place in a modern monarchy.

They'd hoped to demote her as the royal matchmaker, to get her banished from the court.

They'd been unsuccessful, of course. Every time.

Yes, Ying had heard about Mei Po's magic. But *seeing* it firsthand was altogether different. Ying remembered how the mirror-world Mei Po had conjured a tea set out of nowhere after healing Ying's wounds from the gōushé. It had made more sense in that world, a world that ought not to exist.

But in this world?

Mei Po pulled out a vial and tipped its contents into Prince Zhang Lin's mouth. He spluttered a little, still unconscious. Ying sniffed. The liquid smelled cloyingly sweet, like overripe peaches and faint, bloodlike rust.

The scent evoked in Ying a sort of strange nostalgia. There was something, some memory, buried deep in her subconscious, though she couldn't figure out what.

For several seconds, nothing happened. Ying held her breath. Then, with no warning, the prince arched his back, gave a huge gasp, and opened his eyes.

Ying flew to his side and slipped her small hand into his large one. He gave her a weak smile. "Hello, Princess." His voice was raspy. He swung his legs over and sat up slowly, running his hands over his scar, seemingly as surprised as Ying was that it had healed.

Ying stood and turned to Mei Po, her curiosity burning. "What was that elixir you gave him? I—I recognized it."

Mei Po leveled a look at Ying. "Draught of Life. It is the same elixir I gave you, Ying Yue. After I rescued you from the river."

"After you rescued—" Ying's throat seemed to close and she struggled to form more words. "What do you mean . . . ?"

"The day you nearly drowned," Mei Po continued. "You don't remember? You were four years old, and your reflection pulled you into the water."

"Wait." The world began to spin, and Ying clutched her forehead. Pieces of memories were coming back slowly, fitting together like a broken vase. The old woman who had pulled her out of the river. The woman who had just healed the prince. The woman who was now standing before her in this cold and sterile room . . .

They were the same woman.

"It was you!" Ying exclaimed. She hadn't even realized Mei Po had ever visited her house. It made sense, if she thought about it: it was common knowledge that imperial matchmakers regularly trawled each province to make records of all the highborn children. But still, Ying struggled to catch her breath, not quite able to wrap her head around this revelation.

She shot to her feet and began pacing. "You saved me. You saved my life. And you saved Prince Zhang Lin's life, too, and—" Ying raised her eyes, meeting the prince's gaze.

"Xièxie, Madame," Ying said, turning to face Mei Po, trying to shake off her agitation. "Thank you, thank you, thank you. Thank you for saving our lives."

Mei Po gave a low chuckle. "Hush now, child. There's no need to thank me for doing my duty. What you *can* do is tell me why you stumbled across a herd of áoyīn. I assume they came through the mirrors?"

Ying's mouth dropped open. She snapped it shut again, then said, "How do you know—"

"I have known about the mirror world for a very long time, Princess Ying." Mei Po smiled, the lines in her face bunching up like a dried, wrinkled plum. "And your ability to cross it. Why else do you think I chose you for the prince?"

"What do you mean, chose her?" the prince interjected. "You foresaw we would have an auspicious marriage, did you not?"

Mei Po turned and shuffled away. She lowered herself into an armchair in the corner, propped her walking stick against the wall, and looked up at them both.

"I must confess, that was not the only reason, Prince Zhang Lin. There was a prophecy. A thousand years ago."

Ying and the prince said in unison, "A prophecy?"

The old woman inclined her head. "In order for you to understand, we must go back many centuries. As you now know, the mirror world is not like our own."

Ying thought of the monsters. The gōushé and the áoyīn and the glassy-hard skin of the reflections. "Definitely not," she agreed.

"When life began," Mei Po continued, "the two worlds were in parallel. They existed in harmony but independent of one another. The reflective surfaces served to allow us glimpses into each other's universes. For many millennia, contact between the two was limited to brief looks through reflective water—lakes and ponds. That's where legends of merpeople originated.

"But when humans invented mirrors, our contact increased. While both sides were curious, none could cross over into the other world. That is, until a thousand years ago, during the reign of the Crimson Emperor, when the mirror people finally discovered how to breach the barrier. They swarmed through the mirrors and launched an attack. War raged. There were innumerable deaths on both sides. Eventually, the Crimson Emperor forced the enemy back into their own world and sealed the gateway with alchemical spells. He stationed fish spirits and ancient monsters to guard the liminal space between the two worlds, to keep the barrier intact. He then condemned the mirror people to servitude. In recompense for their betrayal of humankind, they were forced to mimic humans, to act as mere reflections."

The prince blew out a breath. "Who would've thought that when we looked at ourselves, what we were really seeing was monsters?" he muttered.

Ying ignored him, turning Mei Po's words over in her mind. Ying's reflection had called the mimicry her duty when, in fact, it was a curse. How long had she been watching Ying, seething with resentment, waiting to break through the mirror?

And that day—the day Ying had nearly died in the river as a child—was it *really* kelp that had dragged her deep into the river's depths? Or had Ying come that close to being murdered by her own reflection?

Her face suddenly felt cold, as though all the blood had pooled in her extremities. She clasped her hands together to keep them from shaking.

Mei Po went on: "Some of the emperor's advisors were against the idea of forcing them to mimic. They were concerned that mimicry would allow them to know too much. They wouldn't just be able to *look* human, but they would also be able to *act* human. Learn our secrets. Learn our ways. But the emperor was stubborn. He wanted to punish the mirror people for their crime. For instigating the war."

"And they've been stuck ever since?" Ying asked, her voice wavering. "Mimicking us?"

Mei Po inclined her head.

"Are they all bad?" Ying asked, thinking of the Mirror Prince.

"No, child." Mei Po chuckled and shook her head. "Just as there are humans with good and bad intentions, so it is for the mirror people. They are all individuals, just like you and me."

The prince made a skeptical noise at the back of his throat. "You really believe that?"

"Of course." The old woman turned her piercing eyes upon him. "I have to believe. What sort of society assumes everyone is a monster?"

"And the prophecy?" Ying asked, trembling slightly. "What does that say?"

"That one day, the gateway will again be opened. It will be opened by a powerful being who takes the form of a fish. And that the mirror people, who have spent all this time preparing for war, will once more breach the barrier and enter this world to attack."

Ying felt faint. What her reflection had said—about reclaiming their world—made sense. "What does this have to do with me?" Her voice sounded thin. Scared.

Mei Po leveled her piercing blue eyes at Ying Yue.

"Everything," she said. "You are the Fish."

18

Ying's mind spiraled at Mei Po's words. She put a hand on her chest, her breaths heaving in and out. "You mean the reason the gateway is open is *me*?"

"It is," Mei Po said simply. "But the prophecy also says the Fish will be the one to close it. For good."

"I thought . . ." Ying shut her eyes and shook her head. "I thought it was the palace . . . the palace that was the gateway."

Mei Po's voice was gentle. "No, Ying Yue. Not the palace. It's you. The palace is just where you've begun to come into your powers."

The prince put his now-warm hand on Ying's shoulder. He turned to Mei Po. "Is she the only one who can get through?"

Mei Po directed her response at Ying. "You, and your reflection. She imbibes your powers, as you do hers."

Cold dread drenched Ying's body. "My reflection," she said slowly, trying to unknot her thoughts. "My reflection wasn't really drowning that day, was she? She was—"

"Just pretending." Mei Po tutted and shook her head. "She knew you were the Fish. She tried to lure you across the barrier—because according to the legend, each time you cross it, it will break down further. But she figured out that day that you did not yet have your powers. That is why she waited so long to try again."

Ying brought her clammy hand to her forehead. "Me crossing it breaks it down further? And now I've crossed it three—no, four—times." Internally, she counted each time: Once when Reflection-Ying dragged her into the mirror world by her hair. A second time in the Mirror Prince's room, waiting for him to return with food, when she stuck her hand through the mirror. A third time when she came back to rescue the real prince. And, if Mei Po was right, the very first time had been when she was four years old and had been tricked into the water by her reflection.

Mei Po gave Ying a shrewd look. "Four times. I see. That makes sense. Seeing as you encountered those áoyīn in this world, then I'm afraid—"

Ying forced the words out. "The barrier is broken." The words held such finality.

"Not fully yet. But it is, at the very least, breaking down."

"What about the áoyīn?" the prince asked. "If the barrier's not fully broken and they're not of this world, how did *they* get through?"

Mei Po reached for her walking stick and rested both hands atop the phoenix-shaped head. "I am not certain. My theory is that they are mythical beasts, with lesser souls, and can cross more easily than we can. Still, they could only come through when the barrier was weakened. The more you traverse it, Ying

Yue, the more it will weaken, until anything can get through. Humans. Reflections. Everything."

"And then?" Ying's throat was thick, her voice almost inaudible. "What does the prophecy say will happen?"

Mei Po's next words were decisive. "War."

A heavy silence descended, and Ying put both hands over her face. What was she supposed to think now? She had been secretly thinking the reason she could cross the mirrors was because her true love, the Mirror Prince, was on the other side. She'd thought the mirrors had only opened so she could be with *him*.

Now she was discovering that wasn't the case. They had opened because of a prophecy so ancient even the history books had forgotten it. And from what Mei Po believed, the four times Ying had passed through the mirrors had broken the barrier down. A queasy feeling rolled through her, making her legs weak. *This is my fault.*

Pressing her hands harder against her closed eyes until light bloomed behind her lids, Ying tried to make sense of it all. The feelings she had for the Mirror Prince were real. And his feelings had seemed real, too. Weren't they?

She'd been wrong to trust her reflection. She knew that now. Maybe, just maybe, she'd been wrong about the Mirror Prince, too.

No, she thought. The pull she'd felt toward him had been so intense. Had felt so right. Hadn't he saved her life and warned her against her own reflection? He'd tried to stop her from going after Reflection-Ying, had tried to keep her safe. That didn't fit the profile of a man who yearned for war.

Ying dropped her hands and turned to face Mei Po. "Okay. So what exactly do I have to do?" She forced her voice to remain even, but inside, she was shaken. Terrified, in fact. And not just because she was afraid of failure. The truth was, she was also a tiny bit afraid of success.

Closing the barrier—if she was even able to—was the right thing to do. But it also meant sealing off the mirror world and all the people in it, including the Mirror Prince. If he was her true destiny . . . was that destiny to be forever stuck on opposite sides of the glass, never to touch again?

In the cold, clinical light of the infirmary, she couldn't begin to answer these questions. They probably weren't even worth asking yet—not until she actually knew how to close the barrier.

Mei Po's voice was gentle. "You opened the barrier, child. You can close it."

"I don't know how I opened it in the first place!" Ying said, raising and then dropping her hands. She looked at Mei Po. "And I don't know how to close it."

Mei Po was silent for a moment but then began to struggle to her feet. The prince moved to assist her; she waved him away, instead using her walking stick as an aid. "Alchemy," she said, leaning on her stick with both hands. Though she was smaller than Ying in stature, somehow she seemed larger. "The answer is alchemy. Alchemy sealed the gateway once. And so it shall again."

"What sort of alchemy?"

The old woman shook her head. "Alas, as to that, I do not know." She raised her translucent eyes to Ying's. "It is said that the Crimson Emperor concealed the secrets of his methods in an ancient text: *The Book of Alchemy*. But it was buried somewhere, and no one has unearthed it since. I have searched for it, mind you. Thus far, though, the information has been lost to time."

Ying dropped her shoulders. The meager hope she'd carried collapsed into emptiness, leaving nothing but a void.

The barrier was broken. The world was in danger. And Princess Ying was responsible for fixing it, even though she had no idea how.

"You're going to try to find it, aren't you?" was the first thing the prince said as they hurried along the corridor. He sounded breathless; despite Mei Po's treatments, he was clearly still affected by his ordeal. "*The Book of Alchemy?*"

Ying, slightly ahead of him, stopped. She waited until the prince had caught up to her. "I have to. You heard what Mei Po said. I have to." The prince opened his mouth to say something, but Ying held up a hand to silence him. "I know, I know. It's dangerous. But I have no choice. It's me or the world."

"I can't convince you to stay? To wait? I can put together a guard to protect—"

"No." Ying shook her head. "Right now, my reflection is unaware that I know about the prophecy. She doesn't know I know about the book. I can't risk her finding out and sabotaging my efforts." She looked up at him. "I have to go right away, Zhang."

"But where?" His tone was insistent. "Where are you planning to go?"

Ying pondered for a moment. She had no idea where to start, but Mei Po had said Ying would need it. Starting at a temple—where priests actually performed it—was as good a plan as any. "The temples," she said with more confidence than she felt. "The priests there have alchemical texts. Maybe they'll have the one we need, or at least know where we should start looking. How many temples are there in Jinshan, Zhang?"

"Ninety-nine," he replied. "But that's madness. It's too many. How will you get through them all?"

Ying's stomach clenched. She didn't have an answer to that.

They'd reached the end of the corridor. The end wall featured a full-length window that faced an internal courtyard. It was night, so Ying couldn't see through the glass. All that was visible were the reflections of the lanterns that lit the corridor, which looked like clustered constellations of suspended suns.

Her reflection was nowhere to be seen.

Ying's heart froze. Where was Reflection-Ying? What was she planning? And where was the prince's reflection? Why had he disappeared, too?

The prince, coming to stand by her side, turned toward the window, staring at the emptiness within. He startled.

Ying understood his reaction. It must've been jarring for him to see his reflection absent. Even she herself was not yet used to seeing an empty mirror.

Placing one hand against the glass, he leaned forward, his eyes wide, unblinking. The surface of the window rippled like water at his touch. Gradually, though, it solidified back into glass. The tightness in Ying's chest loosened very slightly. Despite her sojourns through the mirrors, the prince couldn't quite pass through. Not yet. For humans, at least, the barrier remained mostly intact.

Perhaps there was still time to fix things.

"He isn't here," Ying said, referring to the Mirror Prince. She'd half hoped she would see him, so she could figure out whose side he was on, once and for all. She desperately, desperately wanted to be proven right—that he was one of the good ones.

The real prince ran a hand over the back of his head and gave a huff. "Right," he said. "The *other* prince."

Ignoring his sullen tone, Ying started down the corridor, but he stopped her with a hand on her shoulder. "If you're going to go searching for this *Book of Alchemy*, then I'm coming with you."

They were standing close again. Close enough to feel each other's body heat. Close enough for Ying to see the shadows of his lashes on his cheeks. And then there was his grip on her shoulder—his hand, so warm, so heavy on her skin.

"Why?" Her face heating, Ying twisted herself out of his grip. "We'd probably kill each other."

"You'll get *yourself* killed if you go alone," he shot back. "Do you even know how rough the city is?"

Ying drew herself up to her full height. "I can look after myself!"

"How?" His eyes narrowed.

"I can wield a sword—"

"You can't shoot, though. You said so yourself."

"I shot the áoyīn!" she snapped. *And saved your life.* The words hung between them, unsaid.

"A lucky shot." The prince took a step closer to Ying, his eyes glittering in the lantern light.

Ying glared up at him. She didn't want to admit that he was right. Truthfully, archery was the one thing she'd never bothered to learn—she'd always found it boring compared to the flashiness of swordplay. "Arrows won't help me kill my reflection—"

The prince cut her off. "And swords won't help you find that book!" He stopped short, grimaced, then continued less harshly. "Listen, Ying. Let me come with you. If not for protection, then at least to help you access the temples. You know what the priests are like; they won't take kindly to a young woman roaming about unchaperoned. Plus, I'm more familiar with the temples. I'll know which are more likely to have what we need."

Irritation stabbed at Ying's gut. "We? There's no *we*. I'm the Fish. It's *my* job to close the barrier. I'm the one who caused all this—"

"And it's *my* future empire that's at risk because of it!"

Fuming, Ying opened her mouth to retort, but the words caught in her throat. She couldn't fault his logic, even though it maddened her beyond measure that what he'd said was true.

"Fine. Let's go, then." She tried to shoulder past him, but the prince moved to block her path.

"The temples aren't open yet. We'll go at first light." He narrowed his eyes as though daring her to argue.

At first, Ying didn't answer, irritation filling every crevice of her body. Finally, she nodded grudgingly. "First thing," she muttered.

Without another word, he stepped aside and allowed her to pass. Ying, pushing past him, started down the corridor.

She was some distance away when the prince called after

her: "Remember, Ying. Don't go slipping through any mirrors. Remember Mei Po's warning. The barrier is almost broken. We cannot afford for it to break more."

Ying's step faltered momentarily, but she shook herself and began walking faster.

The sooner they found that stupid book, the better.

19

They spent the next morning touring the temples, pretending the prince was just a proud husband showing off the city to his new, adoring wife. He seemed to enjoy himself, smirking at Ying's feigned reactions whenever he pointed something out. Ying played her part with alacrity, smiling and nodding and gasping in wonder. But she made sure to shoot Prince Zhang venomous glares whenever the priests' backs were turned.

The priests fawned over the visiting royalty. But, to Ying's extreme disappointment, they refused to divulge any secrets. At one point, in desperation, the prince asked about *The Book of Alchemy* outright, but the priest only laughed, the expression not touching his eyes, and declared the book an "unsubstantiated myth."

Dejected, Ying and the prince headed for the last temple they planned to visit that morning: a small, ramshackle building in the Shangren Traders' Quarter. Concealed in the roughest part of town, this one was infamous for the performance of often-illegal alchemy.

"Conceal your face," the prince murmured to Ying as they

approached the traders' district. "It's not safe for us to be recognized in these parts."

Here, the streets were too tight for horses, so they were forced to dismount and enter on foot. Traders called in singsong voices, trying to entice them to their wares. Street vendors tossed food in flaming woks, imbuing clothes and hair alike with savory-scented smoke. Between the stalls, heat shimmered, causing dizzying mirages that shifted and swayed with humidity.

Ying and the prince pushed through the crowd, their cowls drawn low, their faces cast in shadow. Beneath their cloaks, they wore imperial swords sheathed in scabbards. Unbeknownst to the prince, Ying had also strapped a dagger to her thigh. She still didn't entirely trust him.

By now, the dagger was chafing, her feet were aching, and she was sweltering under her heavy cloak. The Shangren temple was built right on the street. A long stone staircase led up to the entrance. Sighing, Ying trudged up the crumbling steps, wishing more than anything that the stonemasons had thought to build it at ground level.

Halfway up, she noticed that the prince was no longer beside her. He was still at the bottom, his head tilted, his eyes narrowed at the double doors.

"What's wrong?" she called down, her words clipped in irritation.

"It's just strange," he said. "The priests don't usually leave the doors open."

Ying spun around to look. One of the doors was slightly ajar. "Perhaps someone just forgot to close it."

The prince gave a most ungentlemanly snort. Shaking his head, he began to climb the steps.

She didn't know what to make of that. But the bigger question was, how did he know? How did he *know* what these temple priests did or didn't do when most of his time was supposedly spent shut up at the palace?

Did he come to the city often? And if so, what for? Was it for necessity—for business—or was it for leisure? Did the palace staff know, or did he have to sneak out?

Ying had so many questions. Once again, she was struck by how little she knew him. But when she chanced a look at the prince's face, she knew now was not the time to ask.

When they reached the top, he motioned silently to Ying to position herself to one side of the double doors. She took her place, drawing her sword, sweat blooming across her brow. The prince unsheathed his own sword and kicked the opposite door open.

Simultaneously, they both spun inward, swords aloft. As their eyes adjusted to the gloom and things came into focus, they saw that the temple had been ransacked. The large, circular space was devoid of anything but rubble. Internal doors hung off their hinges, priceless vases lay smashed, and incense sticks and soot had been trampled all over the shiny marble floor. Even the shrine had been desecrated, to Ying's horror.

The only things intact were the majestic red pillars—nine of them in total, like a forest of bloodstained trees—and an enormous octagonal mirror mounted in the far corner.

They lowered their weapons. Out of respect, Ying began to unlace her boots, but the prince stopped her. "No. Keep them on." He gestured at the debris-strewn floor. It wouldn't be safe to go shoeless.

With a small shrug, Ying gave up on her shoes. She entered, feeling slightly blasphemous as she picked her way through the wreckage. She scanned the room, eyes straining in the darkness, looking for anything the priests might use for alchemical experiments.

"What do you think happened here?" she whispered, wincing at how her voice echoed through the hollow space.

The prince was squatting, examining a broken vase. "Just thieves, hopefully. Bandits. Let's hope it wasn't your reflection." He threw down what he was holding and stood, arching an eyebrow at her. "Either way, I told you the city was dangerous, did I not?"

Suppressing the urge to roll her eyes, Ying turned her attention to the mess. She dug into a pile of trash, cringing at the filth, unearthing nothing more than broken incense sticks and shards of shattered clay. She couldn't help feeling that this was a colossal waste of time; there seemed to be nothing left of value. Since she wasn't sure, though, she had to at least try.

The two of them spent quite some time sorting through piles of rubble, until both were exhausted and covered in grime.

Finally, the prince spoke. "I think we should leave." He

swiped a lock of hair out of his eyes, leaving a trail of soot behind. "There's obviously nothing here—or if there was, it's been taken."

Ying sighed. "Yes, you're probably right—" But then she paused, her attention caught by something on the far side of the temple.

Giving her a quizzical look, Prince Zhang drew nearer. "What is it?"

Ying didn't answer; she just strode away from him. It was subtle, and she wasn't sure if it was just the interplay of light and shadow, but it looked as though maybe, possibly, one floor tile was slightly darker than the rest. Its position suggested that it would previously have been hidden by an altar, which the ransackers had cracked and broken. This was odd, because normally the *exposed* floor should be darker, not the area that had been covered up.

She edged closer, her pulse thudding. Now that she noticed it, she couldn't *unnotice* it. It was completely incongruous with the surrounding tiles.

Falling to her knees, Ying ran both hands across the stone tile and tried to pull it up. Once, twice, three times she tried—throwing all her weight into her efforts—but it didn't budge. She groaned, exasperated.

The prince knelt beside her, their shoulders touching. "Wait," he murmured. "There's something written on the surface." He brushed away the dust. Some writing was etched into the stone, but it was extremely faint, as though it had worn away with time.

Ying tried to make sense of the faded text. WHEN CRIMSON BLOOD FALLS DOWN LIKE RAIN, it read, THE STONES WILL SHIFT LIKE BROKEN EARTH.

"Does it mean"—Ying swallowed the hindrance in her throat—"we need to use . . . our *blood*?"

"Now, come on," the prince replied, in the most patronizing way possible. "You're not afraid of a little blood, are you?"

Scowling, Ying reached for her sword, but the prince stopped her with a hand on her arm. "Come, Ying." His hand tightened a little before he let her go. "I was jesting. Let me do it."

"I don't need you to do it," Ying said peevishly. "I'm perfectly fine with—"

"You do need me." The prince turned his attention back to the tile and frowned. "I don't think it means *any* blood. It says *crimson* blood. I'm guessing it doesn't mean the color. I think it means royal blood. Those of us descended from the Crimson Emperor."

Ying gave him a sour look, annoyed that he'd guessed the riddle before her. But she wouldn't turn down the chance to avoid slicing her own skin. So she shuffled aside to give the prince room, watching as he unsheathed his sword and, with a small grunt, nicked the pad of one finger.

He let a few drops of dark blood splatter onto the stone tile. For several seconds, nothing happened. But then a deep clunk sounded, then a creak, and the tile popped up about an inch off the floor.

Ying's belly clenched. It was clear now why the tile was

darker. Trying to swallow her revulsion, she focused on dragging the tile to one side.

Her hands were clammy. Her pulse roared in her ears. There must be something of value in here—after all, if it wasn't important, why would anyone have gone to all this trouble to hide it?

Beneath the tile was a pit, and inside the pit was . . .

Nothing.

Deflated, Ying swiped her hand across the dirt floor of the cavity. Her fingers caught on something crumpled in the corner. She plucked it out delicately with her thumb and forefinger. It was a note, written on parchment.

She flattened it out against her knee. Oddly, although the pit was dusty, the parchment appeared quite clean, as though it had been placed there recently.

"What's that?" The prince leaned over her shoulder to examine the parchment. Ying's heart sputtered at the way his shoulder pressed against hers. He was so close, if she just turned her head, she'd be able to—

No. She needed to stop this nonsense. She had to be on guard. It was too easy to fall into the trap of confusing him with the Mirror Prince. They looked identical. Sounded identical. Their smiles were the same, caused the same tightness in Ying's chest.

That's the only reason I'm feeling these things, she told herself. Her mind knew better; only her body was confused.

"I'm not sure," she said, trying to clear her head. "It looks like a note."

"What does it say?"

The text was tiny, intershot by sharp creases. Squinting, she read it out loud: "If you are looking for *The Book of Alchemy*, you are too late. I have already stolen it."

Ying gripped the edges of the parchment so hard her fingers blanched bone-white. Someone had gone to great lengths to steal the book. Someone had bypassed the stone tile's blood protection.

The question was: *Who?*

Either it was someone with immense power or someone of royal blood. Slowly, she raised her face to the prince and managed to choke out, "Was this you? Did you steal the book?"

One look at his stricken expression told Ying that was not the case. "No," he said, staring at the piece of parchment. "It wasn't me. Nor would it have been my father, who never leaves the palace compound. My mother doesn't share our blood, and my brother—" He stopped abruptly, then dropped his gaze.

Ying's heart squeezed with pity. The prince's brother was dead.

She thought of the reflections; of their impenetrable, glasslike skin. Of their blackened blood. They bled, certainly, but none of them shared the Crimson Emperor's blood.

Sudden realization dropped into her stomach like a stone. The prince's nose had bled when Reflection-Ying had tried to strangle him. Perhaps she'd stolen his blood.

Her voice dropped to a whisper. "I don't think it was bandits who raided this temple."

The prince's brow creased. "You think it was your reflection?"

"If the book contains important information about how to open and close the mirror gateway, then she'd certainly want it."

"If she stole the book—"

Ying's heart began pounding. "Then it means she knows we're here...."

A scraping sound made them both jump. Icy dread flashed down Ying's spine.

The sound had come from the octagonal mirror.

The prince leapt up, drew his sword, and cautiously approached the mirror. Ying, overcome by an inexplicable urge to yank him away from it, scrambled to her feet.

"Zhang," she said, her voice rising. She stumbled toward him. "Get away from there!"

The prince did not respond. He was completely still, completely silent, squinting into the mirror's depths. And then Ying saw, too late, the shadow within the glass—

Reflection-Ying stood on the opposite side of the mirror. And struggling in the reflection's arms, gagged and bound, was Ying's maid.

Li Ming.

Fear flooded Ying's body; terror seized her mind. Without thinking, she dove for the mirror, her outstretched arms sinking in to her elbows.

"Ying, no!" the prince yelled. He flung his free arm out to block her.

Immediately, the reflection's pale hand shot out of the mirror, seizing Prince Zhang Lin's wrist. He jerked forward, his forearm, then his elbow, disappearing into the glass until finally, his shoulder hit the mirror surface with a bang.

Reflection-Ying bared her teeth in a grin, her inhuman

strength easily allowing her to restrain both Li Ming and the prince.

Zhang Lin's panicked eyes met Ying's. She knew what they were both thinking.

He could get through, too, now.

The barrier was breaking down.

20

Ying caught Prince Zhang Lin's other arm and pulled with all her strength. The parchment fluttered from his hand and fell to the floor, forgotten. Ying's muscles shook with the strain, and she found herself screaming, not daring to contemplate the possibility of letting go.

Somehow, the prince managed to extricate himself from Reflection-Ying's viselike grip. Ying fell backward, carried by momentum. After stumbling momentarily, the prince quickly regained his footing, and—ever the warrior—drew his sword once more. "Get back!" he bellowed at the mirror. He brandished his blade. "BACK!"

Ying's reflection was already retreating, dragging a kicking and screaming Li Ming away and out of sight. *No!* Ying thought, running at the mirror. *Don't go!*

Her efforts to reach Li Ming were thwarted by the prince. Yanking her backward by her collar, he dragged her away from the bronze surface. Ying flailed, trying to jerk out of his grasp.

"Let me go!" she screamed as she lashed out. "It's Li Ming! It's my maid! My maid, my maid!"

The prince did not relent. He just tightened his hold on her collar. "Stop it," he hissed from behind her. "Or you'll get us both killed!"

Ying thrashed again, making a futile effort to break his hold. "I don't care! I'll go through and rescue her myself!"

The prince barked out a single harsh laugh. "What, and break the barrier completely open? That's what they *want*, Ying!"

"It's *already* open!"

"Not fully!" He leaned down, voice low and stern in her ear. "It took effort for my arm to get through. It's still a deterrent, for now. And I won't have you bursting it wide open on some frivolous—"

"Frivolous!" Ying spluttered.

Abruptly, the prince let her go. Ying lurched forward and landed painfully on all fours. She pushed herself upright, gnashing her teeth, and again hurled herself at the mirror.

The prince got there first, ripping it off the wall with merciless strength. He flung it against the floor, and it smashed, glittering shards spraying outward like a shower of fallen stars.

Ying screamed as the mirror shattered. Gone was her chance to go after Li Ming. She had no idea where her reflection had taken her maid. And she had no idea how many hours she would lose trying to find another reflective surface.

And all because of the goddamned prince.

Bastard. The edges of Ying's eyesight wavered until spots formed in her vision. If Li Ming got hurt, or worse, it would be *his* fault. Swinging around, she drew her sword and—to his apparent surprise—sprung at him.

His blade met hers with a clang. She swung at him again, not caring how aggressively she fought or how unhinged her technique was. All she knew was rage; rage that simmered in her veins, that made her hack and slash with reckless abandon.

"Ying." The prince forced her name out through gritted teeth. He was on the defense, deflecting each of her blows with every uttered word. "Stop this." He ducked, then parried another blow. "You won't win."

Snarling, Ying fought harder until she had forced him against the wall. "Oh?" She raised her blade and pressed it against his neck. "Tell me again how I won't win."

Her triumph was brief. In an instant—before she even realized what was happening—the prince had disarmed her, flipped her, and pinned *her* against the wall.

Her sword clattered to the ground. Ying struggled beneath his grip, the stones digging into her back. She gave an outraged cry.

"I would, but . . ." The prince's mouth twisted until it resembled something like a smile. "I am *not* in the habit of repeating myself."

Desperately, Ying groped for her concealed dagger, but with the way the prince had her pinned, she couldn't reach it.

She erupted. "How dare you!" Tendrils of hair had escaped her braid and fallen into her eyes; furious, she blew them away. "How *dare* you stop me from saving her!"

The prince pressed his forearm harder across her chest. "It's too risky!" He leaned in, his black eyes flashing. "Tell me, Ying. Do you ever stop to *think*? Or do you just throw yourself into every ridiculous situation—"

"Ridiculous!" Ying didn't care how loudly her voice was echoing now. "Going after my maid is *ridiculous*?"

The prince towered over her, his anger so palpable she could almost touch it. "She. Is just. A maid. She's not worth breaking the barrier for."

Ying stared up at him, horrified. *Just a maid?* Evidently, the prince was so cold, so inhuman, that he barely thought of staff as people. If Ying weren't so angry, she might have laughed—at the irony of the real prince being such a monster, while the inhuman Mirror Prince had enough humanity for both.

Raising her chin, Ying stared defiantly into the prince's eyes. "She is *not* just a maid," she hissed, seething. "She is a friend. And if you want to stop me from going after her, you'll—you'll have to kill me!"

The prince's eyes widened incrementally, but he quickly schooled his features into his usual mask.

"Kill you?" His words were a sneer. "Very well, then. Where shall I cut you, Ying?" With his right hand, he trailed the point of his sword up Ying's ankle, lifting the hem of her gown. "Here?"

Ying tried, and failed, to hold her breath—instead, she panted, her heartbeat skipping erratically, tears gathering in the corners of her eyes. "Fuck you!"

The prince ignored her. "Or how about . . . up here?" The sword continued its agonizing journey up her calf, toward her knee. The cold steel tingled on her bare skin. Zhang Lin looked down at her, his eyes half-lidded, and leaned into his forearm, pinning her harder. She let out a little whimper, the sting of tears hot on her cheeks.

"Stop this," she whispered. This was hideous. Unbearable. Internally, she was a mess of warring emotions. Fear, certainly. But also . . . something else. The way the prince stared at her was like a tiger crouching, preparing to spring. His murmured threats felt like a lover's caress—terrifying and sensual all at once. And his lips! His lips were so close they were almost brushing hers. So close she could feel their heat. Somehow, this felt more lewd than a real, actual kiss.

"Ah," the prince continued, his voice now just a whisper. He dragged the sword tip still higher, past her knee, until the blade indented the soft flesh of her thigh. His breath tickled her cheek, her hair, the shell-like curve of her ear. "I think, Princess, I've found the perfect spot."

Ying shut her eyes, trembling all over. *He's lost it,* she thought. *He's lost his mind.* The worst thing was that she didn't know—could not at all predict—what he was about to do.

He made a sudden movement, and Ying cried out, but the next moment, he'd released her and backed away. She almost fell over, managing to steady herself against the wall. By the time she'd raised her head to glare at him, he had sheathed his sword, his face a picture of outward calm.

She wanted to scream. In his hand was the blade that had been strapped to her thigh. The leather straps lay on the floor in tatters.

His eyes met hers, and he smirked, twirling the dagger in his fingers. "Couldn't risk you using this on me, could I?" He slid it into his belt. "I mean, you're not too bad with a blade, Ying Yue.

Not as good as me, of course, but that's okay." His smile turned into a satisfied grin. "No one is."

Ying shook with leashed fury. "How did you know . . . ?"

"You were too obvious in your attempt to grab it. An easy mistake to make for a novice."

Fuming, Ying lunged, swiped for it. "Give it back! That's mine!"

He caught her wrist, his reflexes lightning-fast. "Actually," he said, "I think you'll find it's mine." His grin fell away, and he leveled a gaze at Ying. His eyes, blacker and fiercer than she'd ever seen them, flashed as he leaned in closer. "Everything in that palace is mine, Princess. Remember that. *Everything.*"

Ying seethed. Wrenched her wrist from his grasp. She did not need telepathy to know what he was thinking. Everything in the palace was his—including her. To him, she was nothing more than a possession, a plaything, a prize to display on his shelf. In his eyes, she was worth no more than the ornate dagger he had just cut from her thigh.

How lucky it was that they weren't actually married. That she'd managed so far to avoid being bound, spiritually and legally, to this arrogant, insufferable man.

Ying's whole body shook, her insides incandescent with rage. But she forced herself to slow down. Closing her eyes and breathing hard, she stamped down her anger as though quelling a flame.

She was finally realizing: she would never be able to convince him. Her powers of persuasion were no match for a lifetime of privilege. His imperious sense of ownership, his lack of care for the people who lived to serve him. His urge to exert control over *her*. No. It was insurmountable, impossible, to make him see her point of view.

And although it pricked her pride to admit it, she couldn't beat him physically.

What she needed was to somehow slip away. A chance to go into the mirror world and rescue her friend. Li Ming was in danger; Ying couldn't afford to waste more time. She needed to get away from this temple, and fast.

Which meant she needed to play his game.

Slowly, Ying raised her head and looked squarely at the prince. "You're right," she said, willing her voice to remain steady.

The prince stopped. Stared at her, his mouth agape.

"You're right," Ying repeated, giving what she hoped was a nonchalant shrug. "She's just a maid. Besides, I don't even know if it was really Li Ming. It could have been her reflection."

He swallowed hard, then nodded. "Right. It could be a trick to lure you across the mirrors. It's best not to take the chance." He gestured at the smashed mirror. "Not when the stakes are so high."

Ying allowed the prince to lead her back to their horses. She remained silent, compliant, as he helped her mount, her horse falling behind his as they rode toward home. Outwardly, she acted calm, composed. But internally her mind was spinning.

Despite what she'd said, Ying was fairly certain the maid in the mirror was the real version of Li Ming. Reflection-Ying knew how fond Ying was of the girl. She'd been privy to so many personal moments between the two of them. All those nights in front of the mirror, Li Ming fussing over Ying's hair and Ying spilling all her closest secrets.

As her horse plodded along behind the prince's, Ying twisted her brother's opal ring round and round on her finger—a nervous gesture.

Yes, Ying was sure it was the real Li Ming. The maid had most certainly been kidnapped. Ying's reflection knew exactly how to hurt Ying: by targeting the one person in the palace whom Ying considered a friend.

This was a statement. A threat.

It was personal.

This was a declaration of war.

Shooting a covert glance at the prince, Ying tugged her cowl lower. It wouldn't do for him to realize exactly how livid she was—better he not see her face. She never had been good at concealing her feelings.

Once they reached the safety of the palace, the prince offered to escort Ying to her quarters. She was under no illusion that this was a benevolent act. Clearly, he was doing it only to keep her from escaping and running away.

They marched side by side, silent and not touching, an arm's length apart. When they reached her rooms, the prince unlocked the door without a word, and Ying pushed it open slightly. Then she paused, hesitating. Would he try to follow her in? She assumed he would, to keep an eye on her.

Surprisingly, though, he didn't. Nor did he make a move to leave. He just stood there, staring at her, his lips slightly parted.

As though he wanted to say something. A pair of servants rushed past, stopping to kowtow, but he barely noticed them.

Ying drew a shaky breath. This was it. If she went inside her room and closed the door, she'd be cut off from the mirror world completely. There was no longer a mirror in her room; after she'd smashed hers the night before the wedding, a group of servants had been sent to clean up every last stray fragment.

"Well, good evening, then," she said, one hand still on the door. "And thank you. For before."

The prince narrowed his eyes at her, clearly suspicious. "Before? What do you mean?"

"You stopped me from doing something rash. At the temple. You . . . stopped me from going through the mirror."

He frowned. "You were ready to sacrifice yourself—and the world—for your maid."

"I was, Your Highness." Ying dropped her eyes, bowed her head, and tried to look contrite. "I am glad you were there to curb my impulsiveness."

The prince leaned against the doorframe with one shoulder. "Ying," he said after a pause, then sighed.

"Yes, Your Highness?" She blinked up at him, eyes wide.

"You don't have to do this on your own, you know. You're the crown princess—"

"I'm not," Ying corrected quickly. "We're not really married. Remember?"

He gave her an arch look. "Regardless. You have guards, soldiers, entire armies at your disposal. Yet you insist on trying to tackle this yourself. Why?"

"I just . . . don't know if I can trust you."

There was a long pause. The prince's eyes met hers, so dark, so fathomless, so unreadable. "You can trust me," he said finally.

No I can't. Ying's thoughts echoed inside her head like a scream. *I can't, I can't, I can't. I can't trust someone who stops me from saving Li Ming.*

I can't trust someone who thinks she's not worth saving.

She wanted to say this to him, wanted to fling the words until they tore open his skin, until they punched a hole right through his stone-cold chest.

But she didn't. She knew that fighting him wouldn't work. Verbally or physically. He was too strong, too powerful, especially here in the palace—if she tried anything, she was sure he'd just throw her back in her rooms and lock the door. Or perhaps he wouldn't even bother doing it himself. Perhaps he'd just command his guards to do it.

She needed to try a different approach. Something new, something she hadn't tried before.

Reaching out, she slid her hand up his chest. Watched as he froze under the force of her touch. Watched how his pupils dilated, how his breaths became more shallow. His heartbeat quickened beneath her hand.

She continued tracing a path up his neck, along the lines of his muscles, which were taut with tension. His skin burned with heat, which caught her by surprise, though it shouldn't have. She continued her slow caress until her fingers stilled, curled around the back of his neck.

Could she do this? she wondered. Could she play pretend?

For once in her life . . . could she lie?

"Show me," she breathed, moving closer, ignoring the churning in her belly. "Show me how much I can trust you."

And, pulling him down to her, she brought her mouth to his.

21

At first, the prince seemed startled. The kiss was surprisingly gentle, his lips disarmingly soft. But then, with a low groan, he wound his arms around her waist and pulled her closer, the full length of his hard, muscular body nestled against hers.

He did not stop, continuing to kiss her as he backed her into her room and pushed her up against the door. It shut softly behind them with a small click.

Now that they were alone, he became more zealous, his hand sliding up her body until it twisted in her hair. He tilted her head, giving him access to her neck, bringing his lips to the sensitive skin behind her ear. Ying let out a gasp. Heat rushed across her skin. Her breaths came higher, faster. Her fingers raked the prince's broad, muscled back and traveled up into his hair, still disheveled from their trip to the temple.

He tasted like salt. And soot. It occurred to Ying that despite what she'd told herself over and over . . . this did not feel very much like a lie at all.

You don't love him, she forced herself to remember as his warm lips grazed her neck. She bit her lower lip to stifle a moan.

The prince trailed upward, running featherlight kisses along her jaw.

You don't even like him. But then his lips found hers again, and her thoughts just . . . skittered away.

He deepened the kiss, bringing both his hands up to grasp her face, his lips moving hungrily, hurriedly, against hers. Breathing hard, he broke away for a second and looked straight into Ying's eyes.

"Ying," he whispered, his pupils dilated, his hands gripping both sides of her head. "I think—"

She never got to hear what he thought, because a look of sudden panic flashed across his face. He let her go, staggered back a few paces, and fell over—collapsed.

Ying stared, shocked that her plan had actually worked. Then she sank to a crouch and began rummaging through the prince's clothing, ignoring how her cheeks heated when her fingers brushed his bare skin.

It was lucky they were here, alone in her room. No witnesses. Anyone who came across him would just assume he'd passed out drunk.

With some difficulty, she unhooked the sword from his belt. She took her dagger also. Then she rose to her feet and looked down at the sleeping prince.

"Sorry for the inconvenience," she said, though she was not sorry, not really. "Just reclaiming what's mine."

He made no response, of course. Just lay there, his breathing deep and even. Stepping over his slumped form, Ying hurried over to her dresser. She had poisoned the prince. *She had poisoned the prince.* Surely that amounted to something like treason? When he woke in a few hours, groggy, with the taste of her still on his lips . . . would he realize what had happened? What she had done? She didn't know what her plan was, or where her reflection had taken Li Ming. But she did know one thing: she did *not* want to face another fight clad only in a silk dress.

Folded in the bottom dresser drawer were some clothes she'd brought from home. Back when she'd fill her days with horse-riding and roaming the Shuijing He countryside, she'd often wear a short linen tunic and supple leather pants.

Ying brought the tunic to her nose and inhaled. Somehow, after so many months, it still smelled of home. Her tears welled as she stripped off the soiled nightgown and slipped into the familiar outfit.

Once dressed, she scrubbed at her lips with a washcloth, hoping she'd ingested none of the poison herself. When she'd scraped out the residual powder from the empty casing of her ring during the long ride home, she hadn't known if the minuscule amount would even be effective.

But it had worked. And if such a tiny amount of the poison was enough to stupefy the prince—who was both taller and heavier than Ying—what might it do to her?

Flustered, she rubbed harder at her lips until they felt raw. She was a little woozy, certainly. It must be the effects of the toxin. It wasn't like the kiss could have affected her so. She *detested* him, obviously. She'd detested kissing him.

But . . . the thing was, she *hadn't* hated it. She hadn't hated it at all. If she was being honest with herself, she'd liked his lips on her lips, on her neck; she'd liked the way his body felt against hers.

Maybe she just hated that she'd had to resort to it. And even if she hadn't hated it, well, who could blame her? It was nothing more than her treacherous body reacting physically to the attentions of a man.

Now that it was over, she was sure of it.

Irritated with herself, she swiped at her tears with the heel of her hand before knotting a belt around her waist. The sword she strapped on her hip; she tucked the dagger into the waistband of her pants.

Finally, she took off her ring and her betrothal bangle. After a beat, she slipped Hao Yu's ring back on. The betrothal bangle she left atop the dresser.

Chewing her lip, Ying weighed her options. What was the best way of entering the mirror world? She could go through a window or go through the lake. And there were other mirrors around the palace. But was that too obvious? Would it take too much time to get to one, time that would alert her reflection to Ying's plans and give Reflection-Ying a chance to ambush her?

There had to be a better way.

Picking up her boots in one hand, Ying shut the door on the unconscious prince and all but ran across the hall to her maids' room. Ying had never actually been inside. Although she saw Li Ming and Fei fei every day, they always came to her, not the other way around.

Ying's reasoning for coming here was simple: do something

wildly out of the ordinary and she might escape her reflection's notice, even if it was only temporary. Plus, she doubted that the prince would have cared enough about her maids to order that their mirror be removed.

She banged on the door. From within came Fei fei's voice: "Come in!"

As soon as Ying pushed the door open, Fei fei jumped up from her bed. Her eyes were wide, red-rimmed. Immediately, she threw herself on the ground and kowtowed.

"There's no need, Fei. Get up. It's only me."

Fei fei got to her feet, swiping hair out of her face. "But you're a princess now, my lady."

"I'm still the same as before," Ying said. If only she could believe that.

"Have you news about Li Ming?" Fei said, her voice wavering. "I haven't seen her since last night. I'm so worried I've upset her—"

Ying opened her mouth to explain, but stopped herself. Fei apparently didn't know that Li Ming had been kidnapped, and it was kinder not to tell her. "Of course you haven't upset her."

Inspecting the room, Ying was struck by how bare it was. In contrast to the gaudiness of the rest of the palace, this was depressingly bare. Two narrow cast-iron beds were pushed up against opposite corners, and in the middle stood a simple wardrobe made of pine.

"Fei fei," she said, determination in her voice. "Is there a mirror in this room?"

"Yes," the maid replied, pointing with a shaky finger. "On the inside of the wardrobe door. But why, Your Highness?"

Ying didn't answer; she just went to the wardrobe and pulled it open, revealing a plain, rectangular mirror. She hadn't had a chance to get food or a water bladder, but she'd have to do without. The search for the mysterious *Book of Alchemy* would need to wait. Li Ming was in the mirror world. In danger and all alone.

"Fei," Ying said. "I need you to do something. It might be a little scary, but it will really help me out. Will you do it?"

Fei fei's face blanched, but she gave a timid nod. Ying beckoned her to the mirror. "Can you put your hand through this?" She needed to know how permeable the barrier was—since she was about to break it even more.

"My—my hand, Your Highness?"

"Yes. Please."

The maid held up a quivering hand, stretched it out, and touched the surface of the mirror.

Once again, it rippled. There was a slight resistance before Fei fei's hand sank right in.

"Oh!" she cried out, jerking her hand back. Her mouth sagged open, lips pale and bloodless.

Ying eyed the mirror. Its surface undulated slower and slower until eventually it stilled. Her throat felt tight. For a brief moment, she questioned whether she was about to do the right thing.

The barrier was clearly weakening. Going in to save Li Ming would mean opening the gateway more, possibly completely. Could she really risk it?

Li Ming needs me, she thought, and she tightened her jaw, determined. She gave Fei fei a fierce hug. "Whatever you see here, don't mention it to anybody, okay? Don't try to follow me. If anyone asks, tell them you know nothing."

She did not wait for a response before she turned to the mirror and climbed through.

22

True to Ying's memory, the light on this side of the mirror was a little sharper and flatter, as though someone had tried to paint the scene without mastery over depth or dimension. She blinked her eyes, trying to adjust. She hadn't noticed a difference on her first trip through the mirror—back then, her senses weren't so attuned. But now she felt as though she'd be able to tell whether she were in this world or her own.

Reflection–Fei fei was standing, watching her doppelgänger through the mirror with the same wide eyes, the same look of shock.

Ying pulled on her boots, then approached the reflected version of her maid. "Fei," Ying said, waving her hand in front of the reflection-maid's face. Nothing.

Damn, Ying thought. She'd hoped to quiz the reflection on whether she knew where Li Ming was taken. But there was no recognition in those blank brown eyes. As Ying squeezed past her, she noted fine, reticulated cracks on the reflection's face, visible only from close up. As though someone had hit her.

The reflection's eyes flicked toward her before snapping back to the mirror.

A bitter taste rose in Ying's throat. The expression in Reflection-Fei's eyes was pure, unadulterated fear.

Her neck prickling, Ying crept out into the corridor, trying not to dwell on Reflection-Fei's behavior. *Where have you taken her?* Ying thought. What had Ying's reflection done with Li Ming?

Ying deliberated for a moment. If she went one way, she would be heading toward the gardens. If she headed the other way, she'd end up in the Mirror Prince's quarters.

She decided on the prince. And not just because she was desperate to see him, or so she told herself. It was just for information. Surely, he could help her find Li Ming? He'd be familiar enough with Reflection-Ying to know what she'd done with the maid.

Ying rested her hand on the pommel of her sword as she made her way along the corridor. She kept to the shadows, between the flickering lanterns, each footfall landing soundlessly on the plush burgundy carpet.

The antechamber leading to the prince's quarters was precisely as she remembered, with its carved-wood furniture, marble floor, and enormous vases. She remembered from the first night that the prince's door was the first on the right, so with heart hammering, she inched it open and peeked through the crack.

Someone was in there. But not the prince.

It was her reflection.

Reflection-Ying grabbed Ying by the arm, dragged her into the prince's bedroom, and slammed the door.

"You're so predictable," Reflection-Ying said. She shoved Ying against the closed door, her own ornate dagger against Ying's throat. "I *knew* you'd come looking for your precious prince." She spat the last words out, lacing them with acid.

"Go ahead, kill me." Ying clenched her jaw, hoping her bluff would work. Hoping that her reflection still needed Ying, the Fish.

When her reflection didn't move, Ying laughed.

"Ha! I knew you couldn't do it." In a swift movement, Ying kicked out, smashing her foot into Reflection-Ying's knees. The reflection buckled. Ying took the chance to break her opponent's dagger hold. After twisting her arm, Ying slammed Reflection-Ying's head into the door.

Her reflection recoiled a moment, winded, before regrouping and running straight at Ying. Ying ducked to avoid a punch but was smacked on the head by her opponent's elbow. Falling to her knees, she rolled away just as her reflection stomped down with her foot. Ying flipped back onto her feet and sank into a crouch. Her reflection snatched up her dagger, holding it high.

"I know all your moves, Princess," the reflection taunted. "You're deluded if you think you can beat me."

Ying knew they were evenly matched, apart from her reflection's impenetrable skin. She also knew she had one advantage: Reflection-Ying still needed her. Ying was the Fish, the only one who could break down the barrier as Reflection-Ying wanted.

Her reflection couldn't kill her.

Ying launched herself forward, kicking her reflection so hard in the chest she was thrown against the door. Her opponent's rock-hard body splintered the wood, plummeting through it, landing in a crumpled heap on the antechamber floor. Seemingly unhurt, she sprung to her feet and threw the dagger, hard, straight at Ying.

The weapon spun through the air, slashing Ying's cheek and lodging in the wall behind. Ying screamed in shock, clamping her hand to her face. Without thinking, she picked up a molded brass candlestick from a small side table and hurled it at her reflection.

Ying's reflection was too fast. Her arm shot out and caught the candlestick neatly in one hand. Her glassy lips stretched into a slow smile.

"You're going to have to do better than that, *Your Highness.*" She tossed the candlestick away and stalked toward Ying, drawing her sword. Ying drew hers in response.

"Ying!" A voice rang out from behind her. Ying's heart flipped. The Mirror Prince stood at the opposite end of the antechamber, framed by the room's curtained entrance. He was tense, his body coiled, ready to launch an attack.

"Zhang Lin!" both women exclaimed simultaneously. Ying felt her cheeks redden at the sight of him, an awareness that was utterly shameful. If she was smart, she'd rein in her feelings for this man; he was, after all, one of *them*. And no matter how handsome he was, or how pretty his murmured words felt against her skin, she needed to stay impartial. Objective.

For now, at least.

Her reflection's eyes flicked toward Ying with a look that could raze mountains. She then turned her attention back to the prince, narrowed her eyes, and spat out one word.

"Choose." The word was heavy, full of consequence. For how was the prince to choose? How would he even know who was who?

Ying thought quickly. The prince needed to know it was her. If his heart was true and he actually did love her, then he would help her defeat her reflection. Really, it was her only hope of overcoming the other Ying. And if he was one of the mirror people who actually wanted her dead, well . . . she'd deal with that if it came to it.

Shoving her sleeve up past her elbow, Ying held up her forearm. The gōushé scar was a red, angry blemish on her otherwise pristine skin.

The prince took one look at the scar. His eyes met Ying's. It was a loaded glance; in that moment, Ying knew. He did love her. He really did love her. The connection they'd felt on her first trip through the mirrors was genuine. Seeing him brought all her own feelings rushing back, as if her world were tilting.

By some unknown, unuttered signal, they both broke the connection simultaneously and ran full-tilt at Ying's reflection.

The reflection howled with rage but assumed a defensive position.

The prince and Ying's reflection came together with a clash. Almost immediately, the prince unseated his opponent. Reflection-Ying fell, her sword skittering across the marble floor.

The prince advanced upon her, his mouth twisted into a menacing snarl.

"What are you doing?" he roared, his voice echoing around the chamber. "Why are you attacking the woman I love?"

His words halted Ying in her tracks. There he was. There was her prince. *This* was the man she was foretold to love.

Reflection-Ying stared up at the prince, chest heaving. Disheveled hair fell across her eyes. She grinned.

In an instant, Ying's reflection scrambled to her feet. She turned and sprinted away, through the curtains and into the stone corridor. Ying and the prince bolted after her—but not quickly enough. Reflection-Ying had already smashed a window using one of the huge floor vases.

Before Ying could fully grasp what was happening, her reflection had morphed into a glossy raven. Taking flight, she flapped into the night, her great wings carrying her up and up, toward the rising moon.

23

Dropping her sword, Ying ran to the window and leaned out, almost cutting herself on jagged glass. At the last moment, the Mirror Prince grabbed the back of her tunic, pulling her into his arms.

"Careful, now." The coldness of his big arms enveloped her, chilling her body even as heat shot through her core.

She gasped. "She . . . she . . ." Ying gawked out the window where her reflection had disappeared, struggling to form coherent words. Her gaze fell on the Mirror Prince, who was watching her, his black hair in disarray from the short but brutal fight. She traced the lines of his chiseled jaw, his high cheekbones, his enigmatic, catlike eyes. . . .

Her thoughts immediately disappeared, like incense dispersing on a breath of wind.

He was here. *This* was real, and he was here.

The rush of the fight still seared her veins. This, combined with the heady feeling of seeing him again . . . Without thinking, she threw her arms around his neck and—with the ferocity of a tiger—kissed him.

His hands went under her backside, lifting her as he kissed back. She wrapped her legs around his waist, his icy torso freezing her inner thighs. Their kissing was feverish, frenzied. Her hands twisted in his hair. Their breathing became more urgent, more harried, until Ying was forced to break away to catch her breath.

He set her down on a side table, one hand still on her hip. With his other hand, he caressed her neck, running his cool lips along her jaw. Wrapping her legs tighter around him, Ying shuddered, the sensations overwhelming. Ice and heat. Heat and ice.

"Gods, I've missed you, Ying." His words were muffled, his cool breath against her throat. "Talk to me. Distract me. Otherwise, I don't think I can let you go."

Then don't, Ying thought, his words causing something to twist inside her. But as much as she wanted him, this wasn't the time or place.

"I didn't know," Ying started, her voice higher than usual. She gasped when the prince ran his nose along her jawline, inhaling deeply. "I didn't know that my reflection could become a bird."

The prince straightened. With her on the table, they were at a level height.

"We all can," he said. "We can change. That's how we assume your forms."

"What?" Ying gaped at him. "What do *you* become?"

He shrugged. "Loads of things." He caught sight of Ying's face. "No, no. Not like that. It's just the way our world works.

Our duties bind us to the forms we mimic. I can change into any form I've had to mimic in a past life, animal or human."

"In a . . . in a past life?" She drew back to look at him, her head spinning.

"Well, not past life, exactly." He pursed his lips, thoughtful for a moment. "That's the wrong phrase. For us, it's all one life. We're tied to one form—from your world—aging normally. Then, when that form dies, we assume another form, and the cycle of mimicry starts over."

"That must be awful." Ying grimaced.

"What, living forever, shifting at will?" The prince chuckled. "It's not so bad."

"But . . . the pain."

The prince made a face. "The pain we learn to live with. For the most part."

"Some people haven't learned," Ying said. "To live with it, I mean."

"Yes, some of us struggle more than others. They resent their duties." His gaze lingered on Ying's face. "I struggle, too, now . . . when it keeps me from you."

Flushing crimson, Ying remembered how distraught he was when he'd been forced to leave her and she'd been attacked by the gōushé. Her arms tightened around his neck. "And exactly how many of these lives have you had?"

The prince's eyes sparked with something like amusement. "A few."

Ying opened her mouth, then shut it again, trying to make sense of it all.

"Have I scared you, Princess? I know it must seem strange to you."

Ying raised her chin, aiming for bravado. "No. No! Of course not. It makes perfect sense." Nothing could be stranger, really, than the fact there was a mirror world to begin with. Or the fact she was embracing, not her would-be husband, but his possibly immortal, shape-shifter reflection.

"So. Enough about me." The prince's black eyes burned with intensity. "Where the hell have you been? I've been so worried. After you left, I went to get help. But when I got back, I couldn't find you. I hunted for you in every mirror, every lake, within a fifty-mile radius."

He'd been looking for her. That was why the real prince was missing his reflection.

Guilt surged through Ying's chest, images of her time with the other prince flashing through her mind. His warm arms wrapped around her on the narrow bed in his hut. Him tending her wounds at the picnic. His lips. His taste. The way he'd kissed her, clasped her to him, without hesitation, without abandon—before he'd collapsed from the poison on her lips.

She shoved the memories from her mind. "Nowhere," she said, too quickly. "My reflection tried to kill me. I had to get away, lie low for a bit."

"Well, I'm glad you're back," he murmured, running one hand along her leather-clad thigh. He leaned forward and put his mouth to her ear. "I *like* this look, by the way."

Heat rose in Ying's cheeks. She sighed as he brushed her earlobe with his arctic lips.

Remember why you're here. Ying forced herself to concentrate, to ignore the sensations coursing through her as he trailed cold kisses down her neck. Her brain fought with her body, trying to think, trying to remember why she'd come back through the mirror.

It was to see him, yes, but there was something else. There was—

"Li Ming!" Ying's eyes widened as she gasped out the name.

The prince stopped his ministrations. He leveled a look at her. "Your maid?"

"Yes!" Ying put her hands on his shoulders and pushed him away. She slid down to the floor and paced away a few feet before spinning to face the prince. "Li Ming. My handmaiden. She's gone missing! I think my reflection kidnapped her."

He exhaled. "When?"

"Sometime between when I—" Ying stopped, not wanting to mention her late-night escape with the other prince. "Between when I went back to my world and now." Hoping the Mirror Prince hadn't noticed her stumbling over her words, she picked up her sword and resheathed it.

"If your reflection took her, then we'll find her. I swear it." The prince pressed his lips to her forehead. "The other Ying is predictable. I have a pretty good idea where Li Ming might be."

The Mirror Prince led Ying down several flights of stone stairs, descending deep into the bowels of the palace. The atmosphere was colder down here, and damp, pressing on her like a sodden blanket. Hanging in the air was a distinct smell of mold.

"Are we going to the dungeons?" Ying asked, staring at the prince's broad back as he went down the steps in front of her, holding aloft a lantern. Below them, Ying heard the sound of scurrying: rats.

He stopped and looked back up at her. "Yes," he said, holding out his hand. "Are you afraid?"

Ying had heard about the imperial dungeons' fearsome reputation. She slipped her hand into his. "A little," she admitted.

They'd reached the bottom of the staircase. In front of them was an ancient wooden door, crisscrossed with iron beams and heavy, rusted bolts. The prince pushed on it, and it swung open with a high-pitched whine. Beyond the door, a corridor was carved through the rough-hewn rock. Ying took the lantern from the prince and pointed it toward the darkness. Along the left-hand side was a row of iron-barred cells, each around twelve feet wide.

A shiver went down her spine. She turned to the prince, who was leaning against the closed door, his arms crossed. "You think she's down *here*?"

The prince confirmed it with a slight bow of his head.

Ying turned back to face the cells. Her stomach was churning, her forehead drenched in sweat. She hoisted the lantern higher, then paced silently down the corridor. As she passed each cell, she swung the lantern toward it, peering inside.

Most were empty, unlocked, the barred doors standing

open. One or two had floors littered with small skulls and bones, presumably from rodents.

One of them, though, was not empty. Ying stifled a cry at the sight of a cell with a dry, shriveled corpse. The skin was brown and wrinkled, the lips pulled away in a morbid caricature of a smile. The mouth was full of broken teeth. The corpse was propped up against the wall with heavy manacles around its wrists and ankles. Worst of all, swathed around the dried-out body were yards and yards of silk. A hànfú. Was this one of the empresses who had disappeared so many decades ago?

Swallowing her disgust, Ying moved on. The remaining cells were not much better. Many held corpses in various stages of decomposition. Some were already skeletons, all empty eye sockets and macabre grins. Others appeared to be more recent, with strawlike, straggly hair sprouting from leathery scalps. All of them were wearing beautiful silk dresses; every single one was shackled to the walls.

Seven corpses. It was clear now: the missing empresses had not crossed the mirrors to escape.

They'd been taken.

Ying's stomach roiled, and she resisted the urge to retch. Knowing she couldn't do anything to save the poor women, she averted her eyes, whispering a silent prayer for their souls—and one for her own, too.

As she continued down the corridor, a sound of soft rustling emerged from the darkness. *Li Ming!* Abandoning all caution, Ying started running until she reached the very last cell.

This end of the corridor was the dankest of all. Ying raised the lantern, spilling light into the blackness.

Huddled in the back was what looked like a pile of rags. But the pile of rags was moving. Shivering. That was the rustling sound she'd heard. Then the rags shifted, and in the gloom a pale, wan face lifted and stared at Ying.

"Li Ming!" Her maid's face was smudged with tear-streaked dirt. Her hair was unkempt, stringy and tangled, her face half-obscured. And her face itself looked haunted; bruiselike shadows were smudged beneath each eye. As soon as she saw Ying, Li Ming scuttled backward and cringed in the corner.

"Li Ming, it's me!" Ying gripped the bars. "Where is the key?" she yelled over her shoulder. "Gods, Zhang, get me the key!"

The prince had trailed behind her and was standing several paces away. Wordlessly, he stretched out his arm, handing her a shiny brass key.

For a brief moment, Ying wondered where he'd gotten it from, but there was no time to ask. Perhaps it was a palace master key. Perhaps the real prince carried one, so he did, too.

She hung the lantern on a hook and fumbled with the key in the lock. Finally, it turned with a satisfying click. As soon as it swung open, she flew to her maid's side, embraced her, and gave her a kiss on the top of her head.

"Please." Li Ming's voice was croaky from disuse. "Don't hurt me."

"Hurt you? I would never hurt you. Why would you say that?" Realization dawned in Ying's mind. "Oh. You mean the other Ying."

Ying knelt, getting down to Li Ming's level. She smoothed the lank hair away from Li Ming's face, then placed her hand on her cheek. "Can you feel my heat? It's me. The real Ying. We're going to get you out of here, okay? The prince and me. We're going to get you out of the mirror, bring you back—"

Li Ming grabbed the front of Ying's tunic, her thin hands twisting the linen so tightly the tendons on her knuckles stood out. "The . . . the prince?" Her eyes, wild, rolled to and fro. Ying was startled by how bloodshot they looked.

"Yes." Ying covered Li Ming's hands with hers. "He's here. He'll help."

The prince entered the cell and squatted down next to Ying. "Li Ming," he said. "Listen. I'm going to help get you upstairs—"

His words were drowned out by a loud clang, then a click.

Reflection-Ying was at the cell door, grinning, twirling the brass key in her fingers.

Ying's mouth went dry. She had heedlessly left the key in the lock. Slowly, she rose to her feet and turned to face her nemesis. "Open the door," she said, trying to sound authoritative. "My maid is ill. Let us go."

The reflection didn't answer immediately. She just continued to twirl the key for a few seconds, then closed it in her fist.

"You know I can't do that," she said. "I need you down here, out of the way. Really, it was my mistake not to lock you up in the first place. But no matter. Now I have you where I want you."

Ying threw herself at the cell door, her hand swiping through the bars at her reflection. Reflection-Ying laughed and stepped back, just out of reach.

"Why. Are. You. Doing. This?" Ying spoke through gritted teeth.

"You know why," Reflection-Ying said, chuckling. "With you out of the way, I can go out there. No one will know I'm not you. I can take your kind down one by one. The emperor. The empress. The Royal Guard. And the real prince? Well, since his reflection is apparently a traitor . . ." Her lip curled, and she gave the Mirror Prince a pointed look. "I suppose I'll just have to kill both versions."

Ying flushed hot at Reflection-Ying's threat, and her hand curled around her sword handle. A futile effort; it was not as if she could stab her own reflection through the bars. She'd learned the hard way that she couldn't stab her reflection at all. Still, refusing to be cowed, Ying raised her head. "Why not kill me, too?" The words came out surprisingly steady.

The reflection's face twisted in disgust. "Unfortunately, I need you. For some reason, *you* hold the power to break down the barrier, not me."

Ying pressed her further. "Because *I'm* the Fish. Not you. You don't have any power without me. Is that why you stole *The Book of Alchemy*?" She was bluffing, trying to eke more information out of this woman. "So you can work out how to keep the barrier open for good?"

"Book? What book?" A small line appeared between Reflection-Ying's eyebrows. Then her expression smoothed and she gave a tinkling laugh. "Never mind. Don't bother answering. I don't really care, since you won't be alive much longer." She leaned forward and spoke conspiratorially as though divulging a great secret. "When we've infiltrated enough and broken down your pitiful human defenses, it'll be time."

"Time for *what*?" Ying spat the words.

Reflection-Ying smiled, showing entirely too many teeth. "To attack."

Ying screamed and threw herself against the bars, against the cold, unyielding steel. The prince came up behind her and pulled her away.

"Stop, Princess," he murmured, folding her into an icy embrace. "Don't hurt yourself." Ying began sobbing, her tears soaking the front of his shirt.

"Young love," Reflection-Ying said, her tone sarcastic. "*So* sweet. Well, I best be going. I do have a world to conquer." She picked up the lantern. Shadows danced upon the walls.

"You." Ying drew a shaky breath. "You're evil. You'll go to hell for this!"

"Oh, sweet princess." The reflection smiled, white teeth flashing in the gloom. "Don't you realize? We're already in hell. *This* is hell. It has been for a thousand years."

The words twisted in Ying's gut. A thousand years ago was when the Crimson Emperor had cursed the mirror folk.

The reflection turned to go. But she paused, tilted her head, and said one last thing over her shoulder. "I hope you realize I'm doing you a kindness. At least you'll have each other for company. Although, I'm afraid you'll have to comfort each other with an audience." She leered. "Or perhaps you'll let the maid join in. The more the merrier, right?" Her laughter rang out as she strode away, the sound bouncing around the stone walls. The lantern light receded, getting fainter and farther away.

"You *bitch*!" Ying screamed after the retreating figure. "You absolute vile fucking *monster*!"

Ying's screams bounced around the rock walls, ricocheting back and forth until they became a cyclical, taunting chorus. The wooden door slammed shut behind Ying's reflection with a bang. Ying, the prince, and Li Ming were plunged into darkness, left with nothing but Ying's echoed words.

Monster. Monster. Monster. Monster.

Monster.

24

Sinking to her knees, Ying clung to the bars, sobbing into the darkness.

"Princess." Li Ming was at her side. "I'm sorry. You shouldn't have come. You shouldn't have risked yourself."

The maid's face was obscured by darkness, so Ying stretched her hand toward the voice. The tips of her fingers brushed Li Ming's face, and she brought her palm to the warm curve of the girl's cheek.

"I had to," Ying said, her voice thick with tears. "I could never abandon you. Remember, The lakes feed the rivers—"

"And the rivers feed the sea." Li Ming whispered the latter half of the Jiang family motto. The saying meant that everyone, from the lowliest of servants to the highest king, had a part to play for the greater good. And that it was everyone's duty to contribute to achieving a peaceful, harmonious community.

Ying felt dampness on her hand and realized her maid was crying.

"But now we're all trapped here, and I never got to tell Fei—"

"Got to tell Fei what?"

Li Ming withdrew from Ying. "Never mind."

Chewing on her lip, Ying had a sudden thought. She directed her next words toward where she thought the Mirror Prince might be. "Zhang?"

"Yes, Princess?"

"Could you shift into something and slip through the bars?"

There was a brief pause. "No." His voice loomed from the darkness. "I can't say I've ever been that small."

Damn, Ying thought, then climbed to her feet. How were they to escape this mess? Thinking hard, she felt her way along the bars until she reached the cell door. She stretched her arms between the bars, and her fingers found the keyhole. She prodded it, wondering whether...

She could only try.

"Can one of you bring me a rat bone?" Ying asked. "A sharp one?"

The sound of scrabbling on the floor was quickly followed by a small, sharp bone being pushed into her hand.

"Thanks." Ying shoved it into the keyhole and jiggled it around. Nothing happened. It was difficult to get the correct angle from the wrong side of the bars.

"I just need to...get it in properly...." Ying continued pushing and jiggling, hoping for that life-saving click.

Frustrated, she groaned and withdrew the bone. Thinking hard, she wondered whether she could get her arm through farther. If she could get more leverage to insert the bone properly into the keyhole, maybe, just maybe, she'd be able to pick the lock. She'd been shown how by one of the stablehands back home, a boy she'd spent a lot of time with before he finally declared his love for her. She'd turned him down, of course, as graciously as she could, but the conversation was overheard by another servant. Once their secret friendship had been discovered, he'd been sent to work at one of the Jiang's distant outposts.

But she'd learned with hairpins, not rat bones. Pushing up the loose sleeves of her tunic, she shoved her arm through as far as it could possibly go, trying to get the bone in at just the right angle. She was almost there; she just needed to move it a bit to the right—

"Ying! Princess Ying!" Li Ming's cries broke Ying's concentration. She looked around. Her maid was shrinking against the wall, one hand over her mouth, pointing.

"What's wrong, Li Ming?"

"Your arm!"

Ying held up her arm, staring at it. It was glowing.

Or, rather, it was her scar that was shining a sort of phosphorescent green. The light was dim but provided enough illumination to see everything in the cell.

"Wow," Ying said, turning her arm this way and that. "It's the gōushé scar."

The prince caught her arm gently in his hands and traced a cold thumb along the scar. He looked at her. "Magical beasts leave magical scars."

"Magical beasts? Whatever do you mean?" Li Ming sounded scared.

Ying shook her head and forced a smile. "Don't worry about

it, Li Ming." She resolved that she and the prince would get the maid out of here, out of this world, as soon as humanly possible.

Guided by the light from her glowing arm, Ying tried a few more times to get the rat bone in the keyhole, but to no avail. She screamed in rage and threw the bone away. It hit the floor with a hollow sound and broke into two neat pieces.

Ying slid down against the prison bars and sank her head onto her knees.

None of them said anything for a while. Eventually, Ying raised her head.

"What happened to you, Li Ming? Tell us everything. Perhaps we can figure out a plan."

Li Ming recounted the story. The night she'd been kidnapped, she had retired to her chamber after finishing her duties.

"I was at the bed, folding some clean laundry, when something caught my notice. I'd left the wardrobe door open; I saw something in the mirror. Guards—all around me. Of course, I was horrified! I looked around the room, expecting to see them standing right there. But there was nothing. I was alone." Li Ming started crying low, hiccupping sobs.

"Go on," Ying prodded, as gently as she could.

"I panicked. I thought I was losing my mind. I watched in the mirror as the guards grabbed me—my reflection, that is—and dragged me out of the room. But none of it was happening to the real me. And when I looked back at the mirror, there was no reflection."

Ying shivered. "I'm so sorry, Li Ming. That sounds terrifying."

Li Ming looked at Ying with tear-filled eyes. "It was."

"So after you discovered your missing reflection, what happened then?"

"I went to Fei fei. I told her what had happened, about my reflection disappearing. She just kept on saying I must be exhausted, that I should go to bed. She told Madame Yang, and—"

"And then?"

"Madame locked me in my room. I banged and banged on the door, but no one would come. I barricaded the wardrobe. But then . . . then I saw the wardrobe door swing open . . ." She trailed off.

Ying held her breath. ". . . And?"

"It was . . . a reflection. But not my reflection. She climbed out—right through the mirror—and grabbed me. And I was"—Li Ming took a great, shuddering breath—"I was so scared, because . . . because . . . it was . . ." Li Ming didn't seem to be able to choke out the words.

"It was what?" Ying prompted. "Tell me."

"Why, it was *you*, my lady. It was you who dragged me through the mirror."

Ying gritted her teeth. "Not me, Li Ming. My reflection."

The maid gulped and nodded.

Ying continued to probe. "So then they brought you here?"

Li Ming nodded again. "They taunted me. Said that I was not the first human they'd kidnapped, nor would I be the last. I heard the guards boasting about how large their army was. They said everyone I loved would be killed." She covered her face with her hands and began to weep once more.

Ying clenched her jaw, willing herself not to scream. "And what did they do with your reflection? Did you see her?"

"No!" Li Ming wailed. "I don't know!"

"Probably dead," the prince said. "I mean, they attacked Fei's reflection." He threw Ying a dark look. "For trying to warn you to leave this world."

Ying remembered. Reflection-Fei had broken through her curse for an instant, just to tell Ying to leave. She'd tried to protect her. The Mirror Prince had, too. In fact, he'd been trying to protect her every moment, every second, since she first stepped into the mirror world.

Now he was trapped in the dungeons with her, risking himself to help save Li Ming.

It was a relief knowing that at least one mirror person was on her side. In the dark, dank confines of the dungeon, she felt more drawn to him than ever.

Ying rubbed slow circles on Li Ming's back, feeling the maid's small body quivering beneath her hands. "Why is this happening to us, Princess?" Li Ming sobbed through her fingers. "What have I done? Is it punishment?"

"Punishment for what?"

Li Ming lowered her hands. "For my sins. For being lustful."

"Lustful?" Ying stared at her maid, confused. Then, suddenly, she realized. "Fei fei?"

Li Ming nodded. Her voice was a whisper. "It was around the time I started thinking about, um . . ."

"Being intimate?"

The maid nodded again. "It was around that time I started seeing it."

"Seeing what, Li Ming?"

"Movement in the mirrors. Out of the corners of my eyes." Li Ming's face crumpled, defeated.

Ying shifted closer to Li Ming and put her arms around her. "Oh, Li Ming," she said, squeezing her maid tight. "Of course it's not a punishment. There's nothing wrong with—"

"But I'm a maid!" Li Ming wailed, cutting Ying off. "I'm not supposed to have these feelings. You know what Madame says: servants are not supposed to fall in love. Our lives belong to the palace, not to ourselves—"

"Don't you pay mind to what Madame says." Ying's voice was stern. "No one else does."

The corners of Li Ming's mouth turned up the tiniest bit, but then her face settled back into sadness. Ying's eyes skated over Li Ming's hollow cheeks.

"Are you hungry? Have they fed you?" *One day,* Ying thought, flexing her fingers. *One day, I will murder everyone who ever dared to hurt Li Ming.*

"They did," Li Ming said. "But not enough. Only once so far. A small bowl of rice, not enough to feed a child."

Anger flared in Ying's chest. "And did they hurt you?"

"Going through the mirror hurt," whispered the maid. "It was like . . . like being squeezed. Very hard."

Ying's lips thinned. For anyone except her and her reflection, apparently, passage through the partially closed mirrors was still painful. "Let me rephrase this, Li Ming," Ying said, making an effort to keep her voice measured. "Did they *lay their hands on you?*"

Li Ming swallowed. "A little."

Tightening her hands around the cell bars until her knuckles ached, Ying imagined she was squeezing her fingers around Reflection-Ying's pale neck. Whatever that foul creature wanted, going after Li Ming—who had no stake in this war, who had done nothing wrong—was a step too far. Reflection-Ying had kidnapped Ying's friend, had beaten and starved her all to set this elaborate trap.

There were other indignities, too. Ying, sweeping her gaze across the floor, saw that it not only was strewn with bones but also marred with large, dark stains.

"Animals," Ying muttered. She didn't mean the rats.

She sat back on her heels, scanning her surroundings. Sitting just outside the cell was a large wooden pail full to the brim with water.

"Is that for drinking?" she asked the prince.

"No," he said. "That's for washing the floor." Ying pulled a face—she didn't need to ask what needed washing.

An idea was unfolding in her mind. A way that they could all get out. A way they could escape.

Ying went over to the bucket. If she pushed her arm through the bars, she might *just* be able to grab it with her fingertips. Crouching low to the ground, she pushed up her sleeve and reached out—

She cursed. It was just out of reach. As she sat back on her heels, her sword handle hit the bars with a clang, which gave her an idea. . . .

Drawing her sword, Ying threaded it between the bars, then hacked into the bucket's rim. It lodged easily in the water-softened wood. She yanked hard, pulling it over.

It fell over with a thump. The water sloshed out, flooding the floor. It ran along the ground, forming rivulets between the rat bones, spreading out in a slick puddle. The prince jumped to his feet. Li Ming backed up against the far wall.

Ying turned to the others and grinned. "Lucky for us," she said, her voice triumphant, "this didn't occur to the other Ying."

Li Ming's eyes were wide. "What do you mean, my lady?"

"She should have known better than to leave water within my reach." After sheathing her sword, Ying stretched out her hands toward the Mirror Prince and her maid. "Do you two trust me?" The prince took her hand immediately. Li Ming hesitated for a second, then nodded and took the other.

In the light from Ying's glowing arm, the reflection of the cell bars shimmered on the puddle's surface. For the first time, she desperately hoped her last pass through the mirrors had broken the barrier down—enough for her companions to follow, anyway.

Preferably without pain.

She closed her eyes and held her breath. Praying that her plan would work, Ying stepped toward the puddle and jumped.

25

The three of them landed on the stone floor with a crash. It was freezing, and they were soaking wet. Ying sat up, rubbing her sore shoulder. She supposed she should feel guilty that this final trip had probably completely broken the barrier. But she'd rescued Li Ming. She'd escaped the mirror world. Right now, all she felt was relief.

"Lady Ying," her maid asked, "where are we?"

The dungeons were pitch-black, now that the green glow of her arm was gone. Apparently, it glowed only in the mirror world. She could not see but could hear the others struggling to their feet. "Back in our world." Ying stretched out her arms and stumbled in the darkness, searching for the door. She hoped that, just like in the mirror world, the unused cells were left unlocked.

Finally, her fingers touched metal. Ying groped her way along the metal bars and located the crossbars of the cell door. With her heart thumping, she put out a hand and pushed.

The door swung open. Ying exhaled, then called to the others.

"Come. Walk toward my voice."

She tried to ignore the crunching sounds of crumbling bones

as the prince and her maid made their way toward her. Finally, they found one another in the darkness and all grasped hands.

It was difficult navigating the corridor in complete darkness. But after what seemed like a lifetime, several misdirections, and a lot of bumping into walls, they reached the wooden door that led out of the dungeons. This door, too, swung open, eliciting the same high-pitched creak but offering no resistance. Light from hung lanterns filtered in, the brightness almost painful. Ying sighed, relief washing through her limbs.

The air became warmer and less stuffy as they climbed. They'd almost reached the top when Li Ming stumbled. She screamed as she thudded down each stone step.

"Li Ming!" Ying ran back down until she was by Li Ming's side. The maid's eyes were rolling up in her head. Her skin was burning. Her normally pale skin was even paler than usual.

"Li Ming!" Ying cried again, patting her friend on the cheek. "Wake up. Wake up!" She turned to the Mirror Prince, whose glasslike skin was glimmering slightly in the lanternlight. "Can you help me get her to Mei Po, Zhang? Please!"

The prince dragged Li Ming's arm around his neck and struggled to a standing position, but Li Ming just collapsed again.

"I'll carry her," he said, hoisting her over his shoulder.

The maid drifted in and out of consciousness as the three of them hurried to Mei Po's tower.

The old woman must have foreseen their arrival, because she

was waiting for them outside her door. She beckoned them into the room, then gestured at the bed. It was the same one that Ying had lain in only days earlier, although that one had been in the mirror world.

Even in Mei Po's narrow bed, Li Ming looked tiny. Waiflike. Mei Po ran her hands over the maid's face, her expression grave.

"Where has she been?" Mei Po directed her almost-colorless eyes at Ying.

"In the mirror," Ying replied, rushing to get the words out. "In the dungeons. She was kidnapped."

"And her reflection?"

Why was she asking this? Ying shook her head. "I don't know. Probably dead."

Mei Po bent over, inspecting every inch of Li Ming's skin, poking and prodding with the tip of a gnarled finger. Eventually, she straightened.

"It's just exhaustion," she said. "Dehydration. And hunger."

"Yes," Ying said. "They gave her barely anything to eat or drink. Can you help her?"

Mei Po smiled, the corners of her eyes wrinkling. "It will be simple. Wait here."

The prince and Ying clasped hands—Ying finding comfort in his cool, steady grip—as the old woman shuffled across the room and plucked an amber vial from a high shelf. She came back, swirled it around, then unstoppered it, releasing the familiar scent of Draught of Life. This she tipped straight into Li Ming's mouth.

Li Ming coughed and spluttered. Her hands flew to her throat, and she thrashed around, her eyelids snapping open, her eyes bulging.

"Li Ming!" Ying put her hands on her maid's shoulders. "Li Ming! It's me!"

The maid gradually quieted, then lay still. Eventually, she whispered, "Am I dead?"

Tears of relief flooded Ying's eyes. She pulled Li Ming up to a seated position and put her arms around her, embracing her. "No, Li Ming," she whispered into her friend's ear. "You're not dead. You're going to be all right. We all are." Ying hoped she sounded at least somewhat convincing.

Mei Po was watching Li Ming with curiosity. "You've been through the mirrors twice, child?"

Li Ming gave a small sniff, then nodded. "Yes, Madame. Well, the mirror once. The second time was a puddle of water."

"I see." Mei Po stroked her chin. "Áoyīn in this world. Maids going into the other. And you"—she pointed at the Mirror Prince—"you, too, are not in the right place." The old woman's watery eyes sparked. She looked at Ying. "You know what this means."

Ying nodded and stood up abruptly. "The barrier is broken." She stood and began to pace. If the mirrors were open, that meant whatever army her reflection was able to gather could soon infiltrate their world. "But what do I *do*? I'm no closer to finding the answers."

"You are the Fish, Ying Yue." Mei Po seemed oblivious to

Ying's worries. "You are supposed to close the barrier. That is the path you are meant to take, even if you cannot yet see the way."

"Maybe . . ." Ying stopped pacing and bit her lip, agitated. "Maybe it will work only if I die, like all those other empresses who went missing." The memory of dried corpses shackled in the dungeons flashed through her mind. A shiver passed through her body. "I saw them in the dungeons. They were supposed to close the barrier, too, right?"

Mei Po paused, hesitating for a moment. "Yes," she said finally, her expression grave. "For centuries, the Shans have been searching for the Fish, finding women from all over the empire who showed potential promise. The hope was that sending them through the mirrors would be enough to fulfill the prophecy."

Bitter bile rose in Ying's throat. "But it wasn't."

"No. None of them were the Fish. They were just unfortunate women, caught in political maneuvers beyond their control. But you?" Mei Po gave Ying a piercing look. "You are different, Ying Yue."

Ying shook her head. "But I don't understand. How am I so different? None of them were the Fish, yet they were still able to pass through. How?"

"Alchemy." Mei Po's gaze slid away, alighting on the smooth bronze mirror. "The Shans discovered, through experimentation, alchemy that could weaken the barrier. The alchemy could transmute solids into other substances, like liquid or something equally permeable. It worked only for mere moments before the barrier resealed, though. Just enough time to push someone through."

"So the Shans were willing to use this—alchemy—to murder seven women . . . on an assumption? On an unsubstantiated theory?" Ying's voice was rising, unable to disguise her disgust.

"For a while, yes." She turned her gaze on the Mirror Prince, who was listening intently. "Until the other prince's father came into power. The current Emperor Shan. He put a stop to it."

Ying paused to consider this new information. "He—why?"

"Emperor Shan suffered much as a boy. Not only had he lost his mother, who was sent across the mirrors when he was just a child, but his own father became obsessed with the prophecy. So obsessed he neglected everything—even his own son."

"That's awful." Ying's heart ached for the boy emperor, motherless and neglected at such a tender age.

"Yes. As you can imagine, he was scarred by this. As soon as he was crowned emperor, he put a stop to the practice. He chose to believe his advisors who told him the prophecy was a lie. That's why the current empress was able to escape the same fate. And it's why later, when you were four and I found you in that Shuijing He river, he refused to consent to a match between you and his son, despite my recommendations. He believed it to be . . . unnecessary."

Ying nodded, her throat thick. She could see how, after getting it wrong so many times, people would start to disbelieve the prophecy. "Then why did he change his mind?"

"Because of the empress. She believed me. Believed in the prophecy. And since she has quite an . . . influence . . . over her husband... it was she who finally convinced him to sign the betrothal letter."

"So the Shan family meant for me to come and, what, close the barrier? Even despite the risks? Even though I don't know how?"

Mei Po pressed her lips together, silent for a moment. Then she spoke. "They knew about all the past... attempts, with the women who preceded you. They were willing to try again."

"Mā de." Ying shuddered. "And that's what the Shans had planned for me, I suppose."

"They did." Mei Po grimaced, her wrinkles deepening. "They... told Prince Zhang not to get attached to you."

The Mirror Prince uttered a low growl, and Li Ming gasped audibly. But all Ying could do was stare at Mei Po, her horror on full display. This was even worse than she'd thought. They knew. The Shan family knew. Mei Po had told them that Ying was the Fish.

Which meant that the real prince also knew. He *knew*. He knew locking her up with the mirrors would put her in grievous danger...

Yet he did it anyway.

Ying's mind strayed back to the corpses, in various stages of decomposition, the broken teeth in their skeletal smiles. He'd been willing to condemn Ying to that fate. She trembled, her hands balling into fists, the sting of betrayal cutting through her like a blade.

Mei Po's meaning was clear. Ying and Zhang's betrothal was not for compatibility, or because the match was particularly auspicious. It should have been obvious to Ying, really, with how much their personalities clashed. Now that she knew the truth, it made sense: their union had been carefully arranged to exploit Ying's status as the Fish.

They'd used her as an offering in an attempt to fulfill the prophecy. In their eyes, it was a worthwhile sacrifice. Her life—and the lives of seven others—forfeited in order to protect the world.

Everything was starting to make sense. Ying now understood why the Mirror Prince had been so keen to protect her; to keep her hidden in the mirror world. He'd have known what the real-world Shans were planning in an attempt to close the barrier.

Ying bit her cheek so hard she tasted blood. "It didn't work, though. They tried, and it didn't work. Despite their best efforts, I haven't closed the barrier. I still don't know how. Nor have I found *The Book of Alchemy*. We"—she stopped short, the memory of her time with the real prince too raw—"*I* went looking for it. But I didn't find anything."

Briefly, she considered divulging her discovery of the note and its message: *If you are looking for* The Book of Alchemy, *you are too late. I have already stolen it.* It clearly hadn't been her reflection who'd left the note; she'd seemed ignorant of the book when Ying had mentioned it. But if not Reflection-Ying, then who? Who would have access to Shan blood? The real prince had sworn it wasn't him—but maybe he had lied. He had certainly lied before, claiming to know nothing about the mirrors.

Fury crested through her, throbbing through her ears, her head, across the base of her throat. She clenched her fists and turned away, pretending to examine the cluttered shelves. They were identical to the reflected versions in Mirror-Mei Po's tower room, stuffed with jars, vials, and leather-bound books.

It was then that a quiet whispering filled her ears, piercing the silence that had smothered the room.

"What did you say?" she said, spinning back around. If Mei Po, the Mirror Prince, or Li Ming had an idea, surely they should include her, the Fish?

The Mirror Prince frowned. "What do you mean, Ying? No one said anything."

The whispering grew more urgent, more sinister. It slithered up her spine and made her shiver. Could no one else hear it? As she drew closer to the shelves, the whispering became louder, congealing to a constant thrum.

"Ying Yue," Mei Po said sharply as Ying began shoving books and objects aside.

Ying barely heard Mei Po's warning above the ominous whispers, so intent was she on locating the source of the sound. Finally, as the thrumming reached a crescendo which throbbed painfully inside her head, Ying found the source. A book, hidden at the very back of the bookshelf, behind a painted vase.

An ancient book, its spine all creased, bound with old, cracked, lacquered leather. On the cover was an embossed inscription so faint that Ying had to squint to read it.

THE BOOK OF ALCHEMY, it read.

Ying's heart leapt to her throat. The book was here. *The book was here.* The thief who had plundered the Shangren temple wasn't one of the reflections.

The thief was *Mei Po.*

Ying gripped the book hard, her mind spinning. When Mei Po had first told Ying about the prophecy, she'd chosen her words carefully: she'd said no one had "unearthed" the book—*not* that no one had found it.

Mei Po must have already known, even then, where it was hidden. But without the blood of a Crimson heir she'd been unable to access it. All she had needed was a drop of the prince's blood—

Ying's gut twisted. Not long before she and Zhang Lin had discovered the book was missing, the real prince had nearly died from áoyīn wounds. And the person who had saved him, the person who had seen all the blood-soaked moss from the healers, the person who *Ying herself* had called for, was . . .

Mei Po.

All of a sudden, the book felt cursed. Ying had a reckless urge to fling it away. Instead, trembling, she raised her head. *"You,"* she said to Mei Po, her tone accusatory. "You stole the book!"

The old woman used her stick to struggle to her feet. "Yes," she said, her walking stick clacking as she moved toward Ying. She approached unexpectedly quickly, her clear bluish eyes glinting like cut crystal. "Give it to me, and I can explain." Stretching out one hand, she tried to grab the book. "Give it to me, Ying Yue."

Ying slapped Mei Po's hand away, shaking all over. It was

hard, cold, glasslike. Ying cried out, grasping the book to her chest.

"Explain?" Ying backed away, shaking all over. "Explain what? That you're a reflection? That you're one of *them*?"

Mei Po didn't deny it. The light in her watery blue eyes flared, then dulled. Ying noticed, for the first time, the slightly translucent glow of Mei Po's white, white skin and white, white hair. In the dimness of the tower room, it hadn't been obvious before.

Mei Po was a reflection. This was not the woman who had rescued Ying as a child—but the one from the other side of the mirrors. The one who'd left Reflection-Ying to die.

"You stole the book . . . so *you* would have control over the mirror barrier!" Ying's entire body flushed cold. She grabbed Li Ming, nudging the maid behind her. "Where is the real Mei Po? What have you done with her?"

The old woman dropped her hands, resigned. "She is gone."

A pounding began at the base of Ying's skull. *She's been replaced.*

Ying had trusted Mei Po. And now, in this gloomy tower room, she'd learned . . .

Mei Po was one of the monsters.

26

Ying, Li Ming, and the Mirror Prince fled, sprinting down the steps and across the palace grounds to hide out at the stables. Mei Po didn't try to stop them, nor did she chase after the book, a detail that would later strike Ying as ominous. Perhaps by now she knew the contents by heart and could already perform the alchemy.

As Ying ran, thoughts spiraled through her mind. *They're here, they're here, they're already here.* The reflections had already started to infiltrate and replace their doppelgängers. Which meant that from now on, Ying would not be able to trust, well, anyone.

At least she now had the book.

"Mei Po betrayed us," Ying whispered, panting from their flight. "She's one of them."

The prince gave a defensive snort. "We're not all bad!"

"No, but she stole that book from the Shangren temple. Plus," Ying added, "if Mei Po's *reflection* is here, what happened to the real Mei Po?" He didn't have a response to that.

What should Ying do? When she couldn't tell who was real and who was reflection? Mei Po had tried to help them . . . or so Ying had thought. Was Mirror-Mei Po being deliberately vague, sending Ying down the wrong path on purpose? Had she orchestrated everything? She was a mirror person; when had she replaced the real Mei Po? Was it before the áoyīn attack? Had *she* let the áoyīn through the gateway to injure the prince and gain access to his blood?

And then there was the real prince. He'd sworn he didn't know about the mirrors. But Mei Po claimed the empress *had* warned him. Or was the Mirror-Mei Po lying about that, too?

With an enemy—Mei Po, in this case—roaming about, the usual protocol would be to alert the palace guards. The problem was, they belonged to the Shans, and she couldn't trust them either. Not after what they'd tried to do to *her*.

Ying pressed her hands to her temples, trying to untangle her thoughts. Lies, so many lies, all around her. Perhaps they all were lying: Mei Po's reflection, Ying's reflection, the Shan family. All of them deceiving Ying. Using her for their own ends.

The three huddled in an empty stall, spiky straw scratching their skin. Above them, sparrows hopped and flitted in the eaves. In a neighboring stall, Shadow Runner whinnied and stamped his feet. He'd seen the Mirror Prince, who he thought was his master, and was itching to go for a ride.

"I have to close the gateway," Ying said, breathing fast. She had to do it before she became deceived by more lies, more subterfuge. "I have to stop all this. But I don't know how."

"You have the book, though," the Mirror Prince said. "Didn't you say it was important?"

"*Mei Po* said it was important." Ying scrunched her eyes shut, wishing she had the luxury of time. Time to reorder her jumbled thoughts. Time to comb through *The Book of Alchemy*. But time was something she didn't have. With the barrier open, time was running out. "But can we trust her? What if she was trying to sabotage us, to lead us down the wrong path?"

The Mirror Prince gestured at the book. "Only one way to find out."

Ying flipped open the cover, exposing the first page. The book was made of heavy parchment—animal skin, Ying guessed—crammed with tiny columns of text. Her heart sank. The words were unreadable, some ancient dialect she didn't recognize.

"I can't... I can't read this." She drew her eyebrows together, an unuttered scream gathering in her chest. She paged through, frustrated, trying to see if anything was readable—but it was the same the whole way through. "It's written in some sort of traditional text. Can either of you read it?" She held the book out to her companions.

The Mirror Prince just frowned at it. Surprisingly, it was Li Ming who snatched the book from Ying.

"I recognize this!" she exclaimed. The page she was looking at contained nothing except three large glyphs, written in flowing calligraphy. She stabbed a finger at the words. "This says 'jīng, qì, and shén.' My family had these words inscribed on a banner."

Jīng. Qì. Shén. The essences that sustained human life.

Ying sifted through the shadowy recesses of her mind. She remembered sitting through some exceptionally dry lectures from one of the priests back home. Jīng was the essence that a person was born with, before it split into yin and yang. Qì was their life force, the energy that flowed through their body. And shén was the higher essence, a person's spiritual mind. Together, they were known as the Three Treasures, and many alchemists devoted their lives to brewing various elixirs to replenish them. Someone in Li Ming's family must have been interested in alchemy.

"The Three Treasures," Ying repeated, thinking. "What does that have to do with the mirrors?"

"They're in a song," Li Ming said, her eyes widening. "The jīng, qì, and shén. My grandmother was a healer. She sang it a lot."

Ying glanced at her maid. "A song?"

"Everyone knows it." She stopped, then corrected herself. "Every *commoner* knows it. It's a peasant song. Folks sing it when they work the fields. Mothers sing it to their babes at night. My grandmother used to sing it to me at bedtime." She looked at Ying. "I sing it to you sometimes."

Ying's head pounded. The song . . . was it the one Li Ming had always sung? It had been there always, right in front of her, and Ying had never taken notice. Would she even be able to remember the words? "Can you sing it now, Li Ming?"

Li Ming nodded, put her hand on her chest, and closed her eyes. She sang:

> *Jīng is the essence from which all life grows.*
> *Qì is the energy; like water it flows.*

> *Shén is the fir, the forest of trees.*
> *Fire will render the bound spirits free.*
> *Unite the Three Treasures: jing, qi, and shén.*
> *The Phoenix will rise into flame once again.*

It was the song that Ying knew, the very same. Ying joined in for the last few lines, aching with a sweet, nostalgic sorrow. She'd never asked Li Ming where she'd learned the song.

Ying would never have expected her maid to recognize the glyphs. It might have been less surprising had she known more about Li Ming's family. But Ying was suddenly aware that she'd never asked her maid about her childhood. Or what her family was like. Or about the songs her grandmother had sung to soothe her to sleep. Their conversations had always centered on Ying: Ying's needs, Ying's worries, Ying's fascination with supernatural things. It was the nature of the standard employer-servant relationship, Ying supposed, but she was flooded with guilt over the fact she'd never noticed it.

She'd thought the real prince a monster for not caring about his servants, but in some ways, she was just as bad.

When Li Ming stopped singing, it was as though the world had fallen away. Even the birds had gone silent. Ying's eyes were full of tears.

"What does it mean?" the Mirror Prince asked softly, breaking the spell.

Ying shook her head. "I don't know." She closed her eyes, blinking her sorrow away. "Water, forests, fir trees, fire . . . Are those the ingredients I need? To perform the alchemy? What I need to transform myself and close the barrier? Or . . . maybe it's where I need to look—in a lake or a forest . . ."

Ying stood up and paced the length of the stall, thinking hard. Assuming that the nursery rhyme had anything to do with it, where should she even start? It was all so vague.

The Mirror Prince came to Ying's side, twining his icy fingers through hers.

"I'll go with you," he said. "We'll head to the lake—that's water. We'll search for answers together. And we can find whatever it is we're looking for. Together." He tugged on her hand very lightly, drawing her to him.

Ying looked up and into his eyes. It was always discomfiting to look at him, at how similar he was to the real prince. But she knew: behind the façade, he was nothing like the other version. "If I manage to close the barrier, would you . . ." She swallowed, the words catching in her throat. "Would you stay with me?"

She didn't know if it was even possible, but she had to ask. The thought of being separated from him—permanently—felt as though it might fracture her very heart. If she knew they could be together, she knew she could face anything.

"I . . ." The prince blinked, then stared down at her. His eyes were burning, but his voice was soft. "Yes," he said. "Of course I would."

She sighed, the tension in her shoulders ebbing. They kissed, tenderly, gently, their lips in a dance of barely repressed yearning. Ying wished she didn't have to go on this journey. She wished she weren't responsible for the gateway to the mirrors. All she wanted to do was curl up in the prince's ice-like embrace. To pull him down on top of the straw. To bare herself to him, body and soul.

Whatever happened, she told herself, at least they could face it together. That was comfort in itself. Ying tried to pour all her feelings into the kiss: the longing, the love, the relief at having him here with her.

When she pulled away, her insides were a vortex of swirling emotions. She paced away from the prince, tugging on her lower lip, trying to sort her thoughts.

"Li Ming," she said finally. "You said you overheard the guards talking in the mirror world. Did you overhear anything else?"

The maid wrapped her arms around her torso. "Only that they were waiting until the barrier was completely broken. They were planning on sending scouts to figure out when that would be."

Ying paused her pacing and looked up, alarmed. She spoke to the Mirror Prince. "Scouts? Is this true?"

"Yes, Princess," the Mirror Prince said, his expression grim. "That's their usual strategy. They are as yet unsure of the strength of your army and will scope it out first while they gather their forces." He turned to gaze out the window. "They may wait until the fifteenth day of the lunar month. They're at their strongest when it's a full moon."

"Because of the extra light?" Ying asked.

The Mirror Prince gave a curt nod. "Yes. We need light. They will attack during the day so they can feed from the sun.

But if there's also a full moon, then they'll have absorbed all that light through the night, too."

"Okay," Ying said, rubbing her forehead, turning over this new knowledge in her mind. "Do either of you know *when* they'll be sending these scouts?"

There was a brief pause. Then Li Ming spoke: "Um, Princess?" She was staring straight out the stable doors. The stables themselves were next to the Lake of Tranquility, on the side opposite the Lotus Pavilion.

"What is it, Li Ming?"

Slowly, Li Ming got to her feet, one hand going to her mouth, the other pointing in the lake's direction. Her finger shook. "Now," she said. "They're sending them now."

Ying ran to the stable door, her heart pounding. She cursed.

About a dozen leopard-like creatures had emerged from the lake and were stalking in their direction. But unlike the leopards Ying had seen pictures of, these creatures had coats of dark blue, with a metallic patina that shimmered like an oil slick. Their slanted eyes glowed silver. Their mouths hung open, revealing rows of swordlike teeth and long, lolling silver tongues. As they prowled closer, Ying heard them growling—a hissing, low-pitched sound.

"Find help!" Ying told her maid, ushering her out a back door.

"Fēngshēngshòu," the Mirror Prince snarled. "Ying, get out of here!" He grabbed one of the stablehands' brooms.

"No. I'm staying to fight!"

"Ying, for once, please just listen!"

Hearing the commotion, a servant who had been working in

235

the garden straightened and spotted one of the big cats. Too late. He screamed as it sprang toward him.

The Mirror Prince bellowed and sprinted toward the gardener. Holding the broom in two hands like a fighting staff, he cracked the creature over the head. It twisted midair, landing lightly on all four feet. Its head turned, spittle trailing from its open mouth.

"Run!" he shouted to the man, and the gardener scrambled to his feet and fled.

The creature crouched, then pounced, its long claws extended. The prince spun out of the way and whacked the creature's head again. The other beasts turned their heads, sniffing the air, watching the prince bring the staff down again and again and again.

Sweat sprung across Ying's forehead. Her heart hammered in her chest as she began running toward the prince.

The first creature's legs buckled under the Mirror Prince's assault, and it uttered an otherworldly wail as it collapsed onto its side. This seemed to trigger a frenzy in the others. Their growls turned to roars as they bounded toward the prince.

The prince spun and ducked, the broomstick hitting the monsters on their noses, their necks, their heads, their backs. But they were relentless. As they closed in, crowding around him in a circle, the Mirror Prince sank into a crouch, his moves becoming defensive.

Ying screamed his name and ran full-tilt toward him. She drew her sword.

The prince caught sight of her. "No!" he yelled, but his next words were drowned out as one of the creatures pounced. The prince was flung onto his back, the fēngshēngshòu on top of him. The others began to circle, every now and then darting in and attempting to nip at the prince.

Holding the broom horizontally, he fended off the main attacker's snapping jaws. Ying screamed again and brought the sword down on the creature's shimmering, pearlescent neck.

But the sword just glanced off. Their skin was hard, and couldn't be pierced. That must be why the Mirror Prince had grabbed a broom instead of using his sword.

Panic tore a hole in Ying's gut. She remembered now: she'd read about fēngshēngshòu in a storybook as a child. According to the book, of all the mythical creatures, they were the only ones with impenetrable hides.

Except for the reflections, Ying thought, though her storybooks had never referenced the reflections, had never referenced anything about the mirror world at all. How had they escaped mention in any of the written records?

There was something else she was forgetting, something about the fēngshēngshòu. But Ying couldn't remember—not when her mind was so clouded with fear.

She flung away the sword and cast her eyes desperately around for some other blunt object. Remembering the book, she sprinted back to the stables and snatched it up off the straw.

Holding it in both hands, she whacked the creature on its head again and again. Eventually, it briefly relented in its attack on the prince. Taking advantage of the creature's momentary distraction, the prince sprang to his feet and brought the broom down hard on the creature's head. Howling, it stumbled sideways a few steps, then fell on its side. With renewed vigor, Ying and the prince began to fend off the creatures. They fought back-to-back, the prince's broomstick cutting through the air so fast it was barely visible, Ying's book whacking the creatures' heads repeatedly with loud, satisfying thunks.

When they had felled the last beast, it took Ying and the prince a few moments to recognize their victory. Ying was panting. Her fingers were stiff, clutching the heavy book. Cautiously, they both lowered their makeshift weapons.

The creatures looked smaller dead than alive.

"Are they all dead?" she asked.

The Mirror Prince pushed on one with the toe of his boot. "Yes." He turned to face Ying, putting a cold hand on her shoulder. "For now. But we'd better—" He stopped and looked behind her, over her head. He scowled.

"Great," he snapped. "We have company."

Ying turned. A small mob of people was running down the hill toward them.

Palace guards, wearing their distinctive royal blue regalia and scaled armor. Li Ming must have alerted them to the attack. But at the head of the crowd was someone very familiar. . . .

"Zhang Lin," Ying whispered. The Mirror Prince's hand tightened on her shoulder.

The last time Ying had seen the real prince, she had kissed him with poison on her lips. Nausea unfurled in her belly.

He had drawn his sword and was brandishing it. As he drew nearer, she realized: he wasn't running *to* her.

He was running *at* her.

He was going to kill her. And Ying was unarmed; all she held was a book.

"Wait!" she cried. He was already within striking distance, raising his arms to swing his sword.

The Mirror Prince lurched forward, shoving Ying behind his back and drawing his own blade. Ying tripped and fell, her hands scraping the gravel, the book tumbling onto the ground.

The two swords clashed. The men sprang apart, then circled each other, sizing each other up. They looked identical apart from the Mirror Prince's subtle pearlescent glow. The soldiers surrounding them stopped and gaped, their weapons lowered, forgotten.

"You!" The real prince spat the word. "What the *hell* are you doing here?"

"Protecting the princess, since you cannot." The Mirror Prince spat on the ground, then sneered. "Wouldn't expect a lǜmàozi like you to understand."

"What the hell are you talking about, bastard?" The real prince lunged, striking at his reflection. The Mirror Prince blocked the blow, then another, then another.

He thinks I'm my reflection. Ying pushed herself up to her feet. The prince had tried to kill Ying only because he thought she was her reflection.

"Stop," she screeched, and threw herself between the two men. "*Stop!* It's me." She held her arms out and braced herself for a blow. Both of them stopped short, the real prince breathing hard, his face flushed red with fury. In contrast, the Mirror Prince was perfectly composed.

Clearly, the two men had not been evenly matched. A lifetime of mimicking the real prince meant that he had easily preempted his opponent's moves, not even breaking a sweat.

A wave of shock overcame Ying. The real prince's blade had stopped just short of her neck, so close she could feel its faint kiss of steel. She started shaking. "It's me, it's me, it's me," she sobbed, addressing the real prince. "Look at my face. Look at my neck." Ying tugged down the collar of her tunic to reveal the thin red gash from where the reflection had cut her.

The prince lowered his sword, staring at her neck wound. Then he reached out and touched the cut on her cheek with the very tips of two fingers.

"Gods, Ying!" He snatched back his hand and ran it, exasperated, through his hair. "It's really you. I thought you were—"

Ying raised her head, her face wet with tears. "I know what you thought, Zhang Lin."

He said nothing for a moment, then took a great, heaving breath. "Then what"—his hand quivered as he flung it in the direction of the Mirror Prince—"is *he* doing here?"

"He helped to kill the fēngshēngshòu."

"The fēngshēng *what*?"

"Monsters," the Mirror Prince growled. "From the other world."

The real prince's eyes landed on one of the dead creatures, and he startled, having not previously noticed it lying on the ground. "Wǒ cào," he cursed, mostly to himself. Then he reached for Ying's hand. "Come, Princess. Enough of this. Time to come home."

Ying shrank away from him. Bitterness coated her tongue.

"Come home? Why, so you can lock me up again? Mistreat me, like I'm dirt on your fucking sh—"

"Like dirt?" The prince took a step forward, his black eyes narrowed. "You want to talk about playing dirty? You're the one who poisoned *me*!"

"I had no choice!" Ying snapped. "I had to save Li Ming, but you were going to imprison me again, like you did for *months*—"

"It was for your own good! I did it to protect you!"

Ying's anger broke. "No. You did it to SACRIFICE ME!"

The two of them stood, chests heaving, trembling with unleashed fury.

This was the crux of it. The real cause of Ying's rage. She'd been right to hate him—he, along with the rest of his vile family, who'd locked her in with mirrors and left her there to die.

How could she ever have thought the prince was half-decent? To think she'd spent that night with him, up in his mountain cabin, his warmth wrapped around her body and his face buried in her hair. . . .

Ying clenched her fists so hard her nails dug into her palms.

The prince broke the loaded silence with a bitter, hollow laugh. "I see. You think *I'm* the monster. Well, let me tell you, *wife*"—here, he shot a look of pure loathing at the Mirror Prince—"I am *nothing* compared to him."

"What has he ever done to you?" Ying spat. She knew she shouldn't rise to his bait, but she couldn't help it. "Apart from serving you his whole life *as your reflection*?"

He took another step forward, so close she could feel his scorching heat. "He. Stole. My. Fucking. Wife."

Ying tipped her chin up, glowering at him. "He didn't steal me," she said, with as much spite as she could muster. "He just treats me better."

The prince froze, his pupils dilating, and then let out a sharp exhale.

He turned from her, scowling, and addressed his men. "Let's go." Then he pointed his sword at the Mirror Prince. "Go back to where you came from, scum. And take her with you." As he turned to leave, he muttered words under his breath that weren't meant for Ying's ears. But she heard them anyway.

"You two deserve each other."

Ying staggered back and released a sob, her hand on her forehead. The Mirror Prince didn't say anything; he just bundled her into his arms, holding her, stroking her hair with his cold hand as she cried.

Ying just sobbed harder. Why was she so cursed? Finally, *finally* she'd fallen in love. But the man she loved was not meant for her. He was not supposed to be her husband. He was, instead, from the wrong side of the mirrors. . . .

And she was supposed to seal them shut.

She was caught between two princes. Caught between two worlds. One, her own world, a familiar world, in which she was doomed to loneliness. The second, the Mirror Prince's world: cold, vicious, full of monsters. And also love. True, steady, once-in-a-lifetime love.

After how the real prince had betrayed her she could not fathom living with him, maintaining the pretense of a united marriage just for the good of the empire. But could she give up her whole life and join the Mirror Prince in his world? Where she'd be hunted for being a human, targeted for being the Fish, and separated permanently from her family—from her beloved brother Hao Yu?

When the time came to seal the mirrors, which side would she choose?

She pulled back to look at the Mirror Prince's face. The look he gave her was so suffused with love, with compassion, that she immediately knew the answer.

Him, she thought, her heart twisting in her chest. *I choose him.* Wherever he went, she would go. After all, he had offered to do the same for her.

Just then, a breeze stirred, blowing her hair into the air. It kicked up piles of dead autumn leaves until they eddied in the currents like flurries of red-brown snow.

The wind blew into the open mouths of the dead fēngshēng-shòu. Ying watched, horrified, as the animals' chests expanded.

One of them moved.

Ying pushed away from the Mirror Prince and swung around. The slumped, dead corpses were starting to twitch and come back to life. One started growling. At the sound, the real prince's small army stopped and spun around, their eyes scanning the scene.

"They resurrect with a breath of wind," the Mirror Prince said, his jaw set. "Get ready to fight again." He picked up the broomstick and gripped it in two hands, holding it high.

Ying picked up a stick and tossed it to the real prince. "Swords won't work," she shouted.

Zhang Lin caught it, looking momentarily stunned, before he turned and nodded at his men. The palace guards all unhooked the clubs hung at their waists and adopted defensive stances. They were military men, soldiers. They were ready to fight.

Even their resolve seemed to falter as they spotted something else. Something terrifying. Yes, the leopard-like creatures were coming back to life. But still more were swarming up from the lake. A whole herd of them, emerging wet and dripping from the water. And behind them, following them, were three reflections mounted on áoyīn.

The guards shifted on their feet. Ying's palms were slippery with sweat. How could they defend themselves against such monsters?

There was no use thinking that way, though. There was no choice but to fight.

Ying braced herself as the once-dead fēngshēngshòu rose again, brought back to life by the wind.

27

A guard blew a horn, the melancholy sound echoing across the grounds. It was a call for aid, but instead, it seemed to trigger the lake creatures. They swarmed.

Ying and the men roared as they rushed toward the horde. The two groups collided in a melee of teeth, swords, and staffs. Ying brought her book down on one creature before spinning away and cracking the head of another. Vaulting over prone bodies, ducking away from blows, she tried to imagine she was once again a child, learning from her brothers' masters, and this was just a practice fight.

She scanned her surroundings, looking for the prince.

Or princes, rather.

Finally, she spotted one. She ran over, the distance hindering her ability to tell which prince it was. Close up, she saw that it was the real one. He was fending off an attack from one of the big cats. But as he fought, another hurtled into his side, knocking him off his feet.

As he fell, the two creatures pounced, jaws snapping, claws extended.

Ying hesitated for a moment. But then she ran over to help him. As furious as she was with the real prince, he was still technically a human—there was no official species name for asshole. She couldn't just let him die.

Swinging with both hands, Ying whacked one of the creatures over the head with her book, giving the prince a chance to scramble to his feet. Together, they worked to bring both fēngshēngshòu down. The prince kicked the bodies into the lake.

He glanced at Ying, opened his mouth, shut it, then dashed off again.

Ying barely noticed—she'd glimpsed the Mirror Prince fighting his way toward her and started shoving through the crowd to meet him.

Finally, they reached each other. Ying clutched at his chest while his hands roamed across her face, her shoulders, and her arms. "Are you all right?" he asked her, breathing hard, checking her for wounds. "You're not injured?"

"No, my prince." Ying looked up at him. "Are you?"

The Mirror Prince made a face. He glanced around, surveying the battle scene. "I'm fine," he said. "But this is a losing battle, Ying. We must go."

Ying blinked. "What?"

"Leave them. We're outnumbered. And the wind has risen. The fēngshēngshòu keep coming back to life. We can't kill them. Not today."

Ying took a step backward and shook her head. "No. We can't leave the others!"

The prince let loose a feral snarl. "You mean you can't leave *them*?" he said, jerking his chin toward a small group of soldiers who were locked in a battle with a group of fēngshēngshòu. "Or you can't leave *him*?"

Ying was stunned. Was he really questioning her loyalty, midbattle, surrounded by monsters? She didn't have much time to think; already he had his ice-like hand on her shoulder, steering her toward the lake.

"Where are we going?" Ying struggled against his rock-hard grip. "Where are you taking me?"

"Through the lake," he said. "To my world. Where I can keep you safe."

"Safe?" Ying struggled harder. "It's no safer there than it is here. Let. Me. Go!"

"The monsters are all here, Ying." By now, the Mirror Prince had immobilized Ying, one of his icy arms clamped across her chest. There was no use struggling. He was strong, too strong. "I told you we'd go to the lake, remember?"

Ying faltered for a moment, horror-struck by his words. They sounded more like something the real prince would say. Throughout her life, men had always underestimated her, had constantly undermined her, had stubbornly tried to protect her. What they didn't understand—what they never understood—was that she didn't need them to protect her. She needed them to believe in her.

She'd thought the Mirror Prince was different. Yet now he, too, was trying to protect her—against her wishes, no less. . . .

"Please—" Ying said. She never got to say the next word "don't," because the prince pushed her headlong into the water.

She plunged into the frigid depths. As she sank, light from the surface receded, until she was slowly, gradually swallowed by the gloom. But then the darkness parted. A colorful line emerged. It was thin at first, but it then expanded until the colors coalesced and it glared sharp, white, and painfully bright. It was like the lines she'd previously seen out of the corners of her eye, bisecting her own mirror.

She began to panic. *What was going on?* Nothing like this had ever happened when she'd previously crossed between worlds.

The light shone brighter and brighter until suddenly, the line snapped. There was a flash of searing agony, as though all her bones were breaking. Then Ying went numb, and everything went black.

Her hearing was the last sense to recede. All she could hear as she fell was the real prince screaming out her name.

When she resurfaced, all signs of the battle had completely disappeared. Once again, she was in a serene garden, surrounded by the supersaturated colors of the mirror world. But this time, crossing the barrier had felt different. This time, it had felt as if something had severed. Something irreversible, irretrievable.

Gasping for air, she treaded water, trying to regain her bearings. With a jolt, she realized *The Book of Alchemy* had slipped from her grasp and fallen into the lake.

Just as she was about to dive down for it, the Mirror Prince surfaced beside her. One large hand grabbed her upper arm. Despite her protests, he towed her along, swimming to shore.

They reached the Lotus Pavilion. The prince clambered onto it and hauled Ying out of the lake. She doubled over, coughing out a mouthful of water, and then struggled to her feet. He still hadn't released her arm.

"Let me go!" Ying coughed again, then glared at him. "We can't just abandon them! I demand that you let me go." She drew in a sharp breath. "Now!"

"Why?" His eyes burned, his grip as cold as ice. "They're dead, Ying. It's too late."

"It's not too late until *I'm* dead, too."

He growled at that, and Ying balked. What had caused this change in him? Right now, he was acting no better than her would-be husband—restraining her, keeping her from fighting for what she believed was right. She grasped the front of his tunic, feeling the hard, cold lines of muscle beneath. Raising her eyes, she implored him to understand. "Please. It's *not* too late. It's not."

He didn't answer. Instead, his eyes snapped up, his attention diverted by something—or someone—behind her.

What was he looking at? A second later, her question was answered.

"Unfortunately, Princess, it is too late," a familiar voice said behind her. "Too late for you, anyway."

Her own reflection's voice.

Ying whirled around.

The reflection was standing at the entrance to the Lotus Pavilion, framed by trails of wisteria. Immediately, the Mirror Prince dropped Ying's arm and strolled to the edge of the pavilion. One of his hands rested casually upon the pommel of his sword.

A chill tore through Ying's body. Why was he so relaxed? Why wasn't he preparing to fight?

"Is the barrier breached?" Ying's reflection directed the question to the prince, but she kept her eyes on Ying.

"Yes, Princess," he replied. "It is breached."

"Good." Reflection-Ying's mouth twisted into a parody of a smile. "You did well, my prince."

Ying's mouth went dry. What was happening? This couldn't be happening. And yet . . .

"Let me go back," Ying said to the prince, the words sticking in her throat like a lump of sticky rice. "If the barrier is breached, I must help my people."

The Mirror Prince didn't answer immediately. He drew his sword, twirled it around, then resheathed it. When he finally spoke, he sounded calm, almost conversational.

"You know, Ying," he said. "I must say I'm disappointed. You seem like an intelligent woman." He smirked. "I really thought you might have figured it out sooner."

Ying shook her head, trying to clear the fog. "I . . . I don't understand." With faltering footsteps, she approached the prince. She reached her hand out to him, brushing his skin with her fingertips. With snakelike reflexes, he caught her wrist, crushing it beneath his fingers. His icy skin compounded the pain; Ying gave an involuntary cry.

"I mean, you almost made it too easy." He reached out with his other hand and gently cuffed her on the chin. "It really was a very basic mistake."

Ying couldn't breathe. "What was?"

The Mirror Prince's lips spread in a noxious grin. "Trusting me."

Her heart stuttered, her blood pounding against her skin. This prince, *her* prince, was not who he'd claimed to be. The prince she'd risked everything for—her marriage, her reputation, even her life.

She tasted bile. Her head spun as it filled with images of the intimacy they'd shared. His icy embrace. His body pressed against hers. Those cold lips on her neck, cold hands on her hips, the way his velvet voice had whispered words of honey into her ear.

Lies. All lies.

Now she understood. All the feigned compliments, the conspicuous care, the pretense of loyalty and of love. It was all designed for this moment. He and her reflection had lured Ying back and forth through the mirrors, weakening the barrier until, finally, it broke. And now he'd forced her here to meet her own reflection.

She fell to her knees, the edges of her vision shrinking, and vomited lake water all over the floor. The prince wrinkled his nose and jumped back to avoid soiling his feet.

"Now, now, don't tease the poor girl," Ying's reflection said to the Mirror Prince. "She's not the only one who made mistakes. Let's not forget that you, dear Zhang, lost track of her when she went to save her useless husband. You were supposed to seduce her. Distract her. But instead, you lost her."

"I found her again," the prince countered.

"Only because of me." Ying's reflection smiled. "But never mind. It's all water under the bridge now. We finally get the pleasure of killing her."

No! Ying curled over, clawing at her chest.

She'd been so oblivious. So naïve. The Mirror Prince's words when they'd reunited flashed clearly through her mind.

After you left, he'd said, *I couldn't find you. I hunted for you in every mirror, every lake, within a fifty-mile radius.*

He'd said that with his lips on her neck, his hand on her thigh. How had she not noticed the predator behind those words? *Hunted,* not *searched.* He'd hunted her. He'd as good as told her. She just hadn't listened.

"Why are you doing this?" Ying rasped out. She raised her face to the prince. "Why betray me like this?"

The prince's lips quirked up in a half smile. Then, just as fast, his smile vanished. He turned to face the water, propping one foot on a rock, his hand on his thigh.

"Do you have any idea how demeaning it is, Princess, to spend my life mimicking that weakling?"

"He is *not* weak!"

The Mirror Prince chuckled. "He *is* weak. And foolish.

I mean, he kept you locked up for *months*, Ying! Followed his darling mother's orders without question." The prince put on an affected voice. A mocking voice. "All she had to do was tell him you were in danger, and he bent over backward to 'protect you.' The fool didn't even stop to consider where the danger was coming *from*."

Ying's belly twisted. A wave of nausea rolled through her. Was that the truth—that the real prince's actions, however misguided, were out of loyalty to his mother and a desire to keep Ying safe?

"Not weak." Ying shook her head, her voice barely audible. Her throat had closed over. "Kind."

"It *is* weak. And it backfired, didn't it?" His lips curved into a sneer. "He even left you alone on your *wedding day,* in the perfect position for us to grab you. All because he thought you were too drunk on wine. So *honorable.* Bah!"

Ying struggled to her feet. Her head spun. "He . . . he did it out of honor?"

The Mirror Prince snapped out of his tirade. His eyes slid toward Ying, who was supporting herself against a column.

"Rest assured, Princess," he said, bearing down on her. He grabbed her chin, the chill as sharp as a knife. Leaning over her, he kissed her, roughly this time. Her voice was muffled as she struggled and cried out, pushing against his chest in vain.

He broke the kiss, his hand still grasping her chin. Crushing. Hurting. "Rest assured," he repeated, speaking into her ear. A chill tore through Ying's body that had nothing, and everything, to do with his touch. "I wouldn't have left you all drunk and alone. I'd have *destroyed* you. Fuck honor. Honor doesn't mean shit." He let her go, laughing as Ying gasped and stumbled backward.

Ying drew the back of her hand across her mouth and glared at him. She'd been duped. Completely and utterly duped.

And now she was going to die.

Her one chance was to keep the reflections talking while she figured out how to escape. "Why didn't you just kidnap me to begin with? Why bother with—" She stopped, unable to go on. Thinking about how he'd seduced her, and she'd fallen for it, was torture.

The prince rolled his eyes. "Because, Ying, if that little princeling got wind that you'd been kidnapped, he'd have set the ten courts of hell on us as soon as the gateway opened. You've been his intended since you were both children. Again, his insufferable honor and all that." The Mirror Prince's mouth stretched into a savage smile, revealing his even white teeth. Too white. Too bright. They glowed like the rest of him—supernatural. Inhuman.

"It was better coming from you, don't you think?" The Mirror Prince continued, relentless. "After all, it was you who made him think he wasn't wanted. It was *you* who convinced him to stay away. So perfect. So . . . effective."

It was hard for Ying to make sense of the words. They were so at odds with what she thought she knew of the real Zhang Lin. Wasn't it just his pride that had stung, that had made him angry she'd chosen his reflection over him? As if he would have cared that much, to send armies across the worlds to save her! The Mirror Prince must be lying. . . .

And yet, he had spent two decades mimicking the real prince. The Mirror Prince knew him best. Could Ying have misjudged the real prince so badly? Had her infatuation with the Mirror Prince made her insensible to the truth?

"But I don't understand," Ying said, shaking her head. "He wasn't trying to protect me. He *meant* to put me in danger. He locked me up with the mirrors. He knew I was the Fish. . . ."

Reflection-Ying's eyes gleamed, and the corners of her lips turned up in amusement. "Ohhh. You think he *knew*?"

"He didn't know," the Mirror Prince interjected. "The fool believed, without question, what his mother told him—what she, in turn, heard from Mei Po: that you would be attacked. But now you know—"

"Mei Po is on *our* side," Reflection-Ying finished the sentence. "She told the prince exactly what he needed to hear to keep you locked up with a mirror."

Ying, aghast, sagged against the pillar.

Turning his mouth down in an exaggerated frown, the Mirror Prince continued. "Poor, sad, *noble* prince. He thought the threat was *outside* the palace. He ran himself ragged trying to protect you. And after all that, you still don't love him. And people say we're the cold ones!" He threw his head back and laughed, the cheerless sound echoing across the lake and causing a flock of birds to scatter.

Ying bent over, clutching her stomach, fighting the heaviness pervading her body. *He didn't know,* she thought desperately. *All this time, he didn't know.* "You're cruel," she said aloud, though her voice was weak. "You're playing with our lives, and it's cruel—"

"Cruel?" Ying's reflection said. "No, Ying, we're being *merciful*. At least if he hates you, he won't miss you so much when you're gone."

Rage exploded in Ying, and she screamed, launching herself at her reflection. But the Mirror Prince grabbed her. Pinned her arms behind her. Ying struggled, but he had her well and truly trapped.

A convulsion tore through Ying's body, replaced by a frigid, icy chill. And not just because she was being held against the Mirror Prince.

"Before we kill you," Reflection-Ying taunted, pacing closer, "I do want to thank you. I thought the hardest thing would be luring you across the mirrors. But your eagerness to keep rushing across them, to keep breaking them down more and more, was obliging, so helpful." She chuckled as the Mirror Prince maneuvered a struggling Ying toward the edge of the pavilion. "I'm sorry to say, though, Princess, that your services are no longer necessary. Before the gateway was fully open, we needed you."

Reflection-Ying sauntered forward until her face was only inches from Ying's. "Now that it's broken"—she bared her teeth in a smile—"we don't."

Ying thrashed, fought, lunged to bite. But the prince's grip was too strong. He shoved Ying to her knees, grabbed a handful of her hair, and plunged her head into the water.

Ying held her breath for as long as possible, but eventually the urge to breathe took over. She gasped. Water gushed into her mouth, her throat, her lungs.

For a brief moment, the Mirror Prince's grip relented, and Ying reared out of the water, coughing and spluttering. A quick respite, yet fear rendered the scene with alarming clarity; when Ying's reflection spoke, it sounded so loud in Ying's ears.

"Are you sure this will work?" Reflection-Ying said. "Can she even drown if she's the Fish?"

"She's in human form." Ying couldn't see the Mirror Prince's face, but she could hear the scorn in his voice. "Don't worry. It'll work." His fingers tightened in Ying's hair, and she cried out in pain. Before she had a chance to draw another breath, he had shoved her head back underwater.

She jerked and thrashed. The churn of water filled her ears as she flailed.

This was it. Her energy reserves were running low. Bubbles fizzed around her face, obscuring her vision. Every panicked inhale made her aspirate more water, her chest seizing, her rib cage exploding.

Then hypoxia hit. A black, fuzzy feeling enveloped her, closing down her consciousness like a tunnel. She heard voices above her. Muffled, but clearly her reflection asking, "Is she dead?"

Ying forced her body to still, to go limp. This was her only chance of escape. If they thought she was dead, then there was a chance, just a little possibility, that they'd . . .

"She's dead." The Mirror Prince's muted voice filtered in from above. Then he shoved her headfirst into the lake.

It had worked. If Ying could've sighed underwater, she would have. Instead, she allowed herself to go limp and submitted to the darkness.

Her body sank through the murky water, her hair billowing out like a crown. Silence engulfed her, though she couldn't tell if it was just her senses shutting down. A shoal of carp darted up, investigating this new intruder.

It was extraordinarily peaceful, suspended in the silence, shafts of light cutting through from above. Loose pages from *The Book of Alchemy* swirled around her, carried by the water currents. With a gurgled yell, she tried to snatch at pages as she sank, but they spun from her grasp like spiraling leaves.

Any moment now, she told herself, she would cross the barrier and break through to her own world. But she just kept sinking deeper, her salvation slipping away. In her haze of half consciousness, she began to panic.

What if it didn't work this time?

In unison, the carp all darted away. Searing pain tore across the gōushé scar on her back. Something sharp was poking through her skin. Trickles of blood escaped into the water, curling around her like wings. *What the hell is happening?* Ying writhed, unable to scream, unable to escape the pain.

All around her, carp were sprouting manes and legs and beards and claws. As they circled, they grew bigger and bigger, twisting and changing until they were no longer fish at all.

They streaked through the water, weaving and diving, forming a blur of concentrated color. Red, black, white, gold. A few of them snapped playfully at the loose pages of the book, which twirled and tumbled in the swirling currents.

Water—was this related to one of the Three Treasures, qì? *Qì is the energy, like water it flows,* said the song. Was being submerged in water Ying's first step toward gaining control of the mirrors?

By now, the fish were no longer fish. They were dragons, their powerful scaled bodies churning up the water.

It was like the folktale she'd been told as a child, back in her home on the river. In the story, a golden carp who swam upstream would eventually encounter what was known as Longmen, the famous Dragon Gate. The gate, which was high and almost impossible to traverse, was situated at the top of the falls.

A carp that had the fortitude to swim against the current, fight the rapids, scale the waterfall, and leap over the gate would ultimately be rewarded. The reward? Transforming from a lowly fish into the most powerful mythological being of all: a dragon.

It was a story of persistence, of triumph, in the face of insurmountable odds.

Ying was a fish. She was *the* Fish, and now she was transforming. And, like the golden carp of legends past—and the fish that swam around her—she faced a choice: to give up or to prevail.

She could choose to acquiesce, to die, to sink into the silent depths. Or she could choose to complete the transformation. She could choose to have this power. She could leap the Dragon Gate.

She could choose life.

Something large swam beneath her, nudging her back to the

lake's surface, where dark water transitioned into gently dappled light. Dimly, Ying knew she only had to reach there, where there was air, where there was sun, where there was an outside world. She turned her focus upward, almost too weak to raise her head. All she had to do was reach the surface; it was only a few more feet. . . .

Ying snapped back to consciousness just as she exploded from the lake, dripping wet, riding atop a dragon.

28

The dragon soared into the sky, Ying clinging to its mane. It was long and serpentine, its scales a rich crimson color—the color of the carp from which it came. As it flew, it cast a huge shadow over the lake. Wet strands of hair whipped across Ying's face, sticking to it. She took a deep breath, the fogginess from her near-drowning clearing. Under her hands, the dragon's powerful neck muscles flexed and stretched as it wheeled, wingless, through the air.

Bravely, Ying peeked over the side to see both Reflection-Ying and the Mirror Prince staring up at her, stunned.

A wave of exhilaration coursed through her, and she resisted the urge to whoop. Somehow, she knew that she and the dragon were connected; that all she'd need to do would be to give a command and it would understand. To Ying, it was as though she finally felt it, really, truly felt it: she *was* the Fish, she *was* a dragon, and she *would* save her own world and all the people in it.

"Xià!" she shouted, her voice snatched by the wind. "Down!" The dragon dipped its head and swooped down over the Lotus Pavilion. Ying's stomach dropped as the dragon descended with terrifying speed, the turbulence causing the lake's surface to ripple. She took grim satisfaction in the way the Mirror Prince and Ying's reflection both immediately dove for cover.

For a few heart-stopping seconds, it looked as though the dragon might crash into the pavilion. But at the very last moment, and in one smooth motion, it curved back up toward the sky.

Ying considered going back, to wreak revenge on the two tiny figures crouched beneath the bushes. But she decided not to.

After all, she had a world to save.

She concentrated hard on the lake surface. Even without a verbal command, the creature responded, as though dragon and rider were one. Folding its clawed feet against its body, it plummeted, diving right into the center of the lake.

It was disorienting. She'd never traveled through a reflective surface at high speed on a dragon. For a moment, Ying couldn't tell which way was up or down. Moments later, though, the dragon burst from the lake, emerging right into the midst of battle.

Ying's gut contracted at how few soldiers remained. They were heavily outnumbered. The áoyīn were all dead, which made sense, since their hides could be pierced by swords. All the fēngshēngshòu still lived. A dozen or so human guards—or were they reflections?—battled on, caked in mud, fighting between the bodies of fallen comrades.

Ying frantically scanned the scene from where she sat, high in the air, on the back of the dragon. Finally, she spotted the real prince. Soaked as he was in blood and guts and who knew what else, he was barely recognizable. But she could tell it was him from his height, his broad back and shoulders, and his flawless fighting style.

The dragon roared.

Men and beasts alike looked up. A few of the men dove for cover, but the rest just stopped and gawked. Except for the prince, whose eyes locked with Ying's. Somehow, he knew what to do.

"DOWN!" he screamed. "GET DOWN!"

They didn't need to be told a third time.

As the men threw themselves face down on the ground, the dragon dove down, creating a dusty maelstrom as it descended. Then it opened its mouth—and breathed.

Its breath was like nothing Ying had ever witnessed. It was like wind but not wind. There was mist but also ice. There was ancient power in that breath, an ephemeral echo from a time when gods consorted with humans and the heavens were an extension of earth.

The fēngshēngshòu were blown toward the lake. Some screamed with high-pitched keens as they struggled to get away. Most of the creatures, including the two remaining reflections, were frightened enough that they immediately turned and converged upon the lake, scrabbling over each other to dive in.

The dragon circled above the fray, speeding up until Ying felt dizzy. The surface of the lake grew choppy, waves swelling higher and higher. Ying understood: the dragon was now controlling the water. A master of the elements, it was summoning the waves, causing them to come crashing down again and again onto the banks of the lake.

As Ying watched, the water took on a strange, almost sentient sort of movement. A few smaller waves surged outward, followed by a gigantic tidal wave. It engulfed the remaining mirror beasts and dragged them back to the depths of the lake, back to their own world on the other side.

One of the soldiers bellowed, caught up in the vortex. The real prince reached out and grabbed his comrade's wrist, trying to pull him out.

Thinking fast, Ying spurred the dragon down. With a gentleness belied by its colossal size, it plucked the two men from the lake bank and deposited them on higher ground.

Immediately, the waves receded. The lake surface became glassy. All the fēngshēngshòu had been washed away. There was no sign the lake had ever risen, save for a dark tide line.

"Down," Ying instructed, and the dragon descended. The ground shuddered as it landed. It shook its head and bent down to let Ying slide off its back.

"Ying!" The real prince ran toward her. "Ying! It *is* you, right, Ying?" He stopped short several feet away and stared, his eyes flicking to the cut on her cheek.

"Yes. It's me." She flipped her wet hair over her shoulders and away from her face; water dripped down her back.

"You . . . you came back."

"Of course I did." Ying tried to keep the irritation out of her voice. "I'm not a monster."

The prince opened his mouth to say something, but seemed to think better of it and shut it again. Ying rolled her eyes. "I know, I know. *He's* a monster. You don't have to say it."

The prince held up both hands in defense. "I wasn't going to."

Ying turned her face away. "It's okay," she whispered, fighting tears. "You were right all along. He *is* a monster."

There was a pause. "Do you want to talk about it?"

"No."

The prince was silent. He didn't push it.

Bending down, he splashed some lake water on his face. Droplets ran down the bronzed skin of his neck and disappeared below the neckline of his armor. Ying turned her gaze away, her cheeks reddening. The remaining guards were standing on the shore, their heads bowed. So many lost.

"I'm really sorry about your men," she said.

The dragon nosed around the ground and then clamped its jaw around a corpse, eliciting a sickening crunch. Ying flinched.

"They fought bravely." The prince rose to his feet and turned to Ying, his expression mournful. "You arrived just in time, Ying. That's three times you've saved my life now. Perhaps next time I should save yours."

Ying flushed harder, turning back to face him. "It was the dragon that saved us, really."

The prince glanced at the dragon; he winced as it crunched more bones. "Right. The dragon. Where did it come from, anyway?" He kept his tone unnaturally light. Ying could tell he was trying to stay calm in what was truly an unprecedented situation. Dragons were not supposed to exist. Not anymore, at least.

"From the lake," she said. She approached the dragon, stretching out a tentative hand. The creature raised its head as she drew closer.

"It was originally a fish," she said aloud. She placed a hand on the crimson-scaled neck and stroked it. The luminous red skin was unexpectedly smooth, unexpectedly warm. The dragon closed its amber eyes and made a low-pitched rumbling noise deep within its chest. Ying spoke her next words mostly to herself. "*I was a fish.*"

She was the Fish, the fish had become dragons, and maybe... maybe the fish transforming had triggered something in herself, too. Perhaps this was the first step in her journey to closing the mirrors.

But there was one big problem: she still couldn't work out what to do next, couldn't tease out the threads of her theories.

If Li Ming's song was related, Ying was supposed to find, or use, the Three Treasures to perform the alchemy. But what *were* the Three Treasures? While the folk song gave some hints, it was still so vague and unhelpful. And now Ying had lost The Book of Alchemy. She was right back where she'd started.

The prince spoke, snapping Ying out of her despondency. "It does your bidding?" He gestured at the dragon.

"We can communicate, yes." She eyed the dragon, which by now was licking its forelegs. "Whether it does my bidding is a different story."

The prince came to stand beside her and placed his own hand on the dragon's hide.

"I guess it's not surprising you can talk to them," he said, and looked sidelong at Ying. "It's in your family lore, right? That, long ago, you were once lake dwellers. Your ancestors could turn fish into dragons and ride them along riverbeds."

"That's true." Ying gave a small smile. "My ancestors were fond of fairy stories."

"Your ancestors were supposedly very powerful. And notoriously hardheaded." He raised one eyebrow. "That doesn't surprise me either."

Ying tried to suppress her smile. "You seem to know a lot about my family."

They were standing close, so close. The vibration from the dragon's chest was lulling Ying into a sort of daze. Warmth enveloped her, radiating from the dragon's hide and from the prince himself. He tilted his head downward, his breath tickling her cheek. Everything about him was devastating: his face, his presence, how identical he was to the Mirror Prince. Just looking at him was like a knife to the heart.

Ying forced herself to focus on the differences. The heat, for one. And unlike the Mirror Prince, his eyes didn't have the same slightly purple, iridescent sheen. His eyes were a deep, rich brown. So dark they were almost black, as enigmatic as the lake itself.

Had the Mirror Prince spoken the truth before he'd tried to kill her? Had the real Prince Zhang Lin truly been clueless about the mirrors before Reflection-Ying attacked him? Or were the reflections lying to her again, trying to trick her into trusting him? Ying couldn't make sense of anything right now, not with the prince's lips hovering so close to hers. Not with the way he was looking at her, making her light-headed.

He's going to kiss me, she thought, her heart racing. And for the first time ever, she thought that maybe, just maybe, she wanted it.

Abruptly, he stepped back. The spell was broken.

"Of course I know," he said, suddenly brusque. "For a match such as ours, it was only prudent I did my research."

An embarrassed flush rose up Ying's neck. She bit her lip and turned away. She didn't want him to see her face, didn't want him to sense her confusion—how, for a moment, she'd almost thought...

Nothing. It's nothing. She'd thought nothing. Expected nothing. Forcing herself to take a deep breath, she stowed those thoughts away. Residual emotions for the Mirror Prince. That's all this was.

"Thank you," she whispered to the dragon, placing her hand on its neck. It curved into her hand for a moment, then bent its head to the ground and nosed something in her direction. At first, Ying recoiled, but a cursory glance told her it was not part of the dragon's meal.

She picked it up, and the dragon let forth a languid, satisfied purr. "What's this?" Ying whispered, surprised. It was a soggy lump of something.

She smoothed it out, her heart speeding to a gallop.

A piece of parchment.

A soft whisper started unfurling deep in the base of her skull.

It was a page... from *The Book of Alchemy*.

Ying gave a sly, quick glance to check whether Zhang Lin had seen—he hadn't—before scrunching it up and shoving it in her boot. It would take more than the words of two unreliable reflections for Ying to fully trust the prince.

The dragon, now satisfied, lumbered to its feet, forcing Ying and the prince to back away, then uncoiled its gigantic, snakelike body. Blinking one yellow eye at Ying, it shook out its mane, bent its legs, then took off into the arching sky.

Ying and the prince watched the dragon become a shimmering speck in the distance, its elongated body undulating through the air. When it was so high it had almost disappeared, it turned and dove headfirst into the lake, where it disappeared with a small splash and a series of ever-expanding ripples.

"You know what this means, don't you?" Ying stared at the lake, at the spot where the dragon had disappeared.

"Tell me."

She turned around and arched an eyebrow. "The barrier is broken," she said. "The war has begun."

29

When Ying arrived back at the palace, her weariness was temporarily displaced by her reunion with her maids. She hugged them both, tears stinging her eyes, the events of the past few hours finally manifesting in her body.

Later, when she was alone, she would study the page from *The Book of Alchemy*. For now, though, it would have to wait.

Li Ming and Fei fei were ecstatic to see her, although they were less than pleased about her unkempt appearance. "Lady Ying," Li Ming said, looking scandalized. "What did you do to your *hair*?"

"Never mind that," Ying replied. She looked at Fei fei, who stood off to one side, twisting the skirt of her gown in her hands. "Have you . . . ?"

The maids glanced at each other, then erupted into rapturous giggles. Li Ming reached out and clasped Fei fei's hand, her eyes shining with tears.

"After I left you at the stables," Li Ming explained, "I alerted the palace guards. But then I found Fei, and—"

"Oh, Princess," Fei breathed. "Please say you approve? You don't mind?"

Ying blinked at them, confused. "Why would you need *my* approval?"

Fei fei glanced at Li Ming, then back at Ying. "Because . . . because you're our boss, Your Highness."

"Oh, Fei." Ying shook her head and gave a small smile. "That doesn't mean I have *any* say in this." She came forward and took both of their hands. "I'm happy for you, I really am."

She meant it.

Previously, Ying had been too caught up in her own troubles to notice this about her maids: how they moved around each other with practiced familiarity. How they made excuses to touch each other in subtle, endearing ways. How Fei fei's gentle, assiduous nature was the perfect foil for Li Ming's spark. And how they both took such delight—real, genuine delight—in being together, in serving their mistress.

If Ying could have just half their happiness, she'd be content.

Ying's handmaidens were eager to wait on her, to help her clean up. Without their assistance, they argued, she couldn't possibly remedy her disastrous appearance. After several whispered, urgent conversations, which mainly involved their giving each other pointed looks, Ying managed to win the debate. Eventually, with some difficulty, she was able to usher them away.

Being alone allowed Ying to feel the full brunt of the Mirror Prince's betrayal. As she lowered herself into a bath full of pomegranate-scented water—sprinkled with enough petals to render it opaque—she relived the scene on the Lotus Pavilion. The worst thing wasn't that he'd led her on to achieve his own ends, or that he'd turned out to be a conniving bastard. It wasn't even that he was working with Ying's reflection to betray her, kill her, and then invade her world. No, the worst thing was that she'd fallen for it. That she'd fallen for him. For the first time ever, she'd fancied herself in love, and now she had nothing to show for it but an empty, aching pain.

She'd been lured multiple times across the mirrors, broken the gateway down, and lost *The Book of Alchemy* containing the Crimson Emperor's teachings. All because she'd trusted the Mirror Prince, had fallen for the elaborate trap he'd set.

Foolish, foolish girl, Ying told herself. But the real prince had once said she wasn't foolish, but kind. She swore under her breath, cursing *him,* too. What did he know? He barely even knew her—had only the vaguest idea of who she really was.

The water was scalding, but Ying barely felt it. Drawing her knees up, she hugged them to her chest, darkness gnawing through her until it carved a cavernous hole.

When I win the war, she thought, *this heartache will cease to matter.* But how was she to win the war? She needed to close the barrier, and the method for that was outlined in a now-destroyed book. But then—the book! She *had* part of the book. A single page, yes, but a page nonetheless. Ying jumped up, water streaming in sheets off her, and hurriedly dressed in a pale-gold hànfú.

What were the chances that that one page would happen to hold the correct information? The probability was so slim, and yet . . . perhaps fate had brought the parchment to her. What if the dragon, a magical creature, had recognized what it was? What if the dragon had specifically plucked it from the water?

Was it possible that the stars had magically aligned to salvage what she needed most?

After hurriedly knotting the ties of her skirt, she fished the damp, crumpled page out of her discarded boot. Again, that quiet, portentous whisper slithered beneath her skin, making her shudder. She had a sudden sense of being watched.

She took a deep breath, resolving to ignore it.

The parchment was warped and bloated, the tiny text faint and smudged. But it was still by and large intact. Some sort of magic must have protected it from the most egregious effects of the water. With the very tips of her fingers, Ying carried it over to the fireplace and began to dry it out.

The page seemed to relax in the golden glow of the fire; the sound in Ying's head dulling to a hum. She peered at it as it dried, trying to decipher the writing. Most of it wasn't readable, due to age or water damage or both, and the portions that *were* still legible were written in that ancient, incomprehensible script.

Ying ground her teeth. Nothing was ever simple, it seemed. This would take time—and some reference texts—to translate.

Ying strode through the palace, trying her best to look confident, as though she actually belonged. She'd been surprised to find her bedroom door unlocked, for once. Perhaps Prince Zhang was finally trusting her, even if she wasn't yet ready to return the favor. Or it could have just been a mistake, an oversight, on his behalf. Either way, she wasn't sure how much time she had.

Despite her urgency, it took Ying longer than she would have liked—and the help of several servants—to reach her desired destination. The Imperial Library, as Ying discovered, was in the Western quarter, surrounded by a man-made moat. Unlike the rest of the palace buildings, which were bedecked in tones of red and gold and topped with yellow-tiled roofs, this building was an austere structure. Raised on a pavilion, with a square pond out front, it had green-painted pillars, a slate-gray roof, and large, black-framed windows.

At the top of the marble steps, a single guard patrolled the entrance. Upon spotting Ying crossing over the bridge, he immediately threw himself down, face-first, and kowtowed. Ying, feeling awkward, thanked him hurriedly and pushed through the ornate double doors.

The inside of the building was cool and dark. Patterned evening light filtered through the carved-fretwork shutters. Ying stood in the circular entrance hall, her wet hair dripping onto the marble floor, and blinked several times to let her eyes adjust to the gloom. Unsure of where to go, she hesitated for a moment, then started up the sweeping staircase.

She climbed and climbed, bypassing signs pointing out the GOVERNMENT, ACADEMIC, and PRIVATE collections, her breaths coming shorter and faster as she went. Finally, she reached the top level, which had a sign saying SPECIAL INTEREST.

This is it, she thought, and set to browsing the shelves. Her aim was to gather a few books on translation, then set to work interpreting the rescued page from the now-destroyed *Book of Alchemy*.

Pausing momentarily, she reveled in the stillness. She inhaled the familiar smells of camphor and leather and the crisp scent of old paper. Back home, the library had been one of her favorite places to pass time; she'd often used it as a refuge when painting and needlework became too dull. Crouched in the shadows, among rows and rows of books, she would pore over tomes describing witchcraft and magic while steadfastly ignoring her tutors as they frantically called out her name.

The shelves, made from nánmù wood, were packed with all manner of books and scrolls; ladders allowed access to the highest shelves. Ying shrugged off her cloak, draped it over a nearby chair, and started down one of the aisles.

The shelves here held some of the oldest, mustiest-smelling books. As she walked, she trailed the tips of her fingers along the spines, now and then pulling out a book and stacking it in her arms.

Balancing the pile of books in her hands, she scanned the top shelves, squinting in an effort to read the titles.

"What are you looking for?" came a voice behind her, cutting harshly through the hush. Ying jumped and her stack of books fell. They cascaded to the floor with a crash, causing a puff of dust to waft up and make her sneeze.

It was the prince, leaning against a bookshelf, a faint half-smile on his lips.

Ying reddened and bent to gather the books. How had she not heard him enter? "Nothing," she said testily. For some inexplicable reason, she felt as though she'd been caught doing something she shouldn't.

Plus, part of her was still seething over their almost-kiss.

"Oh," the prince said, squatting to help her. "Because I thought, you know, if you want something specific, I can find it for you."

"I'm good, thanks." Ying snatched up the last book, then stood up very quickly. The prince rose, too, and Ying's face heated at how closely they were wedged between the narrow shelves.

She slammed the books down on a nearby desk with more force than was strictly necessary. When she looked up, the prince hadn't moved. He was staring at her.

"What are you doing here, Zhang Lin?" she said, her tone hardening. She turned away from him and started flipping through her books. "Are you following me?"

"No. I'm not following you." The prince edged closer until he was in Ying's peripheral vision. "It's just—one of the servants told me you were wandering the palace halls, looking for the library."

Ying spun to face him, her hands on her hips. "So you did follow me."

He stepped back and raised his hands. "No, Ying. The servant came to find *me*. I was just on my way back from seeing my father—"

Ying's chest tightened. "Your father?" She couldn't help sounding alarmed. Zhang Lin's impromptu meeting could ruin *everything*. Though she was starting to believe that the prince himself hadn't known about Ying being in danger from the mirrors, from what the reflections had said, the emperor and empress *had* known. If they knew that the barrier was finally open, what would stop them from shoving Ying back through it, as their ancestors had done seven times before? No, Emperor and Empress Shan were *not* to be trusted.

"I figured that . . . since war was coming . . ." The prince trailed off, his gaze dropping to somewhere below Ying's left ear. When he spoke again, his words came out in a rush. "He is the most powerful man in the empire, after all, and I just thought that . . ."

"You didn't think, did you?" Ying curbed the impulse to tear at her hair. "Well, what did he say?"

"Not much." The prince frowned. "He was drunk, as usual. Which is odd. He never used to drink. But now he's always so inebriated he can hardly remember what day it is. He even seemed confused as to who I was. At one point he called me by my brother's name." His eyes glazed over, and he blinked and looked away.

Ying faltered, barely able to formulate a response. The prince's elder brother, the one who'd previously been heir but had died in battle. That had been years ago. No wonder the prince looked so hurt.

As much as she pitied him, though, her pity was superseded by spite. Once again, the prince had made a decision for her—one she hadn't been privy to. He'd yet again left her out of his plans. Whether he'd intended to protect her or had just thoughtlessly excluded her didn't matter. It was her job to close the barrier. Her job to win the war. The prophecy centered on *Ying*, and the last thing she needed was the crown prince going off on tangents without her knowledge.

Narrowing her eyes, Ying said, "You still haven't answered my question, Zhang Lin. *What are you doing here?*"

His eyes widened, as though taken aback. "I just thought I'd see if you could use my help."

Tell him, a small internal voice chided. *Tell him about the parchment. He's more familiar with the library than you are. He might be useful.*

"Then help!" Ying exclaimed, exasperated. "If you want to help, help! Don't just *stand* there! Being *useless*!"

The prince's eyes widened slightly, and for a few seconds, he was silent, seemingly lost for words. But then he seemed to gather his wits. "All right," he said. Raising an eyebrow, he added, "As long as you don't poison me again."

"I can't make any promises," Ying muttered. "It depends on how much you annoy me."

The echo of a smile ghosted across the prince's lips. "Fair enough," he replied, then turned serious again. "Well, Ying, what do you need? What will help us unravel the prophecy? Do we need a history book? One about the Crimson Emperor's reign? Or do we need something about"—he moved closer to the desk, tracing the cover of the top book with one finger—"translation?" He gave her a quizzical look.

Ying's pulse began to hammer in her ears. The prince didn't yet know she'd found, and then lost, *The Book of Alchemy*. Even worse, it was because she'd been naïve enough to fall for the Mirror Prince's charms. And while she knew she should tell him, another part of her was afraid of the prince's censure, that he'd think less of her for her folly.

She screwed her eyes shut. She was being silly. Risking the fate of the world because she was *embarrassed*? She needed to swallow her pride and—

"I have a page I need to translate," she said before she changed her mind. "It's some ancient dialect I can't read."

"That should be doable," the prince replied. He held out a hand. "Let's see it, then."

She hesitated for a moment before pulling the crumpled page from the sleeve of her hànfú. Immediately, the same susurrating whispers started, and Ying shoved the parchment at the prince. He took it, smoothed it out, and scanned the page.

She loosed a breath. The whispers had died down. For the first time, she noticed how tense the book was making her.

"Ying, this is about alchemy," he said, his eyebrows lifting in confusion. But then understanding dawned in his expression. His next words came out in a rush. "Does this mean you found it? Is this from *The Book of Alchemy*?"

"Yes. But it was—it was ruined in the lake. This is the only page I could salvage." Ying's cheeks heated, hoping he didn't ask for more detail. "It turns out it was Mei Po who stole it."

The prince gave her a sharp look. "*Mei Po* stole it?"

Ying nodded. "The mirror version of Mei Po. She'd . . . replaced the real Mei Po."

His features twisted in disgust as he considered Ying's words. "Well, she's disappeared now," he said finally, then frowned. "She's been reported missing. No one can find her—either version of her. Perhaps now that you've found her out, the mirror version has run away."

"And perhaps the human version is dead." Ying shuddered.

"Let's hope she's just hiding," the prince replied, though he sounded doubtful.

They lapsed into tense silence before something suddenly occurred to Ying. "Wait," she said. "You said this was about alchemy. Can *you* read it?"

"Yes. I mean, apart from the smudged bits, of course." The prince gave a small shrug. "I had a tutor in ancient languages."

"Of course you did," Ying said faintly. Her heart thudded, her pulse hammering through her veins. This whole time, she'd been so determined to figure out a translation—was prepared to go to such great lengths—when she could have just asked the prince. "So, Mr. Expert-in-ancient-dialects, tell me. . . . What does it say?"

30

"It's a recipe." The prince scrutinized the words, his head tilted to one side. "For some sort of alchemical elixir. It says it's to replenish jīng." He held the parchment out to Ying, who snatched it off him and shoved it back into her sleeve.

She tried to temper her excitement. She didn't want to jump to conclusions. But . . . *jīng*. The first of the Three Treasures, jīng, qì, and shén. What every human is born with, before their energy is split into yin and yang. If this recipe was to increase one's jīng, then perhaps it was another step closer to figuring out the significance of the Three Treasures. "And what is *in* the recipe?"

The prince closed his eyes, as though trying to remember. "There's lead, and cinnabar, and potable gold . . ." He trailed off.

"And?"

"And then it cuts off. There's a whole lot of text at the start, about—I think—jīng again, splitting into yin and yang? Perhaps . . . perhaps this elixir helps that process. It's hard to tell—the ink is so smudged."

Ying's insides churned, as though she was too full of energy that was about to erupt. While she couldn't be sure, it was far too big a coincidence for it not to be interrelated: *The Book of Alchemy* containing information about the Three Treasures. Li Ming's song about the same thing, and referring to bound spirits. *Jing is the essence from which all life grows,* the song said, and then, later, *Fire will render the bound spirits free.*

More than that, Mei Po had spoken of alchemy—how the Crimson Emperor had performed alchemy to seal the mirror gateway, and how Ying herself needed to perform alchemy to do the same.

Maybe, just maybe, this was the start of the alchemical recipe penned by the Crimson Emperor himself. And if *The Book of Alchemy* contained the actual recipe, it was no wonder that Mei Po—a mirror person herself—had stolen it. She either wanted to keep it from Ying . . . or she wanted to use it herself.

It was a shame that Ying was able to rescue only one page. The recipe was incomplete.

She stood for a moment, chewing her lip. Mirror–Mei Po was a problem: she was still at large in the real world, but Ying didn't know where she was or what she planned to do next. What if Mei Po had memorized the alchemy and was already halfway to performing it? Though surely, without Ying, she wouldn't be able to fully control the gateway. Not when Ying was the Fish—the one prophesied to close it off.

Still, there was no time to waste. Mei Po was out there, and Ying needed to hurry. Fortunately, an idea had started to form. "Where's the alchemy section, Zhang Lin?" she called out over her shoulder as she strode away.

The prince jogged a little to catch up with her, then stopped her with a hand on her lower back. Ying gasped. Stumbled a little. Tried not to notice the pressure of Zhang Lin's fingers . . . nor the way his body radiated heat, nor how his sword handle jutted against her hip.

"You're going the wrong way, Princess," he said, his voice low in her ear. Placing his hands on her shoulders, he spun her gently around and pointed. "Try that way."

His warm breath tickled the curve of her ear, and Ying's heartbeat kicked up in both speed and volume. Embarrassed by her reaction, she ducked away from the prince, squared her shoulders, and stalked off in the correct direction.

It was so . . . *annoying* the way he always showed up unannounced. The way he was so smug about everything, even when giving her directions. Granted, it was his own palace, but still. Annoying.

She reached the correct aisle in a fluster and began pulling books off the shelf. She pulled out books about metallurgy, brewing elixirs, energy transfer. . . . And then she spotted a thick black leather tome, high up, that looked extremely promising.

The title on the spine read: IMMORTAL ALCHEMY: NOTES FROM THE CRIMSON EMPEROR ON HOW TO ACHIEVE IMMORTALITY. It wasn't specifically about the Three Treasures, and as far as Ying knew, she didn't need to become immortal. But if the book was written during the Crimson Emperor's reign, then perhaps it would have something of use.

"I need that one," Ying said, dumping her pile of books in the prince's arms. She dragged one of the wooden ladders sideways and lined it up. "Hold this steady for me, will you?"

Carefully, the prince placed the stack of books on the floor and positioned himself at the base of the ladder.

Gathering her skirts close around her legs, Ying began her ascent. The ladder was extremely tall—and whenever she chanced to look down, she felt giddy at the vertiginous height. Luckily, the prince held the ladder with a solid grip, and it didn't budge an inch.

At the top, she leaned over and pulled the book from its place. Did she imagine it, or had it offered some resistance? And what was the whispering sound she could now hear in her ears—so similar to what she had heard from *The Book of Alchemy*?

Ignoring her unsettled feeling, Ying hauled the book off the shelf and clasped it to her chest. It was unusually warm—especially considering that it had been on a shelf in a little-used part of the library—and much heavier than she'd expected. All of a sudden, she didn't want to be holding it. Didn't want it anywhere near her. She felt that if she tried to climb down the ladder with it, she would surely fall.

"Uh, Zhang?" she called down, surprised at how shaky her voice sounded. "It's rather heavy. I don't think I can—"

"Toss it down," he called back up. "I'll catch it."

"Are you sure? I might hit you." She cast a dark, doubtful look at the book.

"Pretend I'm the Mirror Prince," he said jokingly. Ying just glared at him, and he chuckled. "Come on, Ying, throw it down. I'll be all right."

Ying closed her eyes, drew a breath, and dropped the book.

When she risked opening her eyes again, the prince had

caught it and was placing it on top of the stack of books. He didn't seem affected by it at all. Ying shook her head. Perhaps the ancient air of the library, her irritation at having been ambushed by the prince, or the events that had transpired over the past few days were getting to her. Maybe *all* of it was getting to her.

She probably just needed some rest.

The prince continued to hold the ladder steady as Ying descended, now slightly wobbly on her feet. When she had almost reached the bottom, she felt the tip of his right thumb briefly brush her calf.

He sucked in a sharp breath, and Ying froze, sparks spreading outward from where they had touched, skin-to-skin.

Trying to ignore it, Ying continued. She reached the ground and turned around, only to find the prince staring down at her, his hands still gripping the ladder, muscular arms caging her in. Tension radiated from him; his knuckles were white, the muscles of his forearms corded.

Ying pressed herself backward, trying to put some distance between them. The ladder rungs dug into her shoulder blades. But she dared not move. She dared not do anything; she didn't breathe, didn't blink. She just stared back, temporarily immobilized, her eyes locked on his.

This close, she could count every one of his eyelashes. She could see the way his pupils dilated. She could smell his usual scent—wood smoke, white pine. But there was something else, something other than a clean forest smell. Something that was unmistakably, well, *him*.

She licked her lips, which seemed unnaturally dry.

The prince's gaze darkened, watching her mouth. He was so close. Mere inches separated his lips and hers. But the empty space could have held all of history with the amount of heaviness it contained.

Ying trembled, hesitating. Then she raised her chin the tiniest amount and—without overthinking it—

—she closed the distance.

With a groan, the prince responded in kind, his mouth claiming hers. One of his hands grasped her jaw; the other twisted in her hair. They kissed in a tangle of lips and tongue, Ying wrapping her arms around the prince's neck. With one move, he lifted her, propping her up on the ladder, and she grabbed a rung to steady herself.

They kept kissing furiously. For Ying, every sensation, every thought, narrowed down into this fiery, frenetic kiss. She wrapped her legs around his waist, pressing her whole body against his, while the prince grasped her hair still tighter, his other hand making its way to her lower back, her hip....

"Stop!" She broke the kiss and pushed him away, grasping the ladder rung tighter to keep from falling. The prince let go, staggered a few steps backward, then passed the back of his hand over his mouth.

"Gods, Ying!" He turned and walked a few paces away before striding back to her. He had a frayed air about him, like a thread about to snap. "What do you mean, *stop*? You're the one who kissed *me*!" He pushed his disheveled hair out of his eyes. "It's you who needs to stop—*stop* sending mixed signals!"

Ying stood, pressed a hand to her chest, trying to school

her rapid breaths into something resembling calm. She had no idea why she'd done that, no idea why she'd kissed him; it was probably just some nonsensical and vestigial feelings for that vile Mirror Prince. She'd loved that monster so fiercely, so intently, and so quickly that, although he'd betrayed her, and badly, those feelings still festered, like rot.

"Me sending mixed signals?" she said, seething. "What about you?" She fought to keep her voice level, but it still sounded higher than usual. "You're hot one minute and cold the next! You've treated me callously from day one. Why'd you lock me up, Zhang Lin? Why treat me like a prisoner?"

The prince leaned forward, breathing hard, bracing one hand against the ladder above her head. "As I said, it was for your protection. My mother said that Mei Po foresaw you being attacked." The prince's lip curled. "Turns out it didn't matter. Seems you're exceptionally good at putting *yourself* in danger."

"It's a little hard to avoid my own reflection!" she shrieked, not even caring how deranged she sounded. His explanation lined up with what the reflections had said by the lake, but still, somehow, it wasn't enough. It wasn't enough to make up for the months of pain and loneliness that he had subjected her to. "It doesn't explain why you were so cold to me in the first place! You refused to talk to me, or even to see me! You only wanted me after your reflection did. What's *with* that? Were you trying to mark your territory?"

"My *territory*?" The prince spat the words. He glared down at her, and Ying glared right back. "You think *that's* what this is?"

"I know it is." With a furious swipe of her hand, Ying

scrubbed away the tears that had begun to form. Her voice shook as she struggled to gain command over her emotions. "But there's no point, Shan Zhang Lin: I will *never* love you."

The prince flinched when she said the word *love,* and Ying's heart surged with bitter triumph.

He pushed away from the ladder, took a few steps back, and leaned against the opposite bookshelf, head bowed. When he spoke, his voice was muffled.

"If you want the truth, Ying, I . . . I was shaken by the predictions. When I was told that you'd be attacked, even killed, it all seemed so . . . pointless. I was afraid of becoming too attached. It was . . . easier not to see you, not to speak to you, to pretend you didn't exist. I fooled myself into thinking that I was protecting us both. And I'll admit—I resented the thought of marrying someone who'd need constant looking after." He raised his head and looked at her, a weary expression on his face. "But I was wrong about you. Clearly, you can look after yourself."

"Damn right I can." She clenched her fists.

The prince straightened and stood staring at her, his arms by his side. "Ying," he said quietly. "It doesn't excuse my past behavior, but I always hoped I would marry someone I loved. I expected that wouldn't be you. I'm sorry."

Ying bristled. "Then you're an idiot. We both know marriage has nothing to do with love."

A strange look flashed in the prince's eyes, but the next minute, it was gone. "Forgive me, Princess," he said, giving a small bow. "I should've known better."

"Yes, you should have." Ying was still seething, her tears

flowing freely now. "If you crave love so much, why don't you run to one of your concubines? I'm sure they have plenty of love to give."

He sighed. "I don't have any, Ying. Only you."

She drew herself up to her full height. "Maybe you should get some, then."

"Maybe I should," he replied, his eyes hard.

The air between them teemed with tension. In that moment, Ying wanted to take it all back. She wanted *him* to take it all back. But he didn't say anything, nor did she. They just stood there, chests heaving, staring at one another.

Ying was the first to move. She bent down and began gathering the books off the floor—messily, noisily, somewhat clumsily. "I think you should go now," she said, fighting to keep her voice even. "Leave me, please."

There was no response.

The prince could move so silently when he wanted to. Ying didn't even hear him leave. All she heard was the heavy clang of the door slamming shut behind him.

31

Ying cursed as her wolf-hair brush smudged the ink *again*. She was so distracted, so furious—scrawling out a recipe she'd found in *Immortal Alchemy*—that she kept accidentally pressing too hard. In some places, the ink had eroded the paper altogether, leaving it studded with soggy holes.

She'd immediately regretted the fight she'd had with Zhang Lin, even going so far as to run out of the library after him. But as she'd reached the top of the entrance steps, she'd seen him mounted on Shadow Runner, galloping out the gates. She knew the palace guards would never let her leave the grounds unattended, so she'd returned to the library, dejected, resigned to the prospect of figuring things out on her own.

Swirling the brush against the inkstone so forcefully that the bristles splayed, Ying scowled and resumed writing. It had taken several painstaking hours—time she didn't have to waste, really—for her to translate the recipe. Supposedly it was an elixir that rendered the drinker able to transcend different levels of existence. She wasn't even sure she'd gotten it right. Figuring this was as close as she'd get, however, she planned to combine this recipe and the fragments of the one the prince had translated from *The Book of Alchemy*. It wasn't much to go on ... but she had to do *something*. And without any clear direction, what choice did she have?

Finally, she finished. She slammed the black leather book shut. It seemed to shudder. Disconcerted, Ying hurriedly stowed it on a dark corner shelf. There was no way she was attempting the ladder again without someone to keep it steady.

As she tried to walk away, a compulsive pull gripped her, as though she was trudging through sludgy, brackish water. Her chest tightened, her head spun, and she struggled to catch her breath.

What is that? She clutched her head. Ignoring the sensation, she kept walking, and thankfully the effect weakened with distance. Only once she was outside could she breathe freely again.

She paused on the library steps, thinking. Finally, she had the beginnings of a plan. If the Mirror Prince was telling the truth, she had until the full moon to put her plan into motion. Tonight, if the dark sky was anything to go by, was the new moon—day one of the new lunar month. This gave her a shade over two weeks, provided Mei Po—wherever she was—didn't sabotage her first.

She took a deep breath, summoning her courage. Something had happened in the lake when the Mirror Prince had tried to drown her. She remembered the feeling of the bloodlike wings erupting from the gōushé scar on her back. Somehow, she'd caused the fish to transform into dragons. Was it to do with her being submerged in water? Was that the "water" referenced in Li Ming's song?

While she still didn't know how Three Treasures, or the Crimson Emperor's alchemy, would help her seal the mirrors, she at least had a stitched-together recipe she was willing to try. The first Treasure, according to the song, was jīng. And if the real prince was right and the recipe in *The Book of Alchemy* was designed to replenish one's jīng, then perhaps she'd be fulfilling the first part of the prophecy by ingesting the elixir, or something like it. Perhaps she could trigger a transformation, like the one that had allowed her to create the dragons, except this time, maybe it would help her close the mirror barrier.

The mirror barrier. It was open now. She was sure the last thread holding it closed had snapped when the Mirror Prince dragged her through the lake, away from the fēngshēngshòu. The memory of that moment filled her with fury, so she quashed those thoughts.

Instead, she shifted her attention to her current conundrum: how to procure the ingredients. Substances like lead, cinnabar, hematite, and drinkable gold did not just lie around.

Massaging her temples, Ying tried to remember the next part of the song. It mentioned water and mountains, but that didn't help her much.

Well, better she focus on what she did know. What she *could* do. She squinted southward, to where the spires of the imperial temple, known as the Hall of Heavenly Contemplation, were silhouetted by the dying sun. A thin plume of smoke curled up, up into the sky—offerings they burned for the deities day and night, all year long, through all of the twenty-four seasons.

Flinging her cloak back around her shoulders, Ying ran

down the library steps toward the Priests' Precinct . . . and the one person who could help her.

By the time Ying reached the priests' residence, night had well and truly fallen. Servants were beginning to hang rounded red lanterns on their designated hooks. Others stoked braziers full of incense designed to ward off spirits, or wheeled carts full of food and linen along the narrow lanes.

She took a deep breath, then raised a fist and knocked on the huge carved-wood doors. A priest wearing teal robes answered.

"What do you want?" he asked, casting Ying a suspicious look.

"My name is Jiang Ying Yue," she replied, raising her chin and attempting to look regal. Then she added, perhaps unnecessarily, "the crown princess."

Immediately, the priest's eyes widened and he dropped to his knees and performed a kowtow. "Apologies, Your Highness," he said into the polished parquet floor. "I did not recognize you in . . ." Still facing the ground, he made a vague gesture at her outfit.

No longer having a reflection, Ying could not assess her own appearance, but no doubt she looked extremely haggard. She was wrapped up thickly in her travel cloak and her uncombed hair hung long and stringy. She probably didn't look at all like a princess, let alone the future empress of Jinghu Dao.

"No apology necessary," Ying murmured, excusing him, and the priest visibly sagged with relief. "I wish to speak with the Truth Master."

"Certainly, Your Highness," the priest said, jumping to his feet and backing away.

Ying lingered in the entrance hall, an enormous, perfectly square space with a high tile roof. The ceiling was a riotous mix of filigree patterns, dragon and phoenix motifs, and the Shan family's peaked-mountain emblem. Lanterns hung, glowing, around the perimeter of the room.

It seemed an age before one of the internal doors swung open and an old, stooped man approached. He looked smaller than he had from a distance at the tea ceremony. Voluminous red robes embroidered in gold enveloped his slight frame, though the excess fabric did not seem to hinder his movement. He moved with the slow, easy grace of someone who never needed to hurry.

"Your Highness," the Truth Master said, sinking into a deep bow. "It is an honor to formally meet you. I am Master Chen." His voice was whispery, like paper, and Ying immediately thought of the *Immortal Alchemy* book. She swallowed, feeling queasy.

Ying offered the back of her hand, and Master Chen kissed it with his white-whiskered lips, which were reassuringly warm and human. It was a strange feeling, being venerated by the imperial Truth Master. Ying still hadn't adjusted to the idea of her superiority; if anything, it felt like *she* should be bowing to *him*.

"Master Chen," she said when the old man had straightened. "I need your help."

"Certainly." The Master's beard twitched with his smile. "Anything for Her Royal Highness, of course, of course...."

After digging around in the sleeve of her gown, Ying produced the piece of parchment she'd scribbled on in the library. "I need to procure the ingredients for this, Truth Master."

Master Chen tugged on his beard, frowning, as he studied the piece of paper. He was silent a long while. Eventually, he peered at her and said, "But why, Your Highness?"

Feeling her cheeks flush, Ying scrambled for an excuse. But of course, her mind was completely blank. "I just . . . need it. I can't explain."

The old man frowned, reading the words on the paper again, as though hoping they might say something different upon a second read. "Your Highness, I strongly advise—"

Ying, panicking, cut him off. "Master Chen, you are not just a servant of the gods; you are also my servant, and your duty is to obey. Not to question." This was true. In the imperial household, the emperor was a divine being and the highest-ranking man in the empire. His wife, Empress Shan, came second. The prince, being the sole heir, was next, followed by Ying, his supposed wife. Everyone else, according to imperial law, was below them.

Normally, Ying would never have asserted her power so, but fear had seized her mind. Even though she supposedly had almost two weeks to close the barrier, any time wasted risked her plans' being discovered and thwarted by the reflections. Plus, Mirror-Mei Po was still out there, and there was no guarantee the mirror army wouldn't suddenly change their plans and storm the palace sooner.

This was her best opportunity to try the elixir. She was standing on a precipice, facing the fires of hell, and the only way to potentially save the world was to jump right off.

Straightening her posture, she lifted her chin and said, in the haughtiest tone she could muster, "Master Chen, I would strongly advise that you follow my orders."

The Master's wrinkles deepened, and his eyes watered. He paused a second before nodding once, then began to shuffle off.

He moved fast, despite his stooped shoulders, and Ying hurried to keep up. The Master strode through a number of convoluted corridors and ushered Ying through numerous doors. With a lurch, she realized that, if it came to it, she would struggle to find her way back out.

Finally, they arrived at a vast, dark storeroom, its floor-to-ceiling shelves stuffed full of any manner of grotesque things. Some floated in jars; others were contained in wooden boxes. What looked like several shrunken human heads leered down at Ying from one corner.

The Master moved about the room, pulling jars off the shelves, muttering, and emptying things into a little bowl. On more than one occasion, he'd deliberate for a while, his hand hovering between two jars, before he'd grab one to add to his concoction.

Feeling a little faint, Ying made a show of studying the objects on the shelves, reading the neat little labels that categorized each one. She tried to keep her face blank, masking her aversion. Then she gasped, for high up on the Master's shelf was the emperor's own bronze chalice.

Why did the Truth Master have the emperor's cup? Shouldn't the responsibility of mixing the emperor's beverages fall to a cook, or one of the emperor's eunuchs? Ying pressed a hand to her mouth and glanced at Master Chen. Fortunately, he hadn't heard her. She'd have to consider this mystery later.

When he'd added all the ingredients to the bowl, Master Chen took it to a small table in the center of the room and began pounding it. "This is very potent, Your Highness," he said as he worked. "Very potent indeed. Only a small amount needed." From the resulting paste, he strained some thick liquid—dark and red—through a square piece of white silk into a glass vial. Bowing his head, he thrust it toward Ying with both hands. "Here. Take it."

Ying's heart was pounding so loudly it felt like it might escape from her chest. She nearly gagged. It smelled horrid, like dead things, like betrayal. Like bitterness, like tears.

Still, if this is what it took, then she would do it.

She took a deep breath, put it to her lips, and took a sip.

It took every ounce of effort not to retch. It burned, as though fingernails were gouging her from the inside; she doubled over, the vial slipping from her grasp. Was this how replenishing one's jīng was supposed to feel?

She stretched out both arms, trying to grab hold of something. The world was tilting, her eyesight clouding. Rough hands grabbed her upper arms, and the Master, with unexpected strength, began hauling her back the way they'd come.

Ying retched again, but her stomach was empty and nothing came up. Fear gripped her. Her insides felt like they were floating, and she had the unnerving sensation of being nothing more than suspended organs encased in flesh.

By the time they reached the front entrance hall, Ying was no longer able to support her own weight. The Master dragged her to the front door and shoved her through. She collapsed onto her knees, jarring pain bursting from her joints as she hit the stone. "Did you . . . did you poison me?" she rasped, clutching her burning throat.

"No, you foolish girl," Master Chen said. "This was your doing. I did exactly as your recipe asked." He gave her an oily smile, his eyes hardening to steel. "I am, after all, your *humble* servant."

And with that, he slammed the door.

Weakly, Ying pounded on it, but of course there was no answer.

Her vision swaying, Ying spun to face the laneway and blinked. The dim lights of the lanterns were distorted in her vision, like dozens of dancing flames. Of all nights to attempt this, she'd had to choose the new moon—the darkest night of the lunar month.

Terror, along with pain, racked her entire body. Unable to stand, she crawled down the steps, bumping painfully from one to the next. She needed to get to the infirmary, and quickly. Find one of the imperial healers, since Mei Po was no longer an option.

The world was revolving, rolling and blurring like rippling water. Perhaps this was all part of the process, Ying thought desperately. The Crimson Emperor had been lauded for his knowledge. Surely a book written in his own hand would not have described a lethal concoction?

But you didn't follow the recipe, her mind whispered, accusing. *You combined it with another.*

She'd reached the bottom of the steps. The laneway cobblestones scraped her palms, bruised her knees as she crawled, inch by inch, along. Palace staff stopped and stared, some of them tittering behind their hands, some of them whispering and gesturing at her. Two women leaned against the wall, kissing; they briefly glanced up, but then returned to their embrace. None helped her; they probably thought she was a concubine who had overindulged in wine.

At this rate, she'd never make it. Her arms grew shaky, bile rose in her throat, and she tried to climb to her feet once more. The world tipped. Dark spots began to narrow her vision, and numbness spread through her limbs. Ying staggered a few paces, trying to keep her balance, before her entire world darkened and she collapsed onto the ground.

32

When she regained consciousness, Ying was bumping along the ground, the cobblestones scraping the soft flesh of her back. Her mouth was parched, her tongue thick and swollen. She licked her lips, tasting overripe peaches and the sharp, brassy tang of rust. Draught of Life . . . the same elixir that Mei Po used.

But who had given it to her?

Her head hurt. She must have hit it upon impact. Her muddled mind tried to make sense of it all.

She twisted her head. A white fox was tugging her along by the collar of her cloak. Even in the dark its snowy fur gleamed. Ying began to struggle, but the fox did not react. It just continued dragging her into a deserted laneway, before it deposited her on the dirt-crusted ground.

The fox paced back and forth, spending a long time sniffing the ground at the laneway entrance. Ying's head spun as she rolled over and pushed herself to her feet. Though small, this fox was likely dangerous. It was strong enough to drag her here and probably strong enough to attack.

The fox crouched low, silhouetted by lantern light from the

end of the lane. Ying stared, horrified, as the air surrounding began to shimmer. Its shadow grew, then the form unfolded, revealing the shape of an old, bent woman.

"Mei Po!" Ying stumbled backward until she hit a wall. Cold stone permeated her ripped-up cloak. Her heart thumped, fear flooding her veins.

"Nǐ hǎo, Ying Yue," the old woman said. Her face was in shadow, but her eyes shone slightly silver, like a cat's. Surrounding her was a wraithlike glow.

"You're a shape-shifter." Ying forced herself to breathe evenly. It shouldn't have been a surprise, really. Just like the other mirror people, Mei Po could transform into other creatures.

"Yes, Ying Yue. You know we have abilities beyond your own." Mei Po spoke without accusation or fanfare. If anything, she sounded pleasant. Conversational. As though she was discussing the weather and not her status as a mirror-world monster.

"Why have you brought me here?" Ying's voice wavered. She tried her best to tamp down her fear. "What have you done with the real Mei Po?"

The old woman chuckled. Supporting herself on a side wall, she made her way to a stack of wooden crates. After she had lowered herself onto it with some difficulty, she looked up at Ying, one hand braced on each knee. "I brought you here because you were dying. And to answer your second question, I *am* the real Mei Po." She gestured to another stack of crates. "Please, take a seat."

Ying narrowed her eyes but didn't budge. "What do you

mean, you're the real Mei Po? I know you. I felt your skin back in the infirmary. You're ice-cold." She cast her eyes over the old woman's form. "And even now, I can see you're one of them. You're glowing."

"You see it?" Mei Po nodded sagely. "Then the transformation is happening."

"What do you mean? Can't others see it?"

"No, Ying Yue," the old woman said, her puckered lips stretching into a smile. "Only you."

Ying considered this for a moment before stowing the information away to be assessed later. Right now, she was in too much danger. She needed to know what Mirror-Mei Po wanted and where the real Mei Po had gone.

"You stole the book." Ying tried to sound braver than she felt. "Why?"

"I was trying to find the answers as to how to unite the Three Treasures."

"But you hid it from me," Ying said, her tone accusatory. "You tried to stop me from finding it—"

Mei Po held up a wrinkled hand and cut Ying off. "No. I tried to stop Prince Zhang Lin's *reflection* from finding it. With him present, I could not speak frankly. For now, he still thinks I am on his side. I need him to continue believing that." She shook her head very slightly. "Though I fear he may already have guessed that my loyalties lie elsewhere. That's why I've gone into hiding."

"So, what?" Ying raised her eyebrows, incredulous. "You expect me to believe you're on *our* side?"

Mei Po looked at Ying for a moment. "Sit, child, and I will tell you my story. I am not here to hurt you. I am here to help you."

Ying hesitated. If this mirror-world Mei Po wanted to kill her, she would have done so already. But she hadn't; instead, she'd given her the Draught of Life. So while Ying still didn't trust her, at the very least, she could listen to what she had to say.

Without taking her eyes off the old woman, Ying sidled along the laneway until she was nearer the entrance, making sure she was ready to run if needed. "Speak," she said, still suspicious. "I'm listening."

Mei Po folded her hands in her lap and started to speak, her voice low and melodious. "My story starts a thousand years ago," she began. "When I met and fell in love with someone from the other side of the mirror.

"The barrier was closed back then, and though we were separated, we longed for nothing more than to be together. Remember how I told you that alchemy could weaken the barrier, if only for an instant?" Ying nodded, numb all over, and Mei Po went on.

"What I did not tell you before, Ying Yue, was that it was I who invented the alchemy. I was the first living creature to traverse the mirror gateway.

"Finally together, my lover and I met with the Crimson Emperor, and pled our case. All we wanted, I told him, was our two worlds to live in harmony. We wanted to travel freely between the two dimensions rather than being trapped in either one."

Ying swallowed. A familiar story. She thought of her own folly, falling in love with someone from the wrong side of the mirror. She suspected that, like her own, this love story did not have a happy ending.

Mei Po continued: "The emperor was . . . angry. He was a great man. But like so many 'great men,' he was also paranoid, keenly suspicious of those who might steal his power. The idea of his own reflection—someone who bore identical looks, talents, and abilities—coming and going without restriction was too much for him to bear.

"He denied my request. And to teach me a lesson, he"—Mei Po blinked, her bright eyes glistening—"tortured and killed my lover, right in front of me. He made me watch, made me listen to her screaming. He threatened to do the same with anyone else who sought to cross the mirrors again."

Ying pressed a hand to her chest, feeling sick.

The old woman went on. "Heartbroken, I escaped back into my own world and went into hiding. But not before a seed of revenge was planted in my heart. My anger . . . it consumed me. All day, every day, I thought of nothing else. I dreamed of when I could cross the gateway and wreak vengeance on the Crimson Emperor—as well as every other human.

"The other Mei Po, my doppelgänger, was the emperor's favorite consort, the only person he truly loved," Mei Po continued. "So I devised a plan. I would gather an army and breach the barrier. And I would cross into the other realm with one intention: to kill the real Mei Po."

The matchmaker shook her head, her eyes downcast. "But my small army was no match for the Crimson Emperor's trained battalions. The emperor managed to procure and wield his own brand of malevolent magic. Even with our stone-hard skin, our ability to shape-shift, and our immortality, we were quickly overpowered.

"I was, however, successful in capturing my human counterpart. And just before the emperor managed to overthrow the mirror army, I killed my doppelgänger, his one true love." Mei Po's expression hardened. "I made him watch—as he had done to me."

Ying drew in a shaky breath, feeling sick. So there really was only one Mei Po. The other died by this woman's hand.

Mei Po went on, her voice becoming low and hypnotic. "The Crimson Emperor was driven spare with rage. He forced most of my army back into the mirrors and killed the rest. Using alchemy, he sealed the barrier, then burned our only light source, the mirror-world sun. This meant we had to rely on light reflected through the mirrors, making us wholly dependent on your world to survive. His final punishment was a sanction forcing my people to mimic our human counterparts.

"Over time, our resentment grew. We watched as humans became more immoral, more selfish. We were forced to mimic the most violent and depraved acts. And thus, over millennia, my people—a once-peaceful populace—developed a taste for blood."

Mei Po finished speaking. A heavy silence fell, blanketing them both.

Finally, Ying spoke. "Why are you telling me this?" she demanded. "Why did you bring me here? To gloat about how you killed the other Mei Po? To warn me that your kind invaded once and plan to do so again?"

Mei Po shook her head slowly from side to side. "No. I want to help you."

"Help me? But you've been trying to hurt me! You convinced Prince Zhang Lin to lock me up with the mirrors, with no hope of escape!" Ying took a deep, shuddering breath. "Why help me now?"

"The prince played no part in this," Mei Po said firmly. "He thought he was protecting you."

"And the empress?"

"Was just protecting her son." Mei Po closed her eyes and frowned. "No, child. This was all my doing. I thought, in the beginning, that perhaps the sealing of the barrier would happen automatically. That putting you in the proximity of the mirrors would allow you to fulfill the prophecy while avoiding further loss of life." When her eyes reopened, they were sheened with tears. "But I realize now that I was wrong. However much I may wish it, things are not that simple."

Ying's face heated, and she grimaced. An unwelcome memory arose: dried-out corpses down in the mirror dungeons, sheathed in reams of shattered silk. "The seven lost empresses. Was that you, too?" When Mei Po had first spoken about the women, shortly after reviving Li Ming, she'd implied that it was the Shan family who had condemned them. Now it sounded as though Mei Po had been behind it all along.

There was a long stretch of silence. "The wisest among us can still make the wrong choices, Ying Yue, even when trying to make the right ones." Mei Po looked up at Ying with watery eyes.

"*Especially* when trying to make the right ones. It is no excuse, but the truth is, I was trying to stop all this from happening. I have been trying for a very, very long time."

"Why would you even want that?" Ying couldn't help sounding skeptical. Wasn't Mei Po one of the mirror people who *wanted* to attack?

"War is brewing. I want to stop it."

"Yes, but why?"

"I've lived over a thousand years, child. I've seen what war does. I've seen how many lives it destroys." For the first time ever, Mei Po sounded tired. "It's not just those who die in battle. It's also the ones left behind. The trauma amplifies through generations, and neither your people nor mine ever learn."

The ones left behind. The words echoed, resonant, around the hollows of Ying's mind. She flashed back to the battle with the fēngshēngshòu—and the creatures that crawled out of the lake—and the sheer loss of human life the prince's guards had suffered. Those soldiers weren't the first to die because of war, and they wouldn't be the last. The way—the *only* way—to stop further death was for Ying to close the gateway. And the only way to do that was for Ying to find out more.

She didn't need weapons or armies or even dragons. She needed *knowledge*.

"So it was you all this time? Out here"—Ying spread her hands, gesturing to their immediate surroundings—"and in there?"

Mei Po bowed her head.

"And you moved between the worlds using the alchemy you

described? Why? Why not just stay sealed in your world? Why interfere with ours?"

"I was starving, Ying Yue. You see, murdering my own doppelgänger interrupted my usual life cycle. I found myself unable to transmute into another form. Instead, I was stuck looking like her—a lost, untethered reflection. Without her there to reflect the sun, I had no light source. Though I aged as she would have, I became more and more frail, more transparent."

Mei Po's mouth turned down. "Believe me, child, I did not want to cross the barrier. The memories were too painful. But when my light, my energy, had almost run out, I was forced to finally slip through."

Ying rubbed her forehead with both hands. Her reflection had been telling the truth, back when they first met. The mirror folk did need the reflected light from the real world. But if they were able to live in the real world, then they need never starve. Need never rely on anyone else.

It made sense that they wanted to replace the humans. "You began spending more time in our world so you could absorb more light."

"That is correct."

"And that's why the mirror people want this world? To be stronger?"

The old woman inclined her head. "That is one reason, yes."

Ying paused, considering. "And what of the alchemy that can weaken the barrier? Do others know how to do this?" What would be the point of Ying closing the barrier if people could still use alchemy to get through?

Mei Po stared up at Ying. "No. Only me. That is one thing I *did* get right. Even though I opened the barrier at times—for myself, my army, and those seven poor women—I took care to make sure the recipe never fell into the hands of another. Instead, I called it magic and refused to share the method, angering many people in the process."

"Like the priests?" Ying asked. "The ones who are trying to depose you?"

A pause. "Yes."

The two women lapsed into silence again. Ying, her mind racing, ran through everything that Mei Po had said, trying to make sense of the weblike mess.

"So it's on me to fix all this?" Ying said eventually. She dropped her hands. "To close the barrier?"

Mei Po turned her pale blue eyes upon Ying before nodding. "Your role in all this was foretold, Ying Yue. The mirror people—my people—have been biding their time for centuries, waiting for your arrival. They have been anticipating the time when the Fish would break down the barrier for good. It's been their only source of hope. They want freedom. And they believe the only way to obtain it is to wage war."

"By killing us all and taking our places." It wasn't a question, but Mei Po nodded anyway.

"What you're saying"—Ying's voice cracked—"is that if war comes, it will be my fault? All the death, all the suffering—it'll be because of me?"

"You're the Fish that broke the barrier, that's true." Mei Po's eyes slid toward the laneway entrance. "But you're also the one that can close it." Her eyes locked back onto Ying. "My people forget this. But me? I have not forgotten. I have seen it in you. It will be you, child, who shall close the gateway once more."

Trembling, Ying wrapped her arms around her middle and paced a few steps away. Then she spun around to face Mei Po. "But I don't know how." She buried her face in her hands, willing away her tears. "I don't know how," she repeated, more to herself this time.

"You must unite the Three Treasures." Mei Po spoke softly, evenly.

Ying's voice was muffled. "I tried! I tried the alchemy. From a recipe I found in a book. But I failed. I really thought I had the answer. I felt—something strange—emanating from that book, *Immortal Alchemy*. I thought that since it was written by the Crimson Emperor himself, it was the key." Shuddering at the memory of the book's malevolent whispers, Ying added, "If I was wrong and it was not the right book . . . then why did it *speak* to me?"

Something—an indecipherable emotion—flashed fleetingly through the old woman's eyes. "The Crimson Emperor imbued his own brand of dark magic into the books he penned. Ignore it. It is nothing to you."

"Was it the wrong recipe, then?" Ying asked, her mind flailing. "Do I need a different kind of alchemy? Wàidān?" Ying strained to remember everything she'd ever learned about external alchemy.

"No, child." Mei Po used one finger to tap on Ying's chest, at her heart. "Nèidān. Alchemy within the body. You are the Fish. The vessel is within you. The transformation needs to happen inside *you*."

"But how?"

"The transformation. It unifies the Three Treasures." Mei Po checked them off on her fingers. "Jīng." One finger. "Qì." Two fingers. "And shén." She tapped her third finger. "The essences that sustain human life. Only then will you be able to control the flow of energy between the mirror world and this one."

"I don't understand—"

The old woman raised one finger. "You are the Fish, Ying," Mei Po said, then raised a second finger. "But we need the Phoenix."

Ying's impatience was growing. She'd never had a head for riddles. "Phoenix?" she said, trying to keep her voice calm. "Whereabouts would I find a phoenix?"

"Not find a phoenix." Mei Po's voice was patient. "*Be* a phoenix."

"Okay, then," Ying said. "Tell me how to be a phoenix." In fairy tales, phoenixes were made from thunder and lightning. But this didn't really help Ying.

"By uniting the Three Treasures."

Frustration expanded in Ying's chest. This was a circular conversation. Scrunching her eyes shut, she forced herself to take a deep breath. "And *how* do I unite these Three Treasures? What ingredients do I need?"

She heard, rather than saw, Mei Po struggling to her feet.

The old woman shuffled up to her, her feet dragging and causing a swishing sound in the dirt. An ice-cold hand landed on Ying's shoulder.

"Oh, child. You don't need any ingredients. The alchemy is within you, remember? The yin." Mei Po touched Ying on her chest, over her heart. "And the yang."

Ying raised her head. "*Within* me?" Her vision was blurry with tears. She'd spent so long searching for a recipe that would help her complete the transformation. But perhaps she'd gotten it all wrong. Perhaps she didn't need a recipe . . . The elixir she'd taken was supposed to have replenished her jīng. But maybe—being the Fish—the jīng was already *inside* her.

She closed her eyes, rubbing the bridge of her nose in an effort to collect herself. When her eyelids fluttered open again, Mei Po was gone. Ying rushed to the lane entrance, catching a glimpse of a bushy white tail disappearing around the corner. Mei Po's words from their first meeting echoed through her mind.

Remember who the monsters are.

Who were the monsters? It was getting more and more difficult to tell.

Ying shivered, leaning back against the cold stone wall. She was all alone again. The sun was just beginning to peek over the rooftops, limning the clouds with a rosy glow. Briefly, she wondered whether the prince was aware she had gone. *Probably not*, she concluded, a sudden bitterness slicing through her. After their fight in the imperial library, he probably wanted as little to do with her as possible.

Still, she'd best get back before anyone noticed her absence.

Drawing a deep breath, Ying took a single step into the road. Suddenly, a large hand clamped over her mouth, muffling her scream, and hauled her roughly backward.

There was a reason Mei Po had disappeared so suddenly.

Ying wasn't alone after all.

33

Ying gasped and staggered back a few steps, but her attacker had already let go. She spun, ready to defend herself, instead finding herself swept up in a tight embrace.

It was the prince. The real-life, human prince.

"Ying," he breathed. He tightened his warm arms around her and squeezed so hard she gave a squeak. "It's you. I found you. And you're all right!" He drew back, held her at arm's length, and scrutinized her face. "I was so worried. I thought that"—some unreadable emotion flared in his eyes—"you'd been taken . . . by your reflection." With the lightest of touches, he brushed the faint cut on her cheek, grimacing as though it had been he who had inflicted her wound.

"You noticed?" Ying said, slightly faintly. "You noticed I was gone?"

Absentmindedly, the prince brushed a strand of Ying's hair back and away from her face. "Of course I noticed. I shouldn't have run away like that. I shouldn't have left you alone in the library. As soon as I calmed down, I realized. But by the time I'd turned around and come back, you were gone. If you were hurt because of me, then I . . ." He trailed off, then shook his head, his expression pained. "What *happened* to you?"

"It's . . . it's a little hard to explain."

The prince gave Ying's face a searching look. "Are you feeling all right?"

"Not exactly." She shuddered. The effects—and the horror—of her experiment with alchemy still lingered.

Her near-brush with death made everything else seem so trivial. The pettiness, the fighting . . .

She'd always thought of the prince as a monster, someone who delighted in controlling her. But she'd since learned that he'd only locked her up in the misguided notion he was *protecting* her.

And it now occurred to her that Prince Zhang Lin was as much of a puppet in this game as she was. Everyone, from the reflections to his own family, had taken advantage of his honor and sense of duty. Used it against him, to manipulate him. To drive a wedge between them.

She was tired of fighting. She wanted to apologize. Wanted *him* to apologize. Vibrating with nerves, she looked up at him. Held her breath. Tried to find the words.

The prince's eyes locked on hers. "Ying, I—"

"Yes?" Ying could barely get the word out.

"I . . ." He swallowed, his tan throat rippling. Then his gaze hardened, and he turned away. "I should get back to the palace. Let them know I've found you."

The breath died in Ying's throat, and she pressed a hand to

her chest to steady herself. When she looked up, the prince was some way ahead, so she gathered her wits and followed him.

They walked in silence, the awkwardness between them growing heavy. In her mind, Ying replayed the events from the library over and over. The ladder. The kiss. The fight. The hurling of insults at one another.

But then . . . there was the way he'd been so relieved to find her. The way he'd looked at her. The way he'd brushed the hair from her eyes . . .

If she said she was sorry, she wondered, would he forgive her? If he said he was sorry, would she forgive him? Would they ever be able to undo the damage they'd inflicted on one another?

She itched to say all this but couldn't quite work out how. Just contemplating it made her cringe with embarrassment. So instead, she asked, "How did you even find me?"

He gave her a sideways glance and said nothing for a few moments, seemingly weighing his words. "When I realized you were missing, I sent out search parties to scour the palace grounds, since no one at the gates had seen you leave. But I was afraid—"

"That I'd been taken into the mirror world?" Ying said softly.

The prince gave a grim nod. "But also, I know how . . . stubborn you can be." He gave a small, apologetic smile. "Sorry."

"No, you're right," Ying said magnanimously. "So what happened then?"

"I came to the Priests' Precinct to search for you myself. After what we'd found at the library, I figured that on the off chance you hadn't been kidnapped, you'd probably be attempting some sort of alchemy." He frowned, disapproving. "It isn't the first time you've tried to do things all by yourself."

Ying opened her mouth to protest, but then closed it again. If she was being completely honest, the prince was right. She'd been so furious last night when she'd discovered he had spoken to his father without her. Now, though, she was beginning to realize she was guilty of doing the same thing.

The prince continued: "I interrogated the priests. Every single one. Master Chen finally admitted that you'd forced him to create an elixir. He said it wasn't necessarily toxic, as such, but to the uninitiated . . ." The prince shook his head. "He said he'd tried to stop you, but you ran off."

"Ran off?" A burst of anger raced up Ying's spine. "That is *not* what happened—"

"I thought you were dead, Ying," the prince continued, as though he hadn't heard her. His voice was barely audible. "I thought I was combing the streets . . . for a body." He clenched his jaw and looked away.

"Well, I'm not dead," Ying said. How could she explain what had happened? What Mei Po had told her about the alchemy she needed being inside her? She needed time—time to decipher it all, and to explain it to the prince. Time she was aware she didn't have.

They'd arrived at the inner palace gates, a two-layered structure: the outside, a shiny steel portcullis with polished-bronze decorative embellishments; the inside, a heavy, studded wooden door. These were flanked by a huge stone wall, behind which the peaked roofs of the Imperial Palace jutted imposingly into the sky.

"Before we go in," the prince said, turning to face her. "I want to say something."

Something leapt in Ying's chest. What did he have to say?

"I don't want to lock you up anymore, Ying. And I won't. But please—no more late-night excursions."

"What?" Ying said, suddenly annoyed.

"You don't need to do *everything* on your own, you know. I mean, Master Chen might have been able to help if you hadn't run off—"

Anger flared in Ying's chest. "I told you. I didn't *run off*," she snapped. "He threw me out."

The prince gave her a sharp look. "He *what*?"

Ying tried to explain. "After I took the elixir, I got dizzy. Sick. He hauled me out of the temple and slammed the door in my face." She took a deep, shuddering breath, reliving her night of terror. "He called me a 'foolish girl.'"

The prince didn't say anything for a while. He just stood there, his face reddening. When he finally spoke, his voice was a snarl. "I'm going to kill him."

"Not if I get to him first," Ying muttered.

The prince reached out, took Ying's hand, and drew her to him. Surprised, she stared at him and said, "What are you—"

"I'm sorry," he blurted out. "I'm sorry for everything. For assuming this was your fault. For locking you up. For not realizing about the mirrors—"

"I'm sorry, too," Ying interrupted, her heart drumming in her chest. "I'm sorry for . . . for poisoning you."

He gave a low chuckle. "Maybe I deserved it. Maybe . . . I was an ass."

This made Ying laugh. "You were." Then she corrected herself. "You are."

At this, he laughed, too, bringing his free hand up to toy with the collar of her cloak. The tips of his fingers brushed Ying's décolletage, and she shivered, gripped by a sudden and intense longing.

"Ying," he whispered after a protracted silence. "I need to tell you—"

But the next moment, he grabbed Ying and threw her to the ground, landing heavily on top of her.

She opened her mouth to scream, but none came, for she was winded. Before she could regain her breath, the prince lurched to one side, rolling them both over. Ying stared. Her sluggish mind tried to comprehend what she saw: an arrow quivering, upright, stuck into the ground between two cobblestones.

Right where her head had just been.

34

The prince, as quick as a whip, rolled back onto his feet. Ying, still struggling to get her bearings, traced the source of the arrows. They were flying—quickly, consecutively—from within the steel bars of the portcullis gate.

The mirror people! They were on the other side of the reflected surfaces, shooting arrows from one world into the next. Ying started scrambling to her feet. The prince gave her a hand up, and they sprinted for an alcove in the wall. Ying flattened herself, panting, against the rough stone.

They found me. The mirror people had found Ying and were trying to kill her. Unable to fit their bodies through the gate's skinny bars, they were instead shooting right through them.

Now that the gateway was open, they must want to eliminate her—stop her from being able to close the barrier again—before they attacked.

Pushing off the wall, the prince pivoted and shot an arrow at the gate. Even from this distance and half in motion, he managed to send his arrow sailing straight through a narrow bar.

Ying stifled a cry. She'd heard of the prince's archery prowess. But to see it in action was *something else.*

"Let us in!" he roared up to the guard tower, then ducked back into the alcove for safety.

A guard appeared in the open window. After a beat, he called back down. "We've been ordered to keep the gates shut, Your Highness."

An arrow zoomed past, only inches from Ying's face, and hit the wall. It clattered to the ground. The prince swore. "Let us in, goddammit!" Another arrow struck the stone near Ying's neck, and she screamed.

A second guard appeared in the tower window, conferring with the first one. A volley of arrows flew at her and the prince, hitting the wall in a spray of stony debris.

The prince yanked Ying to one side to avoid them, then shot two more arrows into the gate bars. He was deadly accurate, but still it would be no more than a deterrent, a distraction. His arrows couldn't pierce the reflections' impervious skin. What Ying and Zhang needed was to get through the gates, to the wood-reinforced and reflectionless safety beyond.

The prince now raised his bow and pointed it at the guards in the window. "Fuck your orders, man, we are being attacked! Let us in, or I swear to the gods I will put arrows through your heads!" His voice pitched progressively higher, progressively louder, until it was a bellow. "The princess is here, alive! Let us in! I've found the princess!"

One guard disappeared. Moments later, the gate began to creak upward. Ying had never noticed how slowly it opened. It was excruciating to watch as the seconds dribbled by. She turned her thoughts inward and whispered a silent prayer. *Please, gods, let us make it,* she thought. *Please. I need more time to close the barrier. I haven't had enough time.*

The tiniest crack appeared in the bottom of the gate. The prince darted back to Ying, grabbed her hand, and dragged her forward. Together, they bolted for the small opening, narrowly avoiding another volley of arrows. One caught a flap of Ying's cloak as she ran, tearing it. She stumbled and fell.

"Quick." The prince hauled Ying to her feet and half-pushed her toward the gate. They sprinted for the opening, not looking back until they were safely through. Four guards descended upon them, checking their identities, immediately backing off when they confirmed that it was the prince. Another group of guards hurried to close the gate, fastening it with several huge wooden bolts. Luckily, this side of the gates bore no reflective bronze adornments, nor steel bars.

Within the courtyard, a troop of palace guards stood at attention, their scaled armor gleaming reddish in the rising sun. Among them, other palace employees had gathered, drawn by the commotion. Multiple braziers had been lit, burning herbs designed to ward off evil spirits. Smoke rolled over the crowd, and wisps of it hung, suspended.

The prince rounded on one of the guards. "Who ordered that the gates be fastened?" he spat. "You saw us out there! You saw us nearly get killed!"

"Pardon, Your Highness," the guard said, cringing. "With the princess missing, we were told to bar the gates, Your Highness, and let nobody in—"

The prince roared. "By WHOM?"

The guard gulped, his throat bobbing. "By His Holy Highness Emperor Shan, Your Highness."

Ying's stomach lurched. After yesterday's fight at the lake, where they had battled the fēngshēngshòu, Emperor Shan must have ordered the guards to shut the gates. Ying remembered what Mei Po had said of the emperor: that he'd always chosen to believe his advisors who said the prophecy was a lie.

Did the emperor still believe this fallacy? Did he still think the threat was coming from the outside rather than from every reflective surface—even those within the palace?

The prince shook, his face turning puce, the vein on his forehead popping. Although his anger was not directed at her, Ying quaked, her insides clenching. The prince's fury was so forceful it had almost turned corporeal. What was he going to do?

After several drawn-out seconds, he pulled a face and turned away. "Get out of here," he spat at the guard, unmasked disgust in his voice. The man scurried away.

The crowd shuffled and parted, dropping to their knees as Ying and the prince pushed past. Ying ignored them. She scanned the mob looking for familiar faces, looking for—

"Ying!" Someone slammed into her. Arms wound around her tightly, and she screwed up her eyes as her face was covered in kisses. Around them, the crowd shuffled back, giving them space, letting the people through who needed to be there.

"Mā." A weight uncurled and lifted off Ying's chest. "Bàba," she said, turning to hug her father. "You're still here? I thought you'd left days ago—"

"We were about to." Ying's mother wiped away a tear. "After

your wedding, we were told to leave. Told to not contact you again. But then we heard you'd disappeared, and—" She turned to the prince. "Thank you. Thank you. Thank you for saving our daughter."

The prince gave Ying's mother a small bow. "It is the least I could do, Lady Jiang," he said in a quiet, measured voice. His gaze flicked to Ying. "She has, after all, saved me. Many times." His eyes were abnormally bright, with a look that lit Ying's insides on fire.

Lady Jiang gave a sniff and raised her tear-filled eyes. "Thank you anyway, Your Royal Highness."

The prince tore his gaze from Ying, focusing back on Ying's parents. "Please, call me Zhang Lin."

Lord Jiang spoke up for the first time. "We'll call you son. You are family now." Immediately, Ying's father seemed to regret his words. He raised his hands. "Unless you think it impertinent, Your Royal—"

The prince reached out and clasped Lord Jiang's shoulder. "Not at all. We *are* family." He paused, hesitating for a second. "Father."

Ying's father placed his free hand on top of the prince's. They stood there silently, eyes glistening.

Lady Jiang let out another sob, clasping Ying tighter. "Where did you go, Yiyi? What happened to you?"

Ying didn't want to go into too much detail about her brush with death for fear of frightening her mother further. But she explained, as quickly as she could, about the mirror people, the opening of the mirror gateway, and the breakdown of the

Crimson Emperor's curse. "War is almost upon us, Mā," she said. "This is just the beginning."

"War?" Lady Jiang exclaimed, placing a hand on her chest. "Gods save us!"

"Yes, Mā, war." Ying threw a sidelong glance at the prince, a dark, silent undercurrent of dread passing between them. It seemed that Emperor Shan didn't yet know the gravity of the situation, or the fact that the mirror people were threatening to invade. Sure, the prince had already tried to petition the emperor once, but he'd been drunk and in no fit state to listen. And Ying's quest to close the barrier on her own had proven fruitless.

Perhaps, Ying thought, despite her reservations, they ought to go see the emperor again—together.

Ying's father had clearly had the same idea. "It's time, son," he said, clapping Prince Zhang Lin on the shoulder, "to go and see your father."

35

The prince called an emergency meeting with his parents and his generals to discuss the impending war. He was, however, considerate enough to give Ying time to clean up. After almost dying—twice—and a night spent on the streets, she likely looked as feral as she felt.

Hours later, Ying had scrubbed away the street scum that was embedded in her skin, combed out her long hair until it shone like lacquer, and braided her black tresses into an intricate updo. And she'd shoved her complicated feelings for the prince into a closed-off box; a box she planned to forget about until after she'd won the war.

Ying walked into the throne room, her head high, her face a mask of calm indifference. She was dressed in one of her most ornamental outfits, a gown of sky-blue silk. On the skirt was her family emblem: two leaping carp, embroidered in gold thread.

It was a hànfú befitting a Jiang princess, a daughter of the river, a girl who rode dragons. If Ying had learned anything by now, it was that she had a part to play. And this was it. Right now, she looked every bit the princess she had been foretold to be.

The prince was standing at ease, deep in conversation with one of his generals. He, too, had cleaned up and was dressed in ceremonial military regalia: golden-scaled armor, a golden sword, and a pitch-black velvet cloak embroidered with the Shan emblem draped across his shoulders. When he caught sight of her, his posture straightened and he stared. The general dropped into a deep bow in a show of servitude. Ying returned the gesture, and the man took his place behind her.

Ying offered her hand to the prince. He took it and pressed it to his lips, his eyes not leaving hers.

"Husband," Ying said, inclining her head.

A muscle jumped in his jaw. "Wife," he responded. His grip tightened on her hand.

A herald signaled the emperor and empress's arrival, and Ying and the prince turned to face forward. This being only the second time that Ying had met her in-laws, she was surprised to see them enter this meeting with only nine iron-clad guards, one ahead and eight behind. The group ascended the steps to the dais on which the thrones sat, while Ying, the prince, the officials, and the soldiers prostrated themselves on the floor.

The emperor and empress settled themselves onto their thrones, arranging their robes' reams of yellow fabric across their knees. Their headdresses glittered with the reflected light from hundreds of tiny jewels.

When the prince and Ying had finished making their kowtows, they rose to their feet.

"You wished to address me, Zhang Lin?" the emperor said,

bracing himself on the arm of his chair. His throne was gold-framed, with crimson velvet cushions and intricate carvings down each leg. Its back was shaped like a dragon's head, which jutted out over the top. The dragon's mouth was open, midroar, a long, spiked tongue protruding outward. Off to one side, on a lower platform, sat the empress's throne, less ornate and topped with a carved phoenix. The thrones were embedded with precious stones: jade, hematite, lánggān, lapis, and several others that Ying did not recognize.

The entire room was bedecked in shades of red and gold. The steps leading up to the dais were marble, with plush crimson carpet running up the center. Ying had never seen such lavish finery gathered in one place.

The prince stepped forward. "Imperial Majesty," he said, bowing deeply. "I thank the Son of Heaven for gracing me with his audience and hope that now is a more opportune time to discuss . . . recent events. It is a matter of the utmost urgency."

Ying wondered at the formality. While she knew that no one was allowed to address the emperor in a familiar fashion, even his own son, it was still unnerving to see the prince speak to his blood kin in such a cold, detached way.

"What is it?" the emperor snapped, leaning his forehead on one hand. "And keep it short. I have a headache." With his other hand, he beckoned a servant.

The servant boy ran up the steps holding an ornate bronze chalice—the same one, Ying noted, from the tea ceremony. *The same one she'd seen in the storeroom with Master Chen.*

A flicker of unease passed through Ying at the sight of the chalice, a thrill of suspicion she couldn't yet identify.

With his head lowered, the boy presented the cup to the emperor. Emperor Shan snatched it from him and guzzled the entire contents. Once done, he smacked his lips and flung the cup to the ground. The boy picked it up and backed down the steps, bowing the whole way.

With a degree of forbearance suggesting he'd done it many times before, the prince waited until this entire display was over before continuing. "It is well known by now, Imperial Majesty, that we fought a battle yesterday. On the shores of the Lake of Tranquility. I wish to give an update on what has happened since." The prince paused. "Considering . . . we could not speak properly last night."

The emperor's beard twitched, and he narrowed his eyes. "Go on."

Straightening, the prince continued: "Yesterday was not just a random attack. Yesterday was just the beginning. We are being invaded."

The emperor frowned and leaned forward, his hands on the armrests of his throne. "Invaded? Invaded by whom?"

Ying and the prince exchanged a look. Then the prince faced his father again. "Invaded by monsters from the other side of the mirrors."

The room fell silent. Finally, the emperor leaned back on his cushions.

"Impossible!" he said. "The gateway was closed. The Crimson Emperor saw to that."

The prince raised his head and looked squarely at his father. "It is reopened, Imperial Majesty." He clicked his fingers, and six servants hurried in, carrying the enormous body of a dead áoyīn between them. They staggered to the base of the steps and lowered the corpse to the ground. Gesturing at it, the prince said, "Here is the evidence. One of the creatures from the mirror world."

Indoors, the áoyīn looked hazy, almost translucent. Its four horns and strawlike fur glowed a sickly green.

The prince took a step forward and gestured to the beast. "War is coming. We must fight!"

Murmurs swept around the room. The emperor stared at the corpse for several seconds before turning to address his advisor. "Master Chen," he said. "What say the qiú qiān?"

At the mention of Truth Master Chen, the prince's eyes turned pitch-black with hatred. He clenched his fists hard. Ying's heart began to thump. It was so loud she wondered if the emperor could hear it.

From his position, concealed in the crowd at the back of the room, the master shuffled forward, clutching the cylinder of divination sticks to his chest. Ying and the prince watched—Zhang's eyes narrowed, the muscle in his jaw ticking—as the old man made his way to the front.

Out of one of his crimson sleeves, Master Chen produced a small, flat bowl. The same bowl that he'd mixed Ying's alchemical elixir in. This he placed on the bottom of the marble steps. He reached into another pocket, pulled out some powder, and threw it into the dish.

Sparks flew where the powder landed. A smell of incense spread through the room, smoke curling from the concave surface. The master swirled the cylinder of sticks around the smoke column three times, then tipped the cylinder upside down. One stick fell out.

He picked it up, frowning at it.

"I do not see anything to suggest a breach, Holy Highness. The Crimson Emperor's seal is as strong as ever."

"No." The prince spun to face the master, his face reddening. His hand shot out and grabbed the master's collar, dragging upward until the old man spluttered. "You're wrong! You don't know what you're talking about, you . . . yŏngyī!" There was a collective intake of breath. It was blasphemy to call an imperial master a charlatan.

The emperor gave a small wave of his hand, and a dozen guards grabbed the prince, hauled him off the master, and restrained him. With an angry huff, the prince shoved the guards off him and straightened his now-rumpled clothes.

"Enough." The emperor's voice was a warning.

"See this?" The prince waved a hand at the dead áoyīn. "No one can see this and still question my words. The evidence is right here—"

"I see an ox," the emperor said, his voice cold. "With a few extra horns. That is hardly evidence."

Ying's stomach dropped. To her, the beast looked strange, unearthly, with its sickly greenish glow. But she knew that to everyone else, its skin would look completely normal.

"No ox in this world looks like this!" the prince said. "It's an abomination!"

The master raised a withered hand toward the emperor. He looked as if he was supplicating, but his words held a steel edge when he spoke: "Some animals can be born mutated in nature, Holy Highness. It was possibly just an aberration of its kind. Or perhaps the whole herd was diseased, or rabid, and that is why they attacked our men." Turning away from Emperor Shan, Master Chen gave Ying and the prince a sly, unctuous smile.

Rage uncoiled in Ying's belly like a snake. Her fingers twitched; it took every ounce of self-control not to lunge at the master's neck.

"What about the fight yesterday?" The prince gesticulated more wildly. "There were *witnesses*! My soldiers fought creatures that look like blue-and-black leopards, creatures that came from the mirror world. Creatures that didn't die, but instead were revived by the wind..."

"*Your* soldiers, Zhang Lin." Master Chen's voice was cold. "Your soldiers. Of course they would corroborate your story. After all, we know the ... *extent* of their loyalty to *you*."

The prince reddened, his jaw working, before he visibly swallowed and turned away. He turned to the crowd. "Surely some of *you* have noticed something? Haven't you seen inconsistencies in your reflections? In the mirror? I have. My reflection isn't even there anymore. It's up and left me. Pretty soon, all of yours will, too, because they'll be getting together *plotting our demise*."

"Enough!" bellowed the emperor.

The prince whirled back around, drawing himself to his full and formidable height. "Dozens of my men were killed, Imperial Majesty, fighting a horde of undead monsters on the lake. The *princess* and I almost died right outside the gates! And more will die if we don't act soon." His voice rose to a resounding boom, and he jabbed a finger toward the master. "We will *all* die because of that... that quack!"

The emperor glowered at the prince. His tone was cold. "The gods have spoken. The barrier is intact. It would serve you well to remember your place, son." Father and son glared at each other, each unwilling to back down.

Ying had watched the exchange with an increasing sense of despair. Each of the emperor's denials hit her like a wave; she was drowning, drowning in a desolate sea. And for some reason—perhaps the way she'd asserted her rank upon their first meeting—Master Chen seemed determined to sabotage both her and the prince. She was fast learning that a man's pride is a fragile thing, prone to crumbling in the face of the most minor challenge.

How could she convince Emperor Shan?

"Please, Imperial Majesty," she ventured, her voice uncertain. Then she raised her chin and stepped forward, in line with her husband. "Please," she repeated louder.

Beside her, the prince visibly flinched. Everyone fell silent. It was not customary for a subservient to address the emperor without being called upon.

The emperor squinted down at Ying. "What?"

Ying dropped to her knees and stared at the floor. "Holy

Highness, Prince Zhang Lin is right. The barrier is breached. It was . . ." She drew in a breath. "It was I who opened it."

"*You?*" the emperor asked, blinking.

"I . . ." Ying swallowed, then steeled herself. She raised her eyes to meet Emperor Shan's. "Yes. I can demonstrate."

The emperor swelled like a bullfrog. The veins stood out on his neck, looking as if they might burst. Beside him, the empress shifted in her seat. This time, it was she who called over the servant boy with the bronze chalice, who took her husband's cup and handed it to him.

The emperor took another swig; a strange look of calm washed over his face. Ying narrowed her eyes, her gaze flicking between the emperor and Master Chen. What was in the chalice? What was Master Chen brewing to affect the emperor so?

Emperor Shan leaned back in his throne and exhaled. "Proceed" was all he said.

Ying rose to her feet. She cast her eyes around the room, spying a polished bronze mirror mounted on the wall. On trembling legs, she walked over to it, took a deep breath, and stuck her arm right through.

A whisper rushed around the room. Ying withdrew her arm, then turned to face the crowd. "See?" She gestured to the mirror's surface. "I can go right through it. We all can." She turned back toward the emperor. "And it can be seen, Holy Highness, that I have no reflection."

The emperor's eyebrows bunched up. "Why would you do such a thing? Open the gateway?"

"Please." Ying flushed and averted her gaze. "It was not intentional, I swear it. It was a prophecy. According to the prophecy, I am the Fish."

"The prophecy? That matchmaker's garbage?"

Ying raised her chin. "Yes. But it's not garbage. It's true."

The emperor's eyes flicked to the master. "Chen! Did you know about this?"

"No, Holy Highness," the master replied, cringing.

The emperor's mouth twisted, and he stroked his goatee. Then he gave a small nod. "Daughter, you have given me much to think about. I will consult with my advisors and deliver my answer tomorrow."

"We don't have until tomorrow," the prince muttered.

The emperor's eyes snapped to his son. "You don't have a choice." He struggled to his feet, his corpulent frame rendering him slow. "Now go—before I tie you to some stones and throw *you* in the lake."

The prince opened his mouth as though about to retort. But he seemed to think better of it. Instead, he threw his cape back off his shoulders and stormed from the room.

Ying made a quick bow, then scurried after him. It took a bit of running to catch up with his long strides, but she soon fell into step beside him.

His face was a storm cloud, his eyebrows drawn down over thunderous eyes. As they walked, Ying reached out to touch him. He shrugged her hand away. A few paces later, he stopped and turned to face her.

"I'm sorry," he said, his expression softening. "I'm not mad at you, just at my cowardly father. What you did back there, it was—"

"Foolish?"

"No, brave." The prince's mouth twitched, and he relented. "Maybe a little foolish."

Ying smiled in spite of herself. But then she grew grave. "I'm sorry about your father. That he didn't believe you."

"I shouldn't have expected anything different." The prince shrugged, but Ying saw how his shoulders slumped. "He's never been one to listen to me."

Ying placed a hand on his arm, and he tensed. But he didn't move away. "Has it always been so?"

"Not always." A distant look came into the prince's eyes but it quickly disappeared. "I had a brother once, you know."

Ying hesitated, thrown by the prince's abrupt change in subject. "I heard," she said cautiously. "Didn't he die in battle?"

The prince shook his head. "No. That was just what the palace wanted people to think."

"What happened to him?"

"You have to understand what it was like, Ying." The prince spoke with urgency, as though he was trying to convey something important. "My brother was only a year older than me. He was better than me in every way. At least according to my father." Bitterness had crept into the prince's tone.

"My father decided that my brother, as the heir, should get all the attention. He was given the best of everything. The best education, the best fight masters, the best rooms in the palace. My father was so possessive of my brother that he even turned him against my mother. And because I was just a second son, my father shunted me into the army. Had me trained to be a warrior, to be a leader of common men." A pained expression crossed the prince's face like a shadow. "He used to . . . punish me. Physically. Or get his guards to do it. Said it was to 'toughen me up.' He claims now he doesn't remember all the details. And maybe—maybe it's true. His memory *is* failing. But mine isn't. I *do* remember, Ying. I do."

Ying felt suffocated, as if she couldn't breathe. "Then what happened?"

The prince's face crumpled. "I killed him. I killed my brother. My father never forgave me."

Ying's heart stuttered. "You . . . you what?"

Glancing at Ying's face, the prince backtracked. "No, no, not like that. Not directly. It was one of my soldiers. I resented the favoritism my father showed my brother. I'd often complain about it. Only to my closest friends, mind you. Just the ones who fought alongside me, the ones I knew were loyal to me. The ones I trusted with my life.

"The problem was," the prince continued grimly, "they were *too* loyal. They felt the injustice of my father's mistreatment of me as keenly as I did. So one night, a group of my soldiers slipped into the palace under cover of darkness and murdered my brother. They thought they were avenging me, fulfilling my desires. They were all caught and executed, of course. They believed they were sacrificing themselves for my cause."

Ying could barely hide the tremor in her voice. "And was it your cause?"

The prince shook his head. "No. For all my complaining, I was just a kid. Young. Hotheaded. Jealous. Reckless. Sometimes, when I was drinking, I joked about taking my brother's place. But I never really meant it." His voice cracked. "I did love my brother. I did."

The prince's shoulders sagged further. Ying felt the weight of his guilt hanging heavy in the air.

Suddenly, she could see with clarity his reaction to the Mirror Prince. To a person he perceived as bettering him. Someone who was like him in every way, except in personality. And Ying had so casually, so easily, chosen the Mirror Prince over him.

Now, in retrospect, she understood the violence of his reaction. Her heart shattered for the boy he'd been, the boy who'd grown up in his brother's shadow and carried the weight of guilt for his death. And she wished for nothing more than the ability to turn back time and take back every callous word she'd ever uttered.

"It wasn't your fault," she said, her hand tightening around his forearm. But the prince didn't respond. Silence stretched between them.

The prince passed a hand over his face and shook his head. He broke the silence. "I guess we wait for my father's answer, then," he said, blinking and looking away. "Hopefully, he makes the right decision."

To Ying, it didn't sound as if the emperor would make the

right decision. Was it wise to put the fate of the entire empire, the fate of the entire world, in the hands of such a man? One who seemed to put entirely too much trust in the opinion of a corrupt priest?

She placed one hand on the prince's cheek and turned him to face her. "Or we could fight," she said.

He gave Ying a penetrating look. "Fight?"

She nodded. "We could fight with or without your father's support. According to"—she braced herself before continuing—"the Mirror Prince, we have until the fifteenth day of the lunar month. There's still time for us to assemble a small army. You still have soldiers who will take your command, right?"

The prince took her small hand from his cheek and encircled it with his large one. He looked thoughtful for a second, his thumb chafing dull circles across her knuckles.

"Yes," he said slowly, enunciating the words carefully. "Fewer after yesterday's battle, but I'd say there'd be two thousand or so still loyal to me."

"And dragons," Ying added.

"Yes," the prince said, his eyes smoldering with that deep fire, his lips curving up in the shadow of a smile. "And dragons."

The way he was looking at her made Ying's breath catch. Once again, she was struck by how identical he looked to the Mirror Prince, yet how different things felt. It wasn't just the physical differences, like how his skin burned under her hand, or how the coarse hair felt on his forearm. It was also his temperament. While this prince occasionally transformed himself with the slightest hint of a smile, overall, his disposition was taciturn. Stern. The only time she'd seen him completely unguarded was that afternoon on the mountain, away from society, when they'd feasted on loquats and he'd cleaned her wounds.

On the other hand, the Mirror Prince had been quick to laugh, quick to smile, quick to profess his undying love. The prince who had seemed so good, so wholesome, had proven anything but. Ying still couldn't believe she'd gotten him so wrong.

Perhaps she'd been wrong about the real prince, too.

They stood close to one another, so close, their eyes locked. Ying wondered if he could hear her heartbeat, it was so loud in her ears. But her ponderings were interrupted by someone clearing his throat. A guard.

The prince's shoulders stiffened. "What?" he snapped, his gaze still on Ying. But gone was the warmth that had flared in his eyes. Instead, his face had settled into its usual grim expression—the mask of the prince. "Spit it out."

"Your presence is requested at the tower, Your Royal Highness," the guard said in a high, reedy voice.

"Which tower?" The prince still hadn't moved. "Tell me. I'll be there shortly."

"Not *your* presence, Your Royal Highness," the guard replied. Ying raised her head. The man grinned, his cruel eyes cold and calculating, and pointed at Ying. "Hers."

Every single muscle in Ying's body seized, a rabbit cornered by a fox. The prince straightened and turned around slowly. "What do you mean, *hers*?" His eyes narrowed, his voice low, dangerous, deceptively calm.

The guard unrolled a scroll. "On the orders of His Holy Highness, Son of Heaven, Lord of the Kingdom for Ten Thousand Years," the guard read out, his fleshy lips spreading in a smile, "Princess Shan Ying Yue is to be arrested . . . for treason."

36

Before she could protest, Ying was collared by a group of guards, who swept her away from the prince. Zhang tried to launch himself after her, but a dozen more armored guards descended, restraining him. He roared, managing to throw a few off. But he was outnumbered. Horror-struck, he watched as Ying was hauled, still struggling, around a corner.

The guards half dragged, half carried Ying up a stone staircase to the East tower, the one directly opposite Mei Po's. They threw her into the small, circular room at the top. She landed on her hands and knees and heard the door slam shut behind her.

She flew to it, jiggling the handle, but it was locked.

Another locked door.

The room was derelict, with just a narrow bed, a cracked washbasin, and an empty bucket. She searched thoroughly but came up empty: no mirrors, no sources of water, no glass, no metal. Not a single reflective surface had been left in the room. The guards had done their job well. Even the windows had been smashed.

She would have liked to think it was for her protection, to

prevent mirror monsters from getting in. But more likely, it was to stop her getting out.

Ying went to one of the windows and leaned over the sill, her fingers gripping the rough wood. Her jaw clenched so hard she almost ground her teeth to dust. But she couldn't cry. Not yet. She was too angry.

From the window, she had a view of the cobblestone courtyard, in which carpenters were erecting a large wooden structure. Beyond that, past the internal wall, lay the Lake of Tranquility. And beyond that, in the distance, were the mountain ranges that ringed Jinshan province. Jinghu Dao's tallest mountain, Mount Zhixiang, spiked higher than the rest.

She returned her attention to the scene below. The carpenters were busily nailing up some scaffolding. Ying watched them for some time, rehashing the day's events in her mind and growing steadily more irate.

It was unclear to Ying what they were supposed to be building. Perhaps it was a watchtower, to scan for invading armies. She hoped so. Even if the emperor didn't believe the magnitude of their peril, she still retained hope he wished to be prepared.

They'd find out the truth soon enough, for better or worse.

Ying stood motionless for so long she became stiff. Her hands were numb, partially from the cold and partially from gripping the sill. She didn't want to think about why she was up here, trapped in a tower, nor what might happen to her on the morrow. Instead, she focused on the here and now. Dusk was falling, and the temperature was dropping fast.

She jumped when she heard a sound behind her. A small window in the door slid open, and a guard poked a rough wooden tumbler through. *Water,* Ying thought, suddenly thirsty. But when she went to grab it, she backed away, repulsed.

It wasn't water. Instead, the cup contained a measure of thick, dark red liquid. The scent emanating from it smelled like decay.

The royal family had a sick sense of humor: they'd given her the same elixir she'd ordered Master Chen to make.

She held out as long as she could. But after a day and a half, she had still not been given water, and rabid thirst had taken hold. Whether the Shans intended to torture her by making her drink poison—or whether they wanted her to gain her powers while she was imprisoned so they could use her to close the mirrors—she could not say.

Perhaps it was a combination of both.

By the end of night two, she'd been forced to pinch her nose and ingest a small swallow of the foul liquid.

It made her woozy, or woozier than she already was from the effects of dehydration. It took all her willpower not to chug the whole thing. She pushed it far into a dark corner, under her narrow bed, to keep from giving in.

At the end of night three, she was shivering on the narrow bed, clutching the elixir to her chest. Having rationed it, ingesting only a single mouthful at a time—once at dusk and once at dawn—she tossed and turned, awaiting sunrise. If she weren't so thirsty, she might have laughed at the irony. She'd literally handed Master Chen the very recipe he was now using to destroy her.

Her head was foggy, thick with delirium, focused on only one thing: the open window, where she'd see the first sign of sunrise. As soon as dawn light dusted the distant mountains, it was her signal to have a drink. It was close, but not quite there yet. The sickle-shaped moon still floated close to the horizon.

There came a soft knock at the door. Too weak to investigate, Ying squinted at the thin lines she'd scratched in the wall with her nail. If her blurry vision was not deceiving her, it was nine days until the war.

So who would bother coming by *now*?

"Ying, it's me." A low voice. The prince's voice.

She stumbled to the door and crouched down. Through the keyhole, she whispered, "You came!" Her tongue felt thick, too large for her mouth. "What's happening?" What had she missed while she was locked in the tower, so focused on her thirst she thought of almost nothing else?

"Nothing's happened yet. But I've been secretly alerting my men." Ying sighed a relieved breath as the prince went on: "Are you okay?"

Ying shivered. "I'm . . . not great. I'm cold and thirsty." *And poisoned*, she added internally. "I've no water or mirrors, so I can't get out."

She heard the prince exhale. "Nothing can get in, then. That's good."

Ying swallowed, the movement painful. She tried to form coherent thoughts, but they kept petering out to nothing. "It's not good. They've given me nothing to eat or drink. All I have is an elixir—"

"What?" There was a long pause before the prince spoke again. "An elixir? Why? Is it a healing draught?"

"No. It makes me sick." Ying wanted to elaborate; wanted to tell him his family were trying to poison her, but it seemed like too much effort. "It's . . . alchemy."

The prince made a noise of disgust, then said, "Wait." There was a rustling, then a rip, and the prince pushed something under the door. "It's not much, but it's clean."

It was a piece of cloth, torn from his hànfú. He must have soaked it with water from his water bladder. Ying sucked on it ravenously until it was bone dry, then pushed it back under the door.

"Slowly, now," the prince warned, but he soaked it again several times, Ying sucking it dry each time.

"I—I'm working on a way to get you out, I promise," he said once Ying had indicated she'd had enough.

"Yes," Ying said, clutching her forehead. For the first time in days, the fog had lessened just slightly. "So I can get out and help you fight."

"Not to fight, Ying. We can't risk you fighting." The prince's voice was stern.

Ying bristled, sudden fury flashing through her sluggish veins. "If you think I'm going to sit back and watch you risk everything because of me, then—"

"Not because of you. It won't be because of you. I'll be risking myself for my nation—my people. And to give you time to learn how to close the barrier. There's a difference."

Ying huffed. "For you, maybe."

"Let's not argue, Ying," the prince said after a pause. "We don't have much time left, and . . . I don't want to spend it arguing."

A pit opened in Ying's stomach. Did he mean how much time they had left talking through the keyhole tonight?

Or how much time they had left . . . ever?

Either way, he was right. "I don't want to argue either. I know you're trying. And you're only worried because—"

"Because I care," the prince cut in. "Ying, please, you have to believe me. What I told you earlier is the truth. Mei Po did tell me you'd be attacked. But she didn't say *anything* about the mirrors. If I'd had any idea . . ." He trailed off.

"I know," Ying said, pressing up against the door. "I believe you."

The prince was silent for a long while. When he spoke again, he sounded choked. "It's such a relief to hear you say that. If I die in battle"—he took a deep breath—"I'll die knowing that you've forgiven me."

Die? Why was he saying such a thing? "I've seen you fight." Ying's voice cracked. "You *won't* die."

"I don't know. You saw how ferocious those monsters were. And the reflections—you said they can't be cut. Or shot. We've armed ourselves with sticks and clubs, but . . ."

He didn't voice what they both feared: that neither of them

knew what the future held. That he might die fighting a war against his father's wishes. Or that *she* might wither away to dust in this tower, condemned for a crime she didn't commit. Like one of those poor empresses shackled in the dungeons of the mirror world.

That this might be the last time they ever spoke, trapped on different sides of a locked prison door.

She spread her palm out on the splintered wood. "I wish you—you didn't have to do this. It'd be better for you if I'd never come here. If we were never . . . betrothed."

"Don't say that. I—"

"Why not?" Ying's voice rose. "It's the truth. After all, neither of us chose this." And as she said the words, Ying realized how much they stung. The idea that the prince had been forced to accept her against his will had always irked her, even if she didn't want to admit it. "You didn't choose this."

There was another long pause, so long that Ying began to wonder if he was still even there. "Ying, trust me," the prince said eventually. "If I knew you then as I do now, I would have chosen you. A thousand times over. Even though it's wrong."

"What do you mean, wrong?" Ying asked, confused by his contradictory words.

"It's wrong because"—he paused—"because it seems like you're not safe with me. Something's happened, and I don't fully understand what. But when you and I were betrothed, well, it seems like we set something in motion, that's all. Being with me seems to put you in danger."

"No, Zhang," Ying said. She was pressed up against the door, the wood against her cheek, beneath her hand. She couldn't get any closer if she tried. "I'm the Fish. I'm putting *you* in danger."

Silence for a moment. Then he spoke. "I don't care."

Ying closed her eyes. "It's too late to dwell on such things." She pictured the prince sitting on the floor, leaning against the door on the other side.

"It's not too late." His tone was forceful, as if he was trying to convince himself. "We will fight. And we'll win."

Ying leaned her forehead on the door. Her fingers traced the grain of the wood. "I'm going to hold you to those vows, you know."

A low chuckle came through the keyhole. Then it stopped, abruptly. "Speaking of vows." Something scraped along the floor. "Will you . . . will you take this back?"

He had slid something under the door: Ying's betrothal bangle. Her heart fractured into a million pieces. She had been so angry when she'd yanked it off after their fight in the temple. He must have found it abandoned on top of her dresser after she'd gone.

She held her breath as she picked it up and slid it onto her wrist. Her voice was a whisper: "Of course."

From the other side of the door came a sigh of relief. "Now, when the time comes," the prince said, "I can happily ride out to battle. Even if I am facing death out there, I'll know that you're up here, safe. And that maybe . . . just maybe . . . I can have a second chance."

Ying's eyes stung, but she was still too dehydrated to cry. She rubbed at her lids—they felt gritty, as though sand was trapped beneath.

For a long stretch of time, neither of them spoke. Ying pressed herself against the door, wishing she had magic that could make it dematerialize. Every breath she took seemed to take her closer to the breaking dawn and further from the prince.

Eventually, she cast her eyes around the dim, drab room. One question had plagued her for days. "Why do they even have me up here, anyway? Why not the dungeons?" Memories of her stint in the mirror world's dungeons rose unbidden in her mind.

The prince didn't answer immediately. "Ying," he said, his voice strained, "you're safe here. But there's something you need to know, about my family and how they deal with treason. I'll do everything in my power to stop it, but I don't know if I can."

Ying pushed away from the door and sat upright, worried now. "What? Stop what? What do you mean, Zhang?"

"There's a reason they've put you up here with a view over the courtyard. Don't look out the window, no matter what you hear. It's very important, you hear me? Don't look out the window, because—"

He stopped short.

"Because what?"

"Shit! Someone's coming!" he said, and he was gone.

Less than a minute later, there was pounding at the door. "Princess Ying! Your Highness. Wake up!"

Ying trembled at the voice. It was unfamiliar, deep—probably a guard. She waited a while to make it seem as though she had been sleeping, hoping the prince had managed to slip away. Then she called out, feigning fatigue. "Yes?" she said. "Who's there?"

The door burst open, and in marched a group of iron-clad guards. Ying took a couple of steps back and clenched her fists. The first guard bowed, then made an announcement.

"Your Highness, allow me to introduce Her Holy Highness, Her Imperial Majesty. . . ."

Ying couldn't concentrate on the rest of the guard's speech. Her heart started racing, and blood pulsed in her ears.

Her visitor pushed through the wall of guards to stand in front of her.

"Hello, Ying Yue," the visitor said.

Ying dropped to her knees.

It was the empress.

37

The empress didn't say anything at first. She just flicked a hand, a sign for the guards to leave. Ying knelt, staring at the floor, while the guards trudged out. Her knees hurt, raw against the unsealed tower floor. The glow of first light trickled through the eastern window, highlighting knots and whorls in the wood. An ant tottered over the uneven surface, a broken grain of rice upon its back.

"Rise, Princess," the empress said. "Come. Talk with me."

Ying clambered to her feet. Dread clawed at her stomach. She and the empress had never spoken. Not directly, at least.

She couldn't fathom the reason behind the visit. This was the woman who'd ordered that Ying be sacrificed to the mirrors. Had she come to follow through on her plans? Was she the one who'd sent Ying the elixir—and if so, why? To poison her? To punish her? As an experiment?

The empress seated herself on the narrow bed and patted the mattress next to her, gesturing for Ying to sit. She was dressed in a canary-yellow hànfú, with red embroidery adorning each sleeve. Her black hair, with its distinctive slate-gray streak, was scraped back into a high bun that perched birdlike atop her head.

In the muted light of the budding dawn, the empress's skin positively glowed. She seemed too large for the small room.

Since by status, the empress was Ying's superior, she felt compelled to comply. Stiffly, she walked over to the bed and perched on the edge, her hands folded in her lap.

"I am sorry," the empress said, "for my husband's behavior the other day. I came here to reassure you that unlike the emperor, I do believe you."

Ying tried, perhaps unsuccessfully, to hide her shock. First, wives never, *ever* spoke ill of their husbands. This was especially true for royalty. The emperor was considered a deity, a direct line to the gods. Thus, the empress was married to Heaven itself. To question Heaven was blasphemy.

Second, based on everything she'd heard, she had never expected the woman to speak to her with such kindness—let alone apologize.

"He is right to be skeptical, Holy Highness," Ying said in a halting fashion. "It is hard for him when his own advisors are telling him to believe otherwise."

"You mean Master Chen?" The empress gave a hard, bitter laugh. "Yes, that venerated master has a most unusual amount of sway over the emperor. Between you and me, Ying Yue, my husband is a fearful man. He prefers to listen to those who tell him what he wants to hear. And Truth Master Chen does that better than most."

Ying couldn't help blurting out, "But why would he deny it? He is the Truth Master." Ying thought back to the first time she and the master properly met. And how she, though it made her uncomfortable, had asserted her authority over the man. "I know he doesn't like me. But surely, he values the empire? He is a fortune teller! Surely, even he can see that we are all in danger."

The empress gave a delicate snort. "Fortune teller? The Truth Master is no fortune teller. He is nothing more than an ambitious man." Empress Shan fixed her gaze on Ying. "I would counsel you to be wary of him, Ying Yue. That master has no loyalty. He will go to whoever he thinks will elevate his status. He will attempt to depose whoever stands in his way. His hunger for power is outstripped only by his pride."

Ying was taken aback. If the empress wasn't colluding with Master Chen, then who had told him to send the elixir?

"Is that what this is?" she asked slowly, trying to make sense of her jumbled thoughts. "Him trying to depose me? Is that why he's trying to poison me?"

"Poison you?" The empress looked alarmed.

"With this alchemical elixir." Ying picked up the tumbler, which was now half-empty. "It is all I have to drink. I"—her voice faltered—"I don't have any water."

The empress's delicate features creased in disgust. "This is unacceptable. I will have one of my guards send some up." She shook her head. "Clearly, the master is more devious than I thought."

"Devious, Your Holy Highness?"

"Mei Po has long counseled me that alchemy is what will close the mirror gateway. Yet all this time, Master Chen has claimed the prophecy is false. If he is testing alchemy on you, though, then he must realize that he is wrong." The empress paused, as though thinking things through. "After your meeting with the emperor, when you put your arm through the mirror—I think . . . I think he is afraid the truth will be exposed. That he didn't foresee this, any of this. If he can force you to gain your powers while imprisoned, and you manage to close the gateway, he can then quietly dispose of you while pretending none of this ever happened. Do not forget, this is a man who has devoted his life to discrediting Mei Po. He has positioned himself as the emperor's advisor in order to maintain control over the court. If my husband sees through his farce, then he will lose favor with the emperor, something the Truth Master will do anything to avoid."

Ying's heart fell. "Then we are doomed," she whispered, "because of the pride of one man and the cowardice of another."

The empress's expression softened, and she took both of Ying's hands in her own. They were very warm. "Do not lose hope. Not yet. I will do my best to help the prince—my son. With whatever limited resources I have, I will help him win this war."

"But how, Your Imperial Majesty? Surely, you cannot go against the will of your husband?"

The empress dropped Ying's hands and stared down at her own in her lap. "I must," she said very quietly. "I have no other choice. I have already lost one son. I cannot, must not, lose another."

A pang of pity flashed through Ying. The empress was just a mother who grieved the loss of a child. While Ying did not, could not, condone the woman's actions—locking Ying up, being willing to sacrifice her daughter-in-law's life—she could at least understand. If Ying was faced with a choice of saving the world and all the people she loved or saving the life of one stranger . . . which would she choose?

"But . . . won't you be punished?"

"Never mind about me." The empress smiled. "I wouldn't have expected you to be so concerned, Ying Yue. From what I've seen, you are not exactly a subservient wife yourself."

Ying's cheeks burned. "I'll try to do better," she said quickly. The empress might be willing to go against her own husband, but that didn't mean she wanted the same for her son. "I promise."

"No, no." The empress chuckled and placed a warm palm on Ying's cheek. "Dear girl. That's not necessary. Already, I see how good you are for my son. He needs to be challenged, or else he will end up exactly like my useless husband. That was the mistake I made, being docile, never speaking up. I spent my time as a young woman massaging my husband's ego, not knowing I was simultaneously shrinking his courage and resolve." The empress's eyes misted. "Mei Po was right—you were the right choice. Mei Po is always right."

"Mei Po?" Ying sucked in a jagged breath, thinking of her conversation with the old woman in the laneway. She wondered if the empress knew the truth about Mei Po: that she wasn't just a wise matchmaker but actually a thousand-year-old reflection.

The empress nodded. "Yes. She must have known you were what Jinghu Dao really needed."

Ying felt faint. If she was what the empire needed, then she was failing. Badly. Not only had she not found the Three Treasures; she had no idea whether she was on the right path. As far as she could tell, two days and nights of consuming the alchemical elixir hadn't given her additional powers. All it had done was make her sick; it probably would have killed her had she drunk it any faster. Which made her question the relevance of the recipe she'd found in *The Book of Alchemy*.

Not knowing how to respond, Ying rose to her feet. She paced to the window and looked out. A pink blush had begun to spread across the ink-blue sky. Arrows of early morning sunlight shafted down into the courtyard. Workers had already started again on the construction, and the courtyard rang with the sound of hammering, sawing, and the occasional shouts of men.

The structure was almost complete. It consisted of a platform of wooden planks and a long horizontal beam held up by large pillars.

"What are they building?" Ying asked suddenly. The prince's warning still echoed in her mind. Perhaps the empress would be able to enlighten Ying and finish the sentence the prince could not.

The empress joined Ying at the window. Together, they watched the workmen.

"Gallows," the empress said, wrinkling her small nose.

Ying gasped. "For whom?"

The empress turned to Ying, her eyes filling with tears. "Oh, my dear," she said. "Whatever you do, don't watch." She didn't realize she was echoing her son's sentiments from mere minutes earlier. "I must go now. I'll do my best to intervene. Perhaps—perhaps I can convince my husband to issue you a pardon. But in the meantime, don't watch."

A great shout went up, and Ying looked out to see that the gallows had been completed. She meant to question the empress further, but by the time she turned away from the window, the woman had slipped quietly from the room.

Ying turned her attention back to the scene below. How could she ever have been confused as to what the structure was? The workers were now hanging a thick rope noose from the crossbeam, below which was an upturned wooden pail. The courtyard was starting to fill with people, mostly servants and members of court, with the odd guard for good measure.

With a sinking stomach, Ying realized the gallows were probably for her. Not only had she been forced to drink her own elixir, it seemed she'd been also forced to watch as they prepared for her execution. She touched the base of her neck with clammy hands, her pulse beating hot in her ears. The prince said she'd be safe . . . but was he wrong?

The injustice of it all punched a hole in her chest. She was not a traitor. She hadn't intended to open the mirror gateway, hadn't even realized that she had. The only thing she was guilty of was being naïve. She'd trusted the prince's reflection, had fallen victim to his charms. She'd let herself get lured repeatedly across the mirrors until she'd inadvertently broken the barrier.

At the thought of the Mirror Prince, she clenched her teeth so hard they ached. The smug look on his face when he strolled toward her on the pavilion, his steely strength pinning her arms behind her back, his attempt to drown her in the mirror lake . . . He'd feigned having a heart, having a soul, being flesh and blood. But now Ying saw him for what he was: A cold and empty shell. A mere reflection of a man.

And the real prince? Him, she had misjudged. It was he who was full of heart, who was brave and just and loyal and loving. She'd once compared him to a mountain—stern and cold. What she hadn't considered was that mountains were always . . . *there*. Strong, safe, everlasting. Perpetual in their constancy.

Like the Mirror Prince, the real prince had hidden who he really was. The difference is that the former pretended to be a good man, and the latter actually *was* one.

Now the real prince was secretly rallying his troops for a fight, and she was stuck up here, watching the construction of her own gallows. Both of them could die without his knowing how she truly felt.

In the crisp morning light, her feelings crystallized. And through her haze of grief, she finally saw them, stark, naked, pure. The possibility of facing a lifetime, an eternity, without him made her see the truth:

She loved him.

She loved the prince. The reason she had fought it, she now realized, was to guard her tender heart. When she'd first arrived at the palace, his cold reception had shaken her. She didn't know then what she knew now: his mask of coldness, of indifference, was just a way for him to guard *his* heart.

The hurt and humiliation of their first meeting had planted a seed of self-preservation, which over time had grown into a vine-tangled forest. She'd stumbled through this forest, seeing only dead wood and thorns. Not noticing the tinges of green, the damp, fertile soil, the glimpses of sun through the dense canopy. It had been easier to turn away from the real prince—the man she was supposed to marry—and fall into the fantasy of the Mirror Prince's arms. He'd seemed like an easier, better version of the prince she'd so desperately wanted to love.

How wrong she had been.

Setting her jaw, Ying eyed the shards of light reaching from the rising sun. If the prince could face death bravely, she thought, so could she. She would *not* be dragged to the gallows. She would not struggle. She'd walk there herself, on her own two feet, bolstered by the knowledge that she had done nothing wrong. Maybe she and the prince could meet again in another life. Another realm.

A loud cheer went up in the crowd below, jolting Ying back to the present. A line of people, six in total, were being led to the gallows by guards. The prisoners had their hands bound and coarse burlap sacks over their heads. And five more nooses, and five more buckets, had been secured in place.

Ying was confused. The battle hadn't started. Who were these people? Why were they being paraded before the crowd in the courtyard when it was not even much past dawn?

The guards lined the prisoners up. Then, in a synchronized, practiced move, all six of the prisoners had the sacks whipped off their heads.

Ying reeled. She staggered back from the windowsill, her

hand on her chest, the room spinning around her. No longer able to stay upright, she sank to the floor, her soiled silk gown billowing around her.

The six prisoners were not mirror people.

They were her family.

38

It made sense now. The prince's words. The empress's words. *Don't look out the window,* they had warned her. A heavy, hollow feeling punched through her chest. It was painful to breathe. Ying's trial wasn't just Ying's trial.

It was her whole family's trial.

She was too numb to cry. She just sat on the floor, struggling to make sense of the mess of theories swirling around her head. Here she was, locked in a tower, in full view of the gallows on which her family stood. Her beloved mother, her kind and benevolent father, her four older brothers. The emperor wanted her to see them down there, below her window, vulnerable and under threat. Why? Would they be questioned about Ying? Or would the emperor use Ying's family to try to eke a confession out of her?

Before she could answer these questions, the door burst open and a procession of guards marched in, trailed by Master Chen. One of the guards shut and locked the door. Ying scrambled to her feet. The small room was full, too full. It reeked with the stench of men.

The old master flicked his long white beard over one shoulder before reaching into the sleeve of his robes. He produced a neatly rolled parchment scroll; with a shake of his wrinkled hand, it opened. "Jiang Ying Yue, I have come as the ear of the gods, the mouth of His Holy Highness Shan, and, of course"—his mouth curved into a malevolent smile—"your most *humble servant*, to hear your confession. You have been charged with treason for your unauthorized breaching of the mirror gateway established by the esteemed and legendary Crimson Emperor, for conspiring against the crown and the empire, and for placing the people of Jinshan province and all of Jinghu Dao in untold peril." He allowed the roll of parchment to spring closed and added, "Since my elixir appears not to have worked, let us try a different approach."

Ying shook her head. So they believed her now. But with her family in danger it was small comfort. "I didn't," she blabbered. "I didn't open it on purpose."

The master looked at her over the top of his scroll, his black eyes sharp and shrewd. "Princess Ying," he said, "you have six chances to tell us how to close the gateway. Each time you deny us, one of your family will die. Is this what you want, Princess? Think carefully now."

The hollow feeling rose up Ying's throat, making her dizzy, threatening to knock her over. She fought the feeling down, trying to retain her dignity. Raising her head, she glared at the master.

"I can't tell you anything, Master." Her voice wavered. "I don't . . . I don't know how to close it."

The master inclined his head. "Very well, then." He crossed the room to stand in front of the window and raised one hand.

A shout went up. A bang. Then cheering.

Ying ran to the window, her knuckles white, gripping it. What she saw filled her with a horror so palpable, so destructive, that all she could do for a few seconds was stare. But then she put her hands over her mouth, and out of it came a strangled cry.

One of her brothers hung from a rope.

"Did you think we were bluffing?" The master looked sideways at her, the vestige of a smile playing about his lips. "You thought wrong. Emperor Shan does not bluff." He put a withered hand on Ying's shoulder. "And me? I am merely here to *follow orders.*"

She threw him off, her anger rising like a tide. "You . . . you animal!" Ying managed to splutter out before her sobs took over, racking her body with their violence.

"Now," the master said, clasping his hands in front of him as though he was about to recite a verse. "Let's try again, Princess. Tell me how to seal the barrier. How did you breach it in the first place? Have you been conspiring with the mirror army?"

Ying didn't know what to say. It seemed there was no right answer. If she continued to tell the truth, her family would die. But if she lied and pretended to know something, *she* would die. And after the empire had seen to her death, they would probably kill the rest of her family, too, merely for being related to her.

She leaned over the windowsill, her face awash with tears. "Mā!" she screamed. "Bà!"

The master hauled her backward by her collar with a surprising amount of force, but not before she'd seen her father look up, his expression grim, and give her a very subtle shake of his head.

She fought the master's restraint, her fingernails scratching like a wildcat. She struggled back to the windowsill. "Mā!" she screamed again, her cries hoarse with desperation. "Let me go!"

"Have it your way, Princess." The master raised a hand again, and Ying screamed as the executioner kicked over another bucket. Now two of her brothers hung from ropes, one limp, one twitching.

Ying screamed and screamed. Her head felt like it might explode. The crowd jeered, jostling for space, for a better look. As her screams gave way to inconsolable wails, she relented. "Please," she sobbed. "Please. Have mercy. I'll tell you anything. Please, just spare them."

"Very good," the master said, and nodded at the guards, all of whom took a step backward. "Now," he said, rubbing his hands together. "Where were we? Oh yes, you were going to tell me how you opened the gateway. And, most importantly"—he leaned forward, his sour breath fanning Ying's face—"you'll tell us how to close it."

Ying dashed her tears away with the heel of her hand and stared out of the window, refusing to look at Truth Master Chen. She didn't want to look at her brothers either. Or her parents. Somehow that would make this nightmare more real. Instead, she trained her eyes on the lake and whispered a silent prayer. For her family, that the rest may be spared. For herself, that she may stay courageous in the face of death. And for her prince, that they might meet again someday, in this realm or the next.

If anyone is out there, she thought, *then help me. Help me!*

Her mind raced. She could tell the master about *The Book of Alchemy* that she had lost in the lake. Might they be able to salvage the remaining pages and test the alchemy? Mei Po had said that Ying herself was the vessel. They'd probably test the alchemy on her. And considering how badly her body had reacted to the blood-red elixir she'd been consuming, it would probably kill her in the process.

She took a deep breath. If she must be sacrificed, then so be it. Anything to save her family.

"There is something," she said haltingly. "Mei Po found a book—"

The master scoffed. "Mei Po? That old bat?"

Anger surged through Ying's veins, but she concentrated on keeping her face a blank mask.

The master sighed. "Proceed."

Ying opened her mouth, about to disclose what she knew. But then she paused, listening. Something was happening. Unearthly sounds, rumbling sounds, coming from the lake, which lay beyond the palace's inner walls. Down below, people started to shuffle, whispers rising like a rushing tide.

She stared. Normally, the lake was a pale, pastel green. But now the surface was shifting, white froth forming on its peaks. As choppy waves began to cut the water, a mass of reddish-gold coalesced, flashing with the iridescence of a thousand suns. The fish! They must have responded to her silent plea. Ying wondered if she could do it. Could she could connect with them again; could the transformation process be repeated? Would her strange powers work from such a distance?

"Well?" The master's voice was edged with impatience. "What do you have to tell me, girl?"

Ying turned to face him. "Master Chen, I suggest you find somewhere safe," Ying said, her voice flat.

He smiled, scornful. "And why is that?"

Ying said nothing. Just pointed.

The master joined her at the window, his eyes following the direction of Ying's finger. When he saw the lake, he swayed a little and clutched the sill for support. "Gods save us!" he said. "What is it?"

The rumbling increased in volume, causing the very air to vibrate. The ground shook. The crowd in the courtyard began to shout. Collectively, they began to scramble for the exit.

Summoning all her inner strength, Ying closed her eyes, took a deep breath, and commanded the fish to fly.

She opened her eyes. The shoal of fish accelerated, swimming in a giant circle, angling themselves toward the water's surface. And as she watched, the fish transformed themselves into a horde of dragons, which erupted as one from the lake.

39

The swarm of dragons rose high and circled the palace, breathing out puffs of mistlike condensation. The largest dragon, black and serpent-like, rose the highest before letting forth a high-pitched shriek.

This triggered a sort of frenzy in the crowd. They became like cornered animals, jostling and screaming and clawing past each other to reach the exits, the spectacle of the executions completely forgotten.

Frantic, Ying scanned the scene below. The remainder of her family still stood on the gallows, nooses around their necks and hands tied in front.

Her heart skipped a beat. She tore her eyes from the chaos, bending her mind toward the sky and the biggest black dragon. "Lái," she whispered under her breath. "Come."

The dragon did a 180-degree turn in midair and barreled toward her. Master Chen uttered a cry, cringing in fear. When the dragon had nearly reached the tower, it turned a silvery eye upon them. The stare it gave was so deadly, so penetrating, that the master threw up his hands and scrambled for the door, along with all his guards.

Mesmerized, Ying climbed up on the windowsill. She balanced there, arms out, willing the dragon to come closer.

It flew under the open window. Ying saw the broad expanse of its black-scaled back spread beneath her. She closed her eyes, exhaled, and jumped.

The dragon, whose flight before now had been almost leisurely, immediately accelerated. It shot up toward the golden sky, throwing Ying backward. She managed to stop herself from falling by grabbing a handful of the dragon's thick black mane.

Ying found herself suddenly too far away to see much more. The palace was like a doll's house, the masses of people as small as ants. Cold air stung her cheeks, freezing the clinging mist that laced her skin.

"Xià—down," Ying whispered.

It halted in its upward trajectory, turned, and plummeted. Ying's stomach was left behind as the dragon rocketed toward the courtyard. It swooped low, its claws skimming the cobblestones and causing a shower of sparks and debris. The few remaining people on the ground stopped and stared, then dispersed, screaming, before the dragon launched back into the air.

Only Ying's family, who were unable to escape, remained unmoving. Ying wheeled the dragon around. At its approach, her mother's eyes opened wide in fear, then rolled heavenward, glistening with tears. But at the last minute, the dragon swerved, and using one of its razor-sharp claws, sliced through the six ropes as though they were mere cobwebs.

Ying's two hanged brothers dropped like sacks onto the ground. The remainder of her family converged on them, Lady

Jiang howling in anguish. By now, Ying and the dragon were already flying away, but she called down to them, "Quick! Cut your ties!"

Hao Yu looked up at her and nodded. He bent over a guard who'd been trampled by the crowd and began to saw his wrist bindings on the dead man's blade.

Calling to the other dragons, she beckoned them with her mind. *Save them,* she thought. *Take them home.* Immediately, four dragons detached themselves from the sky-bound swarm and flew toward the Jiangs. Ying's mother, father, and two remaining brothers were plucked gently from the ground and lifted high into the sky.

There was no time to say a proper goodbye. Mirror army aside, her family would now be in danger unless Ying obtained a pardon. Otherwise, as long as she lived, as long as the emperor lived, their lives were forfeit. The best she could do was get them far, far away from Jinshan province. Far away from the war, the battles, the lecherous, venomous imperial court. "Stay safe," Ying whispered, swallowing hard.

Once they'd disappeared over the mountains, Ying turned her attention to the scene below. At her command, the dragon descended, landing heavily on the cobblestones. As soon as Ying slid off its back, it took off to join its companions.

Wrenching a sword from a dead soldier's hand, Ying crept forward, past the bodies of the fallen. The sting of tears blurred her vision. Everyone here was dead. Except one man, who lay by the gallows, taking great, gasping breaths. He was alive, but just.

The executioner. Even had he not been wearing his

distinctive white robes, Ying would have recognized his stern and haggard face. That face would be branded on her brain forevermore.

He reached for her and moaned. "Your Highness."

Ying said nothing, just stared. The man clutched at his middle, his chest rattling ominously. His torso, all bloodied, was a mushy mess. He, too, had been trampled.

"Your Highness," he repeated. His words were a croak.

Ice clenched around Ying's heart. She said, through gritted teeth, "What do you want?"

"I'm ... hurt, Your Highness. I will not survive. Please ..."

Ying grimaced, biting back her revulsion. What the man was asking ... She knew what he was asking. The real question was, could she do it? Would she do it?

It would be a kindness. A kindness to put him out of his misery. But Ying—who had just watched him hang two of her brothers—was feeling anything but *kind*. Why should she be kind? Why, when what she really wanted was to slash his belly open further, spilling his guts until they laced the blood-slicked ground? She wanted to watch him howl; wanted to leave him alive for flies to feast on and for crows to peck out his eyes.

She wanted him to suffer as she was suffering.

Her mind buckled as she grappled with indecision. Rage gripped her with unrelenting claws. She wasn't sure who she despised the most: the reflections, who started all this, or the humans. How could she be sure the mirror folk were the monsters when so many humans were just as bad?

It wasn't just the executioner. It was also the emperor. The master. The crowd who jeered as her brothers died, as though it was a spectator sport.

And also . . . Ying herself. A small, salvageable part of her soul was disgusted by her bloodlust, her thirst for revenge. *I should go,* she thought. *Leave him to the threads of fate.*

Adjusting her grip on the handle of her blade, Ying started to turn away.

But the man moaned again, staying her feet. Deep in her heart, her emotions fought an epic battle: mercy . . . or vengeance? Her chest heaved; her belly churned; her resolve spun like the spokes of a wheel.

She turned back.

His eyes were trained on her, one hand stretched out, his lips moving in silent prayer. Before she could change her mind, Ying strode over and slashed the sword, quick and sharp, across the man's neck. Hot blood sprayed her face. He immediately went limp, his hand falling away.

The sword fell with a clatter. Ying staggered over to her brothers' bodies and doubled over, clutching her stomach. She had killed a man. *She had killed a man.* This wasn't like the áoyīn, or the fēngshēngshòu, or even the nonhuman reflections. This man was—or had been—a human. A heinous one, but still a human. And she still couldn't tell if she'd just performed an act of mercy, or one of vengeance. Perhaps it was a bit of both.

"Gods forgive me," she muttered beneath her breath.

Shaking, she fell onto her knees beside her brothers and heaved them over onto their backs. Their eyes were empty, glassy, reflecting the clouds above. Their faces were turgid, blue-tinged, the whites of their eyes filled with blood. "Please, no," she whispered, tears slipping from her eyes and pattering onto her brothers' faces. "Please."

To which entity she was pleading, she did not know. All she knew was that her heart, her blood, her bones, her body, were all begging for this not to be real. To be just a dream. If only she could turn back time, take back what she'd said in the emperor's meeting, so she wouldn't be imprisoned and would not endanger her family.

But this wasn't a dream. And she couldn't reverse time. All she could do was clamp a hand over her mouth, bend over their bodies, and sob and sob until she had no more tears left.

It was here that the prince found her, stooped over her dead brothers. She'd taken their hands—one lifeless hand in each of her own—and had clutched them to her chest.

"Come, Ying," the prince murmured, placing a gentle hand on her back. "You cannot help them now."

Ying let out a wail and clutched her brothers harder. Already, they were cold, their skin mottled.

"You cannot help them," Prince Zhang repeated softly. "But we must leave. The guards are on their way."

Something snapped in Ying's brain when she heard this, and she finally acquiesced, letting her brothers' hands go. Turning her face into the prince's shoulder, she clung to him, sobbing soundlessly into his neck. He wrapped an arm around her shoulder and drew her to her feet before steering her toward the gate.

Shadow Runner was waiting just outside. The prince guided Ying toward the horse and helped her mount. Then he climbed up behind her and spurred the horse to move.

As they rode, Ying did not speak. She just continued to quietly weep. But when the prince pulled the horse to a stop and dismounted, she finally raised her head. "Where are we?" Her eyes were swollen, her throat thick.

They'd stopped in the forest—but since all of Jinshan's forests looked alike, she could not tell how far they'd traveled. Dusk was falling. A soft breeze rustled the branches of ancient pines. Slanting sunbeams limned the tree trunks with a saturated orange glow.

The prince helped her to the ground. "Just a rest stop," he murmured, "so you can catch your breath."

He helped her down, and she collapsed onto the downy moss. Trembling, she leaned against a tree trunk, then curled forward into a ball. The prince said nothing. He draped his cloak around her shaking shoulders and sank to a squat beside her, a silent sentinel to her sorrow.

When her sobs died down, he helped her to sit up, fetched her some water, and guided it to her lips. She gulped down the entire thing, then set upon a substantial piece of jerky he pushed into her hands. She held it with two hands, like a beast.

"I am sorry," the prince said, his voice thick, as she polished off the meat. "About your brothers."

Ying raised her head. "Did you know that would happen?"

"I was hoping . . . that your being the crown princess would offer your family some protection," the prince said. He blew out a long breath, then shook his head. "Although this is the usual protocol, I . . . I did not believe they would actually do it."

Ying said nothing. Her head filled with images of her brothers' bloated faces, their purpled, protruding tongues, the way they'd twitched at the end of the ropes. She drew her legs up to her chest and stared into empty space, too afraid to close her puffy eyes, too afraid to even blink.

"I can't believe . . ." A tear detached itself from Ying's lower lashes, rolled down her cheek, and fell onto her knee. "My brothers. Oh, gods, my brothers." She dissolved again into fresh tears. This time, she leaned into the prince's arms, burying her face against his chest. Reaching up, the prince stroked her hair. Just once.

Ying shivered at the physicality of his touch. She was numb. Half her world had collapsed, and the palace was in uproar. Surely, the prince should be there—appeasing the palace folk, recruiting soldiers to his secret army?

Yet he was here, comforting her. Embracing her. Just being . . . *present*. In a way, he had always been there for her. Or tried to be, even if he hadn't always gotten it right.

It had taken her too long to see it. It had taken facing death for her to see it. Losing her brothers had clarified things with pinpoint accuracy. War was almost upon them. There was no guarantee they'd survive. And Ying knew she should waste no more time in obfuscating her feelings.

She looked up at the prince, into his eyes. His pupils were dilated—pools of black ringed with warm mahogany.

"I am not sure if this is any comfort," he whispered, brushing away one of Ying's tears with a soft swipe of his thumb. "But they died innocent. They died whole. They will enter the afterlife with *honor*."

Ying closed her eyes. Leaned into his touch. All that she had seen, all the death she had witnessed, all the death she herself had caused . . . The only way to stop being consumed by darkness was to inch toward the light. And to her, the prince was light. He was heat, he was life, he was the sun personified.

Before she could overthink it, she leaned over—once again, the taste of tears on her tongue—and pressed her lips to his.

"Don't," he said. He turned his head away.

"What's wrong?" Ying said, pulling back, her cheeks burning.

The prince rose swiftly and stepped away from her. "You shouldn't do this."

"Do what?" Ying was confused. She hugged herself, hurt, humiliated.

He gave her an unhappy look. "You're trying to distract yourself," he said. "You don't know what you're doing."

"I'm not trying to distract myself!" Ying crossed her arms. Shielding her body. Shielding her heart. "I'm . . . I'm . . ."

"You're grieving."

This she could not dispute. Unable to argue, she sat, stunned, her crumpled skirts splayed around her.

By now, the prince was already at Shadow Runner, adjusting the horse's saddle. Ying had no choice but to force herself to stand, stumble over, and allow the prince to help her mount.

"Where are we going?" she asked eventually, when they'd ridden for so long that darkness had fully fallen.

"The Palace of the Crescent Moon," he replied from his position behind her. "It is my summer palace. You can hide out there. Once you're safe, I'll put out a rumor that you escaped on a dragon. I'll pretend we argued and I had no idea what you were planning."

Ying said nothing. It wasn't farfetched to pretend they'd argued, since the truth was they constantly did.

The Moon Palace, as it was colloquially known, was nestled halfway up Mount Zhixiang. It was common knowledge that the prince had been gifted the residence by his mother when he came of age.

A cool, tranquil place, it mostly served the prince as an escape from the overbearing heat of summer—or, if court gossip was to be believed, following quarrels with his father. This was fortuitous, Ying thought, as after yesterday's disastrous meeting, no one would be suspicious if the prince began frequenting the place.

But as Shadow Runner clattered into the entrance courtyard, under full cover of night, Prince Zhang Lin tensed, his posture straightening.

Ying could see why: the Moon Palace was a wreck. All the windows were shattered. Glittering glass shards lay strewn across the path. Flames from lit lanterns danced in the fragments, creating multifaceted reflections. Everything was completely silent.

The prince hastily dismounted, drew his sword, then paced

the perimeter of the courtyard, his lips pressed together so hard they looked white. His footsteps crunched, grinding more glass into the stony ground. Eventually, he slowed, then stopped, right in the center of the courtyard, scanning his surroundings in apparent shock.

Ying slid off Shadow Runner's back and picked her way through piles of splintered glass. She was flooded with unease; her pulse skittered through her veins. When she drew near to the prince, he startled.

"Sorry." His voice was hoarse. "I'm so used to being alone, sometimes I forget that anyone's with me."

She gave him a small, sympathetic nod, then cast a look around the yard. "What happened here?" Her tone was hushed to match the stillness.

As though shaking himself out of a trance, the prince shook his head. "Hopefully, just looters. Hopefully, nothing more sinister—"

He stopped, because he'd heard a noise. Ying had heard it, too. In a flash, the prince had drawn his sword, shoved Ying behind him, and swiveled around.

A figure shrouded in a long black cloak stood in the courtyard shadows.

40

Ying's heart skipped a beat, then resumed pounding at a precipitous pace. Her first thought was that she'd been discovered and this was a palace official. Her second thought was worse: perhaps this was one of the mirror-world reflections.

The figure turned and lowered their hood, and the prince gave a yell. "Mother!"

The empress! Ying drew her cloak tighter around her.

When the empress visited Ying in the tower, she swore to help the prince's cause. Was that what this was? Was the empress here to help? Or had she lied to Ying, as so many others had, and was actually here to rearrest her?

"My boy," Empress Shan said. She stretched both hands out toward the prince. "My son."

Zhang Lin went to his mother and embraced her. The empress accepted the kiss on her cheek with an elegant tilt of her head.

She turned to Ying. "Daughter," she said, holding out her hand.

Ying glanced at the prince, who gave her an encouraging nod. "It's okay," he said.

Moving forward, she kissed the empress's hand, then bowed.

"My respects, Empress Shan, Lady of My Kingdom for Ten Thousand Years."

"Please, just call me Mother," the empress replied, her eyes glistening. "I am very sorry about your brothers, Ying Yue. So very sorry. I had hoped to stop it, but when my husband gets an idea in his head, he . . ." She shook her head. "There is nothing I can say but that I'm sorry."

Once again, grief gouged a hole in Ying's heart. The pain made her whole body tremble. She wanted to scream, cry, smash something, anything. Wanted to track down the emperor, track down Master Chen, run her sword right through both of them, twisting as she went. She wanted to burn down the palace and all the people in it who had jeered as her brothers died. It was all she could do not to pounce on the empress herself.

Clenching her fists, Ying tried to curb her rapid breaths. Tried to rein in her wrath. It was not the empress's fault. Despite being the most powerful woman in Jinghu Dao, the empress would have had little recourse against her husband. Ying knew: in the imperial court, there were very specific, defined roles women were permitted to play. And being a voice of reason—or having any voice at all—was not one of them.

There was, quite simply, very little the empress could have done.

Ying fixed her eyes upon the opposite wall, willing herself not to cry. She was vaguely aware of the prince speaking, but his voice sounded distant, drowned out by the rush of her blood in her ears.

"What are you doing here, Mother?" he was saying. "How did you know where I'd be?"

The empress reached out and grasped her son's shoulders with both hands. "Come, now," she said, her expression soft. "You think I don't know my own son? I know you always escape here after a quarrel with your father."

Prince Zhang frowned. "And where *is* Father? Did he send you? Has he come to see reason?"

The empress did not answer immediately. Instead, she drifted over to a gaping, glassless window.

"He has not," she said finally, placing one hand on the lacquered windowsill. "Your father did not send me. He has taken ill quite suddenly and is now confined to bed."

Ill? Ying was surprised. When they'd last seen the emperor, mere days ago, he'd seemed a little out of shape, certainly. But not infirm enough to be bedridden, unable to command.

The prince sighed, resigned. "Is it the drink again?"

"Not this time." The empress pressed her lips together.

"Will *you* help us then, Mother? I have the support of my soldiers and my guards. But if we have yours as well—"

"Of course," she said. "That is why I'm here, Zhang Lin. Anything you need. Anything at all. I've already taken pains to make sure the two of you will be safe here while we prepare."

For a moment, the prince's brow creased in confusion. But then his eyes flicked to the broken glass scattered all over the ground, and he gave a small nod. "Right. The windows."

Understanding snapped into place for Ying, too. The empress

had ordered that all the reflective surfaces be destroyed to protect them from the mirror people. An odd feeling kindled within Ying. It was something like respect, or admiration. Or both. Ying admired the way the empress was so unafraid of her husband or the possible consequences she'd face defying him. She admired the lengths the empress went to in order to protect her son.

"The mirrors, too. Here and at the main palace." The empress's eyes gleamed, a satisfied smile hovering about her lips. "Oh, don't worry," she continued, catching sight of the prince's face. "I shall leave the ceremonial ones alone. I know how much you despise such desecration." She reached out and patted the prince's arm. "Your gods are safe."

Ying raised her head, her curiosity piqued. The empress had said "*your* gods," as though her loyalties lay elsewhere.

"It would not be the first time I had to destroy a ceremonial mirror," the prince replied, purposely not looking at Ying. "But I appreciate it."

Her face flushing, Ying remembered their visit to the Shangren temple and how he'd smashed the octagonal mirror to stop her from going through it. If the prince was that concerned about the deities, then . . . how desperate must he have been to destroy, without hesitation, such a sacred relic?

The prince was already moving on. "How many guards do you have, Mother? How many can you spare?"

"One thousand," the empress replied, promptly.

Zhang Lin moved to stand beside his mother. Peering through the window, he assessed the interior of his palace and frowned. "Together with my soldiers, that makes about three thousand.

It's not enough. The mirror army will have all of that and more. They have monsters—"

"We have something else, too," the empress said.

The prince half turned. "What?"

"Alchemy. Explosive alchemy." The empress dropped her voice low. "I am not supposed to know this. But your father has been experimenting with it in secret, with Master Chen. Saltpeter, charcoal, sulfur."

"Away from any mirrors?"

Empress Shan nodded. "Deep underground. I followed them. Once."

Ying was impressed at how cunning the empress was, how determined.

The prince paused, considering, but then nodded, his mouth a grim line. "That's good. If we have something the other army won't expect, that's something we can surprise them with."

This is really happening, Ying thought. *War is coming.* She felt faint and flushed and, most of all, furious. She tore her mind away from visions of vengeance and focused back on the present.

The prince was still talking with his mother. "We'll need horses, chariots, armor, weapons. . . ."

The empress nodded. "Yen-gōnggong," she said to the empty courtyard. "Fetch my horse. We need to return to the palace immediately. We need to prepare."

Ying gasped, for a eunuch guard materialized, seemingly out of thin air. Ying realized, with a jolt, that he'd been there the whole time, standing so still Ying had mistaken him for shadow. The eunuch bowed and turned to leave.

"But, Mother." The prince shook his head, his brow creased. "Without Father . . . how . . . ?"

"Do not worry yourself about the emperor," Empress Shan said firmly. The eunuch returned with a slender bay mare and helped the empress mount. After raising the hood of her cloak, she pulled it down low so that it mostly concealed her face.

The cloak was so black that it absorbed every drop of light. It was as though the empress had simply dissolved into the night. "Let me deal with him. For you, son, I have only one request."

The prince gave a visible swallow. "And what's that?"

"Stay safe," the empress murmured, her eyes shining beneath the shadow of her hood. The horse snorted and turned in a circle, ready to go. The empress, sitting tall, steadied her, both reins gathered in one hand. "Please, my darling, just stay alive."

41

The dragons circled the Moon Palace, their bodies knifing through the soft dawn light. Every now and then, one would emit a shriek so shrill and primeval it could have been heralding the birth of a brand-new world.

Ying shivered as her black dragon flew past the window, one silver eye flashing toward her as it passed. For a moment, it looked as though it might collide with the ground, but at the last second it turned, soaring past the snow-dusted mountains and into the gold-hued sky.

Ying did not know where the prince was. When she'd stumbled, exhausted, into the bedroom the previous night, he'd run a bath for her, then insisted she take the bed. He'd then promptly fallen asleep sprawled out on the room's only chair. She remembered lying awake, studying the planes of his face.

His features, caressed by moonlight, had been smooth and unruffled in his sleep. With her eyes, she'd traced the sharp angles of his jaw, his long straight nose, the delicate curves of his eyebrows. One of his hands had rested on his stomach, rising and falling with each breath.

Now the chair was empty, its seat vacant. She sighed and leaned farther out the open window.

"What are you looking at?"

Ying jumped; the prince moved so silently she hadn't heard him enter. "Nothing," she said, her face flushing hot.

He'd bathed and changed. Strands of wet hair fell across his forehead. The linen undershirt he'd donned clung slightly to his still-damp chest. Flushing, Ying forced herself to look away. "I should give back your tunic," she said, plucking despondently at the garment she wore. Since her dress was soiled and virtually unwearable, the prince had given her one of his own shirts to sleep in.

Prince Zhang Lin glanced up. "Keep it." The very edge of his lips tipped up in a smile. "It looks better on you." Ying flushed even deeper.

They were interrupted by sharp rapping at the door. It was Li Ming and Fei fei, bristling with efficiency, carrying piles of Ying's clothing in their arms. Clearly, the prince had sent for them in the night. Behind them, two eunuch guards trailed, each carrying a tray with several enamel dishes, large white jade tureens, and piles of gold-threaded napkins.

The two maids descended on Ying like a flock of birds, tutting and shaking their heads at the state of her hair. They dumped the pile of silks unceremoniously on the bed and ordered her to sit down. The prince just raised his eyebrows and turned to help the servants unload the food onto a round table by the window.

Ying ran her hand over one of the silk dresses and then picked it up. It was emerald green, and beautiful. At any other time, she would have loved it.

Just . . . not now. She looked at her maids. "I'm sorry," she said. "But I can't wear this."

The maids stopped, their mirth dying on their lips. They glanced at each other, then looked at Ying. "Why not, Your Royal Highness? Is the color not to your liking? Shall we exchange it for another?"

Ying shook her head and dropped the dress back down onto the bed. "It's just . . ." She raised her head. "War is coming. I need something that fits under armor. Something I can train in. Something I can *fight* in. I can't be swanning around in a silk dress. It's far too impractical."

Li Ming threw a nervous glance at the prince, who was still busying himself with their breakfast. She and Fei fei shared a brief look before Li Ming leaned forward.

"My lady, this was the prince's *particular* order," she whispered into Ying's ear.

"His what?" Ying spun around and stalked toward the prince, who had thrown himself down on one of the dining chairs and was biting into a piece of sauce-soaked chicken. There was no way—*no way*—she was going to let the prince rob her of the chance to avenge her family. Not this time. She had already killed the executioner who had stolen the life of her brothers. Next, she would kill the emperor. She'd kill the Mirror Prince. She would kill her own reflection. And then she'd kill every other mirror person, until not a single one was left.

"What's going on?" she said to the prince, anger exploding in her chest. "Why did you tell my maids to dress me in silk? You know I can't wear that to fight!"

The prince took a napkin and swiped at his mouth. "But Ying," he said, infuriatingly calm, "*you* won't be fighting at all."

Ying fought the urge to stamp her foot. "Like hell I won't!" Her voice rose, echoing around the room.

Seemingly unruffled, the prince leaned forward and started piling Ying's plate with succulent delicacies: the same soy chicken that he'd been eating, along with pork-stuffed steamed buns, duck and yam hot pot, steamed lotus root atop a glistening bed of glutinous rice, and stir-fried green vegetables studded with plump pink shrimp. "You won't," he repeated as he did so, his tone firm. "We just can't risk bringing you onto the battlefield. The mirror army knows you're the key to closing the gateway—they'd go right for you. No," he continued, "your time would be better spent trying to find the Three Treasures."

"I can do both," she snapped, her fingers curling into fists, refusing to accept the food.

The prince paused for a moment, then placed the plate on the table and slid it toward her. "But, Ying, you don't have to."

Ying forced herself to ignore how good the food smelled. "If you try to stop me," she hissed, "then . . . then I'll just go out the window!"

The prince's eyes widened, flicked toward the window, then back again. "But we're at the top of a tower. You'd die!"

"No, I wouldn't," Ying replied. "I'd use the dragons."

"The dragons!" he exclaimed, incredulous.

"Yes, Zhang Lin. The dragons." She tapped her forehead. "They respond to my commands, remember?"

The prince stared at Ying open-mouthed for a few seconds.

Then he closed his eyes, a pained look on his face. *"Yiiiiiing...,"* he said, drawing out the vowel in her name.

Ying gave him a smile of false sincerity. "Yes, Your Highness?"

"Don't do this. Please." He opened his eyes wide, imploring. His irises were the deepest brown.

"Here's the thing." Ying stood up, her hands braced on the armrests of his chair, looming over the prince. He had to tip his head back to look at her.

"Either I walk out that door and fight." Ying gestured toward the ornate wooden doors. "Or I'll jump out that window and fight. Or, if you bar the windows, I'll find a reflective surface, go into the mirror world, and—"

"Let me guess," the prince interrupted. "You'll fight?"

"Exactly." Ying straightened and crossed her arms. "So. The choice is yours. Which will it be?"

They glared at each other, neither conceding defeat. Finally, the prince stood abruptly, his chair scraping the floor, forcing Ying to take a step back.

"Fei fei, Li Ming," he called, not breaking eye contact with Ying. "Fetch the princess's armor, will you?" He caught a glimpse of Ying's expression, then added, through gritted teeth, *"Please."*

The maids scurried out, Li Ming giving Ying one last apprehensive look before she quietly shut the door. Ying turned back to face the prince; he had not stopped staring at her.

"There. Are you happy now?" he snapped, his eyes flashing.

"Happy?" Ying's voice was higher than usual. Fury snapped like a string within her, painfully sharp in its recoil. "My brothers are dead, the world is ending, and you ask if I am *happy*?"

"You know what I mean." He raked both hands through his hair and exhaled, frustrated. "You're the Fish, Ying. And you're wanted by my father for *treason*. You may as well be going into battle painted with a big red cross. Why do it? Why insist on fighting?"

"Why do you even care?" Ying bit back, seething. He'd made it very clear in the forest that he didn't care about her—not like she cared for him. Or *had* cared for him, before he'd morphed back into his overprotective former self.

"Why do I care?" he said, his face reddening. Ying was aware they were mirroring a conversation they'd had after the tea ceremony, on what was supposed to be their wedding day. "Why do I *care*? Gods, Ying. How could you not see? How could you be so . . . so *clueless*?"

"Me, clueless? I'm not the clueless one! It's *you* who's clueless! You're . . ." Ying grappled for the right words; none of the ones coming to mind were anywhere remotely bad. "You're . . ."

"Completely and utterly in love with you?" he snarled. "That's what you mean, right?"

The effect was immediate. "What?" Ying froze.

"I'm in love with you. Isn't it obvious?" He leaned closer, breathing hard.

Ying was stunned. Trembling, she backed away from him. "But then why . . ." She shook her head, disbelieving. "Why did you push me away? Yesterday. In the forest—"

He turned and paced to the window, bracing both hands on the sill. Dropping his head, he gave a long, drawn-out sigh. "Because I know you don't feel the same way. Because I know for you this is just a sham marriage. I mean, you said it yourself: 'marriage has nothing to do with love.'"

Ying stared at him. Her mind was spinning, sifting through all their past conversations, unable to fully grasp what the prince was saying.

He turned to face her then, his voice becoming hoarse. "I'm a lost man around you, Ying. You're brave, you're beautiful, you . . . infuriate me. Constantly. But I love you. I love everything about you. But if you don't want"—he gestured at the empty space between them, his expression raw—"*this,* then I will respect your wishes. I'm trying to, I really am. The gods know I'm not always successful, but . . . I really am trying to be an honorable man."

Ying said nothing. Her mind had gone completely blank.

The silence expanded; a pregnant pause. Eventually, the prince drew himself to his full height, smoothed his hair, and straightened the hem of his shirt.

"Well," he said, regaining his composure. "I'm going for a walk, if you need me." He didn't look at her. Ying watched his broad back and erect posture as he pushed open the door and went out.

Ying ran to the doorway. "I don't want that," she called out suddenly.

He stopped in the corridor, his shoulders stiffening, but didn't turn around. "I'm aware, Ying." His voice vibrated with strain. "You don't need to repeat yourself. I know you don't want me."

"No." Ying's face and neck were flaming. She was sure she was blushing as red as a yángméi berry. "That's not what I mean."

He spun on his heel. "Then *what*?" He raised his hands in exasperation. "What *do* you want, Ying?"

Ying's voice was tiny. "I don't want you to be honorable."

The prince stopped and dropped his arms. He stood and stared at Ying, seemingly lost for words.

Ying trembled, her face burning hotter than ever. She made the tiniest of moves toward him with her hands, so subtle she was sure he wouldn't notice.

The prince's gaze dropped to her hands. His eyes grew dark. Then, without another word, he strode to her, took her face in his hands, and brought his mouth to hers.

Ying gasped, her lips parting, her hands immediately going to the back of his head. She tugged him toward her until their bodies pressed up against each other, heat burning through her skin and surging in her belly. Their kiss deepened, becoming more frenzied, and Ying moaned when the prince ran his tongue along her lower lip.

He pulled his head back, his eyes boring into hers. "Is this dishonorable enough for you, Princess?"

"Not even close," she breathed, drawing him down again.

Wrapping her arms around his shoulders, she pulled him still closer to her, as though their bodies could merge into one. She felt out of control, as though her blood was pumping too hard in her body and she might just . . . might just explode. Finally, she was kissing the prince! And this wasn't just any kiss. This was a no-barriers, impassioned, feverish kiss.

Ying's head spun, she could barely breathe, but she didn't want to break apart. She wanted to taste him. Needed to taste him.

And she needed his mouth on her mouth, on her neck, on the one shoulder that was exposed through the loose neckline of her shirt. Ying gasped as he trailed burning kisses up and down her throat before skimming his lips along the curve of her collarbone. She fisted her hand in his hair, tugging harder than she meant to.

In response, the prince ran his hand down her back, resting it on her hip. Gripping her soft flesh, he pulled her harder against him as he kissed his way back up her neck. When he finally reached her mouth, they resumed kissing, their tongues colliding urgently, intensely. With his other hand, he twined his fingers in her hair, tilting her head back to look at him.

He gazed down at her, his eyes hooded, his voice husky. "I've changed my mind, Ying. May I . . . may I have my shirt back?"

Ying shivered under his hands. "Yes," she whispered.

The prince gave a low groan as he bent to kiss her again. He let go of her hair, slipped his fingers under her shirt hem, and pulled. Ying raised her arms, shimmying out of the tunic. She tugged on the laces of his trousers, and he stepped back to pull them off. He stripped off his linen shirt, and Ying sucked in a breath at the sight of his muscled chest, the hard ripples of his stomach, the sharp, sloped brackets of his hips.

The two of them stumbled, kissing, toward the bed and tumbled onto the soft silk sheets. The prince's warm weight drove Ying's body into the plush surface, his hands running up and down her sides. He ran his lips along her jawline before moving down her neck. Ying threw her head back, her breaths coming hard and fast.

"You. Are. So. Beautiful." He kissed her exposed skin with

every word, moving down her chest, across her stomach. "My beautiful, brave, reckless wife." His murmur was now against her inner thigh. He glanced up and gave her a questioning look. Biting her lip, Ying gave him a barely perceptible nod.

His gaze lingered for a moment, his hand splayed firmly on her belly. Then, he lowered his head again. . . .

Ying cried out, her senses fracturing at the intensity of it all. Reflexively, she grabbed his head with both hands. The prince chuckled at her reaction and crawled back up to kiss her. Suddenly, his face turned serious. "Do you . . . want to continue? I can stop—"

Ying pulled him closer. "Don't you dare." She needed this. She needed it, needed *him*. After all that had happened, she needed to know they were still alive, that there were still things worth fighting for. Grabbing his face, she made him look at her. "I want you, Zhang Lin." She wrapped both legs around his waist, and her voice dropped low.

She took a deep breath and gave voice to her thoughts: *"I love you."*

The prince shuddered; he leaned down and kissed her hard, passionately. "I love you, too," he murmured against her lips.

Ying kissed him again, winding her arms tightly around his shoulders, her fingers digging in harder than she intended. He deepened the kiss, gathering her in his arms, holding her so close she couldn't tell where she ended and he began.

She cried out; he gasped her name. And then she was exploding, falling, breaking into pieces and being put back together. In this, in the melding of her body and his, she could lose herself.

Rebuild herself. Forget everything: forget about life, about death, forget about ever going back.

"Gods, Ying, you're perfect," he murmured into her ear, one hand in her hair, the other grasping her leg. "You drive me so wild." Yet his touch was light, almost hesitant. As if he was holding back.

As if he was trying to protect her—again.

Ying was panting but managed to choke out a few words. "Well, we're even, then, because you're driving *me* wild."

Ying felt his smile against her skin. "I am?"

"Yes," she said. She pushed him off her and rolled on top of him. He made a move to sit up, but she put her hands on his chest and shoved him back down.

By now, the morning light had reached its full glory, spilling in through the window and tinting them both in golden light. As Ying hovered above him, holding him down by the wrists, she drank in the sight of him—his face flushed, his forehead covered with a fine sheen of sweat, his tan shoulders a contrast against the pale silk of the sheets. She leaned down and gave him an intense, salacious kiss.

"You're driving me wild," she said when she pulled away, "in the most infuriating way."

"What do you mean, Princess?" He stared up at her with a gaze of liquid fire. His free hand caressed her waist.

"You're still being too honorable," she said, and leaned in again.

42

Ying jerked awake. She'd fallen asleep after reading all day, researching alchemy, trying to find more information on the Three Treasures. Since the prince insisted on caution—the palace guards were still searching for her—she'd largely kept herself to their shared bedroom. This meant she'd had little else to do over the past seven days.

During the daytime, that was. From dawn to dusk, Ying was alone in the Moon Palace tower. The prince spent his days at the main palace, working secretly with his mother to plan for the war. But he would return, without fail, every night. The nights were theirs, and theirs alone.

They meant to make the most of their time together. Every sunrise brought them closer and closer to the fifteenth day of the month, the day that war would dawn. And each sunset brought with it an ever-increasing sense of doom. So, as night fell, Ying and Zhang clung to each other, bringing them a temporary reprieve. Those dark hours, full of soft touches and whispered words, were as sweet and as melancholy as a breeze on a still lake, as moonlight spilling onto fresh snow, as the first note sung by a lone bird to greet a breaking dawn.

It was as though their bodies were singing a song of goodbye; as though they both knew every kiss could be their last.

And every morning, the prince would touch his warm lips to Ying's cheek and tell her he had to go. As soon as he'd ridden off on Shadow Runner, Ying would roll out of bed, open one of the books she'd brought back from the Moon Palace library, and begin another all-day session of study.

It was exhausting. Without the distraction, though, she'd just be lying about, idle, in the bedroom all day, reliving her nightmares as though on a loop. Every time she closed her eyes, all she saw was her dead brothers, their faces swollen, their lips blue. When the prince was absent, the only thing that helped was to focus her mind on books.

She rubbed her eyes, even though they stung. Anything to keep them open. How long had she been asleep? How much time had she wasted? Blearily, she squinted at the window; her heart sank as she noted the sun hovering low over the horizon.

Only one more night until the full moon, and she was losing the battle: against time, against the mirror army, against knowledge that she didn't possess. Despite her relentless search, and despite her constant study, she'd gained no further insight into how uniting the Three Treasures might help to close the mirror barrier.

She couldn't shake the feeling that she had failed. She was the Fish. She was supposed to close the barrier, and she had failed. Tomorrow, the mirror army would infiltrate the real world, and thousands of soldiers would likely die, all because she'd failed.

Blinking, Ying stared unseeingly at the book that lay open

atop her lap. It was a dry instructional manual on metallurgy—in desperation, she'd started reading it to see if it referenced alchemy—but she'd fallen asleep. And who could blame her? Instructional manuals were so very dull.

She picked up the book, intending to shut it and move on. Instead, she froze.

It had fallen open to a page featuring a detailed illustration of an ornate embossed-bronze wine goblet. One that looked very similar to the goblet the emperor used. The same one she'd seen in Master Chen's storeroom. She sat up straighter, her eyes glued to the page, skimming the text below the picture.

"Many bronze drinking vessels," the passage read, "contain up to eight percent lead by weight, enough to leach into wine in not-insignificant amounts. One liter of contaminated wine drunk daily is enough to cause chronic lead toxicity, which can lead to . . ."

Ying's hand went to her chest, and her vision wavered as she read the symptoms of lead poisoning. Headaches. Joint pain. Irritation. Memory loss.

All signs the emperor had.

Was this why the emperor was ill? And why would he be drinking from a lead-contaminated vessel unless . . .

Feeling hot, Ying slammed the book shut and dropped it on the floor. Pressing her fingers to her temples, she forced herself to take several deep, steadying breaths.

She shouldn't tell the prince of her suspicions. She couldn't. Not when the war needed his undivided attention. If he went to battle with something like this weighing on his mind—well, it would put him, and the entire army, at risk.

With one foot, she slid the book under the bed. As far as possible into the shadows.

She had no evidence that the emperor was being poisoned. None. There was absolutely no reason to say anything to the prince.

No reason at all.

By the time he arrived that night, Ying was sitting on the bed, staring through the window, watching the waxing gibbous moon.

As he entered, Ying shifted her focus from the window to the prince's face, floating pale amid the room's murky darkness. She was almost surprised to see him. Her mind had been elsewhere, sifting through alternating tableaus of dragons, poisoned wine goblets, and above all, her brothers, her brothers, her brothers.

"Ying." The prince spent some time removing and hanging up his cloak and weapons. "Good news." He strode to her, took her face in both hands, and kissed her. But then he drew back and stared. "You look pale. What's wrong?" He pressed his lips to her forehead, murmuring against her skin, "Is it me? Am I neglecting you? Am I leaving you alone too much?"

His words jolted Ying from her thoughts, and she drew back, blinking at him. "No," she said, shaking her head for emphasis. She knew he was doing important work. "No, no, it's not that."

"Are you worried about the charges, then? Is it getting to you, being cooped up here in the tower? Because I have something that might cheer you up." He dug around his hànfú and pulled out a scroll. "It's a royal pardon. My mother managed to get my father to sign and seal it—although how, I cannot say."

The mention of the emperor made Ying pale even further. Her hand trembled as she took the parchment silently from the prince and stared at it, unblinking.

"Okay," he said gently. "It's not that. Then what?" He tucked a piece of her hair behind her ear.

"It's—" Ying was going to say "nothing," but that wasn't true. She chewed her lip, wondering where she should even start. Should she tell him about her despair at having failed as the Fish? Should she tell him that each time she closed her eyes, her brothers' faces were there, seared on her inner eyelids? Should she tell him that his father might be suffering from chronic lead toxicity, or should she leave him blissfully in the dark about that, too?

I should tell him, she thought recklessly, as she'd already thought a thousand times that night. *He'll probably reassure me that my worries are just a silly notion. . . .* But then again, what if they weren't . . . ?

The prince was still watching her, his face so open, so earnest, that Ying came to a decision. She wouldn't tell him. There was very little to go on, really, just a random picture of a wine goblet that happened to look similar to the emperor's, buried in the back pages of a book.

She could probably find a thousand plausible reasons as to

why the emperor was ill. It could have just been an excess of drink; he could be succumbing to liver sickness. Or he could have been possessed by malevolent spirits. At any rate, there was no point worrying Zhang Lin about it, not when his focus and concentration were needed elsewhere.

The thought of war made Ying's chest crumple. War was coming, it was almost upon them, and that meant she might lose more of those she loved. Losing two of her brothers had nearly broken her—who would be next when the reflections attacked? Her mother? Her father? The man she loved?

She was sick of being strong. She was sick of being stoic. Once, just once in her life, she wanted to let her vulnerability show. To be taken care of. And the only person she would let that close was the prince.

Her husband.

"I'm so afraid," she whispered.

The prince drew her closer. "Of the war?"

"Of losing my family. Losing you." Ying swiped away a tear that was slipping down her cheek. "After what happened to my brothers—"

"Hush," he said soothingly. "You won't. You won't lose more family. You won't lose me."

"But"—Ying drew a shuddering breath—"you can't *know* that! I haven't united the Three Treasures, Zhang! I haven't shut the gateway. If anyone dies . . . if *you* die, then it's all my fault!"

At this, Ying broke down. The prince stroked away her tears, over and over again, kissing the places where his thumbs had been. And where his lips went, his whispers followed: "Ying, Ying, my darling wife, Ying."

It took Ying a while to realize that he had sunk to his knees in front of her, his hands on her thighs. He waited until Ying's sobs had petered out into small, stuttering hiccups. Only then did he speak.

"I cannot predict what tomorrow will bring." He stared up at her, his voice at once both tender and savage. "But I will say this: *none* of this is your fault. None. And every minute, every second, we are fighting"—he kissed her hands, first one, then the next—"I will be fighting to get back to you. Fighting for a better world . . . for *you*."

"Oh, Zhang." Ying looked down at him through a film of tears. "Promise me. Promise you will never leave me."

The prince stared up at her, his gaze raw, intense. "I promise," he said, settling a warm hand on her chest, right over her heart. His voice dropped to a whisper. "Xīngān. I cannot live without you."

Ying was overcome. She couldn't decide whether to smile or sob, laugh or cry. Instead, she grabbed his hand in both of hers and kissed it, trying to show in actions what she could not say in words.

Zhang glanced at the opulent hardwood table that sat by the bed, upon which sat a pitcher of water and two tumblers. It was close enough for him to reach; he poured two cups of water and pushed one into Ying's hand.

She went to drink, but the prince caught her gently by the wrist. "Wait," he said, his voice wavering. "Before you drink, I want to check with you. We don't have wine, only water. Is that enough?"

"What do you—" Ying began, but then understanding dawned and she could only whisper, "The Crossed-Cup Ceremony." It was a ritual usually performed at the wedding ceremony, to bind two souls together. Having swapped with her reflection, Ying had never done it.

He nodded, looking up at her. "We never got a chance to do things properly, and Ying"—he swallowed, his grip tightening—"I want it to be proper. I want us to be married, for real this time. To be a part of you, a part of your soul. If I . . . die . . . in battle, I want to enter the afterlife properly. As your husband."

Ying blinked, and more tears spilled out and ran down her face, although these tasted bittersweet, like memory, like longing. She recalled their wedding day, when the prince had left her alone in their bridal chamber and her reflection had hauled her through the mirrors. How wrong she had been about everything back then.

And now the prince was asking to complete the ritual. To make things right.

She nodded, just once.

The prince stared up into Ying's eyes, tears shining in his own. His gaze was fire, a desert drinking up the rain.

"I am in you," he said, twining his right arm around hers until their arms were locked together. "And you are in me."

They both took a long drink before wordlessly exchanging cups and linking their left arms.

And under the pale light of the moon, they stared at one

another and said the words that would bind them forever. Not merely as husband and wife but as twin souls; like yin and yang, like water and wood, like sun and fire, like wind and rain.

"I am in you, and you are in me," they recited together, and then they drank again.

43

They stood in formation, watching, waiting.

Thousands. Tens of thousands. The Jinghu Dao army. Some on horseback, some on foot, some sitting motionless on the backs of battle chariots. All were clad in intricately patterned iron armor, loose blue tunics, and iron helmets. Each breastplate displayed the Shan family emblem—the three-peaked mountain encircled by a dragon.

Just outside the palace grounds and into the surrounding countryside, they lined up, a black blemish on the once-pristine land. They clustered around every lake, every pond, every estuary, every pool. And within the palace walls, more soldiers stood, silently, guarding every reflective surface.

Ying clung to the back of her black dragon, perched atop the prince's tower, its claws hooked onto the roof tiles. Way down below sat the prince, mounted on an armored war horse. Something twisted in her gut. He was close to the lake. Too close.

The rising sun began to crest the mountains, tinting the jagged peaks red. The sky was a blanket of gray. Just before dawn, Ying had gathered her dragons and commanded them to breathe. They had roared, producing mist, fog, and condensation, which had then coalesced into thick, lumpy clouds. Ying cast a look at the sky and gave a grim smile. While she was here, while her dragons lived, the reflections would not be able to harness the power of the sun.

For a long time, nothing happened. Wind swirled, whispering through the gathered army, stirring the loose strands of Ying's hair that she'd tried to tuck under her helmet. Horses snorted and stamped their feet. But otherwise, no one moved. No one spoke.

Then the rumbling started.

The center of the lake began to bubble and roll. From deep within, there came a sound, soft at first but then building to a crescendo. A shadow billowed just beneath the surface, like a cloud of ink unfurling. The water churned. Waves broke upon the shore.

"It's starting," Ying said to herself under her breath. She narrowed her focus to the lake's center, where the water was at its choppiest and most disturbed.

For several elongated seconds, everything went unnaturally silent, like the breath inhaled before a scream.

Then the water broke.

The mirror army burst from the lake.

Out streamed reflections—hundreds of them. Thousands. Dressed in the livery of the prince's own company, they glowed with green refractile luminescence.

And Ying saw, from her elevated vantage point, that at precisely the same moment, more mirror soldiers were climbing through every reflective surface. The palace windows. The polished bronze statues. Even full buckets of water that were sitting in the courtyard.

At the first sight of the enemy, Prince Zhang Lin rode out in front of his company, bellowing orders. In a colorful, rippling wave, the human army ripped off their outer tunics, revealing scarlet ones below.

Generals hollered. Horns sounded. Drums began to thump, echoing across the plains. And then, like two opposing tidal waves, the two armies clashed.

Heart pounding, Ying launched the dragon into the air. It pushed off the tower roof, fragments of ceramic tiles plummeting to the ground. The dragon drove itself up and up with undulating propulsion, and Ying felt the familiar stomach-dropping feeling of shooting up into the sky.

From up high, Ying saw more mirror people crawling from the lake. More reflections crashed through the palace windows and hauled themselves, bedraggled, out of ponds. Ying's dragons swooped and dove, snatching up mirror people, crushing them in their great claws, tossing their broken bodies back into the water.

As she watched, more and more mirror people emerged, climbing from the reflective surfaces. Her heart plummeted. How would they ever defeat such an indomitable horde?

Frantically, Ying scanned the battle below. Her stomach jolted when she saw a lone figure on horseback break away from the battle and race along the ground after her. It was the prince, mounted on Shadow Runner. She whirled her dragon around to face him, wondering if he needed to tell her something important.

But something was wrong. As she looked more closely, she saw that he was glowing. And the horse he rode wasn't Shadow Runner. This one glinted with a silver luster, as though it had been dipped in starlight and hung out to dry.

It wasn't the prince. It was the Mirror Prince.

His lips spread in a slow grin. Almost lazily, he cut down two soldiers who tried to accost him, then launched himself off the back of his steed. As he shot up into the air, he transformed midflight into an enormous, sleek black eagle.

Ying's stomach roiled with nausea. She'd known, of course, that the Mirror Prince could shift. But seeing her human-looking former lover transform so easily into something not human was . . . disturbing.

He hovered above them, suspended, immobile. Like the prince's hair, the eagle's feathers were as black as night, with a glossy, luminescent sheen. Its wings were large and graceful, tapering into a fine fringe of elongated feathers, the hooked yellow beak a startling contrast.

Without warning, the eagle folded its wings and swooped straight down toward where Ying sat atop the dragon. She swore and ducked as the bird shot past, narrowly missing her head. The dragon gave a violent jerk, snorting out puffs of cold, dense fog, and Ying spun around to see the Mirror Prince standing on its broad, scaled back.

"Hello, Princess." The prince made a show of looking her up and down, his gaze raking her skin. Ying cringed. Where once that look would have filled her with molten desire, now it just chilled her to her core.

Immediately, she launched to her feet and ran at him, landing a kick in his abdomen that sent him staggering backward. The dragon jerked again, and the prince swayed, arms extended. Ying flipped, landed on her feet, and resumed a fighting stance.

"You're good," the prince said, wagging a finger in her direction. Both of them were holding on to the dragon's spines, buffeted by the wind. He leered. "It's a shame I never got to bed you."

Ying let out a derisive laugh. "I have no regrets," she replied. "Tell me, does your cold blood make your cock shrink? Or is it that small all the time?"

The Mirror Prince smirked but didn't get to retort, for an enormous bang sounded, deafening them. The force of the explosion sent them flying sideways; her dragon struggled hard to stay airborne.

The Jinghu Dao army had deployed the cannons. The smell of smoke and gunpowder permeated the air.

Flinging out an arm, Ying managed to grab a big handful of the dragon's mane and hauled herself back up. She spun, just dodging a swing of the Mirror Prince's sword. With a roar, she yanked her club from her belt and parried his next blow.

The Mirror Prince deflected it and gave a brutish laugh. "You think you can fight *me*, human?" He circled her like a predator, and Ying spun, gripping her club handle with both sweat-slicked hands. Close up, his eyes were black; with the cloud cover, they were deprived of sunlight, becoming nothing more than negative space. Empty. Soulless.

Inhuman.

She sprang at him. Their fight was fast, brutal, scrappy—their hair blown wild by the wind. Somehow, they both kept their balance atop the dragon, even as it undulated through the smoky skies and lurched to avoid arrows.

Ying, for all her efforts, was tiring rapidly. She gritted her teeth and bent her mind toward the dragon.

Throw him off, she thought desperately.

The dragon bucked midair. Ying was ready, grabbing one of its bony spines, and just managed to hold on. The Mirror Prince, though, was tossed right off.

Frantically, she scrambled to the edge, trying to see where he was. The height made her giddy. The battling armies looked like insects swarming. The crags of the mountains surrounded them, fog and mist rising in plumes. Was it just the weather, or was it dragon's breath? Dragons were masters of the weather: masters of water, of fog and mist and snow and ice. One command and Ying's dragon could shift the will of the wind, creating typhoons, cyclones, storms, or rain. It could dislodge snowcaps from mountain peaks and send avalanches crashing down their slopes. Could create a storm that made it impossible for the Mirror Prince to see.

The problem was that these things would also affect her own people—perhaps to a greater degree.

Where was he? Ying spurred the dragon higher, looking everywhere for the Mirror Prince. And then . . .

Something solid barreled into her. *Oh,* Ying thought as she hurtled off the dragon's side into free fall. *There he is.* Time slowed to a standstill, then sped up as her brain worked overtime.

She registered everything at once: The jagged mountains

rushing up to meet her. Her dragon, darting sideways to avoid another arrow. The Mirror Prince, who had phased back into the black eagle, hovering high above, watching her with beetle-black eyes.

Bastard. A searing pain flashed across Ying's upper back. There was that feeling again, from when she'd almost drowned in the lake, of something hard poking out through her skin—like a needle trying to push through fine-wrought fabric.

Just before she landed, time slowed even further. She hovered for a moment, six feet in the air, before blackness overcame her and she crashed heavily to the ground.

44

She shouldn't have survived, but she did. She shouldn't have come around, but she did. Groaning, Ying rolled over and coughed, tasting blood. The gōushé scar on her upper back stung, as though she'd sliced it open.

She'd landed right in the middle of the battlefield. The ground was mushy with churned-up mud; around her, people fought, the clash of weapons and piercing screams filling the blood-scented air.

She was alive. *She was alive!* But how? Ying combed back through her memory, those terrifying seconds suspended in the air. Somehow, she'd hovered before she hit the ground. What did that mean? Had the Mirror Prince noticed? Her mind was addled, her vision blurry. A shadow fell across her; she squinted.

The Mirror Prince stood above her, his features lined in fury. He seemed as surprised as Ying was that she was still alive. Winded, she clutched her chest, rolling to one side. Just in time—the Mirror Prince's sword struck the ground, spraying her with stinking mud.

"You're extraordinarily hard to kill, you know that?" he said, wrenching his blade from the mud.

Ying struggled to gain purchase on the slippery ground, bracing herself for the next blow. But none came. Instead, he was jerked backward. Ying struggled to her feet, retching, to see two men tussling in the mud.

The Mirror Prince. And the real prince. But which was which? They were both so dirt-streaked that Ying could not see the color of their tunics. One had gained the upper hand, straddling his opponent and pounding the other man's face over and over again.

Ying stumbled closer, panic tearing up her insides, relieved to see it was her husband, the real prince, sitting astride his reflection. With each blow, he roared: "You. Do. Not. Touch. Her!"

A group of human soldiers had gathered around. As the Mirror Prince's head lolled, Prince Zhang Lin yanked him upright, locking him in a chokehold. His face contorted in fury, his hands went to the Mirror Prince's head, ready to break his neck.

Ying shook, terror knifing through her. In this moment, the prince looked fearsome, his face flushed, his hair plastered to his forehead, his teeth bared. One of his eyes had swelled shut.

A voice behind them interrupted. "Well, well, well," it said. Ying jerked her head around. The voice was familiar. Very familiar. As familiar to Ying as her own.

Reflection-Ying unspooled herself from a crouched position, having just phased from her raven form. She surveyed the scene with her hands on her hips, then smirked. "What have we here?"

"Back off!" Prince Zhang snarled, tightening his chokehold.

"Such a rude reception." Ying's reflection clicked her tongue. "Monstrous, in fact. And here I thought *we* were the monsters."

Birdlike, she cocked her head to one side, raising her eyebrows at Zhang Lin. "I suppose it's not surprising, really. After all, anything *we* learned over the years, we learned from humans like you."

The prince balked, his face twisting in disgust. Then, as if shaken by her words, he let go. The Mirror Prince fell face-forward in the mud.

Ying's grip tightened on the handle of her club, the rough feel of the wood grounding her. Something surged within her veins: Rage. Vengeance. Ugly, vicious emotions, willing her to attack. She knew the mirror people were weakened from the lack of sun. Even now, her reflection looked insubstantial, translucent, as though she was becoming the very glass through which she'd passed. The Mirror Prince was still unconscious. If they worked together, Ying and the real prince could overcome them easily in their depleted state.

But *should* she? She shook with the effort, with the indecision. Prince Zhang Lin had made his choice. But what would she choose? When it came down to it—could she be like Mei Po? Could she kill her own reflection?

Mei Po's words from their first meeting echoed through her mind. *Remember who the monsters are.* For a moment, she saw the scene as though she were an outsider: the Mirror Prince, unconscious in the mud. The real prince, having very nearly killed his own reflection. And Ying herself, brandishing her club, about to finish the Mirror Prince off.

Remember who the monsters are, Mei Po had said.

It was never just about the reflections.

It was about the humans, too.

"Soldiers," she commanded, her voice cracking. She lowered her club. "Throw them in the dungeons." The human soldiers converged and hauled the Mirror Prince's unconscious body up by his armpits. Another group of soldiers grabbed Ying's reflection by her arms, restraining her.

Ying exhaled and turned away. Her bones ached; she felt suddenly weary. She had made her decision, for better or worse; she just hoped she'd live long enough to see the consequences.

The soldiers began to march their prisoners away, the Mirror Prince's feet dragging along the ground, dredging deep tracks through the mud.

Prince Zhang Lin touched her on the shoulder. "Ying," he said. The way he said it sounded . . . portentous.

Ying raised her eyes to meet his. "What's wrong?"

"The . . . water. Look at the water." He pointed.

Turning, Ying saw the center of the lake had become clouded, a swirling black mass coalescing below the surface. *What now?* When would the lake stop yielding horrors from its brown, blood-stained depths?

Ying watched in dismay as the water became a whirlpool.

The blackness surged toward the surface, then burst from the lake. Birds. Like all the other mirror-world creatures, as soon as they entered the real world, they began to glow. But theirs was not a mild green glow. Theirs was painfully bright, like fire.

They flapped skyward, then circled like a golden nebula. The air grew cacophonous with squawking and flapping.

"Huǒ wūyā," the prince breathed, his hand tightening around

Ying's. "Fire crows." Everyone had heard the old stories: birds that burned with the power of ten suns.

"The mirror people have brought their own sunlight," said Ying, staring up at the wheeling flock. Where only seconds earlier the world had been dark, gray, and full of shadows, now it was suffused with golden light. Ying could now see every wound, every gash, every bead of sweat on every soldier.

With rising horror, she recognized the creatures. They were the same crows that had watched Ying on her first trip to the mirror world.

Except this time, they weren't just watching.

Seemingly as one, the birds dove. Like a volley of flaming arrows, they flew at the humans' faces, pecking and flapping, squawking and darting. The humans, including the soldiers restraining the prisoners, dropped whatever they were holding and fought off the birds, arms over their faces, bodies thrashing about.

"Retreat!" the prince bellowed, grabbing Ying's hand and dragging her toward the palace. "Get back. Retreat!" They stumbled away from the lake, using their clubs to fend off the crows.

And among the chaos, Ying's reflection stood, a beatific smile plastered on her face. A face that said, *I did this.*

Ying froze, staring in dismay as a soldier went down, screaming. Blood streamed from his eye sockets. The birds pecked relentlessly at his face.

Prince Zhang, one arm around her torso, pulled her along.

In her peripheral vision, she saw Reflection-Ying dive into the lake; she'd taken advantage of the chaos to make her escape.

Ying could do nothing to stop her. So she ran, the prince running with her. But too many men had been left behind. The prince stopped, torn.

"Go," he said to Ying, urging her away. He drew his sword. "Get out of here!"

"No!" Ying drew her own sword.

"I mean it, Ying! You're needed. I'm—" He was cut off, for a swarm of birds descended upon him. Now, released from reflection-Ying's control, the flock was seemingly swarming anything that moved; attacking indiscriminately.

He spun, his sword hacking and slashing in every direction. Birds squawked. Screamed. As they fell, their bodies turned black before disintegrating into ash. But more came to take their places.

Ying ran toward the attack, taking out birds along the way. She reached the prince; they stood back to back, fending off the attack.

Yet still more birds came.

The swarm grew thicker and thicker. Some birds slipped through Ying's defenses. She screamed as one pecked her hand, splitting her skin. It felt like being burned. Pain jolted up her arm, and she stumbled.

The birds flapped around her, congregating. She squinted against the glare, trying to fight them off, but they were too numerous. This was it. She was going to die.

Not because of the reflections. But because of fucking *birds*.

What was happening, though? They were suddenly thinning out. Leaving her alone. Ying lurched unsteadily to her feet.

Another creature had shown up, running through the crows, moving so fast it was just a blur. The screeches were deafening as monstrous jaws snapped birds from the very air. They flocked, flapping and screeching, a big, messy ball of fire.

What *was* this creature?

It surfaced momentarily from the tussle, and Ying saw who it was. Mei Po, but as the snowy-white fox. She snarled, all snapping teeth and slashing claws.

The prince ran to Ying, clasping her to his side—Mei Po had lured the birds away from both of them.

In the chaos, Ying couldn't properly see what was happening. But then the fox gave a scream that was decidedly human-like, and before Ying's eyes, the fox morphed into the old woman. She'd been thrown onto her back, and the fire crows had congregated around her, pecking at her while she screamed. She was enveloped in a blinding light; fine cracks began to appear on her skin, radiating outward.

"Mei Po!" Ying screamed.

The old woman was panting, her face scrunched in pain. Ying sprinted toward her, walloping birds that were in her way. But Mei Po, her teeth gritted, shook her head.

"Go, both of you!" she ground out. "Go and close the gateway!"

"No!" The sting of tears sliced Ying's eyes. The prince grabbed her upper arm.

Mei Po's voice was getting weaker, drowned out by the screech of the birds. "You must! You need to seal the mirrors!"

Ying shook her head. She was crying now. "But . . . how? I don't know how!"

"You both need to—" Mei Po's faint voice was now totally drowned out by the birds.

"Need to what?" Ying shrieked. "We both need to *what*?"

The prince tugged at her arm. "Princess," he urged, "we need to go."

Looking around, Ying saw that they were now surrounded by the mirror army. Not a single human soldier was in sight; only broken, bloodied bodies remained. And the mirror people were no longer translucent. With the crows' light to bolster them, they bared their teeth, hungry. They closed in on Ying and the prince, drawn by the birds, these false suns—a source of energy.

They were solid. They glowed.

Ying knew enough about battle to know that she and the prince were outnumbered. "Help!" Her broken cry caught in her throat. "Please come! Lái!"

It was enough. In a fraction of a second, the black dragon descended, low enough for Ying and the prince to jump up, grab its mane, and clamber on. "Get the Mirror Prince," Ying yelled, and the dragon closed its claws around his unconscious form. It reared and shot back up into the sky.

Below them, the birds converged. Mei Po gave a wail that transitioned into a scream. Then came a high-pitched sound of splintering, and her glasslike body shattered into pieces.

Ying held on, her body frozen, the dragon taking them still higher. The screams had stopped. The fire crows pecked at the fractured remnants of Mei Po's body.

Ying let out a huge, hacking sob. She hadn't known her long, and she still wasn't sure of her allegiance, but Mei Po, a centuries-old shape-shifting demon, had saved them from the fire crows. And for what? So Ying could close the gateway—something she still didn't know how to do?

The prince put his arms around her. She clung to him, her face against his chest. Below them, the mirror army was advancing, the emperor's army losing ground.

"I wonder why the mirror people are glowing," the prince said suddenly, as though to himself.

Ying looked up at him, her grief briefly giving way to surprise. "They glow for you now, too?"

"Yes." The prince's brow furrowed. "You mean, you've seen them glow before?"

"They've always glowed for me. At least, when they're in our world."

"Not for me," the prince murmured, frowning. "Today is the first time. I wonder what that means?"

Ying didn't get a chance to answer, because the prince suddenly gripped her arm. "Wait." His voice was strained. "We need to go back to the palace. The white banners are up."

Without hesitation, the dragon immediately responded with a smooth turn midair. The prince glanced at Ying. She understood his confusion. The dragon responded to him now, too? She didn't have time to ponder this.

"What does that mean?" she asked, her voice wavering.

"It means," the prince whispered as they sped back to the palace, "the emperor is dying."

45

The black dragon landed in the courtyard, shaking the palace walls and sending up a cloud of dust. Ying and the prince slid off its back. They called to the servants, who hurriedly helped them shed their armor. The prince dashed up the infirmary steps. Before following, Ying turned to a servant and pointed at the Mirror Prince, who was now sprawled on the cobblestones. "Take him to the dungeons," she said, then ran up the steps herself.

The emperor lay, supine, on the infirmary table. A group of healers stood around the perimeter of the room. The empress was by his head, smoothing hair from his pallid face.

The room was silent, the air sour with the smell of sickness. The stillness was oppressive after the racket of the battle, which still raged on outside. Ying reached out, grasping for her husband's hand. They found each other, their fingers entwining, the prince gripping hers with more force than usual.

The lead healer looked up as they approached. "I am sorry," they said to the prince, their voice soft, an expression of commiseration in their dark brown eyes.

The empress let out a wail, bending farther over her husband.

The prince shuddered. He didn't answer. Instead, Ying spoke. "You cannot save him?"

"I cannot, Your Highness," the healer confirmed.

Ying's chest tightened. She supposed she should feel relieved—pleased, even. The emperor had arrested her, locked her up, ordered her brothers' executions. Didn't she want the man dead? An eye for an eye, wasn't that how things worked? But seeing the devastation stamped across Prince Zhang's face made her rage ebb away until there was nothing left in her heart but pity.

The healer's eyes narrowed at the emperor, and they stroked their chin. "If it had been just a simple illness, he might have prevailed. The dysfunctional liver might have regenerated. But the poison . . ." They shook their head. "I'm afraid the effects of that are beyond my abilities to reverse."

"Poison?" The prince had finally found his voice, although it was rougher than usual.

The healer inclined their head. "Yes, Your Royal Highness. Poison." They hovered a finger above the emperor's blanched, bloated face. "The pallor. The swollen joints. It suggests a poison, Your Highness, though I cannot say what."

"But . . . how? Why? What poison . . . ?" the prince said, his face paling, pupils dilating.

The tips of Ying's ears burned. She remembered the carved-bronze tumbler in Master Chen's storeroom. It had looked so like the one in the metallurgy book, purported to cause lead poisoning. She remembered the way the emperor was always swigging from the cup and his blank-faced passivity as he drank from it.

Previously, she had wanted to protect the prince by not mentioning her suspicions. But doing so had led them to this: the emperor dying right in the midst of battle. If anything, this was worse. Much worse.

The realization gripped her: she could not protect anyone by shielding them from the truth.

"Lead," Ying said under her breath. Then, louder, to the room, "Could it be lead?"

The healer turned to Ying. "Lead, Your Highness?"

"The poison His Holy Highness is afflicted with. Is it lead?"

The healer pursed their lips, considering. "The signs are indeed consistent, Your Highness. But—" The healer shook their head. "How would he be exposed . . . to *lead*?"

Turning to one of the waiting servants, Ying voiced a command. "Quick," she said, "go to the emperor's quarters and fetch the vessel from which His Holy Highness drinks. Don't tell anyone what you're doing. Go!"

The servant dashed off. The room settled into an uneasy silence. As soon as he reappeared, Ying snatched up the wine chalice. Her pulse quickened. Close up, it was even more ornate than she'd expected, with an intricate filigree pattern on the outside and a bright-red inner surface. The Shan family name was printed around the rim, over and over, just like the cornices of the Mirror Prince's bedroom. Unease crawled through Ying's veins. Yes, this cup looked almost exactly like the one in the book. But there was something else about it, something that niggled at the corners of Ying's mind, though she couldn't say what or why.

Holding it aloft, she faced the healer. "This. This contains lead."

The healer plucked the chalice from Ying's grasp, mouth downturned in a dubious expression. *"This?"*

Ying raised her chin, her jaw set. "Yes. I read it in a book. *Metallurgy Through the Ages.* You can check if you want." Her tone was more belligerent than she'd intended.

The healer stared at the cup, eyes narrowed. "No, no. I believe you. I don't need to read it."

Ying took a deep inhale. "I saw the cup in the master's storeroom. Truth Master Chen." She paused for emphasis. "The master has been poisoning His Holy Highness."

The healer, stunned, stuttered, "The . . . m-master? But that's not . . . He—he's the emperor's adviser. That *cannot* be right—"

A voice spoke up. "It *is* right."

It was the empress who had spoken, from her place beside the emperor. Everyone turned to face her. She rose to her feet slowly. "The master did it. On *my* orders."

Prince Zhang Lin whirled around. "What?" he spat. "Why?"

Ying watched, numb, as the healer slowly placed the emperor's cup back down on the table.

The prince's closed his eyes and shook his head. "Why?" he repeated, his voice barely audible. Trembling, he opened his eyes, focusing on his mother. "Why would you do such a thing?"

The empress straightened and raised her chin. "I did it for you, son."

The prince's nostrils flared. "You did it for *me*? What do you *mean*? You killed my father!"

"Your *father*?" the empress spat. "Some *father*! He would have sacrificed you in his caprice and cowardice! He would've sacrificed us all. We would not have been ready for this war without my intervention!" In the distance, clashing swords, booming cannons, and screaming men sounded.

"Perhaps," he said, "but . . . Mother! You colluded with the master to kill the *emperor*!"

The empress straightened, her posture regal. "Leadership involves making hard choices, Zhang Lin." She placed a hand on his shoulder. "And many sacrifices—"

He shrugged her off in anger. "Sacrifices?" he scoffed. He shook his head, then continued, his voice low and bitter. "Yes. I once thought as you do, Mother." A pained expression flashed across his face. "I thought that leadership was akin to strength. That power equated to violence. That in order to rule, I had to conquer my enemies, cut down anyone who stood in my path. But you know as well as I do where that led." He raised his head and looked at the empress. "My brother's murder."

The empress looked up at her son, her chest rising and falling with increasingly rapid breaths. Her eyes glistened with unshed tears.

"What if it doesn't have to be that way, Mother?" The prince took a step toward the empress. He reached out and took her hand. "Those reflections out there became what they are because of *us*. From watching us. What if we did things differently from now on? What if we made a choice . . . to rise above violence? To break the cycle?"

For several seconds, the empress did not respond. But then

she tugged her hand from her son's. "That's easy for you to say." Her words were laced with venom. "You are a *man*, Zhang Lin. A prince. You have privileges you cannot begin to understand. Men like you don't have to lurk in the shadows, playing games to court power. Men like you don't need to make empty promises to corrupt priests, just to get things done. That sort of power—you don't need to chase it. It comes to *you*."

Mother and son faced each other, both rigid, jaws clenched, their bodies wound tight with tension. Finally, the prince let out a long exhale, then turned away, shaking his head. "Arrest her," he said through barely moving lips. "Arrest my mother for treason."

A group of guards grabbed the empress by the arms. She made no struggle. "The only thing I'm guilty of, son, is loving you. Protecting you. Remember that."

The prince didn't watch as the guards led their prisoner away. As soon as they exited, he sagged against the wall, spent. Nausea rose in Ying's throat. With an effort, she swallowed it down.

The room fell silent save for the wheezing rattle of the emperor's breaths. Even those were slowing, coming further and further apart. Everyone present watched the ashen form of Zhang's father, the labored rise and fall of his chest. Before long, the emperor gasped, spluttered, then went still.

The healer bowed their head. "He is gone," they said simply.

The prince went to the door, kicked it open, and stormed through. Ying, casting one last frightened look at the emperor's corpse, turned and followed him.

Zhang ran up the final flight of steps, heading for the tower roof. Ying followed as fast as she could, going around and around the spiral staircase before bursting out on top. Although the sky was still radiant from the fire crows, it remained overcast with angry clouds. The air was close and humid, and rain fell; big splashy drops, fat diamonds from a bloated sky. Golden light shimmered, filtering through the raindrops, and over the purpled distance of the horizon arched a luminous double rainbow. The whole scene looked utterly surreal, almost absurd.

Ying found the prince at the far end of the rooftop, soaking wet. As she watched, he punched the battlement wall, his blow leaving a smear of blood on the slippery stone. It stayed there momentarily before washing away in the rain—a transient display of anger, of regret, of hopelessness, of grief.

"Zhang." Ying went to him and put her hand on his broad upper back. He didn't respond, just gave the wall another punch. "Husband." She squeezed his shoulder.

He stopped then, leaning into the wall, pressing his forehead against the rough, damp stone. His body shook, racked with silent sobs. His fingers clawed at the wall, the knuckles bloodied, the tendons standing out on his callused hands.

Ying took a step closer, rubbing circles on his back, feeling how the muscles flexed beneath her hand. She moved even closer; stroking his wet hair from his face, she kissed him on the temple, then on the ear.

With a movement so sudden it startled her, he spun to face her. Grabbing her face in his hands, he brought his lips to hers. Ferocious. Uncompromising. All his grief, all his passion, poured into a kiss. And as he held her face, she pressed up against him, winding her arms around his neck, kissing him back as though this might be it. As though this might actually be the end of the world.

When they broke apart, he leaned his forehead on hers. His face was wet, although Ying couldn't tell if it was with rain or tears or both. He closed his eyes, breathing hard, then drew her to him, burying his nose in her hair. The rain continued driving down. They were soaked.

"I'm sorry, my prince," Ying murmured into his chest. Beneath her ear, she could hear his heart beating; strong, constant, steadfast.

He didn't respond for several moments, just rested his chin on top of her head. Finally, he spoke.

"I shouldn't grieve for him. He never respected me. He never thought I was good enough. I shouldn't miss him, should I?" The prince sounded hesitant, unsure. Not like the confident, measured man he so often pretended to be.

Right now, he sounded so, so young. An echo of the boy he must have been. A boy who craved acceptance from a cold, distant father. A boy who was neglected for a cherished, firstborn brother.

A boy who only ever wanted love.

But this boy, this boy who wanted love, was born into the wrong family. The emperor had poured everything into his firstborn son. The original heir.

And one man's love can only stretch so far.

Ying drew her head back to look up at the prince. His face

was no longer agitated. Instead, his expression just looked pained. Weary. "How can I ever forgive my mother, Ying? How can I ever trust her again?"

"She loves you," Ying murmured. She paused, thinking of the empress's fierce determination. The lengths she went to, the way she put her own life at risk, just to protect her son. "Everything she did was because she loves you."

She put her hand on his heart. "*I* love you," she whispered. "You are loved."

The prince closed his eyes. A line had formed between his eyebrows. He exhaled.

"What's the point anymore, Ying?" he asked, his eyes still closed. He spoke slowly, as though the words themselves caused him pain. "What's even the point? We can't defeat them. We thought we could overthrow them by blocking out their sun. And then they brought their own fucking suns! And the people will hear of the emperor's death, and they'll think we've already lost." He opened his eyes. "We may as well surrender."

"The people still have you. They still have us. We still have each other."

Fire flashed in the prince's gaze, and he snorted and turned away. "No. We don't. Don't you see? I can't even protect you from them! They know you have the power to close the gateway, and they won't stop fighting us until you're dead. Until you're *dead!*" He slumped against the wall and released a ragged breath. "And I don't want to live in a world where you don't exist, Ying. I can't, I can't, I just can't—"

And that was the crux of it. The prince's anguish had less to do with him or even his people. It was about her and his love for her, and how he felt he couldn't shield her. But, Ying thought, anger flaring within her, it wasn't fair to her. It wasn't fair to make this about her, as though she were the only thing worth saving, the only thing worth protecting. By trying to lighten her burden, he only made it heavier.

Ying raised her chin. "No. I don't accept that."

The prince gave a grim laugh. "It's not your decision to make, Ying."

Another flash of irritation twisted in Ying's gut. "It's not about decisions, Zhang," she said. "You don't just *decide* to die. You don't just *decide* to let your people die. You don't get to decide that on my behalf, just so you can protect me. Can't you see that isn't fair? Not to me. Not to them." She took a deep breath. "There is only one decision: We stay. We fight. We win. That's the only option."

"But . . . but how?"

"How?" Ying didn't know whether to laugh at him or slap him. "*How?* Gods, husband. Are you an archer, or are you an archer?"

The prince passed a hand over his face, looking flummoxed. "I don't have a bow."

Ying was already hauling her own bow and quiver off her back. "Take mine," she said, and tossed the weapons to him. "You shoot the fire crows. I'll work on the Three Treasures." She thought of the emperor's bronze chalice, still downstairs in the infirmary, and the feeling she'd had when she'd inspected it. It was like she was missing something, some key piece of the puzzle, and she had an inexplicable urge to take another look.

It was not much to go on, but what else could she do? She needed to pretend she had a plan, if only to pull the prince from despair.

He spurred immediately into action. With the agility of a cat, he sprung up onto one of the battlements, nocked an arrow, and loosed it. A golden bird screeched and fell, now no longer fire-bright but as dark and black as coal. The prince nocked and loosed another arrow, hitting another bird, then another, then another.

His movements were fluid, as though the bow were merely an extension of his arm. Ying resisted the urge to stay, to watch his powerful muscles flex and pull as he wielded the bow with a warrior's grace.

She managed—just—to tear her eyes away before she backed away. Away from the smoke and blood and the growing piles of bodies. Away from all the people still out there on the battlefield. And away from her heart, the center of her universe, shooting arrows from the tower roof.

Turning and running back down the steps, she realized: they couldn't just hope to succeed. They *had* to succeed. For the sake of the world. Its moon, its sun, and all the people in it.

They had to succeed, or die trying.

46

By the time Ying pushed open the door to the infirmary, the healers had already left. The emperor was still lying on the table, awaiting the priests who would prepare his body and dress him in a funerary xiǎoliàn.

Cold, damp sweat broke out across Ying's brow. Gathering her courage, she edged forward—slowly, carefully—and bent to pick the bronze cup up.

What was it about this thing? Certainly, it contained lead, which had been one of the ingredients in the elixir that had almost killed Ying. The ingredient that had slowly and fatally poisoned Emperor Shan. But that wasn't it, surely? Mei Po had already confirmed that Ying didn't need an alchemical *recipe*. Somehow, she needed to complete the alchemy within herself. But how?

Something scraped behind her, and Ying immediately leapt to her feet and pivoted. A person in iron armor was framed by the door. . . .

"Li Ming," Ying said, throwing herself into her friend's arms. The two women hugged fiercely, clinging to each other. Ying was the first to break contact; she held the maid at arm's length. Both their faces were wet with tears.

Li Ming was barely recognizable. Instead of her usual neat muslin dress, she was clad in armor at least two sizes too big. She wore a helmet pushed far back on her head, frizzed tendrils of hair escaping their restraints. And, most alarmingly, her hands were covered in blood.

Ying stared. "What the hell happened to you?"

"I'm fine, Princess. I—" The maid gave a frightened glance at the window, then finished her sentence very quickly. "Fei fei and I have been out on the battlefield, tending the wounded."

"You . . . you're *nursing*?" Ying was shocked. First, women weren't normally allowed in the hospitals of Jinghu Dao. It was thought that their temperaments were too delicate to handle all the gore. And second, her maids had *never* previously expressed interest in anything besides clothes and hair and—as Ying had recently realized—each other.

"Yes. We wanted to help. It wasn't hard to sneak in with all the chaos." Li Ming frowned at Ying. "We saw the white banners. I thought maybe the prince was injured. I needed to check that you were okay." Her eyes widened. "Where is he? Is he hurt?"

Ying looked up, as though she could see through the stone roof. "He's fine. It's the emperor." She gestured at Emperor Shan's corpse, not wanting to look at it. "The prince is up there. Hunting fire crows."

Li Ming glanced at the emperor's body, her face blanching. "Emperor Shan," she whispered in a voice that was very small.

Shan. *Shān.* Something rattled loose in Ying's brain, and she held up the bronze tumbler. Stared at the Shan family name embossed around the rim.

"Li Ming," she said very slowly, "can you repeat that song? The peasant's song you always sing?"

"The song, Your Highness?" Li Ming answered, confused. "But why?"

"No time to explain." Ying tried to keep her voice even. "Please, just sing it."

Li Ming nodded, her face pale, and sang:

> *Jīng is the essence from which all life grows.*
> *Qì is the energy; like water it flows.*
> *Shén is the fir, the forest of trees—*

Ying cut her off. "Stop," she said, and paced away, agitated. "I think we've been getting it wrong, Li Ming."

"Getting wh-what wrong, Your Highness?"

Ying stopped pacing. "I think . . . I wonder . . ." Again she stared at the cup. When Li Ming sang the song, it wasn't in the modern dialect that Ying was accustomed to. It was in a traditional dialect. And in this dialect, the word for fir tree was pronounced *shān*. At least, they'd always *assumed* that the word *shān*, 杉, meant fir tree. It seemed to make sense, since the song mentioned trees. But what if *shān* didn't mean fir? What if it meant . . . something else?

Ying continued, more to herself than to her maid. "We've been assuming the song references fir trees and forests . . . and that *shān* means fir, as in fir trees, right? At least, that's how we've

434

always interpreted it: *Shén is the fir, the forest of trees.* But *shān* also means mountain, like 山, the Shan family name. What if it's actually supposed to be *Shén is the mountain, the forest of trees*? I mean, the pronunciation of the two words is identical; *shān* means both mountain and fir, and none of us truly knows which meaning it's trying to reference." By now, Ying was muttering to herself, trying to unknot the tangle of thoughts in her head.

She continued raving: "And what if over time, as it was sung through generations, the song morphed, and it's not meant to be 'like water it flows'? What if it was originally meant to say—"

Li Ming's eyes grew very round. "River."

Ying clapped a hand to her forehead. "Yes! *Jiang*—river." She stared hard at the ground as everything slotted into place. The prince's family name: Shan, meaning mountain, for a family who had always lived in the mountains. Zhang Lin's given names meant "archer of the forest." And her own family name meant . . .

"River," Ying repeated, as though in a trance. The Jiangs had always been a water family, a boating family. Their last name, Jiang, literally meant "river." These sorts of folk songs were passed down orally, not written down. She could see how over time, the word *river* could have morphed into *water*.

She grasped Li Ming's shoulders. "I need to go to him. Now."

Li Ming nodded. "Then go," she said, and Ying turned and sprinted up the stairs. Up to the top of the tower.

Shān. Lín. Jiang. The names hurtled through her mind as she ran, the key to understanding them so close—but still out of reach. What did it all mean? Were she and the prince somehow the ingredients she'd been searching for all along?

Even more destruction had been wrought by the time she reached the rooftop. The cannons had left large, ugly craters all over the countryside. The air was awash with hazy smoke. Rain clouds had gathered, darkening the sky. Only one fire crow remained, flapping around, spilling its brilliant light.

The mirror army were on the offense, pushing into the humans' ranks. The prince had ordered most of the army to retreat. The majority of the human army were back within the palace grounds, the remaining soldiers folding back toward the gate. Archers lined the walls, shooting flaming arrows into the hordes.

The prince was no longer on the roof. A quick scan of the skies showed he was now mounted on a bronze dragon, chasing the remaining crow. He was now a dragon rider, too.

The dragon wove around the palace towers, avoiding other dragons, while the prince sent arrow after arrow into the smoke-filled air.

The last bird remained just out of his reach. The prince's arrows kept missing, his increasingly reckless shooting betraying his frustration. He shot one last arrow into the ether, going wide by several yards. Ying saw him slump on the dragon's shoulders, spent with the effort, blindsided by disappointment.

He spotted Ying and swooped down. The dragon landed atop the infirmary tower with a resounding boom.

"Mā de!" The prince threw the bow on the ground. He appeared to be grinding his teeth. "That last bird! I've used up all my arrows, and I can't hit the blasted thing." He peered over the side of the battlements. "At least most of our men are inside the walls now. Hopefully, that gives us some time."

He turned to face Ying. Rain had begun to patter down, and Ying stood there, not bothering to keep it, or her tears, from splashing down her face. "Oh gods, Ying. What's happened?"

She couldn't find the words to explain. Instead, she just rushed into his open arms.

"It's darker now," he murmured. "The reflections will be weakened, unless they bring more light. We can do this, Ying. Together. I know we can." Now he was trying to convince *her*.

Ying buried her face in her husband's chest. He was warm, so warm—like the sun. She shivered despite the heat of his touch.

The prince stroked her wet cheek and brushed wet strands of hair from her face with his fingers. "My beautiful, brave wife," he murmured, holding her to his heart. "What's wrong? Tell me."

The fabric of his tunic was tickling her cheek, and his chin rested heavy atop her head. But there was something else, something that dug into the soft flesh of her face. Something that felt awfully familiar . . .

Raising her head, Ying dipped her hand under the neckline of his tunic and pulled it out.

The hair pouch.

It looked decidedly worse for wear. The velvet had rubbed off in patches. It had stiffened with age and from being worn in battle. And the leather tie was frayed. But it was definitely the pouch containing his hair and her own that she'd snipped off so long ago.

"You've been wearing it this whole time?" Ying stared at it, her mind imploding with a million thoughts.

"Yes," the prince replied. "It comforts me, keeping a piece of you close. But it's yours, really. You should have it back." He took it off and handed it to Ying, who took it without a word.

She held up the velvet pouch, which spun back and forth on a long, woven string. A symbol of the union between their two souls. Ying Yue stared at it as though it was something exceptionally precious, something exceptionally rare.

"Ying?" The prince studied her face carefully, his eyebrows knitting in concern. "What is it? Ying?"

Everything snapped into place. The prophecy. The children's song. Their names. The answer was assembling itself from shards of half-formed thoughts.

She was silent for several long moments. When she finally spoke, her voice was just a whisper.

"I know what the Three Treasures are," she said, and let him go.

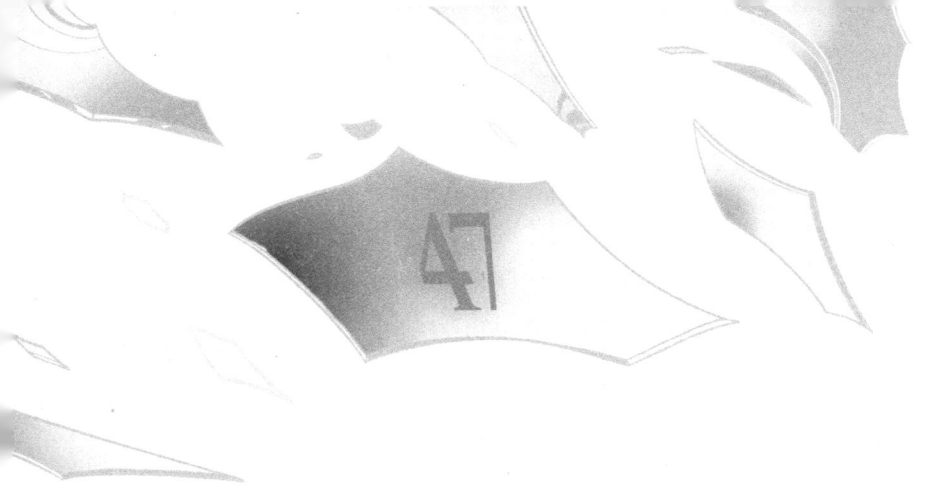

47

"You do?" the prince asked, his brow creasing. "What are they?"

"They're..." Ying inhaled around the lump that had formed in her throat. "They're us."

"Us?" The prince gave her a look. Confusion. Concern.

"There's a song. A folk song. You mightn't know it. Li Ming used to sing it to me. It goes, *Jīng is the essence from which all life grows.*" Ying's words ran into one another; she could barely catch her breath. "*The essence from which all life grows.* It means yin and yang, doesn't it?" She gestured at the empty space between them. "So, jīng—that's us."

"Right." It was common knowledge that yin represented feminine and yang represented masculine energy.

Ying continued: *"Qì is the energy; like a river it flows."* She pointed to herself. "The river—Jiang—that's me. Water is qì." It all made sense now. Why she, the water princess, was chosen for the prince. Why she was chosen to be the Fish. It was her family's heritage: The river family. The water family. It was written into her blood, her bones, her very essence, her qì.

"Shén is the mountain, the forest of trees." She pointed at the prince. "Your names, Shan Zhang Lin: Shan means mountain,

and Lin means forest. You're the shén." The prince said nothing, just stared at her.

Ying finished the song: *"Fire will render the bound spirits free. Unite the Three Treasures: jīng, qì, and shén. The Phoenix will rise into flame once again."* She looked at him. "Uniting the Three Treasures means uniting *us*. Bringing together yin and yang. All we need now is fire."

"Fire?" The prince frowned. "What does *that* mean?"

He paced away for a few steps, running his hands through his hair. A few strands flopped down over his eyes, and he swept them away with an impatient noise.

"You know, I started seeing the reflections glowing only after we performed the Crossed-Cup ceremony. Once we were properly wed." The prince gave Ying a pointed look, and she flushed. "And after that, I could suddenly communicate with the dragons. You know, I think you're right. All this time, we thought the prophecy was just about you, the Fish. But what if it's about both of us . . . together?"

"Mei Po was right," Ying murmured, barely able to speak. "We're meant to be together." As the empress had said: Mei Po was always right.

Lightning flashed across the sky, startling them both, closely followed by a clap of thunder. The dragons patrolled overhead, breathing clouds and ice and mist and fog. Thunder rolled away, rumbling over the plains, echoed by the distant mountains. The sky, swollen with condensation, broke. The rain poured down, faster and faster, until it became a deluge. Wind lashed their faces like a whip.

The storm had restarted, unexpectedly strong, unnaturally sudden. The lone fire crow flashed through the rain's mirage, making the raindrops twinkle like stars. Another flare of lightning illuminated the world, just for an instant, before they were plunged into darkness and rocked once again by thunder.

"We'd better get under cover," the prince shouted over the howling gale, "before—"

Ying cut him off. "Fire!" she yelled suddenly, staring at the sky. Forked lightning streaked across the blackness, patterning it with cracks as if the sky were shattered glass. A relentless, repeating pattern: Lightning. Thunder. Lightning. Thunder.

The dragons soared and twisted high up in the air. Some of them breathed out sparks, sparks that became lightning. The whole time the rain came down in buckets, making everything blur and shimmer.

"What?" the prince yelled over the howl of the wind.

"Fire!" Ying shouted again. "The lightning. That's the fire."

Tears welled in her eyes, lacing her lashes. She now knew what she had to do. The song said that once she'd united the Three Treasures—via the union between herself and the prince—then the Phoenix would be forged in fire and rise in flame.

The Phoenix was *her*. She had been the Fish. And her final transformation would be . . . the Phoenix.

Ying pushed away from the prince. Walked backward a few steps, putting distance between herself and her husband.

The prince had raised his face to the sky, but now he glanced back down at Ying. He made a move to grab her. "Ying, I—"

"Stop." She took another step back. Her tears spilled over,

flashing down her cheeks and mingling with the rain. "Do you remember the stories they used to tell us as children? The ones about how phoenixes are created?"

"Ying, don't . . ."

Ying pressed on. "A phoenix is made when the dragon is struck by lightning and its soul splits." Her nose was running, her voice thick with tears. "Like . . . like two halves of one whole."

The prince made a strangled, tortured sound in the back of his throat. "A fairy story. It means nothing." His eyes burned. He stepped forward and reached for Ying again, but she ducked out of his grasp, backing away.

Ignoring him, she continued: "But it's a test. The dragon who is struck by lightning might survive and be reborn." Ying drew her sleeve under her dripping nose. "But equally, the dragon could be struck by lightning and—"

"You could die!"

Ying took another step back. "Yes. I could die."

The prince roared and lunged at her again, but she held up both hands. A warning. He stopped and stared, his arms hung limp by his side. In his eyes, Ying read despair. Anguish. Desperate, desperate pain.

"Ying, don't do this. Please!"

Ying closed her eyes, squeezing out more tears. "Goodbye," she whispered. "I'll love you forever." Then she turned, ran, and jumped off the tower.

Her dragon swooped up under her, and she landed heavily upon its back. And as she soared into the vicious, monochrome sky, she wondered if she'd ever truly had a choice.

It seemed that her whole life had been funneling her to this point. Her family heritage—their propensity for water, their fish emblem; the prophecies; her ability to open the gateways; her betrothal to the prince.

She could have made another choice, she supposed. She could've stayed with him, fought the war.

In some ways, she wished she could have. They hadn't had enough time. She cursed herself inwardly. If she hadn't been so stubborn, hadn't resisted his love for so long, hadn't been hoodwinked by the Mirror Prince . . . perhaps they would have found each other sooner. Perhaps she would be more at peace with this decision if they'd just had a bit more time.

Lightning forked around her, and then thunder, thunder, rolling thunder. So loud that her ears rang, her body vibrated; she felt as though she'd be thrown off the dragon's back.

Her tears fell freely as she considered the alternative. She could go back. She and the prince could order more cannons, more gunpowder, more soldiers, more weapons. But then what? Without the ability to reseal the gateway, the mirror people would just keep on coming. And, unlike the humans, they wouldn't tire. Her people would be overpowered before long. What chance did the humans have against the mirror army? Against mythical beasts like the fēngshēngshòu?

What chance did mere mortals have against creatures who would never die?

No, she thought, steeling herself. This, here, was her destiny. And she would fulfill it. Even if it led to her death.

The dragon flew higher and higher into the darkened sky. As

they pressed upward into the cloudbank, they were buffeted and jerked around by turbulence. Ying's face and hands were damp with mist. Wet strands of her hair clung to her head. Her eyes stung with the wind, and she squinted, clinging to the dragon's ink-black mane.

Another flash of lightning forked around her. For a moment, in the harsh light, she could see the scene beneath her: The armies fighting. The dragons swooping. The tiny silhouette of her husband, the prince, standing on the roof of the tower. He was yelling something, but she couldn't hear what.

She waited for things to go dark again, her heart clawing up her throat. But they never did.

Instead, the world brightened even further, bathing Ying in an extraordinary light. It was localized, not brightening the ground below but only the immediate vicinity. Ying shielded her eyes with her hand. The webbing of her fingers glowed red. As her eyes adjusted, she saw the final fire crow circling around the dragon, flapping against the rabid wind. The last of the huǒ wūyā. Its feathers were a dazzling gold, and it emitted a dazzling gilded glow. She saw, close up, that its eyes were ruby red. It was large, larger than she expected, larger than a regular crow.

The final sun.

The bird darted inward, pecking at Ying, flapping around her head. *It must still be under Reflection-Ying's control,* Ying thought. *It must be trying to stop me from uniting the Three Treasures.* She slashed her sword at the fog-filled air, catching the end of the crow's wing. It screeched and flew away. A few blackened feathers tumbled on the wind. The bird was gone.

Lightning flashed. Thunder rolled. Ying cringed against the dragon, covering her ears. As soon as the thunder subsided, she swiveled her head again, watching for the bird, waiting for the next attack.

It came from the front. The bird flew in, as fast as a cannon, and flapped around the dragon's head. The dragon uttered a high-pitched shriek, and Ying screamed, too, for she realized now what the bird was doing. It was no longer attacking her. It was doing something far more clever.

It was attacking the dragon.

The bird was pecking out the dragon's eyes. The dragon responded by contorting in midair, filling the sky with an unearthly keen.

Ying hacked at the bird again, but it took off into the sky, its light spilling everywhere. Ying clung onto the dragon as it bucked and spasmed, clawing at its ruined eyes.

She and the dragon fell, writhing and tumbling, toward the infirmary tower. The prince was standing atop the battlements. His loose hair was flying in the wind. He had both hands stretched out toward his wife.

No, Ying thought. *Not there. Not there! You'll kill him!*

The dragon was not listening. It careened toward the tower. Toward death. Its own death, Ying's death . . . and her husband's.

She screamed profanities, pounded on the dragon's neck.

445

She tugged on its mane, trying to alter its flight. But, too preoccupied with its own pain, its blindness, it did not respond.

At the very last moment, right before they collided with the high stone walls, Ying closed her eyes. She pictured the prince's face, pictured him touching her, pictured her lips brushing his, her hands twisting in his hair.

"I love you," she whispered, hoping her message would somehow reach him, in this life or the next.

Whether she died or lived, this was her fate. And her fate, or so it seemed, was tied to his.

At the precise moment the dragon crashed into the tower, Jiang Ying Yue closed her eyes and jumped.

For a moment, it felt as if she were floating, but sensation quickly kicked in. Cold air rushed by her, whistling past her ears. There was a heady feeling of free fall as she plummeted toward the ground.

Then everything went eerily, unnaturally silent. The air prickled. A sharp smell permeated the surroundings. Ying's hair stood on end, splayed around her like a crown. And then a flash, fluorescent, illuminated the whole sky and the clouds and the dark ground that rushed to meet her. The lightning stabbed through her chest, deafening her with an almighty bang.

The impact exploded right down to her bones. She was midair, paralyzed by lightning. Her chest seized; her muscles went rigid. For a second, she couldn't breathe. She was entirely numb.

Then, almost instantaneously, every feeling rushed back. Starting with her chest, then searing outward until every single inch of her body blazed with white-hot pain.

Fire, she thought as time seemingly skidded to a stop. As she tumbled down and down, the pain surged with the force of an exploding sun.

And Ying, the Fish, blacked out, knowing she was about to die.

Ying came to in a world of flickering shadows. She was lying prone, her head turned to one side, surrounded by blurry, ghost-like apparitions.

So. This was the afterlife. This was what it was like to die.

She was not in pain. In fact, she could barely feel her body. She could barely feel anything. But then she curled her fingers. Beneath them was a bed of powder, as fine as dust, or cornstarch, or the finely milled rice her handmaidens often caked upon her face. And her cheek was resting in this soft substance.

Some of it wafted up and tickled her nose. Ying sneezed.

This is when she realized: If this was indeed the afterlife, well . . . she wouldn't have sneezed, would she?

She blinked, squeezing her eyes shut, then opened them again. The figures surrounding her gradually sharpened into focus, becoming more and more corporeal as her eyes adjusted. The more she looked, the more she realized: The crowd gathering around her were not ghosts. They weren't guǐ, spirits trapped in the fissure between life and death. They were people.

And Ying herself wasn't dead. She had flown into the storm, been struck by lightning, and survived.

She was very, very much alive.

Ying climbed slowly to her feet. Now that her lucidity was returning, her senses were too. Her limbs were stiff, as though they'd been fixed in one position for too long. Her exposed skin stung all over. Her feet were bare, buried in a layer of ash. Where had all this ash come from?

Deep down, she knew. The ash was her old self. This, her raw, aching body, was the new version. The final version. She was the Phoenix, reborn.

Her whole life had led to this.

The breeze stirred over her bare skin. Ying's clothing was in tatters, the burned edges curled and crusty. She wrapped her arms around herself in protection, hoping desperately she was covered enough.

She'd landed in the courtyard. The rain had subsided, and the storm had dispersed. Blue sky peeked through wisps of cottony clouds. Shafts of sunlight beamed through the gaps. How long had she been unconscious?

A crowd of people—some soldiers, some servants—pressed in around her. Most of them looked curious, some looked slightly scared. Mercifully, one of the soldiers dashed forward, swinging his cloak off his shoulders. He covered Ying with it, and she clutched it around herself and nodded at him. He bowed his head and melted back into the crowd.

The mass of people parted, shuffling and staring, as Ying made her way toward the wreckage of the ruined tower. The breeze danced again, and the smell of her singed clothes shot up her nostrils. She blinked, her eyes stinging.

The smell... It reminded her of campfires, and of the prince, and of better times.

It reminded her of a different life. A life belonging to a different girl.

Now the prince was gone. There was no way he could have survived being knocked off the tower.

The realization tore afresh the hole in Ying's heart. A hole that expanded outward with every torturous breath. Fracturing, fragmenting, cracking her apart until she resembled nothing more than burned paper—so brittle, so delicate, that a mere breath of air could send her to pieces.

She hadn't just lost her old self. She'd lost her other self, her other half. She'd lost a piece of her very soul.

Feeling barely tethered to the ground, she drifted to the tower's base, drawn to the sight of a small black fish. It was flopping about on the cold stone ground, its gills flaring, its mouth gaping as it drew in useless air. A sick feeling rose in Ying's stomach when she saw that its eyes were just gaping, bloodied holes.

Her dragon.

"Hand me a blade," she said hoarsely, to no one in particular. Immediately, a soldier came forward, sank to one knee, and held a dagger handle upright. Ying wrapped her stiff fingers around the hilt. But then she caught a glimpse of the soldier's face and gasped.

"Fei fei!"

Her maid raised her round, tear-streaked face. "Princess," she whispered. "Did you do it? Did you find the Three Treasures?"

Ying touched the girl's disheveled hair. "I did," she said, her voice barely sounding like her own. The figurative hole in Ying's chest cracked even wider, and she blinked, dislodging tears. It was true, she *had* found them. But she'd lost a vital part of herself in the process.

"You can seal the gateway, then." Fei fei raised her chin. "You can save us all. Right?" She stared up at her mistress with an uncharacteristic look of fierce determination, and the last of Ying's resolve broke and flew away, up toward the heavens.

Ying Yue's tears rained down on the fish as she took Fei fei's proffered dagger and drove the blade through the poor creature's head. It gave two more feeble jerks with its tail, then lay quite still. Ying bowed her head, feeling like her heart would break from trying to cram in another piece of grief.

Her magnificent black dragon would cross the threshold of this life as nothing more than a simple fish. And what of the prince? Would he be perpetually condemned to be a restless spirit? Trapped forever in the shadows of a ruined tower, unable to access this life *or* the next?

Dashing away her tears, she wiped the dagger on her cloak and straightened.

The crowd was still watching her. Now was not the time to go to pieces. Later. She could do it later. She would hold it together for the sake of her people. For the sake of her prince.

"Where is His Highness's body?" she asked the crowd, ignoring the tremor in her voice.

The people shuffled. Whispers swelled before a soldier stepped forward. He was the one who had given her his cloak, and from his livery, she knew he'd been one of the prince's men.

"His body has not been found." The soldier's eyes were downcast, his face lined with grief. Ying scanned the crowd. It wasn't just him. Every soldier, every servant, had their shoulders slumped with grief. The prince was loved by his people.

Or had been, rather.

Ying forced herself to focus. She pushed her sadness deep into her chest, ready to be retrieved and dissected later. Right now, she had a job to do. And that was to overthrow the mirror army and seal the gateway. After all, with both the emperor and the prince dead and the empress imprisoned, who else was there to do it? Who else would take charge?

"Soldier." Ying gathered her scattered thoughts and raised her chin. "Tell me what is happening with the battle. Quickly, now."

The soldier gave her a rapid summary. After Ying had flown into the storm, the prince had sent down a command for the remaining army to retreat. When the dragon exploded into the infirmary tower in a shower of rubble and stone, the prince's army continued to follow his orders, valiantly fighting as they inched their way back to the palace. Many soldiers fell, but eventually the ones remaining managed to crowd back through the palace gates and shut them firmly against their foes.

"And what has the enemy been doing since?" Ying asked.

"They are just standing quietly outside the gate."

"Is it a siege?" In Jinghu Dao, sieges were an uncommon strategy, but who knew what the mirror army was planning?

He gave a small, exhausted shrug. "We cannot be sure."

Ying drew the soldier's cloak around her tighter. It was heavy and slightly too long. But the drape of the fabric felt like armor. It made her feel strong. Or, rather, it made her look strong, even if she didn't feel it.

She climbed a few steps and addressed the crowd.

"My dear people," she said, sheathing herself with a calm exterior despite the turmoil within. "We appear to be safe in here. But we may be trapped for some time." She began to give orders, hesitantly at first, but gathering in momentum as she continued. Instructions to reinforce the gates, to station extra guards at every weak point, to take stock of their food supply and calculate how best to ration it. The soldiers and servants wasted no time in executing her instructions, jumping to attention as soon as she spoke, responding to her authoritative tone.

When she had given the final instruction, she stopped beside the cloakless soldier. "Xièxie," she said, placing a hand on his shoulder. "Thank you. For everything you did for him."

"It was an honor to serve such a man." The soldier paused. "Just as it will be an honor to serve you." He bent low, kowtowing. "I am your obedient servant, Your Imperial Majesty."

Ying's heart stuttered. Imperial Majesty? She wasn't the empress . . . yet.

The crowd dispersed to their respective tasks, and Ying set about sorting through the tower rubble. Right now, her one objective was to find the prince's body. To embrace him, to bring him home, to prepare him for a suitable entry into the afterlife.

She had only just started when she heard the cry.

It was piercing, like the wail of a human baby. Except it

didn't come from the hordes of humans milling around her. It came from above. Harsh, brilliant light fell across the entire courtyard.

Ying looked up, squinting her eyes, trying to locate the source. A bird, blazing with light, obliterated the sky.

The final fire crow. It soared overhead, its high, piercing cries filling the air, its flaming feathers emitting painful brightness. The humans, along with Ying, screwed shut their eyes. Pressed their palms over their ears, doubling over, trying to block out the light, the noise.

The fire crow—the one that had killed Ying's dragon—was back.

And it had come to claim its next victim.

49

It wailed again, the sound so terrible that several humans dropped into fetal positions. Still others crawled along the ground, searching for shelter, faces contorted with pain. Even the archers on the walls threw down their bows and dropped to their knees, hands over their ears.

The sound was not coming from the outside, Ying realized, her own hands pressed over her ears. The sound was within her, inside her head. It was inside everyone's heads.

Then the booms started. At every door, every gate. Rhythmic. Forceful. It didn't take long to work out what the noise was: it was the mirror army battering down the gates.

With icy dread, Ying watched the fire crow dive down at a soldier. Its powerful beak ripped right through his iron armor as though it were silk. The man screamed as the bird tore his flesh.

Ying ran toward them even as others recoiled. She didn't know what she was going to do, but her body flushed hot with anger, prickles surging across her skin. As if she were being struck again by lightning—except this time, instead of shrouding her entire body, the prickling flowed into her hands. Her palms became searingly hot.

And as Ying raised her hands toward the man-eating bird, a shaft of sunlight fell across her open palms....

The next moment, the bird was on fire. The soldier himself was unburned, but he collapsed to the ground like a lifeless doll. The bird wailed again with its otherworldly, baby-like cry, and writhed in the air. It thrashed for a few short seconds before it combusted, spraying the immediate vicinity with ash.

Ying glanced down at her palms. They glowed red, but they weren't burned. And then the sun fell on her again, and she understood.

She was harnessing the power of the sun. She'd become the Phoenix and was now immune to fire. In fact, she could control heat, as though she herself were a mirror. A yángsuì, a sun mirror, that could pull fire from the very sun.

She could do this. She could save the world. So that all the deaths would not be in vain.

She turned her attention to the mirror army outside.

Lái, Ying thought, calling one of her dragons. With a powerful whoosh, a crimson dragon landed on the scarred rubble of the infirmary tower.

Ying hopped up the broken staircase, leaping from step to step with newfound agility. Her cloak flapped in the wind, held only by the fastened neck.

Hoisting herself onto the dragon's back, she clambered between its shoulders. "Come on," she said, giving its neck a pat. "Let's go save the world."

The dragon roared, flexed its powerful back, and took off into the sky.

Ying's hair whipped across her face as the dragon ascended into the big expanse of blue. With the power of the sun beating down on her exposed neck and hands, the energy running through her surged until flashes of light sparked off her skin.

She eyed the hordes of mirror people below. They had successfully broken down one of the gates and were barging into the courtyard. The human army, her people, fought back with renewed vigor—as though her triumph over the last fire crow had rejuvenated their morale. The roar of both armies' battle cries filled the air.

Squeezing her eyes shut, Ying concentrated hard. She turned her thoughts inward and blocked out the sounds of battle, the shouts and the screams and the thud of steel hitting bone. She blocked out the smells: horse shit and soggy soil and the acrid stench of blood.

I am a dragon rider, she thought. *I am the Fish. I am the Keeper of the Gateway.*

Forcing her mind into a state of blank stillness, she took a slow breath—in, then out.

I am the Phoenix, reborn.

Energy swelled within her. Her insides burned with a fire that swirled in her blood and sang in her veins, that beat against her skin as though trying to escape.

And it did. The dam broke. The energy released. She

raised her palms, deflecting sunlight straight into the mirror crowd.

It hit the ground, igniting small fires everywhere. Whole swathes of mirror people were caught in the reflected rays of sun—flashing red-hot before bursting into flames. Ablaze, they rolled around on the ground, screaming.

These mirror people, who thrived on light, were now being defeated by fire. Ying quashed her horror, her guilt, her fear, her pain, and continued to gather sunlight in her hands. She bombarded the enemies. She torched the bushy scrub and forests, burned the woods to the ground. She shot fire at the mirror army; shot fire at their hideous beasts. Those that were still able to run bolted for the lake, slipping, slithering, and diving in. There seemed to be never-ending throngs of creatures from the mirror world.

Eventually the crowd thinned. The lake swallowed up the last of the enemies.

Ying gasped, nearly falling off the dragon. Just in time, she managed to right herself. The grounds around the lake were still, save for twitching bodies, the lick of flames, and billowing smoke floating languorously above the wastelands.

It was time. Time to seal the gateway. She hadn't known how before, but now she knew. Deep in her bones, she knew it—in her belly, in her heart.

She didn't only have the power to deflect the sun's energy, to create fire, to wield the world's heat as though it were a whip. She also had the ability to absorb it. To keep it sheltered. To keep it safe. To hold it in her body—her new body. The old body had simply been a vessel, a case of flesh to contain the alchemy. Within her resurrected form, she'd united the Three Treasures. And what emerged had been forged from ash and bone and blood and fire, and had been born anew.

Ying closed her eyes, concentrating hard, sweat springing across her forehead. She turned every thought outward until her entire mind, her entire being, was bent toward the lake. And she *focused,* intent on drawing the heat from its depths.

Slowly, steam curled from the water, condensing into elaborate spirals. Heat rose, amorphous, shimmering, from the surface. The bolus of heat took shape, narrowing into a column, and streamed up toward Ying. It permeated her body, entering her, filling her up.

She burned. Her skin glowed ember-red. The air around her wavered with the mounting temperature, and she was hot, too hot, as though she might explode.

Her body, drenched in sweat, shook with the strain. Everything hurt. But when she stared through the shimmering mirage of heat, she saw that the lake was icing over. Crystalline frost was creeping across, sealing the lake surface. Patchy at first, but then getting thicker, more opaque, more solid, more strong. She didn't stop. She felt as though she might die from the exertion, but she didn't stop.

Her hair caught fire. Her fingertips were aglow. Sparks flew off her body, spraying cinders into the surrounding air.

She did not stop.

The remaining humans, fewer now that the battle in the courtyard had been fought, ran out of the open gates. They gaped at Ying, stared at the lake, shouting and pointing and grabbing their heads.

Still, she did not stop.

The lake was now just a solid white island in the center of the battlefield. Around the lake and extending for many miles was trampled, grassless ground. Devoid of plant life. Devoid of flowers. The entire landscape was awash with pools of red-black blood and the bodies of fallen soldiers. Even the willow trees had been uprooted and thrown into the water. Still farther away, the twisted, charred remains of the forest smoldered.

The humans dragged off their helmets, holding them reverently in their hands or dropping them onto the ground. This, Ying saw in her peripheral vision. Yet, still, she did not stop.

She didn't stop until the entire lake had frozen over. Completely. Unnaturally. Right down to the bottom. The trees, a smattering of fish, and a couple of eels were frozen in an eerie tableau, immortally suspended in ice.

There was no heat left in the lake. Now, instead of drawing warmth, the energy she was drawing was freezing cold. It knifed through her body, making her shiver. Lacy icicles formed on her skin before sizzling and melting away. Gasping, she broke the connection and dropped her hands.

The last of the magic prickled over her skin, and she sent it scattering into the atmosphere. It whirled around like a million tiny sparkles, then dispersed in every direction. The surface of the lake glowed, sealed by magic. And Ying knew that across the empire and around the entire world, the sparks were traveling to each reflective surface, sealing them in the exact same way.

The crimson dragon thundered to the ground, and Ying slid off, her knees buckling. She swayed for a moment before collapsing face-first onto the ground. Broken. Exhausted. Empty.

Spent.

50

A group of soldiers ran to her, but Ying did not move.

She scrunched her eyes shut, blocking out the light. Blocking out the world. Blocking out the sounds of people calling out her name.

There was no joy in her triumph. She'd managed to force the mirror army back into their own world. She'd managed to seal the gateway, just as Mei Po had predicted. But she didn't feel relieved. She just felt...

Desolate.

Yes, she had saved the world. But she had lost her prince in the process. She knew in her heart it had been necessary, unavoidable. That it was a worthy trade. The prince would have sacrificed himself if it meant saving his people. Saving her. She just couldn't shake the thought, couldn't shake the idea...

It should have been me, Ying thought. It was supposed to be her. She'd been the Fish. And now she was the Phoenix. She was the one who was supposed to die, who was supposed to trade her life to protect humankind. Not the prince. Not her kind, serious, benevolent prince. His people *needed* him.

Ying was numb all over, her eyes dry and stinging. Hands

reached for her, helping her to her feet. Her knees almost gave way, but someone propped her up. It was the soldier who had given her his cloak, his dirt-streaked face tracked with tears. More strong hands supported her under her armpits and began steering her gently back to the palace.

When they reached the ruin of the infirmary tower, Ying saw a horse standing at its base, nosing at an enormous block of stone rubble.

A jet-black horse, iridescent in the light.

"Shadow Runner," Ying whispered, the name snagging against her tongue. "Help me," she blurted to the soldiers accompanying her. "The prince is under there. He's under there!"

She ran. She ran toward Shadow Runner, fear clutching her heart. Together, she and the soldiers hefted the stone out of the way.

The prince lay there, ice-cold. Shadow Runner nuzzled him, then let out a soft puff of air. Raising his head, he blinked one eye at Ying; she swore there was grief welling in those clear blue depths.

Ying crouched down next to the prince. His face was pale, his lips a bruised-blue smudge. Although his eyes were open, they were glassy, flat. There was none of the usual brilliance, none of the shifting light that usually shone from within.

With shaking fingers, Ying felt for a pulse. Then she placed her hand over his chest. Nothing. No pulse, no heartbeat.

"He's dead," she whispered. She didn't want to believe it, couldn't believe it, even though the evidence was right there. Looking up at the circle of soldiers who had surrounded her, she raised her voice. "He's dead," she repeated, still numb, her mind rebelling against the truth.

Seeing the soldiers' reactions hit Ying like a typhoon. One of them crumpled over, folding like a piece of paper, needing to be held upright by his peers. Ying tore her gaze away from him and pressed her lips to the prince's cold ones.

She shuddered. This wasn't him. He wasn't supposed to be cold, like his reflection. This prince, her prince, was fire. He was the sun personified. He was her heat, her anchor, her molten core.

But now that heat had gone.

She lowered her forehead to his chest, and the silence there echoed louder than a scream. "You promised," she whispered. "Remember? You said you'd never leave me."

The prince did not respond. He said nothing. Did nothing. Just lay there looking up at the heavens with his empty, ground-glass stare. No longer burdened by this lifetime, nor by this world.

Her tears finally came.

They gushed out like a tide, like the sky that had opened mere hours earlier. Ying found herself bent in half, sobbing over the prince's prostrate body. Sobbing over the time they'd lost in misunderstandings, in miscommunications, in the sheer force of her own stubbornness. She loved him. She loved him. They hadn't had enough time. Even if they'd lived a thousand lifetimes together, it still wouldn't have been enough time.

"Xīngān." Her words converged into silent, racking sobs. "I cannot live without you. I cannot, I cannot. . . ." She was repeating to Prince Zhang the words he'd said to her.

Her tears slid down her cheeks, down her nose, splashed

over the prince's frozen face. She knelt on the ground, clasping his hands and kissing them over and over. His hands were icicles, the knuckles still raw; they still bore the damage he'd self-inflicted in grieving for his father.

She did not notice that her own heat was starting to leach out of her. So focused was she on the prince that she barely noticed her body cooling. And she barely noticed *him* thawing, warming, until suddenly, she heard a gasp.

He took a breath.

Ying's eyes snapped open. She clamped a hand to her mouth and let out an enormous, hacking sob. Her other hand gripped his as he blinked, his eyes coming into focus. He coughed, then drew a long, shaking breath.

"Ying." His voice was hoarse, as though from years of disuse. The color was gradually coming back into his cheeks, into the rest of his face. His hands were still cold, but less so. They were starting to feel more like the cool glass of a mirror and not blocks of ice.

Ying didn't reply. She only sobbed harder. The prince placed his hand on her damp cheek. With the pad of his thumb, he stroked away a tear. "Why are you crying?"

In response, Ying threw herself down on top of him, her whole body shaking with the force of her tears. She hugged him fiercely, possessively.

And everywhere her body touched his, she felt the sun's heat, her magic, her life force, her qì, flowing out of her and into him.

He had been cold. Dead. And now he was not.

The prince didn't say anything more. He just hugged her

back, one of his hands in her hair, the other splayed across her lower back.

Eventually, she calmed herself enough to speak. "You were dead," she whispered.

The prince's eyes widened. "Was I?" He touched his head, where a bruise was blooming, and then shook it slowly from side to side. "I don't remember anything," he said. "I only remember you flying into the storm. Did that really happen?"

Ying rolled over onto the ground and sat up, helping him upright. With a small, protesting groan, the prince tugged her onto his lap and cradled her against him.

"It did." Ying placed her hand on his chest, feeling his reassuring heartbeat. "I survived the lightning strike. I threw back the mirror army, I burned them, I pushed them back into their world." She raised her head to look at him. She looked and looked, like dry earth drinking the rain, like she would not ever—could not ever—stop looking. "I became the Phoenix and I—I sealed the gateway."

The prince caressed her cheek, tears gathering at the corners of his eyes. "You're . . ." He shook his head, just slightly. "You're amazing. I'm sorry I ever doubted you. You're just"—he kissed her forehead and spoke against her skin—"amazing."

Ying bit her lip and looked away, her eyes scanning the carnage that surrounded them. The soldiers had all backed away, giving Ying and the prince some space.

"You were dead," Ying repeated, her voice distant. "But now you're not. I don't understand."

The prince drew her closer and buried his nose in her hair. Then he spoke. "It's the Three Treasures."

"What do you mean?"

"You and me. We're like yin and yang. Dragon and phoenix. Two halves of one whole." He took her face in his hands, caressing her. "One of us can't exist without the other. You are water and fire. And I'm the wood and the mountains. It's all related—that's what the alchemy is."

"The alchemy?"

"The song. *Jīng is the essence from which all life grows.* It's love, Ying, don't you see? It's always been love. The key to sealing the mirrors. Your love saved me. Your love closed the gateway."

Ying had gotten it wrong. She'd thought she needed something tangible, something like alchemical ingredients, to create the Three Treasures.

Now she understood. The power lay with her. The alchemy was always inside her.

Nèidān, Mei Po had once said. *The vessel is within you. The transformation needs to happen . . . inside you.*

"I carried the heat of the sun," Ying murmured. "And when you were cold, I gave it back to you." She smiled at him, her eyes brimming with fresh tears. "But you got one thing wrong."

"What's that?"

"It wasn't my love," she said. "It was *our* love. It was our love that saved the world."

51

It was a while before Zhang Lin regained enough strength to clamber to his feet. He leaned on Ying as they began making their way back to the palace. The soldiers trailed behind them, keeping the crowds back so they didn't overwhelm the prince.

As they passed, people stopped, dropped to their knees, and kowtowed. Aware of how exhausted they must be, Ying and the prince repeatedly urged them not to bow, murmuring, "Bùyóng jūgōng." But the people ignored the words, choosing to bend their foreheads to the ground, displaying deep deference and respect. They rose to their feet only once Ying and the prince had passed.

The two of them took a slow, meandering path through the courtyard. Ying's heart twisted when they passed groups of family members comforting each other, wailing and wringing their hands over their fallen. So deep in the throes of despair they did not see Ying and Zhang Lin pass, too preoccupied were they with their own grief.

Ying blinked, tears threatening to spill out again, but she and the prince walked on.

Finally, they reached the palace. Placing her hand under her husband's elbow, Ying guided him up the stone staircase. She'd already noticed him getting stronger, his skin growing warmer, his movements becoming more assured. It was their prolonged contact, she realized. Since he'd been revived, they hadn't stopped touching each other, whether consciously or unconsciously—not even once. They held hands or linked arms or leaned on one another. To Ying, it felt dangerous to let go, like he might just slip out of her reach for good if she did.

She wasn't far wrong. The longer she touched him, the more heat flowed out of her and into him. He needed her touch to heal, to survive. And with each passing minute, he became stronger, more animated, less reliant on Ying to ascend the steps. By the time they reached the top, he was as strong and as steady as ever. His hand, large and warm, encircled hers. His eyes flashed dark and radiant. And when he leaned down to kiss her, she gasped at how his lips burned. He broke away too soon.

"Ready?" he asked, searching her face.

Ying took a deep breath and nodded.

The front doors swung open as they approached, pulled smoothly apart by two eunuchs. They—along with servants, soldiers, and courtiers—bent low as Ying and the prince approached the throne room, and no amount of reassurance could make them get up again. Many of them even did the liùkòu, three sets of kowtows, standing up in between. Ying and the prince threw each other puzzled looks, but when they reached the throne room, they suddenly understood.

A great cheer went up. The people milling about the throne room all scrambled to their places, the most noble of them finding hollow tiles on which to knock their heads. And with the solemnity of templegoers, they performed sānguì jiǔkòu, the most deferential bows of all. Nine kneelings, nine knocks of the head on the resounding tiles—a greeting reserved for the emperor, and the emperor alone.

"Of course." Ying turned to her husband. "You're the emperor now."

Zhang Lin blinked. "My mother—"

"Your mother is still imprisoned, Your Imperial Majesty," said a man. He was dressed in eunuch's robes, but Ying couldn't see who it was. He was still face down, talking to the floor. They all were.

"Well!" was all Zhang managed to say. He stared up the long carpet, his gaze lingering on the dragon throne.

Ying gave his arm a reassuring squeeze and tugged him along. He followed, seemingly in a trance. A lost man among a sea of subjects.

"Go," she whispered when they reached the steps that led to the throne. She gave him a little push, and slowly, stiffly, he ascended.

As soon as he let go of her hand, Ying felt bereft, as though part of her soul had been severed. Her husband clearly felt it, too, because he stopped and turned. "Come with me," he murmured, and held out a hand.

Relieved, she took it, following him up the steps. When they reached the dais, they both turned to face the room full of kowtowing people.

"Please rise," Zhang Lin said.

The people rose to their knees but stayed kneeling, cupping their hands to their chests in an ongoing sign of respect. Ying's heart swelled when she spied Li Ming and Fei fei, still armored, holding hands.

The space where her family should be, however, was empty. She'd sent them home to keep them safe. But not all of them were safe. Not all of them had survived. She was torn between relief for those in her family who'd escaped and profound grief for those who hadn't.

Zhang stood before the throne, grasping Ying's hand. As royalty, he was accustomed to addressing a roomful of people, exuding an air of calm confidence. But only Ying knew how hard his fingers gripped hers. Only Ying could sense the tension in his shoulders, in the set of his jaw, in the undercurrent of sadness he still carried in his heart. Guilt, anger, grief over his father and his mother and his long-dead, murdered brother. He didn't want this title.

He'd only ever wanted love.

And he had it. Fierce pride erupted in Ying's chest. She looked at the sea of faces turned toward them, at their tear-filled eyes. He was loved. Not just by Ying but by every person in this room. Every person in the palace. He just hadn't realized it yet.

"My dear subjects," he said, addressing the crowd. "We have fought valiantly. We have fought loyally. We have fought hard.

And we have won!" He raised his and Ying's joined hands above his head.

A huge cheer went up. The prince waited until the sound died down.

"But although the battle is won, we must remember. We must remember the fallen; the brave individuals who gave their lives to save ours. We must remember and support their families, their loved ones, the ones they left behind."

He closed his eyes and took a deep breath, punctuating the silence that had settled in the room. Then he gathered himself, opened his eyes, and spoke again.

"Most of all, we must remember ourselves. We must remember who *we* are. We must be kind to ourselves and to each other. We must rebuild ourselves, rebuild the dynasty, rebuild our world. But not just any world. A better world. The monsters in the mirror spent the last thousand years as our reflections. Mimicking us. Learning from us. Becoming us. And if there's one thing we can learn from this war, it's that perhaps they weren't the only monsters."

He raised his chin. "Perhaps we were, too."

The hall was completely silent.

Taking another breath, he dropped his voice low. "Let us not forget this day. Yes, let us mourn the bloodshed, grieve our loved ones, heal from the trauma of war. But let us also remember. By remembering, we honor the fallen. By remembering, we can build a better future."

For a moment, no one moved. No one spoke. But then one of the courtiers started clapping. Then another. Then another.

Soon, the entire room erupted in applause. And the people rose to their feet, tears streaming down their faces.

"Take the throne, Emperor Shan!" someone shouted, and Zhang, stunned, turned to look at it.

"My husband," Ying whispered, a smile on her lips. She kissed him. "My love."

He wasn't the prince anymore. He wasn't the lonely boy who just wanted love.

He was the emperor, the most powerful man in the land.

Emperor Zhang Lin strode to the throne. He swept the skirt of his tunic aside and began to sit. But halfway down, he hesitated, paused, and rose back to his feet.

"No," he said, shaking his head. "No. It's not mine."

"What's not yours?" Ying was confused.

He gestured to the throne. "This. It isn't mine."

Ying's mind reeled. "What? What do you mean? That's the dragon throne! You're the emperor, of course it's—"

"It's yours." He took a step toward Ying. "It's always been yours."

Ying was speechless. The applause had died away, and again, all was quiet. The silence pressed in until all Ying heard was roaring in her ears.

"B-but," she spluttered, "I'm . . . I'm not . . ."

"You're the Fish. You're the Phoenix." He took another step toward her. "You survived the lightning strike. You beat the mirror army. You drove them back into their world. You sealed the gateway. *You* won the war." He closed the distance and took both her hands in his. "This empire is yours, Empress Ying." He leaned forward and spoke in her ear, his warm breath tickling the sensitive skin on her neck. "*I am yours.*"

Ying's breath caught, hindered by the lump that had formed in her throat.

He turned to face the crowd. "My wife," he said, his sonorous voice rumbling around the room, "my wife is your true leader. With her courage, her tenacity, her intelligence, her spirit, she saved us all. She saved the world. I hereby bestow upon her the Mandate of Heaven, the highest power in the empire. May she lead us into a time of peace, prosperity, and harmony."

And with that, Shan Zhang Lin—her husband, the emperor of all of Jinghu Dao—sank to one knee, smiling up at her, her hands still in both of his.

He was bowing. To her.

"You can't do this!" Ying said, only just managing to find her voice.

He gave her a surreptitious wink. "I'm the emperor. I can do what I want."

Ying stared at him, not knowing what to say. Around the hall, whispers started, stealing through the crowd like a warm summer breeze. How would the people react? Would they accept her, a woman, as the highest authority in the land? Would they listen to her as they'd listened to Zhang Lin's father, the late emperor, and his father, his father's father, and all the emperors before that?

As if in response, a shout went up from somewhere at the

back of the crowd. "All hail Empress Ying!" And then more shouts, and more cheers, and the crowd collectively sank into more sānguì jiǔkòu. The hall was filled with joyous cries and the resonant sound of heads knocking hollow tiles.

Ying's eyes roved the crowd, scarcely daring to believe it. She couldn't believe it—they were accepting it. Accepting Emperor Zhang Lin's words.

Accepting her.

Stunned, she turned her gaze back onto Zhang Lin. Even now, after all that had happened, looking at him made her heart beat faster. The brilliance of his dark eyes, his fierce feline grace. The broadness of his shoulders, his strong jaw, his tousled, jet-black hair. And even underneath his clothing, she could see the planes of his well-muscled torso, the long lines of his battle-honed legs. She swallowed, her mouth suddenly dry.

Whatever happened, he was her prince. He'd always be her prince. Whoever ruled, whoever had the Mandate of Heaven, whoever had the ultimate authority . . .

They belonged to one another.

"So." Ying smiled down at her husband. "If I have the authority, I can order you to do anything, right?"

"Within reason!" he protested, though he was grinning. "But yes. I've given you the highest power. Whatever you say goes. Whatever you want is yours."

"Well, then, husband, I have my first order."

Zhang raised his eyebrows, surprised. "Oh?"

Ying gave a low chuckle, then tugged him back to standing.

Her breaths were coming low and fast, her heart pounding in her chest.

"Kiss me," she said, barely able to breathe. "Please."

Her husband smiled down at her, his eyes luminous, his warm hands grasping hers.

"Gladly," he said, and leaned in.

Their kiss was gentle at first, just a brush of lips. Then the prince moaned against her mouth; his hands clamped around her waist and crushed her body to his. Ying sighed. Her lips parted. She wrapped her arms around his neck.

Ying was vaguely aware of the audience clapping, but as Zhang Lin deepened his kiss, the entire room seemed to fade away. As though they were the only two people in the room. As though they were the only two in the world. Their tongues touched—tentatively at first, but then getting bolder, deeper, more passionate. His hand snaked up into her hair, his fingers clasping the back of her head.

Nothing else mattered, nothing except this kiss. She kissed him with the fervor of someone who had walked through hell to fight for and retrieve her lover. And he kissed her back as though his life depended on it, which, in a way, it did.

When they finally broke apart, both of them were panting. The background noise of applause, whoops, and cheers swelled to a deafening crescendo, hitting Ying like a wave. Emperor Zhang Lin rested his forehead on Ying's, trying to calm his breathing, his eyes locked on hers.

For a while, they couldn't speak.

"I have a second order," Ying whispered finally. She took a deep, steadying breath. "If I rule, you rule with me. Together."

Her husband smiled in response.

"Together," he agreed, and kissed her on the forehead.

"Forever."

Acknowledgments

This book exists only because of the collective efforts of all those who have helped me. And while it's tempting to write something witty, I have many, *many* people to thank. So in the interest of brevity, I'll try to keep this short.

Firstly I'd like to acknowledge the Traditional Owners of the unceded land on which I live and work, the Wurundjeri people of the Kulin nation, and pay tribute to Elders past, present, and emerging.

To my literary agent, Tricia Lawrence. Thank you for championing my book and its characters with such passion. I am so glad we connected during #DVPit! It has been wonderful having you in my corner.

To my editor, Lydia Gregovic, for the best editorial experience an author could ask for. Your considered, intelligent feedback has completely transformed this book for the better, and your willingness to answer my many questions is so appreciated! I could not have found a better partner to bring this book to life.

To the team at Delacorte Press and Random House Children's Books: Krista Marino, Beverly Horowitz, Colleen Fellingham, Candice Gianetti, Zhui Ning Chang, Jillian Vandall, Natali Cavanagh, Michelle Campbell, Caroline Kirk, Tamar Schwartz, and Michael Caiati, as well as Barbara Marcus, Judith Haut, and the entire RHCB publishing office and sales team. Thank you for helping to bring *The Girl with No Reflection* into the world. I've admired Delacorte from afar for so long that it still feels like a dream to be part of the family. Thank you, also, to my publishing teams around the world—especially Calah at Hodderscape and Zoe, Jess D, Rosie, Jess B, and Bec at Penguin Australia.

To cover designer Casey Moses and illustrator Victo Ngai: I am in awe of the both of you; your talent and creativity have resulted in the most stunningly gorgeous cover *ever*! It is beyond anything I could have ever imagined! Also, to Megan Shortt, who designed the interior, and Virginia Allyn, who created the breathtaking map, thank you, thank you, thank you.

This book has been through a (frankly ridiculous) number of revisions. I'd like to thank all the beta readers who so generously volunteered their time and expertise. In alphabetical order: Lindo Forbes, Bria Fournier, R. Lee Fryar, Shaylin Gandhi, Manuia Heinrich, Al Hess, Rina McAlpine, Nick Petrou, Pine, Raidah Shah Idil, and Nisha Tuli. I could not have done it without you, and I am forever grateful.

To my wonderful mentors Chloe Gong, Brian D. Kennedy, and Louie Stowell: for all the advice you gave to me, a newbie author, and for being such incredible cheerleaders and friends.

To my writer friends, who make navigating a tough industry so much easier. Especially Frances, Al (again), Raidah (again), Sher, Belinda, Kate, Kara, Lizzie, Nisha, and everyone in the Write or Die Growlery: Sunyi, JT, Shay (again), Ronnie, Clay, Essa, Wayne, Kim, Mike, Akiva, Richard, Ryan, Scott, and

Torrens. Plus the other groups who have been such major parts of my publishing journey: The Submission Slog, APIary, WMC, Writers Helping Writers, Moms Who Write, all the AoC 2021 mentees, my fellow 2024 debuts, and many more.

To Mr. Brian Merlo, who taught me English for three years in high school. Thank you for your encouragement and for opening my mind up to different styles of storytelling. I can tell you that I still hum songs from *Cabaret*—and that I have never again cheapened the narrative by making it "all a dream."

To the judges of the 2022 Victorian Premier's Literary Awards Prize for an Unpublished Manuscript, R.W.R McDonald, Tresa LeClerc, and Ronnie Scott: for plucking my manuscript from the contest entries and seeing its potential. It truly was the biggest surprise of my life to win, and I will be eternally grateful for the honor.

To my cats, who gave up their rightful place on my keyboard but then proceeded to steal my chair: thanks for keeping my seat warm, and for all the random extra letters you probably inserted into the book. (Side note: if you notice any typos, then please blame the cats.)

To the most important people of all: my family. To Mum, Dad, Kevin, and Keli, thank you for tolerating me reading absolutely *everything* in the house. To Ginny, for your unwavering support. To my kids, Ada and Callan: you taught me how to use my time more wisely, how to live in the present, and how to grab life with both hands. Without you I would have never had the bravery to take the leap and write a book. And thank you most of all to Lachie, my husband and staunchest supporter, for all the time, help, and support you've gifted me. In this new chapter of our lives—and my journey into authorhood—I cannot imagine having anyone else by my side.

And finally, many thanks to you, the reader. I am so humbled that you have chosen to read my words.

About the Author

Keshe Chow is a multi-award-winning Chinese Australian author of fantasy, romance, and speculative fiction. Born in Malaysia, Keshe moved to Australia when she was two years old. Currently she resides in Naarm (Melbourne) with her partner, two kids, one cat, and way too many houseplants.

keshechow.com